small blessings

small blessings

MARTHA WOODROOF

St. Martin's Press ⚒ New York

This is a work of fiction. All of the characters, organizations, and events portrayed in this novel are either products of the author's imagination or are used fictitiously.

www.stmartins.com

Library of Congress Cataloging-in-Publication Data

Woodroof, Martha, 1947–
   Small blessings: a novel / Martha Woodroof.
      p. cm.
   ISBN 978-1-250-04052-7 (hardcover)   55729064   08/14
   ISBN 978-1-4668-3588-7 (e-book)
   1. College teachers—Fiction.   2. Husband and wife—Fiction.   3. Life change events—Fiction.   4. Fathers and sons—Fiction.   5. Domestic fiction.   I. Title.
   PS3623.O6685S63 2014
   813'.6—dc23
                                                            2014000134

St. Martin's Press books may be purchased for educational, business, or promotional use. For information on bulk purchases, please contact Macmillan Corporate and Premium Sales Department at 1-800-221-7945, extension 5442, or write specialmarkets@macmillan.com.

First Edition: August 2014

10 9 8 7 6 5 4 3 2 1

To Charlie and my daughter, Liz Gipson.
And to my friend Marcia Robertson because she is, as The Boss puts it,
tougher than the rest.

acknowledgments

First and foremost, thanks to the great Loretta Williams for her story skills and her friendship. Thanks to Kate Garrick, my agent, and Hilary Teeman, my editor, for taking me on; and to Skipper Fitts, director of The Sweet Briar College Book Store back during its heyday, for hiring me to run his brand-new espresso machine.

A big shout-out to Kip Carrico, Jeffrey Freymann-Weyr, "Doodling" Judy Dilts, all my lunch-loving friends, and to my pals at WMRA Public Radio (the little public radio station that *can!*) at James Madison University in Harrisonburg, Virginia.

I'd also like to applaud my English instructor mother, the late Ruth Hege, who may have loved words as much as she loved me. And great gratitude goes to Pop for telling me when I left for boarding school that I must never have more luggage than I can handle on my own.

'Tis the gift to be simple. 'Tis the gift to be free.
'Tis the gift to come down where you want to be.
And when you find yourself in the place just right
You will be in the Valley of Love and Delight.

—SHAKER HYMN

Decide that you want it more than you are afraid of it.

—ATTRIBUTED TO BILL COSBY

part one

chapter 1

There she was, as welcome in this insular community as fresh air in a multiplex, a woman who, rumor had it, risked being happy. Tom had heard the most about her from Russell Jacobs, his colleague in the English Department, and now he was looking at her in the flesh, at this tall, slender, dark-haired creature, oddly stylish in her ill-fitting, baggy trousers and white T-shirt.

She stood not twenty feet away from him in the new coffee room, listening attentively to one of a coterie of retired faculty members who, according to Russ, had glommed on to the Book Store's new assistant director as soon as she'd set foot on campus. For Tom it was a moment to treasure. Here, at this isolated seat of southern learning, where everyone clung to busy-ness as though it were proof of an importance in the larger, more meaningful world, was a person who dared to seem relaxed, as though she had time to draw breath and listen to what someone was saying and even think about it for a moment or two. Imagine that!

Her name, Tom knew, was Rose Callahan, and she'd been hired by Ted Pitts, director of the Book Store, to manage the coffee room and "to re-energize the community's co-curricular life of the mind through programming in the college bookstore." Whatever that meant. Over the last couple of years, Ted Pitts had become pleasantly obsessed with what he called "building community." Everyone applauded his efforts except the college's new VP of finance, an attractive, fortyish Darden School graduate referred to unaffectionately by the faculty as "the Harpy."

The new VP had been hired a year ago, when the post-9/11 economy had forced the college to dip into its substantial endowment. Ever since her arrival, the Harpy had worried publicly that such frivolities as Mr. Pitts's "community building" further eroded the college's bottom line, which appeared to be the beginning and end of her concerns. Ted Pitts's hiring of Rose Callahan as assistant director (and community-builder-in-chief) was seen by everyone as open defiance of the Harpy's clawlike grip on the soul of the college. Much to the faculty's delight, Ted had always operated with quasi-independence, paying the Book Store's expenses with textbook sales, reinvesting the profits from trade books, gifts, and coffee sales in his "community building" efforts.

Rose Callahan had been at the college for a full month, usually plenty of time for every detail of a person's past to be ferreted out and vetted. But, according to Russ (who was the campus gossip coordinator and so would know), there was remarkably little dirt to dish about Rose Callahan. She was thirty-seven and originally from Texas. She was either never married or amicably divorced—Russ wasn't sure which, only that she appeared to live alone and didn't seem inclined to bite men's heads off. She was to move into one of the tumbledown cottages down by the old barn as soon as some busted pipes were repaired; until then she was staying at the College Inn. She had moved down to take the Book Store job from Charlottesville, where she'd managed an independent bookstore on the Charlottesville Downtown Mall for the last two years, reportedly changing the color of its bottom line from red to black with her innovative programming. Rose Callahan could talk about books intelligently, Russ said, including the literature of the eighteenth century, which was Russ's own domain, and the students had begun pouring out their troubles to her on their first day back from summer break, which had been yesterday. She ate her meals in the dining hall and seemed equally comfortable sitting by herself or with a table of strangers, and she had been sighted walking miles from campus after work hours carrying binoculars, which indicated she was either a spy or a birdwatcher. Russ had thought probably the latter.

"She's not at all pretty," Russ had said, leaning over Tom's desk in that stilted, locker-room way he saved for male colleagues who were part of his regular poker nights. "I mean, her nose has been broken, playing high school basketball, of all things! Next to your beautiful wife, she'd look like Olive Oyl." Russ, who was long divorced and nearing retirement age, still liked to think of himself as a gay young blade. He'd raised his bushy eyebrows. "She's remarkably *self-contained,* if you know what I mean. Everyone on campus is completely intrigued by her, because she's here all by herself and is still so obviously un-*needy.* And she never blows her own horn. Never. In fact, Rose Callahan doesn't talk much about herself at *all.* I don't even know whether she has a lover—or if the woman is heterosexual, for that matter. I don't mean to imply she's necessarily keeping secrets or anything like that. She simply appears to find other people's lives more interesting to talk about than her own. But for all her frustrating reserve, Thomas, Rose Callahan's got something about her that will make the man in you sit up and take notice. Yes, Professor Putnam, even you."

Tom had laughed at this, his eyes on his cluttered desktop, and thought for perhaps the four-thousandth time what a harmless old ass Russ was. Up until this moment in the Book Store, Tom would have bet his retirement fund there wasn't enough man left in him to lift its little finger, let alone sit up. But now, there Rose Callahan was, and here he was, alert as a small boy who smells freshly baked cookies.

At that moment Rose looked up and smiled. Something inside Tom heaved and shifted and he thought, channeling his idol: *The very instant that I saw you, did my heart fly to your service.*

And just like that he, Thomas Marvin Putnam—lover of Shakespeare, educated at Amherst College and the University of Virginia, dysfunctionally married for twenty years—was a joyous, carefree child somersaulting down a hill, joining Alice in falling, falling, falling somewhere he had never contemplated going.

Tom's impulse was to run, but Marjory had begun plucking at the sleeve of his tweed jacket, her nervous fingers working into the hole under the leather patch that was coming off again.

They were there for the Book Store's first annual "Teaching English Afternoon." As Rose's inaugural program, its astute purpose was to bring the college's English Department faculty and current majors together with area high school English teachers and their best students, who were potential majors.

The event, which had been a howling success for Admissions, was winding down. All other members of the English Department had left, but Marjory, who hadn't wanted to come, was now refusing to leave. "There's the new assistant director," she whispered. "Let's go over and introduce ourselves."

"Not *now*," Tom hissed, wondering that his riotously pounding heart did not burst through the front of his jacket and flop down on the display of new books spread out before them; wondering that his knees didn't buckle; wondering that he just stood there, probably still looking like the tall, dull, inoffensive, pleasant full professor of English that he was. But it was too late. Rose Callahan had excused herself from the retired faculty member and was coming toward them, her hand held out to Marjory. Her voice was warm and slightly twangy. "I'm Rose Callahan, and I'm new at the Book Store. I don't think we've met."

Tom saw with astonishment that Marjory was charmed into momentary sanity. She never shook hands anymore. Since his regrettable affair with a poet, she'd developed wild phobias about germs and obscure diseases. Yet she shook hands with Rose Callahan and spoke to her as pleasantly as you please. "I'm Marjory Putnam, and this is my husband, Tom. He's in the English Department."

"It's very nice to meet you, Marjory," Rose said, taking a moment to focus on this fragile, nervous woman, standing there buttoned up to the chin in inappropriately immature flowered chintz. Tom was grateful for this small courtesy paid to Marjory. But he was even more grateful when Rose, at last, turned to him. "Rose Callahan," she said simply, holding out her hand to him. "You must be a colleague of Russell Jacobs."

Her touch was cool, her hand unusually long-fingered and strong. Her handshake conveyed conviction and hardiness, both considered suspect feminine traits on this campus where some young women still wore strings of real pearls with their designer jeans. Tom felt a small jolt as their palms connected. Rose looked down at their hands with an expression he could not read. "Yes," he said. "I am." He intended to say something else, something witty about Russ, but not another word came out of his mouth.

There was an infinitesimal pause before Rose said to Marjory, "Russell has been very nice to me." Tom noticed she was much taller than Marjory, who only came up to his own heart. For an instant, Tom saw his wife the way he'd first seen her, as an exquisite china doll, immensely chippable. It was, perhaps, the most accurate read he could have taken of her.

"Oh," Marjory said, battling nervousness again, looking down and picking at the clasp of her purse. Marjory was profoundly uncomfortable around Russ. He was too confident for her by half.

Rose smiled, but then thinking about Russ made most people other than Marjory smile. Rose turned to Tom again. "Russell has introduced me to a dizzying number of people and told me all about them." Now their eyes were meeting. Rose Callahan's eyes were truly blue, Paul Newman blue, and as he looked into them her whole being seemed to glow, as though she herself generated light.

The Bard, ever present in Tom's head and ever willing to think the right words when he could not, pointed out that *light, seeking light, doth light of light beguile.* "Yes," he managed. "Russ is the self-proclaimed social maven around here." Tom was pleased with himself for using the word "maven" and then immediately uncomfortable with feeling pleased. It had been years since he'd been concerned about the impression he was making on anyone. The back of Tom's neck began to itch unbearably, and his left middle toe threatened to cramp. He wished he'd remembered to get a haircut. His brown hair became a mass of rampaging cowlicks when he put off going to the barber.

Marjory stirred by his side, letting off an unusual little pop of energy. "Why don't you come have supper with us this Friday night, Rose? We'll celebrate getting through the first week of having the students back. We live right on campus, and we'd love to have you, wouldn't we, Tom?"

Tom stopped staring at Rose Callahan and turned to stare at his wife. Marjory hadn't issued a social invitation in ten years. Was she drunk at three o'clock in the afternoon? Had she taken too many of her happy pills? A decade ago, his wife had sunk into pathological timidity and indecisiveness, especially around strange women.

"Wouldn't we, Tom?" Marjory repeated, as calmly as though there were nothing at all unusual about what she'd said.

"Of course." The words came out rather louder than Tom would have wished. He turned back to Rose Callahan, feeling a rush of almost adolescent despair. She would think he was a dolt now, for sure. One of those moldy academics who can't really function in any world other than the one inside his own head. "Do come," he said, hearing himself, with just those two words, sound as though he were begging.

"I'd love to," she said, smiling at Marjory. "It's so nice of you to ask me."

It was as though some of Rose Callahan's calm, some of her *sanity*, had flowed into Marjory by osmosis. This was the longest social interaction Tom could remember his wife having in years. "Good," she said. "Shall we say seven o'clock? We live at the very end of Faculty Row—the big, square brick house that's a bit set back from the rest. My mother lives with us, and I'm sure she'll want to join us."

"How very nice. It will be a treat to eat dinner again in a real house with a real family for a change," Rose said, sounding as though the prospect of spending an evening with Marjory's mother really did fill her with pleasurable expectation. Of course, rumor could work both ways, and the stories Rose would have heard about his mother-in-law might have intrigued her. "I'll see you on Friday, then, if not before," Rose said to Marjory. Then she turned to Tom again. "You know," she said, almost shyly, "I've decided to go back to school and finish my degree, and I'm signed up for one of your classes— Shakespeare 402 that meets on Tuesday and Thursday afternoons?"

The light was there again, flaring out as though someone had set off a Roman candle behind Rose Callahan's head. "Oh," Tom said. His heart did another flop, and his left middle toe seized up like an oil-less engine. "It meets from two thirty until four forty-five tomorrow."

"Yes." Rose Callahan smiled again, still shy, and added, "Well then, I'll see *you* tomorrow afternoon."

Tom looked quickly at his wife to see if she minded this. Marjory had been known to start keening like an Irish mother if he so much as nodded to another woman at a party. But Marjory was smiling as though she were as normal as the next person.

*   *   *

Rose leaned against the archway that separated the coffee room from the main part of the Book Store and watched the Putnams leave. She'd been at the college for three weeks and three days and had already heard a lot about Marjory Putnam, particularly from Russell Jacobs. Everyone had said Marjory was very peculiar, but no one had said a word about how lovely she was. Or that she was so friendly. To be fair to the gossipers, Marjory was obviously a tad high-strung. There had been real effort behind her friendliness, as though it were rusty or in disrepair. And Marjory's fingers had begun to hop around like grasshoppers in the folds of her dress when Russell's name had come up. But those two things, on their own, didn't have to mean Marjory Putnam was *peculiar*, only that she was shy and the thought of bombastic Russell Jacobs made her nervous.

As Rose watched from her archway, the Putnams stopped abruptly beside one of the many glass shelves of knickknacks in the Book Store's front room. The two of them stood there, whispering together; or rather Professor Putnam whispered while Marjory lowered her head, wrung her hands, and listened. Professor Putnam then put a hand on his wife's arm in an obvious attempt to get her moving again, but Marjory shook her head like an obstinate child, took a step away from him, and turned back to look at Rose. Her body had gone rigid as a poker, and her face was a blank. She didn't wave, but Rose did wave at her, and in response Marjory lifted her hand and held it in the air. The two stood looking at each other, and Rose felt something protective rear up inside her and attach itself to the other woman. She would have sworn Marjory recognized this, for she nodded once and smiled for a beat of Rose's heart. She then went back to staring. Only it wasn't a simple stare. It was the stare of a blind woman who sees with her entire being, senses things beyond what other people are capable of noticing.

She's been potty for years, Russell had said, with absolutely no compunction about branding someone Rose had never met as a loony. *You can ask anyone, Rose, my dear. Everyone has Marjory stories to tell. Anyone except for Tom would have fled years ago. But Professor Putnam is our campus Boy Scout, our token nice guy. The only man I know who can act truly selflessly. Although God only knows what the man feels. I'm sure he'd like to murder Marjory sometime, just for an hour's freedom from worrying about her.*

Marjory remained wooden and still for perhaps ten more beats of Rose's heart, wearing anxious fragility like a sandwich board: *I apologize for everything I do.* Perhaps Marjory Putnam knew exactly how people talked about her and thought it entirely her fault that they did? This thought made Rose want to

rear back and punch the next person who told her a story about Marjory—
who would probably be Russell Jacobs—in the nose.

Now, finally, Professor Putnam put a hand gently on his wife's arm
again, and this time Marjory allowed herself to be turned back. The Putnams
were again on the march, and Rose saw with real regret that lovely Marjory
was beginning to act more as advertised, leading her husband on an awkward
zigzag course through the Book Store that was only vaguely canted toward
the front door. She was like a two-year-old, drawn to every colorful knick-
knack she passed. And still Professor Putnam managed to smile bravely at
everyone they passed, as well as smile and nod at whatever his wife was saying, his expression as set and pleasant as a bobbing-head doll's.

Rose stood there in the archway and watched them, watched all the
pitying looks that passed among other faculty members and the suppressed student giggles, and found that she'd stopped concentrating on lovely Marjory and
begun, instead, to study Professor Putnam. Rose didn't usually admire people
who lived obviously muddled lives, but something about this man, about the
way he made no effort to distance himself from his wife's noticeably odd behavior, pinged her well-defended heart. Rose, who never hesitated to change or
move on if life got complicated, began to wonder if this man might have a kind
of remarkable bravery. Might he be one of the rare few who had the courage to
accept—without malice—other people exactly as they were, even when this
meant he found himself joined for life with Marjory?

Rose folded her arms and sighed. She had never inspired anything like
such loyalty from another person—except her mother, Mavis, of course. Nor
had she given it. Rose hated the infrequent occasions when the imperma-
nence of her own life left her feeling vaguely distressed instead of gloriously
freewheeling. And that was exactly how Professor Putnam's dealings with his
damaged wife were making her feel.

Mavis Callahan, who was never without a theory, especially about her
only child, said that Rose, who was brave in every other way, had always been
a coward when it came to accepting *anything* she didn't have a complete handle on. Mavis said that Rose always kept one foot out the door of wherever she
was so as to be ready to move on if things got confusing. Mavis would go on to
say that this was not really Rose's fault, it was the way she'd been raised. But,
Mavis would add, she herself had finally managed to stick somewhere, and so

Rose, *God willing and the crik don't rise*—one of Mavis's all-purpose sayings—probably had enough guts to stick somewhere, someday, as well. Her daughter was no coward, Mavis would always end with a flourish, just challenged in the acceptance department. The way she, Mavis, had been for the first forty-some years of her life. Before she'd come nose-to-nose with her professor and realized she'd better develop some staying power if she didn't want to screw up her last best chance to have a real permanent mailing address.

Her professor . . .

"So you've finally met the redoubtable Putnams, man and wife," said a voice at Rose's elbow.

Rose turned to find Iris Benson, standing too close as usual. It was, Rose suspected, a way for her to launch any interaction as an offensive. According to Russ, Iris Benson loved all confrontation, great and small.

Rose calmly stepped away from her archway and moved back to a comfortable speaking distance. "Hello, Iris. How are you?"

Iris Benson was dressed in the color of her namesake flower, in purple from head to toe. This, too, was as usual. Iris would never be called pretty by anyone, but Rose found her quite theatrically handsome—which was certainly appropriate since she'd tried for a career as an actress during a decade of regional rep and summer stock before retreating to graduate school. Iris had wild red hair, green eyes, a strong nose, and high cheekbones that were always blushed a bright pink. All these were assembled around, and within, a delicate, heart-shaped face. She was, Rose thought, a valentine delivering a call to battle. Rose liked talking to Iris, but then, as Mavis Callahan's daughter, she would be drawn to anyone with rough edges. *I like talking to someone who's a bit of an adventure,* Rose had heard her mother say often enough from behind whatever bar Mavis was tending.

"How am I?" Iris frowned and looked fiercely at something over Rose's left shoulder. "I'm not sure. But then I don't suppose you really care." She looked accusingly at Rose.

"I don't really have time to care now," Rose said, calmly looking back at her and smiling. "I'm hosting an event."

Was it her imagination or did Iris Benson flush slightly under all that blusher? "I'm sorry," Iris said unexpectedly. "That was rude. And I have no call to be rude to you. Yet." With that, she turned around and stalked away.

It was like Iris to attack, unlike her to apologize. Was she all right? Rose wondered. And if she weren't all right, why should she, who'd been here such a short time, be suckered into caring? Surely Iris had real friends who *liked* caring about her? Then again, and here Rose loosed another sigh, perhaps not. Being Iris's friend would be a prickly business.

A student sitting with a group at one of the tables behind her let out a shriek, which was followed by a flood of giggles from the whole group. They would be laughing *at* someone, of course; that was what students *did*. Compassion bloomed late in most people. Rose turned her back on them and allowed herself a quick break from socializing to straighten bookshelves. Books were the main reason Rose worked in bookstores, for no matter how chaotic and strange the worlds in them might be, it would always be a finite chaos, one in which you could safely immerse yourself without getting stuck. It was so different from the low-keyed, never-ending, creeping chaos of real life.

She gave a matched set of Emerson a vigorous push, so it was no longer hanging over the edge of its shelf. The simple truth was now what the simple truth had always been: Reality, with all its attendant complexities—i.e., other people—was inescapable. As Mavis had put it to her sodden customers, "Real life, darling, is the only game in town."

*   *   *

His mother-in-law, Agnes Tattle, paid Tom a rare visit that night in his office. He'd escaped upstairs right after dinner, announcing he had to make final notes for tomorrow's inaugural meeting of his Shakespeare class. The one thing Tom remained clear about was that he was morally bound to teach as effectively as possible. Just because his home life might be difficult, that did not relieve him of the responsibility to keep things in the classroom fresh and interesting. If *he* wasn't engaged by what he was saying, how could he expect anyone else to be?

Tom had indeed made some notes about the BBC production of *Midsummer Night's Dream* with Helen Mirren as Titania. (*My Oberon! What visions have I seen! Methought I was enamoured of an ass.*) When Agnes arrived, though, he discovered he'd begun doodling roses.

"What the hell is wrong with Marjory?" Agnes demanded in her froggy voice. She'd smoked unfiltered Camels for decades, then quit cold turkey when she'd moved in with them, as her son-in-law was allergic to smoke.

Tom's office was on the third floor of the house in what was really a still-unfinished attic. The rough room he'd fashioned for himself under the eaves was hot as hell in the summer and cold as a deep freeze in the winter. The college would have insulated it fully for him if he'd asked, but he never had. He had no wish to turn it into a comfortable room in which his wife and mother-in-law might want to visit him more regularly. As the years crept by, he was turning more and more into Greta Garbo, *vanting to be alone.* Agnes glared at him from the doorway, dabbing at her damp face with a Kleenex she'd fished out of what she called her "reticule," a kind of at-home fabric purse she carried with her from room to room. "It's hot as hell up here," she said crossly. "I don't understand why you don't work on the second floor where it's air-conditioned."

"What was that you asked about Marjory?" Tom ignored her comment about the heat. She said the same thing every time she came up here. Tom liked his mother-in-law. She'd been molded by the lingering effects of the Depression and World War II with all their deprivations and opportunities for soldiering through. Oddly enough, she had graduated from this very college back in the mid-fifties, magna cum laude in mathematics of all things.

Agnes never complained about the big things—such as her daughter's chronic mental illness or her own considerable holdings in Enron—just the little ones, such as the location of his office. She had moved in with them when Marjory had gotten bad enough to need a keeper. Tom hadn't asked for her help. What would he have said—*your daughter's gone completely crazy at last? It's my fault because I had a stupid, three-week affair, but I still can't cope?* Nine years ago, Agnes had simply shown up with a suitcase and announced she was there to stay for a while. Tom would be eternally grateful to her, even though she had a bossy side that gave him one more reason to flee to his attic.

Agnes came a step or two into the low-ceilinged room, looking around as though she'd never been there before and didn't see any reason ever to come again, another ritual of visitation. "I said, 'What the hell is wrong with Marjory?' She's down in the kitchen baking macaroons."

Tom was not above enjoying a chance to shock. He leaned back in his chair, tented his hands, and carefully composed his face into its mildest expression. "Your daughter has invited company for dinner on Friday. The macaroons must be for dessert. If I remember right, they have to age for a day or two to reach their full potential."

Agnes was satisfactorily bamboozled. She stared at her son-in-law open-mouthed for perhaps ten seconds. Then she turned and very slowly removed a pile of books from the only other chair in the room and sat down. "What the hell is going on?"

Tom shrugged. "Got me," he said, quite cheerfully. "Rose Callahan, the new assistant director of the Book Store, introduced herself this afternoon, and before you could say Jack Robinson, Marjory had asked her to dinner on Friday."

"Was she drunk?" Agnes asked, leaning forward, still whispering. "I don't see how she could have been. I watched her all afternoon until you took her to the Book Store. As far as I could tell, she spent the whole time sitting at the table in the sunroom working on her goddamn scrapbooks." Marjory's scrapbooks were picture books of her rampaging pathology. She bought and read piles of women's and self-help magazines, cutting out articles about such things as "How to Keep Your Long-Term Partner Interested in Your Mind" and "Ten Steps to Staying Young Forever" and pasted them into an endless succession of photo albums. Agnes had wanted to make her daughter give up such nonsense years ago, but Dr. Simms, her psychiatrist, had forbidden her to intervene. The updated scrapbooks went off with Marjory to Charlottesville for her twice-weekly appointments with the good doctor, her only allowed solo trips these days. Privately, Tom thought, his wife's psychiatrist must be bored out of his tree spending two hours a week with Marjory rehashing her husband's one, ten-year-old, three-week-long transgression. The scrapbooks at least gave him something new to look at.

Tom shook his head. "She seemed perfectly sober to me," he said. "Maybe Dr. Simms changed her medication and found something that actually helps?"

"Nope," Agnes said, sitting back. "No such luck."

Tom shrugged again. "Well then," he said, "the impetus for the invitation and the resulting macaroons remains a mystery."

Agnes narrowed her eyes and looked at him. She was, Tom knew, his committed partner in this mess. They had these moments of closeness, when

Tom felt, in some cockeyed way, that he and Agnes were man and wife, and Marjory was their hopelessly dependent child. Agnes Tattle was the only person he'd ever met who was strong enough to look life right in the eye and spit. It must be the mathematics in her background. Such courageous realism certainly didn't come from the study of English literature.

"Well, I'll be!" Agnes sighed and got up to go. At the door, she turned around and looked at him again. There really was nothing else for them to discuss. Marjory was a custodial issue between them, not a source of pleasant conversation. "I'm going to go down, unlock the Scotch, and have a drink. May I bring you one?"

"No thanks," Tom said. Had Agnes noticed the roses he'd doodled? She was looking at him with her usual inscrutable glare. If anyone could read minds, it was Agnes Tattle.

"Well then, Professor. I'll leave you with your mail."

The envelope Agnes withdrew from her reticule was small, lavender, and self-consciously feminine. It was addressed in brown ink, postmarked New Orleans, and the return address was confined to the initials R.T. Agnes looked Tom squarely in the eye as she handed it to him. "This came registered mail today. I beat Marjory to the door, which is probably just as well."

And then, before Tom could so much as blink, she was gone.

There was no need to tear open the small envelope. He had all evening to revisit one of the most boneheaded mistakes he had ever made.

Tom Putnam's affair had been with a visiting poet, Retesia Turnball; another wispy, dreamy woman, much like Marjory when he'd first met her, barely connected enough to the here and now to grocery shop. Retesia, who had been quite a good poet, had written a lot about her Nordic ancestry. What Tom mainly remembered about her was how pale she was.

Retesia had been in residence at the college for exactly one month, laboring doggedly with a few overly self-involved students at turning angst into words. At the time, she had been newly widowed and grieving desperately, and Tom had just been desperate—desperate for life, for a meaningful connection with another human being—and so he'd ignored his usual overriding caution and had sex with Retesia a half-dozen times on the couch in her office. Then she was gone, never to be heard from again until now, and it had been he who was grieving—not so much for Retesia as for everything he'd wanted her to be.

Why, Tom wondered, had he been so attracted to unhappy women in those days? Unhappiness repelled him now. He'd had enough of it.

He'd written Retesia one letter, just a chatty compilation of college happenings, which he'd never mailed, but hadn't thrown away either. Marjory had found it a month later. Even though there was nothing in the letter that hinted he and Retesia had been lovers, his wife's decompensation, which had been proceeding for years at a sedate pace, had quickly accelerated.

Within two months she was officially Mad as a Hatter.

Tom hadn't had sex or a normal, intimate conversation with a woman since. His punishment for his transgression was to live life as a caged eunuch. Why hadn't he at least strayed with a woman who made him laugh? Why had he picked another struggling soul who, like Marjory, cried out for rescuing?

Marjory. His wife. What a sad woman she was and had probably always been. But when he'd married her, he was sure their marriage would make all the difference in her life. She was so lovely and so lost, this girl child of the emphatic Agnes and her flyboy husband, who had flown off into the skies of Del Rio on an air force training mission and never come back. Some kind of engine failure, the family was told. Just *pfft*, a fireball, and he was gone.

Agnes had evidently loved her flyboy passionately, for she'd remained fiercely single ever since. The flyboy had left her—his then just-pregnant wife— with a nice slice of family money, a pretty Charlottesville house, and an extended family of overbearing in-laws with stultifying ideas about femininity. Agnes had declined to join her mother-in-law's garden club and had instead taken herself off to the UVA law school, rising to be editor of the *Law Review* and graduating third in her class. According to Agnes, her mother-in-law had been appalled.

After graduation, Lawyer Tattle had quickly become the champion of middle-aged women who'd been dumped by their husbands, delighting in making the bastards pay through the nose for their disloyalty. Marjory—a physically frail child—had spent her formative years listening to her mother's tales of browbeating unfaithful men and prodding unassertive women to buck up and not take no for an answer. Tom had met his future wife during his first year in grad school at UVA. Marjory had been a lovely, pathologically shy graduate of this same women's college, already within shouting distance of thirty, back home living with Agnes, without an inkling of how to survive on her own. He'd been introduced to her at some Legal Aid shindig. What he was doing there, Tom could never remember, but he did remember meeting Marjory for the first time. She had stood before him shyly, lovely as spring's first daffodil, a dribble of punch spilled down her buttoned-up white blouse, while over the PA Fontella Bass had belted out "Rescue Me."

What he'd learned most painfully over the next quarter of a century was that you cannot do that. One human being, with the best will and intentions in the world, cannot fix what is wrong with someone else. There was enough left of Marjory to cling, but not to connect. Tom picked up his pen and absently doodled another rose. The past was always there, wasn't it? Waiting to be sorted out and connected to the present. He must have been terribly lonely when he'd met Marjory—grad school had been so different from the easy, boys' club atmosphere of Amherst. He'd slept with a few women in college, but they were all from Mount Holyoke and could jolly well take care of themselves. His Achilles' heel, back in that lonely year, had been a wish to feel special, not just another likable Joe in the crowd. His collegiate longing to help save the world had somehow perverted itself into a longing to save another person.

Agnes had tried to tell him before the wedding that her daughter was not marriage material. She'd sat him down and—as direct in this as in everything—said there was something missing in Marjory that neither she nor the doctors seemed to be able to do anything about. With the accumulated wisdom of twenty years behind him, however, Tom had politely but firmly told Agnes and her advice to take a hike. The truth was—Tom could see this plainly now, sitting at his desk in this dim, hot attic—that he'd been a little lost himself in those days; another sheltered intellectual trying to figure out how to *live*. And so he'd constructed the convenient fantasy that two straws, if bound together, would make an adequate broom.

Agnes had been right, of course. The marriage had been a mess from the get-go. Marjory had been frightened of sex, frightened of being with people, frightened of being left alone and abandoned. Tom frowned and stabbed his latest rose with the point of his pen. It was so easy to see now that he should have gotten out during the first year when it was obvious to all—and most importantly to himself—that whatever was wrong with Marjory was not his fault. But she'd been so lovely and so desperate, she'd told him over and over again how hard she was trying, and so he'd stayed that year and the next and the next, and then it was hard not to feel that some of her troubles were indeed his fault.

Tom stared out the small, dark dormer window at the great blank sky. *Whatever,* as his current crop of students would say. There was no point in fuming now about the gods' need of a good black joke at humankind's expense. As Van Morrison had put it: *It ain't why, why, why, why, why; it just is.* If it weren't for Agnes, Tom sometimes thought—giving in to his latent penchant for melodrama after a couple of late-night Scotches—he would have hanged himself up here in the attic just to have done something different with his day. The truth was he had made a muddle of his life and there was nothing he could do about it.

The small square lavender envelope in his hand felt hot to the touch. What the hell. A letter was just a letter. Why not read it now and get on with it, whatever it was.

Dear Tom,

I know this will probably be a big surprise, but I hope it will not be an unwelcome one. You are the father of a ten-year-old boy named Henry. On his tenth birthday, which was three weeks ago, I informed Henry of this as well. He had long wanted to know who his father is, but I had held back the information to make it a kind of rite of passage for him when he turned ten.

My life has changed completely in the past few years, and is now much more satisfying and exciting. The change was triggered by my realization that poetry is for losers. I started writing romance novels instead and I have been extremely successful. I write under a pseudonym (which is now also my legal name) that you do not need to know.

Anyway, my agent and publisher have put together a three-month world "lecture" tour, and rather than coming with me, Henry has decided to come and live with you.

We both thought it would be best just to surprise you, so I'm putting your son on a train from New Orleans that will arrive in Charlottesville at 7:09 A.M. on Monday, September 5.

Don't try to find me. I have most definitely moved on with my life. I will be in touch at the end of the tour or shortly thereafter.

Give my best to Marjory.

Affectionately,
Retesia

Tom gripped the small piece of paper and stared down at the hand that was doing the gripping. He'd taken in nothing after the second sentence, the one that announced he'd fathered a boy named Henry. It took tremendous effort for him to unstick his mind enough to spew forth anything, which naturally turned out to be a couple of comforting lines from Shakespeare.

It is a pretty mocking of the life. And nature must obey necessity.

Could Retesia possibly be making this up? Was there any reason to doubt this bombshell?

No, there really wasn't. For a poet, Retesia was strangely lacking in imagination. If she said he had a son, he had a son.

It is a wise father that knows his own child.

A child! *His* child.

Something deep inside Tom began elbowing its way to the front of his crowded consciousness, and that something seemed, unexpectedly, to be *excited.*

He focused on the letter again. What didn't seem at *all* like Retesia was the brown ink and lavender paper. She'd had, as he remembered it, a real *thing* for Emily Post, who, as an etiquettarian, made Ms. Manners look casual. But whether or not the notepaper and ink were customary for Retesia, the letter had to be from her, because he, she, Marjory, and Russell (to whom he'd impulsively confided just after Marjory had found the ridiculous letter) were the only people in the world who knew that he and she had done what it takes to produce a child.

Someone else was coming up the stairs. Tom immediately stuffed the letter into his chair cushions and waited. It wasn't Agnes; the steps were far too hesitant. From their sound, Tom would have thought it was Marjory, but he couldn't remember the last time she'd been up here. Marjory always referred to his "office" in verbal quotation marks, as though its real purposes in his life were well known and unmentionable. Why, oh why, thought Tom, enduring a wave of defeat, did Marjory have to be so relentlessly unstable? Who knew what she'd do once Henry showed up?

Without thinking, Tom picked up the legal pad with its doodled roses and turned it over on his desk. His daydreams of the afternoon had taken place in another lifetime.

"Tom?"

Angels and ministers of grace defend us! It *was* Marjory. Tom was up in an instant. "Come in!" he sang out, too heartily. "This *is* a pleasant surprise."

Marjory had a damaged person's ability to read another's reaction, and she shrank back before the mild blast of his greeting. One of her hands began pinching the flesh on the back of the other.

"I know I'm interrupting," she said.

"No, you're not," Tom said, reining in the last shred of heartiness. He forced himself to walk slowly and carefully over to his wife, approaching her as he might a wounded bird fluttering on the grass. When he got within range, he gently lifted his arm and touched the hand that was doing the picking. "Come over and sit down. Please."

He drew her over to the chair. Marjory's eyes stayed on the floor, following the progress of her own feet. She perched on the seat's edge. Even in the dim light, Tom could see she'd carefully applied fresh makeup for this visit. When he released her hand, it immediately began dancing within the folds of her skirt.

Tom sat down in his desk chair and slowly rolled around to face her. There was absolutely no point in feigning chitchat. His wife would not have come up here without some serious purpose. It took too much effort. "Yes," he said, in his kindest voice. "Did you need something, my dear?"

Marjory's eyes drifted upward until she looked him straight in the eye. She spoke in a rush. "I just wanted to say that I like Rose Callahan very much, and I think she will make a nice friend for both of us. I think she needs friends as well." Her words sounded rehearsed, as though she'd written them down and memorized them once the macaroons were in the oven.

"I beg your pardon?" Tom was stunned. For Marjory, other women were threats, not nice friends.

Marjory dutifully repeated herself. "I wanted to say I like Rose Callahan very much. I think she will make a nice friend for both of us. And I think she needs friends as well." Then, wonder of wonders, she smiled—truly smiled—at him and added, "I'm glad she's coming to dinner. I thought I would make spaghetti."

This outpouring was perhaps the biggest, pleasantest bombshell Marjory had lobbed during their last, long decade together. His wife was trying to tell him something tremendously important, he was sure of it; much more important than that she was making spaghetti. But whatever did she mean by saying she thought Rose Callahan needed friends? That, Tom thought, was preposterous. Rose Callahan was obviously as quietly self-sufficient as they came. Besides, everyone on campus seemed to have taken to her immediately.

Marjory was still looking at him, her eyes uncharacteristically focused. *What now?* Tom thought. "Yes, my dear?"

"I'm glad you like her," she said. "And I want you to know I understand completely about . . ." Here Marjory faltered. Her eyes drifted down until she seemed to be talking to Tom's third shirt button. "About that other thing." The words came out in an almost unintelligible mumble.

Tom had no idea what she meant. Had she finally forgiven him for his affair with Retesia? "What was that? I'm not quite sure I understand your meaning?"

Marjory's hands were back among the folds of her skirt, her eyes on her hands. "It was nothing. The important things I wanted to say were about this afternoon and about the spaghetti."

It occurred to Tom that something truly significant must have passed between his wife and Rose Callahan earlier today. It had to have been when Marjory stopped and mulishly insisted on turning back. He'd been quite cross with her at the time; all he'd wanted was to get out of there before Marjory became Marjory again. He'd wanted Rose Callahan to think—just for a little while—that they were a normal couple living a normal life. "Spaghetti would be lovely," he said, deciding to concentrate on less disturbing issues.

Marjory stood up. She'd either said all she needed to say or she'd run out of courage to say more. "I'll leave you, then," she said, whispering again. "I know you have a lot of work to do." And with that she scuttled out the door and was gone. Tom listened to her creep back down the stairs and shut the door at the bottom of the attic steps. The house was once again as quiet as though it were uninhabited. Over the silence, he heard a faint aria wafting in through the small open window. Lost love, set to music. It came from the neighbors, a nice, childless couple, both in the Music Department, who were in the throes of fertility counseling.

Tom sat for quite a while staring at the blank doorway. He tried and failed to grasp that he was the father of a ten-year-old son. He tried and failed to wonder if his wife had somehow figured this out. His mind resolutely remained as blank as the doorway—a state with which Tom was familiar and quite comfortable. It came on when he needed a rest from bewilderment and had nothing orderly to think about. It was a signal he should give up trying to sort things out, at least for a while. What was there to sort out, anyway? He couldn't, no matter what it did to Marjory or to himself, tell a ten-year-old boy that his father didn't want anything to do with him. Even though Retesia's letter had not sounded at all like the wispy poet he remembered, Henry was relentlessly on his way. Tomorrow, he, Tom, would get up, go to class as though life were, quote-unquote "normal," then come home and dump the whole mess in Agnes's capable lap.

There was also no point in trying to fathom Marjory's visit. It would remain forever a source of indecipherable wonderment. But Tom couldn't help wondering about Marjory's extraordinary statement about Rose Callahan needing friends. He remembered a similarly oddball statement she'd once made about Russ. Out of the blue, Marjory had looked up from her scrapbook one evening and said, "Russell has secrets, you know. It's why he is the way he is." Then she'd calmly gone back to cutting out an article from *Glamour*. Marjory had also from time to time made such extreme statements about other people, all of which except—so far—the one about Russ had turned out to be astoundingly accurate. It was as though other people's inner workings gave off a scent that only Marjory could smell.

The faint aria changed to a faint duet that was much more joyous in tone. Perhaps the lost love had been found again? Tom stopped staring at the blank doorway and swiveled around to stare out the square, blank window. A bead of sweat ran off his chin and plummeted down onto the back of the legal pad. The small sound startled him out of his suspended state. He turned the pad back over and looked at his doodled roses. They were old-fashioned single roses, the kind you could find in the garden at Monticello, graceful, curving stems ending in clusters of simple blooms. They would smell of apples and fresh air and romance.

Rose. Rose Callahan. Russ was right, she wasn't pretty. She was a Modigliani painting; her face, too long; her nose, too crooked; her hair—to use his favorite word gleaned from the novels of Patrick O'Brian—all ahoo. But there was nothing pinched or mean or petty in her unpretty face. She had an aliveness, a *presentness*, that had reached out and shaken a hopeful part of him awake that had been snoozing for decades. With one chance encounter, quirky Rose Callahan had beamed herself into the center of his heart.

Her smiling face danced across Tom's notebook page, looking out from under her cloud of hair, not at him, but at Marjory. No one had bothered to be truly kind to Marjory in years. It was hardly worth the trouble. Marjory would take whatever anyone said to her and turn it into an embarrassment. But Marjory had responded to Rose's kindness with a properly phrased invitation. Would Marjory's propriety last through the dinner? Probably not. But perhaps they all owed Marjory the right to try one more time. Part of him remained fiercely protective of his wife against everything but his own despair. And somehow whatever errant shots Marjory let fly, Tom was sure that Rose Callahan would be no less kind to her than she'd been in the Book Store.

Tom took his pen and carefully sketched another flower. *Yet mark'd I where the bolt of Cupid fell . . .*

chapter 2

Rose rolled over on her back and stared at the plastered ceiling. Today appeared to be starting in the same way yesterday had ended, in the company of Marjory Putnam. As soon as the alarm had gone off, there she was again, in her elaborately flowered dress with its poufy sleeves and fussy collar, turning back from ten paces away with *that look* in her eye; the look that had made it perfectly clear to Rose that this woman knew something about her that she herself did not.

Mavis always said that people who hung out in bars wasted a lot of energy avoiding the truth about themselves. As it did not take the wisdom of Solomon to see that Mavis herself was wise, Rose had vowed early on never to waste one second in self-delusion. So what the hell had she missed about her own makeup that Marjory Putnam had not?

The bedside clock ticked relentlessly. If she was going to have her morning run, there was nothing for it but to get up. Rose threw back the covers, rolled out of bed, and padded soundlessly across the thick carpet to the bathroom. Once there, she turned on the ornate lamp over the sink and stared at herself in the mirror.

What if humans were simply hardwired to avoid knowing themselves completely?

"Oh, for pity's sake!" Rose said aloud. She'd never before had much desire to root around on the dark side of her psyche. After all, you didn't need to turn over every rock on a riverbank in order to have a good time on a picnic.

A particularly lusty white-throated sparrow shouted at her through the bathroom's open window. Marjory Putnam. There she was again, looking back like some latter-day Lot's wife with psychic abilities. And there beside her was her sad, brave, Shakespearean husband; so steady, so kind-looking, so—so something else Rose could not quite put into words. A flash went off in her brain, exploding like a tiny, trod-on land mine. Was it possible she was feeling out of sorts because she had developed an instantaneous *thing* for Professor Putnam and had to face him again this afternoon in class? Surely not. Oh, surely, surely, surely not. And yet there had been that something—that *jolt*—when their hands had touched briefly in the Book Store.

Mavis spoke up again inside her head: *The worst thing you can do in this life is turn away from it, my dear.*

* * *

Tom Putnam felt surprisingly energetic as he straightened the stack of papers on the lectern, peered out at his class, and continued not to think about his newly discovered paternity. He'd made an appointment to talk privately with Agnes this evening. They would sneak out into the backyard and be assured of their privacy, as Marjory had wild theories about killer mosquitoes that kept her predictably indoors after dark.

His eyes dutifully scanned the students until they reached Rose Callahan. She sat off to his right, the spine of her paperback copy of *Dream* thoroughly creased from reading, a pad and pen laid out beside it for note taking. Today, Tom noted with intense interest, she wore a black T-shirt and brown pants, and there was a heavy silver band on the middle finger of each hand. Tom's heart gave a little jolt as he caught himself relishing this detail. He brought his eyes smartly back to the lectern, reminding himself sternly that, while she sat in this room, Rose Callahan was just another student. As such, she was someone in whom he should have no personal interest. Rose Callahan was here to learn about Shakespeare, *not* to be ogled by her professor.

The thirteen other students were all familiar to Tom. They were English majors, mostly seniors, with a few juniors and one particularly bright, albeit shy and gawky, sophomore who had petitioned to be let into the class.

The bell struck half past. Fourteen pairs of eyes looked up at him more or less expectantly. "So," he said. "What did you think of Mr. Shakespeare's play?"

Twelve pairs of eyes looked thoughtful but noncommittal. Getting conversation going on the first day was always difficult. The sophomore, a freckle-faced sprig named Susan Mason, timidly raised her hand. He nodded; she spoke. "I liked it a lot," she said. "I thought it was good."

Not a lot to work with there, but probably enough to get started. Tom looked down at his remarks, recopied without the roses. He took in a breath and began his lecture. It was difficult for him not to deliver it solely to Rose Callahan, who paid close attention most of the time and took careful notes, although it did seem to take some effort for her to stay focused. He noticed her hands disappeared below the seminar table and her shoulders hunched as though she were gripping the edges of her chair.

Occasionally she shot him a surprised look that seemed to his hyperattentive inner self to say: *I'm in a bit of trouble here, but please pay no attention.*

Tom couldn't help himself; he stopped her after class. "Ms. Callahan!" he called out rather sharply. He always addressed his students formally. In that way, he remained stubbornly old-fashioned. He might submit to the dean's pressure to grade on the curve or pass full-pay students who had done inferior work, but he refused to submit to the instant familiarity of first names.

Not only Rose but the other half-dozen students remaining in the seminar room turned to him. What was he thinking of, calling her back in front of so many others? "May I speak to you for a moment?" he said more softly, hoping his sudden, colossal confusion didn't show.

"Of course." Rose's brown sandals made soft scuffing sounds as she walked toward him, holding her book and her pad tightly against her breasts. Her fingers did indeed look long and strong enough to dribble a basketball with authority. Hadn't Russ said that playing high school basketball was how she'd broken her nose? Maybe she still played? Tom had a sudden vision of her pushing a basketball down the court, her inner light glowing like a small sun.

The rest of the students drifted away, giggling and whispering. Rose stopped four feet away from him. "Yes?"

Tom realized he had thought of nothing to say to her. He'd called her back on impulse, simply because he wanted her in the room. Marjory's face

floated before him. Marjory was with her shrink at this exact moment. Maybe
she was telling Dr. Simms about inviting company for dinner instead of spending the hour pointlessly resurrecting his affair with the poet. Maybe she was
talking about why she liked Rose Callahan. "Are we still on for dinner tomorrow night?" he asked.

"Of course," Rose said, smiling—quite happily, he thought. Her eyes
skittered up to meet his, then skittered away to something over his left shoulder. "May I bring something for dessert? Or maybe the wine?"

The back of Tom's neck began to itch again, and one of his eyes felt as
though it had developed a tic. Was he going to itch and twitch every time he
spoke to this woman? "Just yourself. That's all that's needed."

Rose pushed her fingers into her unruly hair and attempted to drive it
back. The attempt was not successful. "I think I met your mother-in-law this
afternoon at the Book Store," she said. "Agnes Tattle? Doesn't she belong to
you?" Rose laughed when she said this, understanding that the idea of Agnes
Tattle's belonging to anyone was pleasantly ridiculous.

"All mine," he said, catching up the joke. "She's a pistol, isn't she?"

"I liked her. She said she came in to size me up. I think I must have
passed muster, because she stayed to chat for a while." Rose smiled again, and
Tom felt slightly dizzy from the impact. "Anyway, I'm looking forward to tomorrow night."

"Me, too," Tom said, aware of faint, alien stirrings of rivalry directed
toward his mother-in-law, of all people. Then he remembered the look Rose
had given him once or twice in class, the one that had seemed to be asking
for some kind of help.

"Was everything all right during class?" he heard himself say to her.
Amazing. He never asked students anything remotely personal. Of course, if
any other student had sent out distress signals during class, he would have asked
her to stay just as he asked Rose Callahan, and then he would have asked *her*
what was wrong. He would have felt such an inquiry was nothing short of his
duty as a professor. But with Ms. Callahan here, it felt—oh, for Pete's sake,
whom was he kidding—it *was* personal. It was he himself who wanted to know
if anything was wrong; not Professor Putnam, the dutiful academic.

Rose appeared to be deciding whether she should tell him about whatever it was. He held his breath. Please, please, *please* let her . . .

"Professor Putnam." Susan Mason's face appeared again in the doorway. Tom dragged his eyes away from Rose. "Yes, Miss Mason?"

The child was peering around the doorframe like the Country Mouse in the Beatrix Potter book once adored by Tom's cousins. The sight of her irritated the living daylights out of him, but then the sight of *anybody* would have done that at this moment. "I wonder if I might ask you some questions," she squeaked. "I know I should have asked them in class, but I only just thought of them."

Rose was leaving. "I'll see you tomorrow night," she called from the door.

Tom instinctively looked at Miss Mason to see if she thought this odd, but Miss Mason's freckled nose was buried in her gigantic backpack, and she didn't seem to have heard.

"Tom!" Iris Benson accosted him in the hall, throwing back her curtain of emphatically red hair and leading with her pelvis. Man, woman, or beast, Iris Benson sent the same message: *Let's tangle and see what happens!* There was nothing personal about it. As Russ said, every campus needs an Iris to keep complacency in check.

Iris's office was four doors down from his. She was up for tenure this year in American Studies; her specialty—what a surprise!—was the history of women's suffrage and women's rights in general. Her style in the classroom was the polar opposite of Tom's—she was "Iris" to one and all, and she regularly had her favorite students, her groupies, over to her house for dinner. Tom privately thought that if Iris made tenure, it would have as much to do with the volume of her voice as the volume of her scholarship. His fellow sheltered academics often confused aggression with competence.

"I want to talk with you," Iris said, backing him up against the wall with her flying hair.

"So talk."

"Not here. Someplace more private. Could we go into your office?"

Tom hesitated. It had been when the two of them were alone in his office that Iris had once come so close to him that her formidable breasts had actually made contact with his shirtfront. Iris was not an unattractive woman, and goodness knows, Tom was starved for sex. He was afraid that even guilt and personal distaste would not be armor enough to withstand a direct seduction, and sex with Iris would be even stupider than sex with his poet had been. Even considering the just-discovered results.

"No," he said, "we couldn't."

Iris stared at him, obviously surprised at receiving a direct refusal. It pleased Tom to have asserted himself quietly before one of her onslaughts. But then his innate good manners took over and he added, "I'm sorry, but I need to get home." *To huddle with my mother-in-law about how to prepare my crazy wife for the arrival of my ten-year-old son I didn't know existed until yesterday,* Tom added in his own head.

There was instant derision in Iris's eyes. "And how is Marjory these days? Still cutting and pasting?"

"Yes, I'm afraid so." Tom experienced that odd flash of loyalty that came on whenever his wife was under attack. "What was it you wanted?"

Iris Benson tossed her head. Red hair flew around and settled over one shoulder. "It's not anything to do with tenure. I wanted to ask your advice on something of a personal nature," she said, not quite meeting his eye. "I'm worried about"—she shot him a quick, almost beseeching look—"about something I . . . I may have done. For very good reasons, of course," she finished lamely.

Tom thought about all the things Iris had done that had *not* worried her: throwing tantrums in faculty meetings, failing to meet classes, asking her students to turn in chocolates with their papers, all the tales of her polymorphous perversity. But it was too small a campus to simply tell a troublesome colleague to take a hike. "Could we get together tomorrow, Iris? I've got office hours at ten, but I'm not expecting much business this early in the semester. We'd have to leave the door open, but we should be fairly private."

Iris seemed to shrink inside her clothes. She was wearing some kind of flowing purple shirt over black jeans. How old was she? Tom wondered. His age? Mid-forties? She looked much older at this moment, almost haggard, diminished by her own flood of hair.

"I guess that will have to do," she said, taking a step backward, releasing him from the wall. Tom was immediately certain he'd been unfair—surely even Iris Benson could have normal human troubles and was entitled to seek comfort from another human being. But God help him if Iris Benson had slated him as a confidant.

"Are you all right, Iris?" he asked, impulsively reaching for her hand.

She looked up at him. "No, I'm not. I'm afraid I've finally gotten myself into something I can't get out of just by yelling."

If he hadn't been standing against a wall, Tom would have leapt backward. *Why tell me about it?* he wanted to shout. *What can I do?* He stood there frozen, holding her hand. The idea of Iris Benson telling him her secrets filled him with dread. He had enough trouble dealing with Russ's occasional confidences. He hadn't talked about himself to anyone other than Agnes in years.

Iris was looking down at their intertwined hands. "You've always seemed so kind, you know, Tom. And I have to talk to someone. I'm not sure I'll make it otherwise."

Was this real suffering or just another of Iris's mood swings? "I can call home and say I'll be late if this is some kind of emergency," he said.

Iris looked up at him gratefully. "I was right, then. You are kind, Tom." Iris gave him a wan smile. "It's not really an emergency, I guess. I'm sure I'll feel just as desperate tomorrow. Thanks anyway."

"Certainly."

They stood there awkwardly, unsure of what to say next, both momentarily yanked out of their accustomed roles. *But then,* Tom thought, *Marjory has decided to become a hostess, and I am about to dive into fatherhood. Why not try friendship with Iris Benson?*

Down in the parking lot, Tom handed Iris into her Toyota Corolla like the fusty, old-school academic he was, and she accepted his outdated courtesy without derision. "I'll see you tomorrow, then," he said, standing back and giving her a little wave.

"Yes," she said though her open window. "Have a good evening."

"You, too."

Not much chance of that for either of us, he thought, watching her back out of her parking space. Iris reportedly lived in some improbable cabin up in the hills the students thought was way cool. Russ said she had a half-dozen dogs, and she told tales in class of letting them all sleep with her when she was feeling blue. Tom felt a wave of pity for her. Iris must be as lonely as he was and a lot more needy—or maybe just a lot less conveniently repressed. It occurred to Tom that he had never seen Iris Benson consistently with the same person, man or woman, colleague or lover, for more than a few months running. She had plenty of groupies among the students and the junior faculty, but did she have any friends?

Iris swung her car around and drove off through the rows of parked cars. A couple of passing students waved enthusiastically, but Iris didn't respond. Tom stood and watched Iris's car until it disappeared, then turned and began the walk home, his briefcase clutched in his right hand, full of work that he wouldn't do. It was the last week in August and the early chrysanthemums were coming into bloom. The campus was beautifully planted, beautifully tended. The administration put a lot of emphasis on this, as though education were a still-life rather than a process. But then most things in life were like that, the emphasis on surface rather than substance.

Did he have any friends? The question nipped at him like a small dog.

Well, there was certainly Russ. Tom was genuinely fond of Russ and thought that Russ was fond of him. But did Russ really *know* him? Could he talk to Russ about Henry, for example, and expect to receive wise counsel tailored exclusively for him? Probably not. Russell would certainly listen, certainly care, certainly give advice. But in the end, he was probably too bombastic, too intent on his own performance. In order for true closeness to develop between people, there had to be times of something quieter, less showy, more honestly forthcoming than what Russ offered—less driven by a need for response.

Tom walked on, taking the long way home, one of his small personal indulgences in good weather. He stopped in front of a particularly brilliant display of bright purple mums. *Agnes*. What about her? Could he count his mother-in-law as a friend?

The first hint of fall was in the air. The late afternoon light slanted at a sharper angle; the maples showed an errant red leaf or two. Tom decided to extend his already wandering way home and take the path through the woods that began just below the soccer field and would take him around behind the houses on Faculty Row. Who knew? He might run into Rose Callahan. Russ had said she wandered around out in the woods with her binoculars.

Tom's sense of obligation immediately began needling him. A conscience was such a delicate balancing act. There was what he knew was right, what he ought to think was right, and what he wanted to do, all to be considered. It

was the ultimate moral chess match, and it was the only game that mismatched married people got to play.

It seemed to Tom the birds were exceptionally active as he entered the
woods. He recognized most of the ones that flitted about the campus—robins
and cardinals and mockingbirds—but over there he spotted a giant striped
woodpecker that looked like a throwback to dinosaur times. It was pecking
ferociously at a dead tree. Tom carefully noticed its "field marks," as a colleague
in the Biology Department called a bird's distinguishing characteristics. That
way, he'd have something to talk about with Rose Callahan tomorrow night.

Tom stopped dead in his tracks. He was actually looking forward to tomorrow night. And so, it appeared, was his wife. My God, he felt *happy*! Who
cared that the feeling couldn't last beyond the next ten minutes? They would
be the best ten minutes he'd had in years, and he was going to enjoy them!

The path brought Tom up behind his house. The sun shone directly
into his eyes. He squinted into the strong light, and immediately all joy fell
out of him. Agnes sat on the back porch steps *smoking*! What had Marjory
done now?

The last time his wife had gone bonkers in public—what he thought
of as the Incident—was the last time she'd been allowed out alone except for
trips to the doctor. One glorious afternoon last April, Marjory had driven the
car into Lynchburg, gone into a sleazy little beer joint called the Dahlia, sat
down all by herself at the bar, and gotten completely smashed. Then she'd
taken a longneck beer bottle outside, smashed it on the sidewalk, sat herself
down on the curb, and proceeded to trace ribbons of blood on her arms with
the broken bottle. According to the police she'd screamed, "*I want to feel
something!*" over and over all the way to the hospital, but that had been the
last thing she'd said for three weeks. Marjory had sat silent and stoic on the
edge of her hospital bed, not responding to her husband, her mother, her doctors, the Pink Ladies, anyone, until one day she'd asked a startled orderly to
please turn down the air-conditioning and that had been that—Marjory had
been back to whatever passed in her head for normal. He and Agnes had
brought her home and taken away her car keys. End of the Incident. End of
Marjory's freedom.

Agnes sat with one elbow on a knee, her head in her hand. The only
time she lifted her face was to draw in smoke from her cigarette and let it out

in the long stream of a habitual smoker. Tom couldn't see her expression from the bottom of the yard, but he could read her body language. Agnes Tattle had momentarily despaired.

He squared his shoulders and hurried up the weedy back walk. The college maintained the front yard, since parents of prospective students might wander down Faculty Row, but the backyard was as unkempt as the lives hidden inside the house. "Agnes!" he called out. "Agnes! What is it? What's wrong?"

She looked up, a Camel dangling between her fingers. Her eyes were expressionless.

He stared at her. Suddenly he didn't want to *know*. "You're—you're smoking!" was all he could bring himself to say.

Agnes Tattle would try to joke if she were inside the open mouth of Jaws. "So," she said tiredly, "you think it's only small boys who sneak out back for a smoke?"

Tom put down his briefcase and sat beside her on the steps. Neither one of them said anything. He watched the smoke of her cigarette rise into the bright, slanted light and disappear. After a moment, he put his arm around her. He didn't pull her close but just rested it on her shoulders, reminding them both that the other was there.

"Okay," he said. "Let's have it."

"Marjory is dead," Agnes said, in the exact same tired tone of voice. "She either had a wreck or deliberately ran her car off the road, on that curvy part of 29 about fifteen miles south of Charlottesville. The police left about ten minutes ago, but they said they'd be back to talk to you."

Tom was used to emergencies involving Marjory. At first, this registered as just another one of those. His response was purely practical. "Have you talked to Dr. Simms?"

"Nope. And I hope I never will." Agnes stared out across the weeds toward the woods where ten minutes ago her son-in-law had stood thumping his chest. "It's not his fault, of course, but he didn't help all that much either."

"He tried. At least he kept seeing her."

"Sure. We kept paying him, remember?"

Tom experienced his first blip of realization that this escapade of Marjory's stood apart from all her other escapades. And with this blip, there came a rush of feeling. Guilt, of course—it would be. Not about Marjory herself, but about the fact that it had been his mother-in-law's money that had kept the good doctor's attention after the college's inadequate mental health coverage had dried up. The irony was that he'd been the one who'd actually thought Dr. Simms had made a difference in the quality of Marjory's life, raised it from hopeless to pathetic. Agnes had always said the man was a nincompoop.

Marjory is dead, Tom said to himself, trying to take it in. *I don't have to get up and go in there and sit with her and hear about Charlottesville. She won't be staring at me at supper. I will never have to explain Henry to her. Marjory is no longer here.*

Shakespeare spoke up inside his head as Shakespeare always did in times of perplexity or stress. The Bard's words were easier for Tom to process, somehow, than his own.

And all our yesterdays have lighted fools the way to dusty death.

The weakest kind of fruit drops earliest to the ground.

Tom had experienced death before. His father had died of a stroke; his mother was all but dead from dementia. Both losses had caused him quiet, painful grief that had come upon him in waves and surprised him still, years after acceptance of the fact that his parents were gone. He had loved them both and missed them in his life. His wife's death felt—initially at least— more like a release and a relief. So what did this say about Marjory? What did it say about him?

But Marjory's death also meant the death of hope—and wasn't that what he'd just been feeling in the woods? The magical, expansive hope that somehow everyone's efforts would finally pay off, and Marjory would actually begin to live; the smaller, encapsulated hope that tomorrow night the four of them would, thanks to the healing elixir of Rose Callahan's presence, actually have a good time. And now it was not going to happen. Not tomorrow night. Not ever. The final verdict on his and Marjory's coupledom was in. Their twenty years of married life had done neither of them any good, and now it was over. There was no chance of redemption.

The trouble was that Marjory had never really *been,* and now she would never *be.* The harshness of this truth struck him like a kick. Marjory had come and gone, and he had made no real difference to her. Their marriage had accomplished absolutely nothing good.

Agnes moved slightly inside his arm. A guttural sound escaped her, the noise someone trying to breathe after being punched in the stomach might make. The hand holding the Camel began to shake violently. It occurred to Tom with a kind of hazy wonder that he loved his mother-in-law. Agnes had written the book on *being*. You had to love the woman in order to be able to live with her.

Tom took the cigarette gently out of her hand and crushed it out under his shoe. Then he sat there quietly staring off into the woods with his arm around his mother-in-law while Agnes's sobs struggled to get out from the depths of her broken heart.

Tom fixed scrambled eggs and toast for supper, then gave Agnes a double Scotch and one of Marjory's sleeping pills and sent her off to bed. It had taken him a while to find the capsules—his wife had a frightening array of prescriptions in the medicine cabinet. Agnes, who never went to the doctor and rarely took an aspirin, accepted the pill without complaint. She'd hardly spoken at dinner, and did not say anything but good night as she headed upstairs to her bedroom. Tom watched her climb the stairs and thought how frail she looked, clinging to the banister like an old woman. Poor Marjory had been so difficult to love, it had never occurred to him that Agnes might have loved her simply because she was her daughter, the child of her flyboy, the man who had flown away with her heart so long ago.

Instead of going up to his office, Tom sat down at the kitchen table. Agnes's bedroom was directly above him. For a few moments, she continued to move around, her steps as light as a child's. Then he heard the creak of bedsprings and the house was still.

Tom moved himself to one of the battered wing chairs by the parlor fireplace that faced the double windows looking out over the front lawn. It was not quite dark outside. Fireflies dotted the college's manicured grass, rising up toward the tree branches like minute floating bonfires lit by enterprising hobgoblins. Tom had always loved fireflies. As a child he'd sometimes caught and kept them in a jar overnight, shaking them to make them light up in his room. But they'd lit up only halfway, and there was always a dead one in the morning, and gradually Tom had realized he didn't really enjoy keeping fireflies in a jar but preferred them loose in the backyard where they belonged. He smiled to himself, thinking of how he and his friends must have looked like dancers in a pagan ritual, whirling and spinning in the half-light of summer evenings. How near those summer evenings seemed, as though his years with Marjory were not only over but had dissolved, had never been, and he was once again a young man with his childhood just over and a whole life of possibilities stretching out before him.

He should get up, go call Russ and tell him about Marjory. Russ always expected to be telephoned immediately when things happened, so that he could bustle in and help sort things out. But the truth was that right now Tom had no desire to sort things out. Right now, he wanted rather fiercely to be left alone to imagine what it would be like simply to live, to let life and his ten-year-old son come to him and see what happened, now that its constant, central crisis had been removed—or at least rejiggered into the shape of a small boy. Tomorrow he would feel guilty about allowing himself such a guilt-free evening on the day his wife had died. Tomorrow he would dutifully call Russ, which would effectively loose the news on campus. But tonight he seemed to be on some kind of weird post-traumatic high. Tonight all he wanted was to sit still and try to take in that he was a free man. He and Henry could move to Nova Scotia, where he would write rugged, manly poetry. They could move to Idaho and—

"I *still* can't sleep," Agnes announced loudly from the hall door. "Those pills of Marjory's are worthless."

Tom jumped as though his mother-in-law had set off a firecracker. "My goodness, you scared me! I didn't hear you coming down the stairs."

"Sorry," Agnes said shortly, coming into the room. It was hard to see in the dim light, but she seemed to be wearing an ancient pair of men's striped pajamas. She crossed in front of him and sat down in the other wing chair. Tom thought she seemed slightly more like herself and less like her own ghost. "What were you thinking about?" Agnes asked, snapping on the floor light beside her chair.

"When?"

"Just now. Just before I scared the living daylights out of you."

He sat back. "Fireflies, I think."

Agnes studied him with what he thought of as her I'm-reading-your-mind look. "You won't miss her, will you?"

There was no point in lying to her. Or to himself, for that matter. "No.

I don't think I will. I'm sad, I feel a horrible sense of loss, but I guess that's not the same thing as actually missing her presence."

To his surprise Agnes nodded agreement. "Good for you."

"I beg your pardon?"

"I said, 'Good for you.' I hate pretense between people who are supposed to respect each other."

Tom felt himself flush with pleasure. Had Agnes really meant to imply he was someone she respected?

His mother-in-law turned and looked out the window. It was dark now. With the light on inside, there was nothing at all to look at but blank, dark squares of glass. "The truth is I won't miss her much either," Agnes said softly. "I loved her, but I won't miss having to deal with her. Marjory was hard work from the day after she turned three. That was the day I started law school, and she was too attached to me for her own good. She had her first real attack of the howls when I left for my first class. She kept screaming, 'Don't leave me, Mama,' as though I were leaving forever." Agnes stared down at the backs of her hands. She still wore her wedding ring on her right ring finger. She'd mentioned once in passing that she'd moved it over there the day after her husband had been killed as an exercise in reality testing. "And this was even though I'd told her over and over that I'd be back for lunch, and Millie was right there to take care of her." Millie was the unliberated, old-school nanny who'd practically raised Marjory's father and who, at that point in Marjory's three-year-long life, had probably been with her every day.

Tom said nothing. It had been exhausting just to *live* with Marjory over the past two decades. What would it have been like to love her? She'd been so relentlessly dysfunctional for so long, so persistent in turning everyone's efforts to help into nonsense.

"It makes me sad," Agnes said, talking again to the blank, dark squares of the windows.

"I'm sorry," Tom said, because he had to say something.

But Agnes hadn't finished yet. "I'm not sad for myself, you understand, I'm sad for my daughter. The best thing she ever did in life was to give up on it. And that's as bleak as a life can get."

Tom had no idea what to say to that. Agnes was right, but where was the kindness in agreeing? They sat in silence, Agnes staring at the window while he stared at her. *What will she do now?* Tom wondered. *Will she go back to Charlottesville?* Something almost like panic flickered inside him. It hadn't occurred to him that Marjory's death might mean his mother-in-law would leave. And it had certainly never occurred to him how much he would miss her if she did. How little he knew his own heart. But then what had been the point? How he'd felt about anything had been irrelevant for a long time.

"Would you like a drink, Agnes?" Tom said, standing up.

"No, thank you. I have quite enough stuff inside me already. I just came down for some company."

"You don't mind if I get one, do you?"

She turned to him with that look on her face again, the one that made him despair of ever keeping anything secret Agnes Tattle wanted to know. She still looked haggard and old, but there was strength and humor in her eyes again. "Have two," she said, "and make them both doubles. This might be the night Scotch was invented for."

Tom started toward the kitchen where the Scotch was kept, only to have Agnes snag his arm and stop him. "Listen, Tom. I know that letter you got had something in it we have to deal with, but is it something that will keep for twenty-four hours? Say, till Saturday morning?"

"Sure." He smiled down at her. *Life's uncertain voyage.*

How would he think if Shakespeare had never been? Tom wondered.

On the move toward the kitchen again, he felt almost giddy with relief. In talking about the something that had to be dealt with, Agnes had said "we" instead of "you."

chapter 3

When she was sixteen, Miss Mavis Callahan of San Marcos, Texas, had spent a long, hot summer living in a boxcar with Janis Joplin. That experience, and others like it, had largely formed the character of Rose Callahan's mother. For her, life was to be lived at full-tilt boogie within the bounds of practicality. Mavis Callahan had no desire to flirt with drug addiction or to romanticize doomed love. Whatever was real was good enough for her, and so—like mother, like daughter—it had always been good enough for Rose.

Mavis had poured drinks for a living. Rose had grown up in a series of cramped apartments over noisy bars. Mavis had stuck to working in college towns after she'd had a child, figuring her customers there could contribute the most to her daughter's education. Rose had done her homework perched on phone directories placed on bar stools, books and papers spread out before her on glass-ringed slabs of mahogany. Mavis had kept a close eye on her daughter's progress while she dispensed drinks and traded wisecracks with friendly men and women who did indeed recite T. S. Eliot to Rose, explain the mathematical complexities of the moon's orbit on bar napkins, and otherwise fill in as Rose's supervision when Mavis had her hands full.

The two of them had moved around a lot. Mavis, like Merle Haggard (to whom she had four times, in four different towns, served an evening's worth of whiskey), had had ramblin' fever. Only once did Rose go to the same school for two years in a row. Only twice did she celebrate Christmas in the same apartment. Had she felt deprived by her disorderly childhood? Not a bit.

Rose considered that she'd learned much that was valuable from growing up with Mavis. She'd learned to make friends quickly, to be cheerful when life wasn't perfect, to accept the fact that change was all you could count on in this life—except, of course, when it came to Mavis, who was rock-solid and would always be exactly the same. And sitting, bellied up to all those bars, listening to and watching all those strangers, Rose had early on formed the opinion that an awful lot of people had their hearts broken in ways they could have easily avoided. Miss Mavis Callahan (always with a decided emphasis on the *Miss*, thank you very much) had not raised a dreamer.

Perhaps the hardest lesson Rose had learned was that change was not only dependable, it was omnivorous. When she was a restless nineteen and poised to drop out of Rice, Rose had been forced to realize she could not even count on Mavis to remain the same. It was then that her mother, who had just turned thirty-eight, abruptly came to rest in Williamstown, Massachusetts, where, three years later, at the age of forty-one, she married a widowed college professor thirteen years her senior and became happily domesticated. She continued, however, to introduce herself emphatically as *Miss* Mavis Callahan. Her husband—Stu, a kindly professor of ancient history, whom Rose liked very much but had never felt the slightest pressure to love—did not seem to mind this at all.

*   *   *

There were a half-dozen cars parked in front of the Putnams', and another three in the driveway. *My goodness*, Rose thought, *it's a party, and here I am in a wrinkled dress, holding an old canning jar of backyard roses.*

Her move out of the College Inn and into her cottage that day had happened without warning. Rose had gotten a call late yesterday afternoon at the Book Store saying her cottage was ready. Mr. Pitts had said why not take the next day off, since it was a Friday, and have a long weekend to get settled in? He'd even volunteered his two hulking teenaged sons to help get her things out of storage in the big barn next to the cottage. The boys had worked like stevedores, but even so, the last box of books had not been put down on the living room floor until late afternoon. Miss Mavis Callahan, however, had not raised a daughter who was late to dinner, so here Rose was, at seven on the dot, standing on the Putnams' front stoop.

Rose heard footsteps behind her. She turned and looked back down the walk. A man she dimly recognized from the Book Store was walking down the central path between the facing lines of houses on Faculty Row. "Good evening," he called, just loudly enough to be heard. He paused and shook his head. "So sad."

"Isn't it," Rose said, wondering what news she had missed during the day. Surely there hadn't been another terrorist attack?

"I'll be over in a little while," the man said. "As soon as I change."

"Good," Rose answered. What else was she to say?

The man, still shaking his head, went on his way. Rose inadvertently gave her unruly hair a shove. It immediately sprang back to its starting point, as independent as the rest of her. The man had mentioned changing. Whatever was going on at the Putnams', it was obvious that she was not adequately turned out. Her blue cotton dress was too casual and too discouraged looking. She had put it on only because lovely Marjory Putnam had worn such a fussy, flowery number when they'd met in the Book Store, and it was difficult to imagine her entertaining casually at home dressed in blue jeans and a tank top. The dress hung unimpeded to well below her knees, and her sandal-clad feet were clearly visible below. Rose sighed again. Growing up, she'd seen the attention her mother's breasts had attracted. She herself had not particularly liked attention, so one night she'd gone outside and wished upon a star that she would never grow boobs.

Obviously the star had listened.

Standing there on the Putnams' front stoop, Rose had one of her odd moments, blips of time when she felt as though she were waiting for something. What that might be—adventure, true love, Godot—who knew? Rose didn't like these moments at all. They smacked of the kind of pointless, existential quest for meaning that Mavis's customers had carried out through the bottom of a glass.

How funny life was, Rose thought. Two months ago she'd been living in Charlottesville with everything rolling merrily along. Now here she was awash in unknowns again. The only remaining constants were her furniture, her books, and her boyfriend, Ray. And Ray was a constant only because he lived in Washington, and their relationship was a commuter one. Rose was certain the two of them wouldn't have lasted six weeks in the same town. If they were separated by only a couple of Metro stops, Ray would have almost certainly wanted things from her she'd always assumed she didn't have to give and didn't want to have.

Rose looked down at her jar of blossoms. She'd picked them from the overgrown bush that sprawled along the cottage's back fence, not wanting to arrive at Marjory Putnam's house for dinner empty-handed. They were old-fashioned roses, blooming single and double on the same stem, the color of a baby's ear. Their lush scent was tinged with clove.

The protectiveness Rose had felt for Marjory in the Book Store came back to her. She immediately lifted her free hand to ring the bell, but then stopped and listened with her finger poised and pointing at the door. How quiet it was. There was no music, no sound of laughter. If this was a party, it must be a very dull one.

Ring the bell, she told herself sternly. *This is your life now, these are your people, and this is what passes for a party. Get on with it . . .*

The door was quickly opened by Russell Jacobs—tall, bushy browed, with a silver leonine mane of carefully styled hair.

He struck a pose. "Rose, my dear. How nice of you to come!" In spite of the pose, Russell seemed unnaturally constrained. In the Book Store, he always took stage like an old actor. "I didn't expect to see you here tonight," he went on in this new, queer, quiet way. "I stopped by the Book Store today just to say hello, and Mr. Pitts said you were moving."

"I did move," Rose said, conscious of her jar of roses and her wrinkled dress—Russell was nattily turned out; Tom Wolfe, gone provincial. "That's why I'm such a mess. But Marjory was kind enough to invite me, and so here I am."

Russell's jaw dropped. "*Marjory* invited you?"

"Yes. The day before yesterday. She and Professor Putnam came into the Book Store together."

"Invited you to *what?*" Russell spoke sotto voce like a TV golf announcer.

"Why, to this!" Rose gestured at the parked cars. "I'd thought it was to be a casual dinner for the three of us, but from the cars and from your answering the door, I can see it's a party."

Russell stepped outside and firmly took her arm, drawing her to the edge of the tiny stoop as though there they were to have some kind of chummy tête-à-tête. Rose looked at him closely. Was he drunk? She couldn't smell any booze, and he didn't seem drunk, just peculiar, even for Russ. "You don't know, do you?" he asked in a hoarse whisper.

"Know what?" Rose looked up at him blankly.

"Marjory is dead," Russell said softly. "I'm sorry. I guess nobody knew about your invitation to dinner tonight, and so nobody thought to find you and let you know."

Rose stared at him. *People overuse the word "sudden,"* she thought. *It should be saved for times like this, when something comes at you so quickly it smacks the sense out of you.* Russell was looking down at her solicitously, his eyes politely sad and concerned, but not really distressed. "My goodness! I had no idea," she said. "I'm so sorry."

"I know you are." Russell patted her arm. "We all are."

There was a slight pause. Rose looked down at her jar of flowers. "How did it happen? What did poor Marjory do?"

Russell shook his head. "'Poor Marjory' had a car wreck yesterday. She ran off the side of Route 29 in that section south of Charlottesville where the drop-off is so very steep. She was dead by the time they got to her."

An image of a squashed car with that lovely woman trapped inside, people milling around it, yelling, flashed before Rose. *I'll never know what Marjory saw in me,* she thought. "How brutal," she said.

"Yes. It is. Particularly since Marjory was such a flimsy creature."

Flimsy? What an unkind word to use about someone who's just been killed. But accurate, Rose suspected, when it came to Marjory Putnam.

"Do you want to come in?" Russell asked. "Or would you rather sneak away into the night and escape? It's not very festive in there. Of course, there's a lot of truly awful food—casseroles and Jell-O and such—and you must be hungry if you've been moving all day and were expecting dinner."

Someone walked heavily across the floor of the foyer and Iris Benson appeared in the doorway, swathed in a lime green, vaguely African-looking ensemble and carrying an almost empty highball glass. Was it possible her hair was even redder than yesterday? "Rosie!" she bellowed, striding out onto the front stoop, pushing Russell out of the way and attempting to fling her arms around Rose before she was stopped by the thorny bouquet in the canning jar. "My, my," Iris said, swaying slightly. "It's our newest college star come with flowers to honor the passing of the little woman. How sweet."

Iris was clearly very drunk, so drunk that standing was problematic.

She grasped Russell's arm. "Have you ever noticed that we are both named for flowers?"

"Yes," Russell said. "I have."

Iris turned to face Russell's chest. "Isn't that sweet? Isn't *she* sweet?"

Russell let go of Rose and put his arm around Iris to steady her. "Yes, it is, and yes, she is. Now perhaps we'd better get you back inside, Iris, and see if someone will give you a ride home."

But Iris was not to be corralled. She lunged for Rose and caught her by her free arm. "Not without Rosie!" she said, her voice soaring. "I won't go back in unless Rosie comes, too!"

Russell shrugged and looked across Iris's fiery head toward Rose. "Do you mind? It would save a scene. Iris is quite capable of a scene when she *hasn't* been drinking. When she has, the sky's the limit."

Iris listed back toward Rose. "You got that right!" she said cheerfully. "The sky's the limit!"

"Of course not," Rose said.

Together, each grasping one of Iris's arms, they hauled her into the house and shut the front door. The foyer was dim and cluttered. Piles of newspapers, books, and unread junk mail littered a wooden bench. More books lined the walls. Faint sounds of conversation and Bach drifted out from the back of the house, sounding like a gathering of polite, musical ghosts.

Rose and Russell lowered Iris onto the bench, wedging her in between a stack of paperbacks and a pile of back issues of the *Sunday Book Review*. Iris waved her highball glass at Russell. "I need another drink."

Russell crossed his arms. "No, you don't, Iris. You're already as drunk as a frat boy on Saturday night. And this is not an occasion where even *you* want to lose control."

Iris's face grew ugly. "Get me a drink, you goddamn pompous hack!" she bellowed.

Russell turned bright red, took the glass without a word, and disappeared into the hall, slamming the foyer door shut behind him.

Iris grinned up at Rose. "I'd have said 'asshole' to anyone else. But 'hack' is more effective with Russell. People do so hate to hear the truth." She spoke as though her mouth were full of hot oatmeal.

"Still, it wasn't very kind," Rose said.

Iris's eyes filled with tears. "He isn't kind to me, why should I be kind back? Only Tom is kind. He's the only one."

"Tom?"

"Tom Putnam. Widower Tom. The grieving husband of the dead Marjory. Who the hell do you think I mean?" Iris swayed on her bench.

"I'm sorry. I have yet to think of him as a Tom. I'm taking his class, so he's Professor Putnam to me."

Iris nodded solemnly, regarding her green knees. "He's as old-fashioned as they come. But he's not a hack, and he's not mean. Tom Putnam is a very good teacher and a very kind man! Very kind!" She lifted damp eyes to Rose. "Did I already tell you that?"

"Yes, you did."

"Sorry 'bout that." Iris grinned sheepishly. "Had a little too much to drink. Don't do it all that often anymore, but I've sure as hell done it tonight. Makes me mix up what I say with what I think." She screwed her face up as though she were trying to entertain a baby. "Does that make any sense?"

"Perfect sense," Rose said.

The music finished and didn't begin again. There was a burst of laughter, quickly suppressed. Rose wished she could get rid of the roses. Their scent was overpowering in the enclosed space.

Abruptly, with a single sweeping motion, Iris pushed the stack of books onto the floor and patted the cleared space beside her. "Sit here, Rosie. I wanna tell you a secret."

Rose hesitated. She didn't like secrets. She didn't have many herself, and she didn't like knowing other people's. But perhaps at this moment she didn't have a choice. "All right," she said, sitting down and placing the jar of flowers on her knees.

Iris swayed into her. "Rosie, Rosie, Rosie," she chanted. "Rosie, Rosie, Rosie with her posies!"

Rose nodded. "That's me!"

Iris wagged a finger. Her red hair might go on forever, but her nails were bitten to the quick. "'That's I,'" she chided. "If you're in the house of a distinguished member of the English Department of this undistinguished college, you must be grammatical and say 'That's I.'" Iris leaned against Rose, not for comradeship but for balance.

"Certainly. *I* stand corrected."

Iris didn't get the joke. She wagged her head along with her finger. "You shouldn't be so cheerful about it when I correct you like that. You should tell me to go to hell. That's what I would do, if someone said that to me."

Rose shifted the jar of flowers to one side so she could put an arm around the sagging Iris. It wouldn't do to have her land in a heap on the floor. "Well, I'm not you."

Iris moved closer and settled in against her. "That's for sure. Tom's nice and you're nice. How come you're so nice to everyone, Rosie?"

"I don't know. It keeps life simple, I guess."

"Oh. Hmmm. Never thought of that." Iris's head dropped on Rose's shoulder. Her lime-green-clad body slumped.

She's passed out, Rose thought. *What do I do now?*

The only other piece of furniture in the foyer was a grandfather clock that looked very, very old. Its sedate face stared down at them. Rose stared back and listened to the clock's insistent ticking. There was almost no sound coming from the rear of the house now. Was everyone talking in whispers? Russell had obviously decided not to come back. And who could blame him?

She and Iris were forgotten and abandoned, snuggled up together in this dark box. Still, everything was fine, really, if only she weren't so hungry.

Iris abruptly pulled herself upright, shaking off Rose's arm. "I think I'm in trouble," she said, mush no longer clinging to her words. "Did I already tell you that?"

"No," Rose said cautiously. "You didn't."

"Well, I certainly haven't told anyone else," Iris said crossly.

"Well then," Rose said. "It really is a secret, I guess."

"What do you mean by that?" Iris turned on her, ready to fight.

"You were going to tell me a secret, remember?"

Iris looked blank. "I was?"

"Yes."

Iris subsided into muddled thought. Rose stared at the clock again, wishing it had a visible pendulum, just so she could watch it move. Her stomach growled. Outside, children shouted and were quickly silenced. This was a house of grief. Time must be allowed to pass quietly, with as few intrusions as possible.

"I'm all mixed up," Iris said.

No surprises there. "I'm sorry." Rose's stomach had begun a low, constant droning.

"I was going to tell Tom this morning and then *this* happened." She gestured vaguely at a stack of junk mail on the floor.

Rose had begun thinking about tuna casserole. There had to be one somewhere in this house. People weren't allowed to die in America without tuna casserole, were they? "What was that?"

Iris lifted her head like a she-wolf preparing to howl. *"God dammit! Everything's gone to hell, again!"* This time she shouted loud enough for anyone on the planet to hear.

"Nothing's ever as bad as it looks through the bottom of a bottle," Rose said automatically. It had been Mavis's standard response to drunks who whined.

"Don't say that!" Iris wailed. "It's so demeaning!" She burst into noisy tears.

At that moment the overhead light in the foyer flicked on, the hallway door opened again, and the president of the college appeared, followed by Professor Putnam.

Rose stood up, clasping her jar of flowers. She liked the president, who often came over to the Book Store for what she called her "afternoon decompression." She was a slightly overweight, aggressively chic frosted blonde from Dallas, who affected stiletto heels around this country campus, but was still, in Rose's book, a good and interesting person because she was smart and unafraid to be herself.

The president came clicking across the wooden floor in her signature stilettos. "Hello, Rose," she said. "It's nice to see you. Although I'm sorry it's not under our usual more cheerful circumstances."

"Yes," Rose said.

The president then turned to Iris, who'd begun sobbing extravagantly, making loud honking noises, and so was oblivious to everything except her own painful inner drummer. "How sad." The president patted Iris's bright green shoulders with the tips of her manicured fingers. "She and Marjory must have been very close."

Professor Putnam still stood in the doorway. His look of amusement was there and gone in an instant, but Rose had seen it. There was a refreshing lack of pretense in allowing yourself to be amused in public by anything the day after your wife was killed. It made him seem more like a person and less like a caricature. How old was Professor Putnam? she wondered. Mid-forties? It was hard to tell the age of someone so self-effacing. He was as tall as Russell, but more stooped and without any of Russell's swagger. He looked tired, but not really devastated, not at all like a man who had just lost someone he loved. Perhaps "off-balance" would be the word to describe Professor Putnam, like someone who has pushed and pushed for a long time against a great weight that has suddenly and inexplicably disappeared.

Once the president had made her usual gracious exit, there was still Iris to deal with. She'd gone to sleep slumped over the pile of *Sunday Book Reviews*. Rose and Professor Putnam stood over her side by side, clamped together in this strangely comic interlude.

"I'm sorry about this," Rose said.

Professor Putnam smiled. "Why? It's not your fault." He'd taken the jar of roses from her. He stood with both his hands wrapped around it, the flowers' thorny stalks pressed against his chest, his warm dark brown eyes looking down at her. "This is Russ's doing. Everyone knows Iris drinks too much if you let her. Well, actually she hasn't for a while, but it looks as though she's back at it again. Iris hates Russell for some reason, says really nasty things about his ideas in faculty meetings. Russ himself hasn't had a drink in years, but he feels perfectly justified in getting Iris drunk. He baits her until she says something that makes him mad, then he storms off and leaves her for someone else to deal with."

"My, my," Rose said quietly. "What a dysfunctional little couple they are."

Professor Putnam smiled again from behind the roses. "I'd never thought of it in that way, but that's precisely what they are."

"Where does Iris live?" Rose asked.

"Miles from here. Somewhere on the side of a mountain up around Lovingston. I don't know exactly. I doubt if anyone here has ever been to her house."

"Oh dear."

They looked down at the fallen woman. Rose was unsure whether her first order of business should be dealing with Iris or offering condolences about Marjory's death. She decided on condolences. "I'm very sorry about your wife. I didn't know about her death until I got here. I'm afraid I've intruded. I . . . I thought I was just coming for dinner. That's why I brought the roses. They were for Marjory."

"Really!" Professor Putnam's grip on the jar of flowers tightened. For the first time, he seemed to be in real pain. "That was terribly thoughtful of you. Marjory would have been tremendously pleased. No one else around here has ever thought of treating her like that."

Like what? Rose wondered. "It's nothing."

He turned to her, frowning. "Didn't you get my message?"

"What message?"

"About Marjory's accident. I called the Book Store to tell you, but no one seemed to know where you were. So I called the inn and left a message. Didn't you get it?"

Rose shook her head. "I was moving today. I haven't been back to the inn since about seven o'clock this morning."

Professor Putnam stood looking down at her, still frowning. "No one at the Book Store said anything about your moving."

This was the closest Rose had ever been to him. Drunken Iris was right, the man emanated kindness, even now. What in the name of the eyes of Texas had made her so anxious yesterday in his class? "It doesn't matter in the least," she said. "I'm only sorry that I've intruded into an evening obviously meant for much older friends."

He moved a step closer and took her arm. It was a completely unselfconscious gesture of concern. "But you must be starving. Have you had anything to eat?"

"No, but that's nothing for you to worry about," Rose said. "Really. I'd better be going. You should get back to your guests."

"But you're Marjory's guest," Professor Putnam said with quiet, deliberate emphasis. Rose was moved. If this man wasn't shattered by his wife's death, at least he honored her place in this house. Not only did Professor Putnam have the courage to live with Marjory, he had enough courage to be honest in the wake of her death. Rose had long ago decided that she would be no good dealing with the complexities of a long-term relationship. She'd always called this self-assessment wisdom, but could it, perhaps, be fear?

Rose looked down at Professor Putnam's hand resting lightly on her arm. Abruptly all the confusion, all the bustle of the day, stopped, and she was perfectly contented to stand there.

Rose had always wondered what had first attracted Mavis to her professor, what had caused her to abandon the restless habits of a lifetime. Could it have been a moment such as this? Could it have been that in the midst of all the roar and hubbub, he'd taken her arm and, for just an instant, made her rackety life stand still?

Rose removed her arm. She immediately pushed back her hair, not wanting Professor Putnam to think she was deliberately breaking contact with him. He'd meant nothing personal by touching her. He was simply a host concerned about a guest's comfort.

Of this, she was almost certain.

chapter 4

Agnes Tattle was the only woman that evening not wearing a dress. She had thought about putting one on earlier, just to blend in, but then she'd decided to hell with blending in, and she'd put on slacks and a cotton sweater instead.

People had begun showing up about five thirty. Agnes had known they would appear as soon as they could according to their own rigid social code, which would naturally include precise times for coming over uninvited to comfort and feed the bereaved. Besides, with this particular death, there would be an eruption of collective guilt among her fellow campus residents. Marjory had been the Old Faithful subject around here for years. This evening would be the last, best chance for the campus to exorcise its communal guilt.

And sure enough, once the front door bell began to ring at five thirty, it didn't stop. Through the door marched a steady stream of food-bearing women, their plumage appropriately subdued (except for Iris, in her glorious lime green costume, who'd gotten drunk as a fart) and trailed by their soberly dressed men. The house had filled up quickly, but you would have never guessed how packed it was from the noise. Everyone talked very quietly, and no one laughed. After her second Scotch, Agnes began to wonder if these people might not be secretly afraid that if they let out a loud enough guffaw, Marjory would rise up from her casket, hitch a ride over from Peterson's funeral home, and haunt them. Would that her daughter had the guts to do that. Marjory, Agnes thought, was due a little payback.

Finally, about eight thirty, she'd had enough sanctimonious twaddle and slipped into the kitchen to pour herself a fresh drink. Her plan was to sneak out onto the back porch, smoke a cigarette, have another Scotch, and spend a few quiet moments away from all these whispering, well-meaning, *platitudinous*— was that a word?—college people. Most of all, her plan was to be *alone* out on the back porch, but when she quietly opened the door, Agnes found that Rose Callahan had gotten there before her. She sat sideways on the third step down with her back against a railing post, busily stuffing herself with tuna casserole and peanut butter pie. Agnes was surprised to see that Rose, too, had on a dress; certainly unfashionable and unironed, but still a dress. Her hair, however, was a spectacular mess—all over the place in some kind of anti-hairdo.

"Damn!" Agnes said before she could stop herself.

Rose immediately looked up at Agnes and—wonder of wonders in this evening of stylized gloom—smiled. "I could leave. Or just promise not to talk. I'll bet you could use a break from talking."

Agnes hesitated. Rose Callahan must have had one of the longest interactions with Marjory anyone had had in years—besides herself and Tom and Dr. Simms, of course. If Marjory were alive, the four of them might right now be eating dinner together. And there could have been a miracle, and Marjory might actually have been *enjoying* herself. "It's not talking I need a break from," she said. "It's listening to claptrap." She sat down on the top step and lit a Camel.

Rose smiled again and went back to eating. She ate vigorously, Agnes noticed, like someone who'd never heard of calories. Agnes took a generous sip of Scotch. She herself was not at all hungry, might never be hungry again, but she did think she might be a little tight. Just a little. Just tight enough not to mind quite as much. She would mind tomorrow. Tonight she had to endure all these chatty people, whose words drifted out to her now through the open windows at the back of the house. They seemed to have already put aside Marjory's death and be talking disdainfully about some new cost-cutting measures introduced at last week's faculty meeting. Agnes sniffed. Get a group of academics together for any reason, give them all a drink, and they would automatically begin bad-mouthing their administration—no matter who had just died. At least Rose Callahan had the sense to be quiet. It *was* nice to have someone around right now. Nicer still when that someone wasn't saying anything.

Agnes propped an elbow on a knee and contemplated what remained of the three fingers of Scotch she'd poured in her Foghorn Leghorn jelly glass. "My daughter gave me six of these things for Christmas last year. They're the same jelly glasses I threw away for years. Marjory paid a fortune for them on eBay. Said they reminded her of her childhood."

"How very nice," Rose said.

Agnes rolled on, talking not so much *to* someone as because someone was there. "The problem was that Marjory wasn't a happy child. Other children frightened her. I'd take her to the park, and she wouldn't want to get out of the car." Agnes stared hard at Foghorn. Did she have *any* happy memories of Marjory after the age of about six? Any at *all*? "Why, in heaven's name, would someone say they wanted to remember a childhood like that? I'd have thought she was being ironic, except Marjory didn't have enough self-confidence to be ironic. That was my province." She waved her cigarette at Rose's water glass. "Don't you drink?"

Rose shook her head. "Not often. I grew up around bars. It dims your enthusiasm for alcohol."

"Does it bother you if I drink?"

"Nope. I liked growing up in bars."

Agnes leaned sideways and eyed her. Rose Callahan was quite the Buddha, really, when you thought about it, sort of enigmatically happy. "You didn't have some kind of Gothic deprived childhood, did you?"

"Heavens, no. I had a happy childhood. Unusual, perhaps, by middle-class standards, but it was a lot of fun."

"Then what were you doing hanging out in bars?"

"My mother was a bartender, and she kept me on a pretty tight leash." Agnes snorted. "Good for her!"

"Uh-huh. She always said she'd made all the mistakes, so I didn't have to."

"And was she right?"

"In what sense?"

"Have you made mistakes?"

Rose grinned. "Certainly. How else would I have grown up?"

"Hmmm." Agnes took a deep drag off her Camel and blew out a stream of smoke. "Marjory never deliberately made a mistake in her life."

"I beg your pardon?"

Agnes watched the smoke from her Camel reach the blank blackness of the night sky. "My daughter never once disobeyed me that I can remember. I don't think she ever disobeyed anyone. I wish she had. If she'd been able to act on her own, she might have been happier."

The protectiveness Rose had felt for Marjory came back in a rush. "She invited me to dinner. She did that on her own."

Agnes's face contorted. "I know. I wish you'd come around earlier. You seemed to have reached something sturdy inside her that the rest of us couldn't. It made me quite hopeful. My daughter always had such a fragile heart."

An unwanted thought came into Rose's head: *I, too, have a fragile heart . . .*

A soft breeze stirred. The trees at the bottom of the yard moved about like great, dark, cloaked figures.

Agnes stared at the glowing tip of her cigarette. "This must be why I started to smoke again. It gives me something to look at when I don't want to think, and I certainly don't want to feel." Her voice was bleak. "My daughter was damaged in ways nobody, including myself, could ever understand. I had no patience with her. I loved her, but I had no patience. She was always some-one I found it difficult to be around. Even when she was a small child. Every-thing that came easily to me was hard work for her."

"I think I might have liked her," Rose said quietly.

Agnes waved her cigarette in the air. "How could you possibly think that? Marjory was so broken. Her own feelings frightened her. I don't know what possessed me to let Tom marry her. I should have stopped it, for his sake, but I let it happen because I was terribly sorry for myself in those days and wanted someone else to deal with Marjory for a while. The result was that Tom's been in prison for twenty years, and I never really got out of it. It's foolish to think you can ever run away from your own child." She took another drag on her Camel, another swig of Scotch. "Have you had any real pain in your life?"

Rose hesitated. "Not really. I guess I've never stayed anywhere long enough."

Agnes eyed the younger woman curiously, storing this information away. Then she turned back to the night sky and pushed up the sleeve of her sweater. It was an old, stretched-out one she'd had for years. The sleeves kept flopping down over her hands and irritating her. And she was irritated enough already. No, that was inaccurate. She wasn't irritated, she wasn't annoyed, she wasn't "out of spirits," as her mother-in-law would have put it. She was flat-out, full-steam, blow-your-top *angry*. "Pain is an overrated experience. It's better to be happy."

"I suppose so," Rose said. "I have enough sense to know I've been lucky." Which was true. Nothing awful had ever happened to her.

From inside the house, Rose heard her boss, Mr. Pitts, laugh and call out something about the Red Sox. It was the loudest anyone—except for Iris—had spoken since Rose had arrived.

"Perhaps," Agnes said. "Or perhaps you're brave. It takes courage to be happy, you know—even when you keep moving. It takes guts to accept things as they really are and not blame life for being what it is." She swept her hand fiercely across the backyard. Ice cubes sloshed against the edge of her glass. "Look at this goddamn place. No one's really happy here, but they cling to it like leeches because it looks pretty and pastoral, and they think it's safe. If any of them had any guts they'd get the hell out! And that includes me and my son-in-law. My son-in-law especially, since he's got a little life left."

As if on cue, a neighbor, out walking his dog, passed by in the alley between the small backyard and the woods. He was careful not to look in their direction. In this tiny, enclosed world, it took discipline to maintain the illusion of privacy. The man's feet crunched loudly on last year's dead, dry leaves.

Agnes drained her Scotch. "Would you believe the one thing Marjory showed promise in was art? When she was little, she drew beautiful, expressive pictures. In the ninth grade, she won the city-wide art contest for high school students. In the ninth grade! She beat out kids who were years older than she was. It was the one time in her life she competed at something, and she won! I thought she was turning things around, finding herself. I framed that picture and hung it on the wall of my office and showed it off to everybody. But right after that Marjory folded up as though someone had let the air out of her. I took her to doctors all over the country. But nothing and nobody helped."

"I'm sorry," Rose said.

Agnes turned on her, ready to fend off any insincere sympathy, but something in Rose's face stopped her. "I believe you really are. Amazing." She turned away again and stared up at the black, blank sky. There was too much light on that part of the campus for stars to penetrate.

"May I get you some more Scotch?" Rose asked.

Agnes hesitated, then shook her head decidedly. "No. I'm teetering on the edge of maudlin as it is. I hate maudlin drunks."

"It beats argumentative ones."

Agnes gave another snort. "I've argued enough without drinking."

"Oh? How's that?"

"I was a lawyer. A divorce lawyer. A good one. I was a huge fan of alimony for a long time. There's many a woman holed up in Charlottesville living a bitter life on gigantic alimony checks thanks to me, when what she should have done is said good-bye to the past along with her bastard exhusband and made a new start." Agnes tossed her ice cubes out onto the ragged grass. "At the time, however, I thought I was God's gift to women."

Rose Callahan was sitting close enough for Agnes's shin to brush her knee. The woman actually *felt* calm. Agnes found herself floating back and forth in her own life. It was a feeling she rarely experienced. Usually she was all *now*. "I'm going to tell you something," she said softly. It felt as though some stranger were channeling through her, prepared to spill the beans.

"All right."

There was the past. Right there. As present as anything within reach. "My husband was killed on a routine training run out of Laughlin Air Force Base. The last morning I saw him, I snapped at him. I'd just found out I was pregnant. I was sick as a dog, puking up soda crackers, and I took it out on him. Not badly, but enough. I wish I hadn't been such a bitch."

Rose reached instinctively for the old lady's hand. It was such a small sin, being unfairly snappish with someone, but Mavis, the forthright mother confessor behind the bar, had always maintained it was people's small sins that, unshriven, became their damnation.

Agnes shook her off. She was all business again, back firmly in the present. "I don't want comfort. I wanted to tell someone, that's all. I didn't say a word about it as long as Marjory was alive, but now she's dead and I decided to spill the beans to you. Can you understand that?"

"Of course." If there was one thing Rose was sure of, it was that the mysteries of the human heart must always speak for themselves.

Agnes stared hard at the woods and let out her breath. It felt as though she'd held it in for decades. "Good, because I sure as hell couldn't explain it to you." Footsteps sounded again, and the neighbor walked by, heading home, the small dog trotting jauntily ahead, straining at its leash. Agnes stubbed her cigarette out on a step and tossed it out into the grass. "Goddamn mutt gets loose and craps in the yard," she said, once the neighbor was safely out of earshot.

*   *   *

"You don't have a choice," Russell said, trotting out his charm as a matter of course. He'd bumped into Rose Callahan in the foyer, both of them on their way out. "It's late, you're a lady, and I'm going to walk you home. It's the way southern men of my generation do things."

"All right," Rose said. "If you insist."

"I *do* insist." Russell gave her a little bow to hide the fact that he was not quite comfortable. He was leaving without saying good night to Tom, which left this dreadful evening feeling dreadfully unfinished. But Tom had disappeared, and no one seemed to know where he was or how long he might be. For a bad few moments, Russell had had the uncomfortable thought that Tom had gone somewhere private with Rose Callahan, but then here she was, so maybe Tom had just given up and gone to bed. He was fully capable of wandering off from a gathering in his own house, wasn't he?

Russell realized he was frowning at Rose. She seemed as unfinished as the evening, standing there in that ridiculously rumpled dress with her arms hanging down at her sides. "Don't you have a purse or anything like that you need to get?"

"No," Rose said, looking up at him as though the question amused her, "I don't."

Of course she wouldn't, now that he thought about it. Rose Callahan didn't wear makeup, didn't comb her hair every five minutes, probably hadn't even locked her front door. Why would she need a purse? "Well then, we're off." Russell reached down for the umbrella he'd wedged between the wall and a stack of magazines. What a dunce he'd been to tote that thing along just because the Channel 13 weatherman had mentioned a slight possibility of late evening showers. When would he learn not to pay attention to *anything* said on TV? The sky had been cloudless all evening.

Tom Putnam appeared in the hall doorway. "You're leaving, then?" he said. His eyes, Russell noticed, were on Rose.

"Yes." Russell tried hard not to sound too happy about it. My God, it had been a long evening, full of awkward moments—which was only appropriate, since the cause of the gathering was the death of poor, pathetic Marjory. Tom's wife had always made Russell extremely uncomfortable, as she'd taken him straight back to his own squalid, disordered childhood, which he'd spent his whole adult life trying not to think about. "We're off. I looked for you to say good night, but I couldn't find you," he said.

Tom made a vague upward gesture with one hand. "I went upstairs for a moment to look for Agnes. I found her sitting in the hall chair with the lights off, so I sat down on the floor and chatted with her. You know, just to be sure she was all right."

Russell nodded. "Of course. Well then, we'll be going. Unless, that is, there's anything at all we can do for you?" Tom Putnam was still looking at Rose. Really, he was *staring* at her. Russell glanced down at the top of her tousled head. Rose Callahan wasn't all *that* wonderful, was she? Just different, really; more like a refugee from an artist colony than a college employee.

"No, thank you, Russ," Tom was saying. "Agnes and I just need some sleep. We've got a lot to see to tomorrow. You know how it is."

Tom offered his hand. Russell shook it, warmly. Really, Tom Putnam was a fine fellow; it was hard to see him in such an exhausting muddle. It was difficult to imagine what it must be like, not loving your wife at all, but still sticking with her and ordering everything you did around her. Then one day you come home from work, and—*poof!*—she's gone.

Rose had taken a couple of steps toward Tom and put her hand on his arm. What was this about? Russell wondered. She'd never put her hand on *his* arm, and he'd talked to her every day for four weeks. As far as Russell knew, Tom had only met her that one brief time in the Book Store. Of course, she was taking his Shakespeare class. And the two of them had had to deal with horrid Iris tonight when she'd begun wailing like a banshee in front of the president and passed out right there on that bench. Russell felt an internal stab when he thought about Iris. He'd have to call Lewis, his AA sponsor, when he got home and confess he'd been goading her again. What was even worse—and what he might leave out of his confession, because he didn't want to hear AA Lewis *not* being judgmental about it—was that he'd been goading Iris *and* plying her with alcohol. How many AA venal sins had he commit-ted by doing that? But it was so hard to resist egging awful Iris on, and it was so much easier to do when she was drinking; besides, awful Iris was mean as a snake to him every time she got the chance. Really, the woman was insufferable. Completely insufferable. She wasn't the right sort for this college, at all. At this, Russell felt another stab. He could hear Lewis's pa-tient reply if he voiced *that* sentiment. *Russell,* he would say, *perhaps the fact that you think such a thing about a colleague actually says something about you that might be worth thinking about as a recovering alcoholic.* God, Russell hated trying to be good!

"I'm so sorry," Rose was saying, her hand still on Tom Putnam's arm, her eyes looking up at Tom Putnam's face. Russell felt another stab—jealousy this time, something else about which AA Lewis would have a few disgust-ingly tolerant words to say. Why was he feeling jealous? He liked smooth, glossy, finished-looking women. Graduates of St. Catherine's or St. Anne's— that sort. Not someone as casually turned out as Rose Callahan. Sure, she was fun to talk to, but not the real deal as a woman, at all!

"Thank you," Tom said, not even bothering to put his hand on hers and give it a little squeeze, which Russell certainly would have done. "And thank you for the flowers. Marjory would have been so pleased."

Russell looked at his old friend more closely. My God! There were tears in Tom Putnam's eyes. Here he'd gone through the whole evening dry-eyed, stoically enduring the crowd at his house like a politician who'd just lost an election. And now, just because Rose Callahan had brought his dead, unlov-able wife a bunch of thorny roses from her backyard, *now* he was tearing up. If Russell didn't know Tom better, he'd suspect him of making a show of grief for Rose Callahan's benefit, the way he, Russell, might have been tempted to do. But since he *did* know Tom, Russell could only conclude that the tears really had something to do with what he was saying to Rose Callahan, that her silly posies would have pleased dead, unlovable Marjory.

Russell hunched his shoulders and squinted at the lighted doorway be-hind Tom's head. He did not like complicated emotions. The straightforwardness of Alcoholics Anonymous was the one thing that probably kept him in the program. "Keep It Simple!" was plastered everywhere you looked at an AA meeting and was often chosen as a topic for discussion. Russell took "Keep It Simple!" to mean that you shouldn't dig around too far under the surface of your own emotions, thoughts, or impulses. Just turn your life over to your Higher Power, whatever that was, and plow full steam ahead. And right now— keeping it simple!—what Russell wanted was Rose Callahan's hand on *his* arm so that he could plow full steam ahead out of there. "Shall we?" he said, stepping toward her, offering his arm.

Tom immediately stepped back, well trained by his marriage not to be caught doing anything, under any circumstances, that might be considered flirtatious. In that way, Russell thought sadly, Marjory would haunt him for years.

Instead of taking his arm, however, Rose simply let her hand fall. She didn't bother with any feminine ruse, either, such as pretending she hadn't seen his offered arm. She simply noticed it was there and didn't take it. "Good night, Professor Putnam," she said. "Please tell Agnes good night for me as well. We had a nice chat out on the back steps."

"I will," Tom said formally, like the old schoolmaster he was. "Thank you both for coming."

Enough was enough. Tom Putnam might be his very good friend (another stab—oh, for heaven's sake, Russell! *Keep it simple!*), but Tom was single now and, whether he knew it or not, competition for feminine attentions. Russell firmly exorcised all ambivalence about leaving and propelled Rose ahead of him toward the front door. "Good night, Tom," he called over his shoulder.

*　　*　　*

It was a truly lovely night, clear as a polished shot glass, with just a hint of sharpness. Russell walked briskly along the sidewalk toward the main campus, swinging his umbrella, feeling unashamedly glad to be alive. If Rose Callahan hadn't taken his arm, at least she was beside him, loping along in her ugly dress and sloppy sandals, exuding what he'd come to think of as "Rosiness," a quiet, contained, removed quality that—for whatever strange reason— drew him to her like a sugar ant to a chocolate cake. He'd never spent time around a woman before who didn't seem to care at *all* what he thought of her. Even horrible Iris sought some kind of reaction from him, but Rose just hung out in his presence if he happened to be there, probably exactly as she'd been before he showed up and exactly as she'd still be once he left her. The other women he knew seemed to have a thousand personality permutations. They adjusted this and muted that as people—particularly men—drifted in and out of their sphere. And he, Russell, was much the same, now that he thought about it. He made constant minor adjustments, depending upon whatever company he was in. But this didn't seem to work around Rose Callahan. He'd tried hard to find the right note with her, subtly struck this pose and that, only to find her slight air of distance and—dare he think it!—*disinterest* deepening. Rose had seemed the most interested in what he had to say the other day when he'd talked to her seriously about an article he'd been reading about Spenser.

Russell glanced down at her. Her dowdy blue dress blew back against her in the slight breeze. Rose really was thin as a whippet. Maybe she ran marathons? Maybe she had a high metabolism? Really, he knew almost nothing about her—he couldn't remember Rose Callahan answering one direct personal question satisfactorily. Her complete self-possession made such questions pointless, anyway. Russell usually asked women about themselves to help them feel more at ease with *him*, but Rose had been at ease with him from the moment he'd come up to her in the Book Store and introduced himself. If he was honest—which was another thing AA demanded, even though honesty often seemed the antithesis of keeping it simple—it was he who'd needed to be put at his ease around Rose. And this she must have done, because here the two of them were at the end of Faculty Row, and they had yet to exchange a word. How strange. He'd actually been *thinking* in a woman's company, instead of chattering—something he couldn't remember doing since he'd escaped the stultifying boredom of his brief marriage.

Russell glanced up. There was a bright demi-moon sailing loftily across the sky. It would light their way perfectly if they left the well-lit campus. "Let's go this way," he said, pointing off to the right toward a hockey field. "It's a nice shortcut to your house."

"All right," Rose said. There was no bridling. No pretending they were teenagers and he was cooking up some ruse to get her off somewhere private so he could feel her up. Russell sighed. Would that they were teenagers. He'd wasted his teen years studying and worrying about his drunken, impossible mother. He looked down at Rose's hands, swinging freely by her sides, and briefly considered catching one up and giving it a little squeeze. But, for reasons he didn't understand and didn't want to understand, Tom Putnam's sad, befuddled face intruded and he gave up the idea. Instead he asked, "Will you be going to Marjory's funeral on Tuesday? I'd be glad to give you a ride if you need one."

Rose shook her head. "I don't think so. I just met Marjory the one time. I only came tonight by mistake, remember?"

Russell found himself giving her another little bow without breaking stride. He did a lot of this bowing stuff, didn't he? "I'll bet you're one of those people who's never met a stranger, Rose. You fit in here as though you've been around us all for years. And we're not always an easy bunch to get along with."

"Thank you," she said, with that mystifyingly straightforward look of hers that went straight to some unfamiliar place inside him. "My mother and I moved around a lot when I was a child. It helps you learn to adapt to new situations."

"Oh?" Russell was immediately interested. Here was the perfect opening for a personal question. "Was your father in the military?"

She shook her head. "I don't think so. I can't imagine that he was."

What did she mean by that? Surely she *knew* whether or not her father had been in the military? If it had been anyone but Rose, Russell would have thought she was playing with him. "That's interesting," he said, hoping it was obvious he would like more information.

But Rose walked on silently beside him. A paper cup skipped across the ground, a rare piece of litter on the immaculate campus. They had reached the center of the hockey field. Russell found himself conversationally stymied. For once, he didn't want to be charming. All he wanted was to ask Rose what her father had done for a living that had kept him on the move. What he *wanted*, Russell realized, was to ask Rose Callahan about herself and have her give him a straight answer. Before he could stop himself, he heard himself saying, "Would you have dinner with me tomorrow night, Rose?"

She didn't even pretend to consider. "No, I won't, Russell. Or any other night either. But thanks for the invitation."

"My, my, aren't we direct?" Russell knew he sounded testy, but what the hell—he *felt* testy, and directness was a two-way street.

Rose's eyes were on the moon. "My mother was a bartender. She always dealt very openly and directly with men."

"Ahh," Russell said. So he had stumbled onto a little personal information tonight, found out he'd just been derailed from possible entanglement with the daughter of a bartender. That was probably a blessing, even though it might not feel like one at the moment. Most of the women he went out with had ancestors who had helped form the country and once ruled in the South. Russell began to feel better. "I knew the first time I met you that you were an unusual child of unusual parents."

"Parent. There was only my mother."

Russell finally did put his hand on her arm, not to flirt, but to make a point. "That, my dear, is a biological impossibility."

"Says you," Rose said, still talking to the moon. Russell considered this. It didn't seem like the time or the place to argue biology. And back to her bartender lineage. Surely that didn't mean he couldn't enjoy her company? "So how about lunch? Surely we could have lunch together?"

"Of course we could. I eat in the college dining hall almost every day at noon. I'd be glad of your company."

The college dining hall! Russell hadn't eaten in the college dining hall for years.

They had reached the end of the hockey field. In front of them was a short hill. They climbed it together. Russell kept his hand under her arm, and Rose didn't object. She was having trouble with her floppy sandals slipping on the wet grass. It made him feel pleasantly straightforward to be in physical contact with her at last, and have it be for some useful reason. At the top of the hill was the main entrance road into the college. Farmhouse Lane stretched just ahead of them on the left. Russell let go of Rose's arm. "I'm almost home!" she said, sounding surprised.

They walked together past the dark houses, first the sprawling residence of the director of the Riding Program, then the increasingly humble cottages of the college's lesser souls. Rose had left on her front porch light, and a lamp burned brightly in her front room. Russell peered in from the road, unabashedly curious. The room inside reminded him of his graduate school adviser's office at the university—run-down furniture and piles of books everywhere. "You have a lot of books," he said. "And your furniture looks a bit—shall I say—eclectic."

"Right on both counts." Rose stopped at the end of her front walk and extended her hand. "Thanks for seeing me home."

Russell took her hand, shook it, and let it go again immediately. The straightforward feeling of the hill had lingered, and he didn't want to lose it by trying to force some romance into the evening. "Thanks for letting me."

She turned away and headed for her door.

"Rose?"

"Yes?"

Russell stood there with shoulders hunched and his hands stuffed in his pockets. What on earth did he want to say to her? She had turned around and was looking back at him, a dark, slim silhouette against the porch light. Surely she knew all about him, even if she hadn't filled in all the details. He felt as exposed as a streaker, but there was nowhere to go with this other than forward, wherever that took him. "I know I can be an awful blowhard sometimes," Russell heard himself say.

"Yes, you can." Rose's tone was completely neutral, and there was no way to know whether or not she was smiling.

Enough was enough. Russell swung back into character. He straightened his back and gave her the smart bow of a movie butler. Whatever he was, he was, and it would have to do. "Sure, and it's part of me charm," he said in what he'd often been told was a stellar imitation of an Irish brogue.

"If you say so!" Rose turned again and walked up the two steps of her newly painted front stoop. Russell waited until she had opened her front door, then took off again toward the main road. His own house was on the other side of campus, on a tree-lined, manicured street where deans, high-level administrators, and the president dwelt imposingly in brick. He walked very fast, because something kept pulling him backward, as though he were trying to drive a car with the brakes on.

chapter 5

Saturday morning, Tom Putnam sat up and looked around. The room he and Marjory had shared for most of their long, blank years together was strewn with her stuff; half-used pots of this and that, stacks and stacks of self-help books, the contraption she'd strapped under her chin every night that was supposed to keep her neck from turning into a turkey's. Every object offered its own mute and separate reproach that he'd not been able to make its owner whole again—or at least somewhat functional.

Tom heard Agnes open the door of her room and stomp down the hall toward the back stairs. For years the two of them had eaten a painfully polite breakfast with Marjory, then sent her off to do some failure-proof task while they sat on together at the kitchen table and chatted about what they planned to do with their days and how they felt about various unimportant subjects, like whether or not Agnes should start texting. Nothing they said would have held a thimbleful of interest for anyone else on the planet, but Tom had always found these morning conversations deeply satisfying. Talking to your mother-in-law might seem like small potatoes to people who luxuriated in more richly felt lives, but it had been enough for him to build a bearable day on. *Small blessings*, as his mother had so often said, shaking her head as though the wisdom of Solomon had been compressed into those two words. *Small blessings.*

Tom rolled out of bed and peered through the open window. Today appeared to be shaping up much like yesterday, golden-lit and clear. He shaded his eyes and peered out at the ancient oak that spread its lofty arms over the backyard. Every October, its dull red leaves blew down across the lane and carpeted his yard. He'd spent one glorious Saturday morning every year raking them up, glad to have a worthwhile task to do. It was one of the few mornings during the year he'd been able to count on not having to battle dull anger at Marjory's absolute inability ever to let anything go. He knew this inability came from what Dr. Simms called "her pathological lack of self-esteem." He *knew* that. But her whole life, Marjory had been allowed to demand what she could never give—nonstop understanding and forgiveness.

Tom stretched his arms high over his head and listened for signs of life downstairs. On most mornings Agnes banged her way around the kitchen, but today, she'd clumped down the stairs, and then . . . nothing.

Abruptly Tom was a man on a mission. He dressed and raced down to the kitchen, certain he would find the room empty except for a note on the table saying, *I'm outta here!* But there she was! Agnes Tattle, his crusty, cigarette-smoking mother-in-law. Tom could have kissed her—thrown his long arms around Agnes's small body and smacked her loudly on whatever part of her he reached first.

At a quick glance, everything looked relatively normal. Agnes sat in her usual place at the big kitchen table, working on the day's to-do lists with a ballpoint pen. But then Tom saw that his mother-in-law was not only smoking a Camel, she was still wearing those enormous men's pajamas. This was aberrant behavior in the extreme, for Agnes always dressed before coming downstairs in the morning. *Always.*

"Good morning!" he sang out, a shade too heartily.

Agnes eyed him over her cigarette. She looked worn out, like a bag lady who'd spent the night on a subway vent. "Don't be so loud right off the bat," she snapped, putting down her ballpoint. "Give me a moment to get used to being awake."

"Okay," Tom said cheerfully, glad to find Agnes had at least recovered some of her habitual bark. The kitchen windows were open. A slight breeze pushed cigarette smoke in his direction, and he sneezed. It was a real blast, out before he could even attempt to muffle it.

"*Gesundheit,*" Agnes said.

"Thank you."

The Braun hissed and spluttered on the kitchen counter, announcing it was through dripping. It was Tom's job to put the coffee together at night, Agnes's to turn it on in the morning. Each of them had come through as usual, at least in the coffee department. It might be a small scrap of structure to cling to, but it was something. A ripple of dread slapped at Tom. What would happen to their comfortingly familiar routine now that Marjory was gone and Henry was on his way?

Agnes was watching him, wearing her I-know-what-*you're*-thinking look. "Are you going to stand there looking rabbity or are you going to get us some coffee?"

"I'm going to get us some coffee, of course." Tom crossed over to the counter, got their usual mugs down from the cupboard (both awkward gifts from Marjory—his said "World's Greatest Husband"; hers, "World's Greatest Mom"), poured coffee into them, placed Agnes's mug in front of her, and sat down across from her at the table.

Agnes stubbed out her half-finished Camel in the jar lid she was using as an ashtray. "I'm sorry about the smoke. I know it makes you clog up. This breakfast will be the last time I smoke in the house. I may smoke out on the back porch where no one can see me for quite a while, though. Who knows?" She gestured down at her pajamas. "These were my husband's."

"You're kidding." Tom looked at the pajamas more closely. They were exactly like a pair his father had had, years and years ago. Agnes rarely mentioned her husband to him. Why was she wearing his pajamas?

"Nope, I'm not kidding. I wear these things on the rare nights I need comfort. I think I've had them on ten times in the past four and a half decades, but I've needed them for the last two nights. I seem to have lost most of my self-discipline along with my daughter. Ever since the police were here, I've been drinking like a fish, smoking like a chimney, and fighting a desire to curl up and suck my thumb."

"You'll get hold of yourself again," Tom said, meaning it. Agnes *was* self-discipline. Self-destruction was not her thing.

"Sure." Agnes lit another Camel, sucked in smoke, blew it out her nose, and eyed Tom over Rose Callahan's jar of roses, which someone (Agnes herself?) had placed in the center of the kitchen table. The flowers bloomed away as though nothing in the world were awry. "Look," Agnes said, "I know that letter you got night before last contained some bomb you've got to detonate this morning, but before all that, I'd just like to say that I think Rose Callahan is a nice person."

"You would?" Tom experienced a blast of confusion.

"I think she's a safe person, too," Agnes went on. "And I don't say that about many people. I certainly can't say it about myself."

"What do you mean by 'safe'?"

"I mean she doesn't need a lot from other people. She was raised in a series of apartments over bars."

"She was?" Tom's own hopelessly conventional upbringing loomed before him like an eighteen-year-long episode of *Leave It to Beaver*.

"Yep. She was. She evidently moved around a lot."

"Really?" The image of a skinny, ten-year-old Rose Callahan eating lunch by herself in yet another new school cafeteria tugged at Tom's heart. He'd had the same group of friends all through high school. "You know," he said, "night before last, Marjory came up to my office to tell me that she liked Rose Callahan very much, and that she thought Rose needed friends."

"Really?" Agnes eyed him.

"Yes. Really. It's hard to imagine, but that's what Marjory said." Tom stared at a fallen rose petal that lay just beyond his coffee cup. "Do you think it could possibly be true? It seems so unlikely."

Agnes shrugged. "Got me. Rose *is* remarkably self-contained. That's part of the reason Marjory responded to her the way she did. Rose Callahan instantly sized up poor, crazy Marjory and let her be who she was. The rest of us were always trying to force Marjory to act some way she wasn't capable of, just so *we* could feel a little better."

"The rest of us had to live with her," Tom said.

"That's true. We did have to do that. And Rose is new on the scene. She'd never had to deal with Marjory bursting into tears because her scissors were dull, or having an anxiety attack over which doughnut to choose. Oh, dear." Agnes drew in a long, shuddering breath. "What a tortured human being my daughter was. Marjory is, I really do think, better off dead. I don't know what dead is, of course, but it's got to be more fun than my daughter's life was."

Another rose petal fluttered to the tabletop. Tom picked it up. It felt like thin velvet between his fingers. The truth was that his mother-in-law often said things he was too timid even to think, things such as *Marjory is better off dead.* When he actually considered it, though, that statement seemed pretty likely to be true. Twenty years of marriage, and the woman he'd been married to was better off dead. Tom tried to picture Rose Callahan's oddly peaceful face, but it eluded him. He knew Agnes was waiting for him to say something. "I wish," he said, "that Marjory could have figured out a way to be more relaxed about things. I really do. But she didn't seem to have much capacity for relaxation."

Agnes snorted. "The master of understatement speaks again!"

Tom put the petal carefully back where it had fallen on the table. "I guess you've got that right." It was a great relief to find that he and Agnes could still talk; that the two of them were joined in a way that had, initially anyway, survived Marjory's death. He would at least have a comfortable beginning to this long tumultuous day. *Small blessings.* There was his mother again. Louise Putnam was in a New Jersey nursing home, smoothing her apron and planning to bake brownies for him and her dead husband, blissfully convinced it was 1967. Growing up, Tom had thought she was mostly hopeless, only able to grasp the occasional big picture, such as civil rights. But now he knew she'd been wise, taking sustenance from the simple pleasures of everyday things. When you got down to actual survival, that *was* the big picture.

Agnes ground out her Camel. "So let's have it," she said around a final blast of smoke. "I think I've put off knowing long enough."

It didn't occur to Tom to be disingenuous, to ask, "Have what?" or to stall for time by talking about what he was about to talk about. He took a deep breath and addressed the jar of roses. "I have a ten-year-old son named Henry who's arriving in Charlottesville on the Monday morning train. I had no idea he existed until that letter arrived."

"Hmmm." Agnes lit another Camel. Tom heard her sucking and blowing, but other than that, nothing. The silence was unbearable, so he rattled on. "I had a short affair with a visiting poet the year before you came to live with us. It only lasted three weeks, but I guess that was long enough to produce Henry. I'm so, so sorry."

"Why?" Agnes asked.

"Because I was a self-centered fool?" Tom heard the question in his voice, as though he were being quizzed and wasn't sure of the correct answer.

Agnes made a disgusted sound around her Camel. "I didn't mean why did you have the affair. I've known about that for a long, long time. I meant why are you *sorry* you had the affair?"

"Oh." Tom's eyes were still on the roses. "I see. I guess I'm sorry because Marjory somehow sussed it out and it made her worse."

"Hmmm," Agnes said again. "And am I right in supposing that was the only affair you had during your two decades of marriage to my daughter?"

"Yes."

Another suck. Another blow. "It was with that really pale Nordic poet, wasn't it? The one you said had just lost her husband and gone all needy?"

"Yes."

"Pity. I remember I drove down to the college from Charlottesville for her reading. I thought she was quite a good poet, but she wasn't very jolly, and twenty years is a long time."

Tom finally looked at his mother-in-law. Had she just implied she wished he'd had *more* affairs? "What did you say?"

"You heard me."

Tom would have never guessed that one person could bestow forgiveness and understanding on another person so efficiently. "I did hear you. Thank you."

"The reality of all this is, Tom Putnam, that Marjory deserves peace. And you, Tom Putnam, deserve a life."

His heart jolted unpleasantly. *What's that?*

Agnes grinned. "Scared you, didn't I?"

"A bit." Tom put both hands around his coffee mug. Its warmth felt good. "I guess living isn't a concept I'm familiar with. I'm used to spending my days hurrying through this to get to that."

"Until you climb the stairs to that office in the evening and bury yourself in Shakespeare."

He shrugged. "Yes, until then." *Let every man be master of his time.*

"Well, I haven't done so hot myself in the productivity department over the last few years," Agnes said. "The truth is I'm seventy-two years old, and I have no idea whether I can still really think, let alone prepare a brief or argue a case. No wonder all the women around here don't talk about anything that hasn't happened in their own backyards. The brain atrophies just like everything else. And God knows I've certainly felt sorry for myself." Agnes made a face. "Self-pity is poison. I kept telling myself to quit whining, to accept Marjory as she was, and get on with it. But I couldn't do it. And now she's dead, for heaven's sake, and yet I keep right on punishing her for being who she was, and punishing myself because I couldn't fix her." She shook her head. "Who the hell do I think I am, anyway? God?"

"Probably."

She shot him a look. "Speaking of God," she said, pulling herself up straight and squaring her shoulders. This must be the Agnes Tattle who had sat behind a desk and told mealymouthed women exactly what to do about their worthless soon-to-be-ex husbands. "You know, Tom, just between you and me, I don't think for one moment that Marjory killed herself. I think that, for some reason, my daughter was as close to happy as she was ever going to get, and if there is a God, that God is a merciful one who decided Marjory should be allowed to die when things were looking up. We both know in our heart of hearts that she couldn't have sustained even marginally upbeat feelings for long, but Marjory was as upbeat as I've seen her in ages when she got in the car with her goddamn scrapbooks and left for Charlottesville. If she killed herself, it was a Thelma and Louise thing. You know, there she was in her car, driving back to what she had to know would soon turn into the same old, same old, when she sees this glorious drop-off beside the road, and she has the impulse to fly away."

Tom had dropped acid once in college. He still remembered the feeling it had given him, of being free from all boundaries, loose in a world with no natural laws. Was it too much to hope that Marjory had known something close to that?

"I hope you're right," he said.

"Me, too," Agnes said. "And you know, considering that Henry's on his way, her timing couldn't have been better. But while I'm on this talking jag, I want to say one more thing to you, Tom Putnam, before we seriously get down to the Henry thing."

He smiled at her. Did he have a choice? "Okay."

She glared at him. "I know you didn't love Marjory. Who could? But you stuck it out because she was helpless and wouldn't have lasted a month without you. I know I helped out with the daily maintenance, but you were the one who provided my daughter with an identity and a place to live where she could feel reasonably safe. And while you may have indulged freely in self-pity, you never lapsed into bitterness, and you never hated her, and you never abandoned her. I think you are one of the few people I've ever met who really has a heart and a conscience."

Tom stared at her, his mind a whirl of caveats, disclaimers, denials. Agnes raised her hand. "I don't care whether your motives were grounded in inertia instead of high-mindedness. The truth is I don't really care what you *think*. That is the way you *acted*. It was a mixed-up mess of a situation, and no one could have been kinder to Marjory than you were."

She stopped, waiting for him to respond. "Thank you," he said, meaning it perhaps as much as he'd ever meant anything.

"You're welcome." Agnes nodded decisively. Case closed. "Now, let's put all this aside for a while and move on to Henry. Have you thought about where he'll go to school?"

Tom realized his mouth was still open. He shut it, opened it again, and said, "No, I haven't. The truth is I'm not sure I've really *thought* anything. I'm still working on believing. I've yet to progress much beyond being stunned."

"I see." Agnes stubbed out her cigarette. "Well, while you work on believing, I'll work on to-do lists."

chapter 6

The Book Store closed at two on Saturday. At twenty minutes past two, her workday over, Rose walked down the dappled, leafy lane that led to her cottage, admiring the fields, the sky, the venerable old bank barn; in fact, admiring everything. Until, that is, she swung her eyes toward her own cottage—*whoosh!*—all joy wisped away. Ray's car was in her driveway, and Ray himself sat on her front steps, talking forcefully into his cell phone.

Any dolt could tell that Rose had bruised both Ray's feelings and his ego by moving fifty miles farther away from him. "You haven't even looked for work in Washington," he'd said to her on their last weekend together before she'd left Charlottesville. "I'm sure you could find something up in D.C. or northern Virginia, and then we could try living together."

Ray had taken her hand at that point and looked at her in a way he'd meant to be appealing but Rose had found exasperating. She'd taken her hand back immediately and said, "No, we couldn't. I live by myself, remember?"

Ray *had* remembered, of that she was certain, but he stubbornly refused to accept that her stance about their living together was caused by anything other than logistics. In Ray's mind, if Rose moved to Washington, then there would be no reason for them *not* to live together. She, however, knew better. What her moving to Washington would mean was that, in a very short time, they wouldn't be seeing each other at all.

Ray was an arts editor for National Public Radio, a position he frequently equated to being pecked to death by ducks. Ten more steps and she could hear his end of the conversation. "I don't know what other options there *are* at this point, Frederick. They need more sound to mix the story, and they need it by ten tonight. So *you* need to get yourself back out there and get some!" He punched OFF, obviously furious throughout his entire being. When, Rose wondered, was the last time she had felt that angry at anyone? That *anything* at anyone? Opportunities for strong emotion generally made her feel what she was feeling now, ponderous and inert.

She trudged another few steps and was there. Home. The current iteration. "Hi, Ray," she said.

"Freelancers!" Ray momentarily glared up at her, as though she were one of them.

"I'm sorry," Rose said. Which she was, but not about anything to do with freelancers. She was sorry because her weekend had become so . . . so *cluttered.*

Not that Ray would notice how she was feeling. In his mind it was delightful for them both that he was here. Predictably, he shook off his phone call, smiled up at her, and with a very Ray-like flourish held up a wrapped package. "I brought you a cottage-warming present," he said. "And I brought myself! I'm here to help you unpack!"

The problem was that Rose hadn't *wanted* help unpacking. And now here it was, Sunday morning, and here, still, was Ray. He sat across from her at the breakfast table, scarfing down walnut pancakes that she, for some strange, throwback *housewifely* reason, had felt obligated to fix.

Why hadn't she just told him yesterday, kindly but directly, that she didn't want him to stay? Usually she could tell anyone anything. Or almost anyone practically anything. So, as unpleasant as it was to face first thing on a Sunday morning, the unsettling truth was that Ray shut parts of her down rather than opening parts of her up. And surely, Rose thought, if she were really meant to be with someone, that wouldn't be happening. The cottage was quiet except for the sound of Ray's chewing and the aggressive ticking of his cottage-warming present, an antique pine shoe box of a clock with an appealingly primitive face. It banged away from its new home atop her pie safe. Something about *hearing* time pass unsettled Rose, made her discomfortingly aware of all the things she was *not* doing.

"I *love* these pancakes!" Ray said again, grinning at her like the small boy he so often became when delighted. Ray's moods tended toward the mercurial; excesses of joy trod the heels of excesses of angst and irritation. "I could eat your walnut pancakes until I pop!"

Rose made an effort to smile back at him. "Relationship," she thought, was the wrong word to describe this thing she had going with Ray. A ship was too stable, too steadily on course. Relation-*boat* would be better. A little tippy boat that drifted with the wind and the ripples.

"I'm glad you like them," she said, pushing her own plate of pancakes to one side, half-eaten. The half she had eaten sat lumpishly inside her. Or could that sodden lump be her heart? A thought came, unbidden and unwelcome: *There is no happily ever after for me. There is only serial monogamy with a succession of Rays.* "What would you like to do today?" she asked politely.

Ray was eyeing her unfinished pancakes. "You going to eat those?"

"Nope. They're yours if you want them."

Ray pushed aside his own empty plate and slid hers into position. "Yum!"

The kitchen window was wide open. Sunshine shone through it onto the black-and-white linoleum floor tiles like a stage light. Professor Putnam floated by among all the dancing dust motes. *But you're Marjory's guest . . .*

When Rose was little she had fallen in love with "The Walrus and the Carpenter." For several years, Mavis had kept a copy behind whatever bar she was tending, and certain customers had been allowed to read it to Rose before she'd been sent upstairs to bed.

One stanza floated back to her. Ray's clock beat its time like a metronome.

> The moon was shining sulkily,
> Because she thought the sun
> Had got no business to be there
> After the day was done—
> "It's very rude of him," she said,
> "To come and spoil the fun!"

"I don't think we should see each other any longer, Ray," she said.

Ray had just forked a good-sized chunk of pancakes into his mouth. "Wha'?" he managed.

Ray, showered and packed, was ready to leave in twenty minutes. When he emerged from the bedroom carrying the old Boy Scout knapsack he used as an overnight bag, Rose was sitting on the floor of her tiny living room, sorting through a box of books. She started to get up, but he shook his head.

"Don't come out with me" was all he said as he headed out the front door.

And that, evidently, was that. The end of the affair.

Rose just had time to think about how sad it was that the two of them were to end in such paltry fashion before Ray was back. "My car won't start," he announced. "Now what?"

Now not much, Rose thought. Ray's car was a 1969 Volvo 1800S sports car. Its only dependable feature was its undependability. Ray drove it because he loved the way driving it made him feel about himself. When it was driv-able, that is.

The tiny town attached to the college shut up tight on Sundays. Nary a mechanic would be available until tomorrow. Besides, they'd probably have to have it towed to Charlottesville in order to find a mechanic who could work on it.

It's just as Mavis always says, Rose thought. *Life can't go long without showing its funny side.*

chapter 7

A crash from below woke Agnes while it was still full dark on Monday morning. Her bedroom was directly over the kitchen. She rolled over, looked at the illuminated face of the clock, and read 3:48. She and Tom had agreed to leave to pick up Henry in Charlottesville by five. She'd set her alarm for 4:15 in order to have a half hour on the back steps to drink coffee, smoke cigarettes, and prepare herself for whatever was to come. If she went back to sleep now, chances were she'd have more weird dreams about Marjory. Why not just get up and get on with it?

Agnes pulled on the clothes she'd laid out the night before—navy putter pants, a navy zip-top, and navy Keds. Tom was moving around below her—or rather, *clomping* around. The man was a klutz; he made noise by existing. Heading down the stairs, Agnes wondered what he'd broken this time. Please, please, *please* don't let it be the coffeepot!

It was not the coffeepot but an ugly antique chicken figurine Marjory had taken a fancy to on eBay, paid way too much for, stuck on a high shelf, and, after a week of frenzied delight, forgotten. Amazingly, the thing hadn't shattered but had broken into three neat chunks. When Agnes reached the kitchen, Tom was staring down at the chunks as though he could read them like tea leaves. "I was trying to get down my travel mug, and *this* happened."

"Oh, for Pete's sake!" Agnes hoped Tom knew the disgust in her voice was directed at the chicken and not at him. Hurriedly she scooped up the chunks and dumped them into the trash. "Good riddance to bad rubbish! Literally!"

"I was going to do that," Tom said. "Clean up the mess, I mean. I'm sorry I woke you."

"Don't be. Getting rid of that ugly chicken was worth losing a little sleep."

Abruptly they were grinning; two naughties who'd gotten away with something. Once again.

"Do you want some coffee?" Tom asked.

"Heavens, yes."

Agnes sat down in her usual chair. Perhaps someday soon she'd shake up her morning routine by sitting in a different one, but things were going to be shaken up enough today without that.

The kitchen table was littered with rose petals from Rose Callahan's bouquet. It struck Agnes that of all the detritus left in the wake of Marjory's sad existence, those roses were the one thing that didn't make her either sad or angry. Agnes reached out and touched one. It felt soft and cool and *calm*, somehow. After the funeral tomorrow, she and Tom would be drowning in floral arrangements, but Agnes didn't expect to be calmed by any of them. Not one of them would really be about Marjory. She and Tom had asked for contributions to the college scholarship fund in lieu of, but that meant nothing. Other people *knew* when you sent flowers to a funeral. And around here, what other people knew mattered much more than any scholarship fund. And much, *much* more than Marjory.

"Here you go!" Tom placed the mug of coffee before her using two hands, as though it might be inclined to follow the chicken into flight.

Agnes took a tentative sip and sighed with satisfaction. Very hot, very strong, just the way she liked it. She watched her son-in-law pour his own mug, dilute it with hot water from the sink (he was *such* a coffee wuss), come back to the table, and take his customary seat directly across the table from her. Not, Agnes thought, that it would ever occur to him to take any other seat. Routine was life to Tom Putnam, sweet, dutiful, loyal guy that he was.

"*L'chaim!*" Agnes raised her mug.

"*L'chaim!*" Tom raised his mug in return. But then he put it back down on the kitchen table. "The thing that really worries me," he said, "is that I'm now part of Henry's future. I'm not sure I can handle dealing with someone who needs to be opened up, instead of, you know, *contained*."

Ah yes! The Big Switch. Tom was concerned about being able to convert from the caretaker of a damaged adult to the caretaker of a small boy. But then who, in Tom's unpolished shoes, wouldn't be? What man could mutate smoothly overnight from custodian into daddy?

Agnes took another swig of coffee. "Henry got any other options in the dad department at the moment?"

"Well, no, of course not. But what—what if I screw this up? I mean, he's lived ten whole years of life and suddenly I'm his *father*. It makes me think about all the important, necessary things my father did for me. And did so well. Just because he was my father and he had these fatherly instincts. And I'm not sure I have any of those at *all*."

Agnes badly needed a cigarette. "Well, what about me?"

Tom looked startled. "You?"

"Yes, me. I didn't do so hot in the parenting department, did I?"

"You mean because of Marjory? But you were *wonderful* with her. You never stopped trying. You did the very best you could."

"Exactly," Agnes said. "And that's all any of us can do."

It took, she thought, almost a full minute for Tom to get her point.

Although it was only 6:20 on Monday morning, the Charlottesville Amtrak waiting room was already half full of people waiting for the 7:08 train. They banged away on laptops and yakked away on cell phones, as though the whole rest of the world were awake and wanting to hear from them.

She and Tom went together up to the ticket window. "Excuse me," Tom said, addressing the large, round caricature of a railroad employee who beamed out at them from behind his grate. "Can you tell me if the *Crescent*'s still on time?"

"The *Crescent*'s on time, doing fine!" the round man sang out. "How ya'll doing this beautiful morning?"

It was Agnes's opinion that if this oppressively cheerful gentleman would bother to *look* at them, he'd see how they were doing. They were tired and nervous and sad.

"Fine, thank you," Tom said politely.

"So, who you got coming to visit you?" the man asked. His face, Agnes decided, was really too small for his features. There was very little space left, once you crammed in the man's extra-large eyes, nose, mouth, and sprouty eyebrows.

"A little boy," Tom said. *Not*, Agnes noticed, "*my son.*"

"A little boy, huh? Like a nephew or something?"

"Or something." Tom's politeness was unwavering.

"How old is he?"

"He's ten."

Concern clouded the round man's eyes. "Only ten? He got someone traveling with him? Like his mother?"

"No," Tom said. "I don't believe he does."

Worry was now writ large on the man's face. "Well, don't you think that's a bit young for a boy to be on the train by hisself? Where's he coming from?"

"New Orleans. At least, I think that's where he boarded."

Worry galloped toward alarm. "From *New Orleans*! All that way by *hisself*! A ten-year-old *boy*? That's against company policy!"

Agnes could stand it no longer. Politeness was not going to cut it in this situation. "He's a Katrina orphan," she said, stepping forward. "We're taking him in."

Tom gasped. Without looking at him, Agnes knew he was staring at her openmouthed. What an innocent Tom Putnam was. If she hadn't cut in and lied decisively, who knew what hassles Henry would have been subjected to by this righteous arm of Amtrak? The words "Katrina" and "orphan," however, were magic; an instant free pass for her and Tom and Henry to get away with anything.

The round man beamed. "God bless you both!" he sang out, loud enough for the entire waiting room to hear. Around them was a blur of movement, as people briefly disconnected from their e-worlds to check in on this one. "Praise Jesus," the ticket window man said in an even louder voice. "Praise Him, who said suffer the little children to come unto me! Thank you, Lord, for putting these two good people before me on this earth, and God bless them and their poor little orphan boy!"

"Amen!" said several people.

For once, Agnes was unoffended by a public display of religiosity. She

figured that she, Tom, and Henry—especially Henry—could use any blessings any deities cared to send their way.

The *Crescent* arrived ten minutes late.

So, Agnes thought, *the world has turned and Henry has arrived.* Outside
this building there was a small boy who needed her time, her efforts, her *heart,*
for God's sake. She stood up and her insides did what felt like a swan dive. A
wave of dizziness followed, and she was forced to clutch Tom's arm to keep from
having to sit down again. Agnes had never in her whole life experienced anything like this. Had she kept going through her husband's and Marjory's deaths
and all that had happened in between, only to be felled by Henry's arrival?

Tom's arm felt surprisingly steady as they moved slowly toward the
platform. He patted her hand and snugged it up against him, smiling down at
her and murmuring sotto voce, "Heeeeeere's Henry!" in a bad imitation of
that man who used to introduce Johnny Carson on *The Tonight Show.*

A fine clear morning greeted them outside. Mr. Jefferson's small, smug
city, Agnes thought, could not have done itself any prouder. If she were the
one arriving, she would have taken heart from the brilliant blue skies and the
distant Blue Ridge Mountains. But then she was not the one arriving. Who
knew what shape Henry's ten-year-old heart would be in, after a day and a
half on a train chugging away from everything and everyone he knew.

The *Crescent* was still in the process of huffing to a stop as they stationed
themselves on the platform. It seemed to take several centuries for the long
beast to finally and completely settle. Then it took another hundred or so years
for the porter to climb down, position the steps, and hand down passengers.
Agnes watched as eight people got off: two couples, three women, one man.

That was it. No one else got off the train.

Tom stepped forward, as assured as anyone in the world. "Excuse me,"
he said to the porter, "but we're here to meet a boy named Henry, who is from
New Orleans."

"Oh, *Henry,*" the porter said, shaking his head, climbing the steps, and
disappearing back into the train.

The porter reappeared a few minutes later half guiding, half carrying a
very small boy clutching a large blue backpack. He was neatly dressed in blue
jeans, a checked shirt, and boy-sized Nike basketball shoes. This small boy

and his backpack were all the way down the steps, being guided toward them, before it registered on Agnes that this must be Henry. And that Henry was years younger than ten and most definitely a person of color.

Agnes moved forward to stand beside her son-in-law. Tom's eyes, fastened on the advancing boy, were calm and confident and *welcoming*. Whatever there was of steel in him had taken him over. For better or for worse, Tom Putnam was ready for Henry.

*   *   *

They were late, but it was not really her fault. Rose had allowed fifty-five minutes for the trip, which was her customary drive-time to Charlottesville. Ray, however—after spending most of yesterday silently pouting and last night sleeping on the couch—had insisted on talking during the drive about their *issues*. Having to explain the inexplicable, i.e., herself, had slowed Rose down.

Why, Rose wondered, had she not driven him to the car rental place at the Lynchburg airport yesterday? Why had she come up with the cockamamie idea that Ray should take the Monday morning train back to Washington?

At the time, it had seemed to her that another twenty-four hours together might defuse the tension between them, get Ray used to the idea of their not being together. In the 20/20 vision of a clear Monday morning, however, it was clear to Rose she'd been off her rocker to think any such thing.

The train—*hallelujah!*—was still there. Rose gunned her Honda directly up to the station entrance. Ray flung open the passenger door, grabbed his bag from the backseat, and sprinted into the building with nary a backward glance.

"I'll park and come in," she yelled after him.

Ray's response was a dismissive wave, which Rose knew was meant to send the message that he would prefer to see himself off. To hell with that. Mavis had drummed manners into her, and manners declared it rude to dump someone out at the station and drive away.

Rose parked the Honda some way from the squat brick building and impulsively inspected herself in the rearview mirror. She looked as she always did, only more tired. *Oh, what are you afraid of?* she asked herself angrily. *Another scathing glance from another former lover?*

The station waiting room was deserted by the time she entered. Rose pushed through the swinging doors to the track platform. Ray wasn't there either; but Professor Putnam was, coming toward her in the company of Agnes Tattle and a small brown boy whom Rose had never seen before. The three of them walked hand in hand, the boy in the middle. He was hunched under the weight of an enormous backpack.

"Hello!" Rose sang out, waving as vigorously as though Tom, Agnes, and the small brown boy were just dots in the distance.

Agnes waved back and kept walking, while Professor Putnam stopped and stared. The small brown boy, caught between the moving woman and the stationary man, yelped, "Please! You're *stretching* me!"

Agnes immediately dropped the boy's hand, while Professor Putnam stepped forward still grasping the one he held. The child, obviously very sleepy, moved forward with him. They stopped a few feet away from Rose. "Henry," Professor Putnam said, "I'd like you to meet Rose Callahan. Rose is a friend of your grandmother's and mine from the college." He smiled then, not at her, but at the top of Henry's head, and Rose thought his smile was simply grand.

"Rose Callahan," he said, looking now at her, "I'd like you to meet my—my son, Henry Putnam."

Behind the professor, Ray's train had begun slowly lumbering northward. Rose, however, couldn't bring herself to care. Trains came and trains went, but surely smiling fathers and their small brown sons were eternal.

Rose held out her hand. Henry stared at it briefly with his great blue eyes; then, as though pushed by some unseen adult urging him to mind his manners, he stepped forward and shook it. "I'm very pleased to meet you," he said, not quite looking at anybody.

chapter 8

"So," Tom said, standing with Henry in the middle of the guest room. "This is your room for as long as you're here."

Henry looked around at the stodgy furniture and limp curtains and said nothing. Which was pretty much what he'd said since he'd announced to Rose that he was pleased to meet her. Henry, as Tom put it to himself, was choosing to stand mute, as any smart prisoner would who didn't have a clue what was going on.

The one thing the boy had volunteered had been on the ride home. Out of the blue, he'd piped up from the backseat and said, "I know you're not my real father, but my mother said you're nice and I have to be with you because she can't take care of me, because she knows she's going out."

And then he'd gone mute again.

That was the moment Tom had realized that biology had nothing to do with the right and wrong of this situation. If Henry wasn't biologically his, he was still his in the sense that homeless kittens were his. All his life, Tom had taken in homeless kittens, fed them, had them checked over by vets, found them good homes. It might take him a while to figure out what constituted the equivalent treatment of Henry, but just turning him over to the SPCA—i.e., taking him to social services—was out of the question.

A sigh drifted up from around his knees. As Henry making any sound was big news, Tom hitched up his trousers and squatted down to look him in the eye. The boy's eyes were large, long-lashed, and astoundingly blue—

perhaps the one stamp his mother had left on him, although Retesia's eyes had been much, much paler. Henry's froth of tightly curled brown hair might need to be cut or might need to be left alone. *Oh dear,* Tom thought. *Three months of responsibility for the length of this child's hair.*

Henry regarded him solemnly over his spiffy backpack. The only time he'd abandoned the thing had been in McDonald's, where the three of them and Rose Callahan had gone for breakfast. Tom had suggested this, not wanting to let go of Rose's company quite yet and thinking that there was no child on the planet who didn't like McDonald's.

It was only Rose who'd appeared at all relaxed during the McExperience. She'd sat herself down across from Henry and proceeded to employ the same social procedures with him she used with everyone: I am who I am, you are who you are, and with that as a given, why shouldn't the two of us get along just fine? It hadn't seemed to matter at *all* to her that Henry didn't talk. Rose chatted away as though they'd known each other since the dawn of time, talking about places she'd discovered in the woods that Henry might like to visit, asking him if he'd like to go to the gym with her one afternoon and shoot hoops. Henry had mostly stared down at his backpack while she talked, but occasionally he'd looked up at her with something in his eyes akin to wonder. Tom had empathized with the boy. How could anyone be as comfortable as Rose Callahan appeared to be in weird situations?

Tom's knees were beginning to hurt. Perhaps squatting down to look Henry in the eye had not been a good idea. Yet he couldn't just stand up again without saying *something,* could he?

He asked the first question that came to him. "How old are you, Henry?"

To Tom's amazement, Henry responded by lowering his backpack to the floor, unzipping the front compartment, and extracting a folded piece of paper that he handed (wordlessly) to Tom. Tom unfolded the paper and saw that it was a Xeroxed copy of a birth certificate for one Henry Thomas Putnam, born September 23, 1998, at Tulane Hospital in New Orleans. His mother was listed as Serafine Despré; which, to Tom, sounded very much like a name Retesia might have made up on the spot.

His father was listed as one Thomas Marvin Putnam.

So there it was in black and white: a physical impossibility masquerading as a legal responsibility. What had Retesia done, arbitrarily picked a father for her son out of her past? What chaos had this child been born into?

Tom looked up to find Henry watching him anxiously, savvy enough already to know a Rubicon when he faced one. "So," Tom said, careful not to sound too hearty, "you're six years old, about to turn seven, then. You've got a birthday coming up in just a couple of weeks! We'll have to celebrate."

Instead of answering, or even nodding, Henry reached for his paper. Tom handed it back and watched Henry carefully refold it, zip it back in its compartment, pick up his backpack, and hug it close.

Both knees cracked as Tom stood up. "Thank you for showing me your birth certificate, Henry. It made me feel quite proud to see myself written down there officially as your father."

Henry's eyes snapped upward, and Tom thought he saw doubt flicker through their composure. This he construed as a good thing, for Tom was pretty sure Henry had gotten off the train expecting things *not* to work out.

Marjory was suddenly in his head, more perspicacious in memory than she'd ever been in life. *Henry,* she whispered, *is not me. He can still be all right.*

Tom looked down at the small, brown, abandoned six-year-old standing before him, separated from his own heart by only the bulk of a blue backpack. He reached down and grasped a strap. "May I put this down for a moment, Henry?"

Henry allowed his backpack to be dislodged without protest. Tom put it carefully on the floor at the boy's feet. He thought of Rose Callahan's ease with the boy; of how she'd treated him as she would treat any small boy with whom she was breakfasting. *If I'm to be this child's caretaker for three months,* he thought, *I need to let him know I care.*

Reaching down, Tom picked up the boy and held him close. Henry didn't respond, but neither did he struggle. Which, Tom figured, was a start.

So here they were, father and son, in the world according to Retesia Turnball. He held this strange, contained child as close as he dared, his heart suddenly quite fierce with feeling, his head ticking off all the things to be done in preparation for Marjory's funeral tomorrow. Of course, Agnes would right now be roaring through to-do lists with an efficiency he could only dream of. Besides, what he really *wanted* to do was take Henry shopping for bunches of new room stuff. Did that mean he was trying to buy some kind of relationship with him?

Marjory's ugly chicken loomed, whole again and on its shelf. The fact of the matter was the hideous thing had delighted her, made her happy for almost a whole week. So who was he to sneer at it? Who was he to monitor other people's happiness? If a new bedspread and matching jammies would bring a smile to Henry's face, why should he give his own motives for buying them a second thought? If this boy needed anything, he needed a reason to smile.

Tom carried Henry over to the bed, planning to sit down. This turned awkward when he had to physically maneuver the boy into his lap, first bending him in the middle and then folding his legs down. But he managed it, and put both arms around the little boy. Henry sat straight-backed as any marine.

Now what?

It came to Tom that the one thing he didn't have to do was hurry. Today would pass; he'd get done what he got done; Henry would either relax a bit or he wouldn't. The thing to do was for him, Tom, to relax and take his time. Let things come to him instead of rushing at them as he usually did.

Tom looked down at Henry's froth of tight curls and thought again of his own father. Eddie Putnam had never talked down to his son; he had always talked *to* him. He might have dumbed his language down a bit or simplified his sentence structure, but with the exception of Santa Claus, his father had never, at least as far as Tom could remember, tweaked his presentation of reality.

"Henry," he said. "I want to talk with you about this father-son business."

Henry blinked and, as if this were possible, seemed to stiffen.

Tom soldiered on. "Here's the way it seems to me. It seems to me that your birth certificate says I'm your father and that's one thing to consider. But it's not, perhaps, the most *important* thing."

Henry blinked again. Tom thought he could *feel* the boy waiting for the next in his short lifetime's long line of dropping footwear to fall. *Here, said they, is the terror of the French, The scarecrow that affrights our children so . . .*

"It seems to me, Henry, that the most important thing is how you and I *feel* about being father and son. Isn't that what you think?"

Henry's eyebrows ran together. *Is he thinking?* Tom wondered. *Or is he just worrying harder?* "I don't know," Henry said, in a voice just loud enough to be a voice.

"Well, that's fine. But what I really want to say to you right now is that I *do* know. Okay?"

Henry said nothing.

Tom gently tipped Henry over against his chest, holding him, patting him, trying his best to transmit his own surprisingly profound sense that everything was okay now and was soon to get even better. "What I want you to understand, Henry, is that I feel just grand about your being here."

Silence. Then a slight movement from Henry. "Am I going to school here?" he asked in the same whispery voice.

"Of course. We have to get ourselves through tomorrow. Through my wife's funeral that I was telling you about on the ride home today . . ." Tom's voice caught and he stopped, as Marjory was there again. Just for that moment, he missed her. Missed *her*. Marjory, as she'd actually been; defeated by life from the get-go, but always, *always* trying to figure out why, so she could fix herself.

Tom looked down to find Henry looking up at him, his blue eyes fastened directly on Tom's own. "I'm sorry your wife died," he whispered.

Tom suddenly couldn't stop himself; he hugged Henry to his chest so tightly that, if one of them were drowning and the other one were rescuing, it would have been impossible to tell which was which.

Around nine thirty, Tom was in the kitchen eating a bowl of rocky road ice cream when Agnes came in carrying Henry's backpack. "That's—that's Henry's!" he said, shocked at Agnes's behavior. "We can't just rummage around in Henry's stuff!"

Agnes waved Henry's privacy aside like a fly. "Have you *looked* in this thing?"

"Of course not! It's Henry's private space."

"Oh, please." Agnes plunked the backpack down on the kitchen table, finally swept clean of rose petals. "The last thing Henry needs is us not giving a damn about the details of his life. Would you like to know what's in here?"

Tom stared at the big blue thing. "Would that be right?"

"Right or wrong, I've already looked. And believe me there are things our boy Henry needs much more than his space. So, you want to know what Henry's mother sent along with him?"

"He already showed me his birth certificate." Tom felt again the weight of that small boy in his arms. "Did you see that?"

"I did. Who the hell is Serafine Despré?"

"I'm assuming it's a name Retesia made up for some reason."

"Why would she do that?"

Tom shrugged. "Because she's Retesia?"

Agnes thought for a moment and then nodded, as though Retesia being Retesia were excuse enough for anything. "So, did you notice the date of Henry's birth?"

Tom nodded, acknowledging that whoever Henry's biological father might be, it wasn't he.

"Speaking as a lawyer," Agnes said, "your name listed as Henry's father on his birth certificate means that unless some guy comes forward claiming *he's* the father and backs up that claim with DNA testing, legally you *are* Henry's father. Speaking as a person, however, legalities are not the best organizing principles when it comes to six-year-old boys. This boy needs you and me to step up and sort his life out."

Tom realized he'd been holding his breath only when he let it out. "I couldn't agree more."

Agnes nodded. "Good. Now, for the third time, do you want to know what's in Henry's backpack?"

"Yes," Tom said. "I do."

"Well," Agnes said, "first of all, there's not one ticket stub but two, and they're from Picayune, Mississippi, to Charlottesville, not from New Orleans to Charlottesville."

"You're kidding."

"I'm not kidding. You want to see them?"

Tom's curiosity once unbound, had taken over. "No, no, I'll take your word for that. What else did you find?"

"One change of clothes, one pair of pajamas, underwear, and socks, all of which are brand-new. There's also one brand-new teddy bear from the Vermont Teddy Bear Company—which means Teddy is a very pricey bear."

Tom frowned. "That's not a lot, is it? For such a long visit."

"Maybe not, but that's all there was room for," Agnes said.

Tom knew his mother-in-law loved nothing more than bombshells. "And why is that all there was room for?"

Agnes leaned forward and jammed a finger into Henry's backpack. "Because there are fifty thousand dollars' worth of hundreds in here, as well as a cashier's check for four hundred and fifty thousand more dollars."

"*What?*" Tom stared down at the blue backpack, trying to comprehend that it did indeed contain half a million dollars. That made Henry, the small, mute boy asleep in the upstairs guest room, a demi-millionaire. No wonder he'd held on to the thing. Tom imagined Retesia hovering over him, telling him again and again not to let go of it for *any* reason!

"So?" Agnes demanded.

"You're kidding?" Tom said.

Agnes threw both hands up. "Stop asking me that. I am *not* kidding! What the hell is the story with this child? You knew his mother. Do you have a clue?"

Tom fiddled his spoon around in the melting pond of rocky road. "I didn't really *know* her, you see. That—that wasn't the point of our relationship."

"Of course it wasn't the point! But I thought you two might have talked *occasionally.*"

Tom began pulling at his right earlobe, as though that might help him remember. "Her family came from either Iceland or Norway, I think. Or maybe Sweden. But wherever they came from, it was a couple of generations ago. Retesia never talked about them—I mean in terms of seeing them or having any contact with them."

Agnes was now in full lawyer mode. "You said she was newly widowed. Is Turnball her married name or her maiden name?"

Tom pulled harder on his earlobe. "I . . . I don't know. I don't even know if that's her real name or just her poet name. She could be Susan Smith for all I know."

"Had she been living in New Orleans before she came here ten years ago?"

"Not that I remember. I think she'd been living in Detroit. Although maybe it was St. Louis."

"Well, I Googled her before I came down here. There wasn't much— nothing at all after 2002. There was a little flutter in 2000 when she won something called the Dorothy Prize for her poetry. It looks as though she was living in San Francisco at the time. I couldn't find any reference to her teaching anywhere after she left here."

Tom gave up on his earlobe. "I'm sorry. I wish I could remember something helpful, but I just can't."

They sat in silence for a couple of minutes. *What now?* Tom thought. Taking in a lost boy was one thing; taking in a lost boy with a half-million bucks in his backpack was something else entirely.

Agnes stood up. "That's enough for today. Henry's okay, we're okay, the money's okay, and I'm going to bed." She reached for the backpack. "I'll take this back up to Henry's room. We don't want him thinking we're nosey or anything."

"Could I look at it first?" Tom asked.

"Look at what?"

"The money. I think this would all seem more real if I saw it."

Agnes, being Agnes, understood. "Sure," she said, sitting down again. "Take all the time you need."

Tom got up and pulled the backpack toward himself. He unclicked the front straps and folded back the covering flap. The clothes and the teddy bear were on top. He removed them carefully and stacked them on the table in reverse order.

Underneath the clothes was what looked like a large blue nylon lunch box encrusted with appliquéd dinosaurs. Tom pulled it out.

Years ago, just out of Amherst and briefly considering writing fiction for a living, Tom had produced one good short story, based on his mother's experience as, of all things, a freedom rider in the early sixties. On a whim, he'd sent it off to *The New Yorker,* and wonder of wonders, it was accepted. The result was a check in the mail for five hundred whole dollars.

Tom had never had that much money at one time before, and the prospect of lots of cash made him giddy. He'd taken the check to the bank and asked for all one-dollar bills. The teller, well versed in the quirks of human nature, had unquestioningly done as he'd asked. Tom had taken those five hundred one-dollar bills home and put them in a shoe box. For a couple of days, until the rent was due and he'd needed some of the money, he had taken out that shoe box, looked at those dollars, and felt irrationally optimistic about everything.

Gazing down now at Henry's money, Tom realized that five hundred one-hundred-dollar bills in a lunch box looked the same as five hundred one-dollar bills in a shoe box. Which, to him, seemed both strange and wonderful.

He didn't bother to look for the cashier's check. If Agnes said it was there, it was there.

The phone rang a few minutes after eleven. Tom, alone again at the kitchen table, made no move to get up and answer it.

In due course, the ringing stopped, and Tom's voice requested that the caller leave a message. There was pause, a click, and Rose Callahan began speaking. "Hello, Professor, Agnes, and Henry, this is Rose Callahan. I'm sorry to call so late, but—"

Tom had gone from immobile to picking up the receiver in one and a half sentences. "Hello? Hello, Rose, is that you?"

"Oh, so you *are* there," said Rose, laughing. "Yes, it's me."

"I'm here," said Tom, simultaneously noting Rose's flawed grammar and wondering if she could hear his pounding heart. "How are you? No ill effects from your Egg McMuffin, I trust?"

"None at all. And I didn't have to eat again until the middle of the afternoon. Whatever that cheese stuff is they put on those things really hangs around."

Tom gloried in her laughter and the hint of Texas twang in her speech. They made him feel less pressure to be *sensible*, which was a relief. "It was a great pleasure to have you join us."

"I sure enjoyed myself. Listen, I'm sorry to call so late, but I've only just had an idea."

"Oh? And what idea is that?" Might this mean she'd been thinking about him? Tom wondered. Although it was more likely she'd been thinking about Henry.

"Well, it occurred to me that it might be easier for you and Agnes if you didn't have to take Henry with you to your wife's funeral tomorrow. But then I thought, as Henry just got here and seems a bit shy, you might not want to leave him with a strange sitter. So, since he and I are sort of friends already, I thought I would offer to look after him tomorrow while you and

Agnes take care of what you need to take care of. I've already checked with Mr. Pitts and gotten his okay to take tomorrow off. So, anyway," she finished in a rush, "I'm available to take care of Henry tomorrow if you'd like me to."

Tom was so flooded with gratitude he had to sit down. Henry hadn't known Marjory at all. And funerals were so weird, once you stopped and thought about them; putting dead people in boxes and lowering them into the ground while everyone stood around getting emotional. "Thank you so much, Rose. That is so kind."

"It is? Oh, good. I'm glad there's something I can do to help."

Tom could *hear* her smiling.

"What time should I come over?"

Marjory's funeral was at two o'clock in Charlottesville. "Shall we say noon?"

"Noon it is. Bye now."

Click and she was gone. Tom put the phone down carefully as though this could maintain a connection between the two of them. Or, more accurately, among the three of them. Whatever tenuous connection he'd had with Rose before this morning now had Henry squarely in its middle, which somehow, in some complicated way Tom could not begin to parse, planted Rose Callahan much more firmly in his heart.

chapter 9

"I'm here!" Rose said when Tom opened the door a little before noon the next day.

And so she was, in jeans, clogs, and a white T-shirt.

"Yes, you are." Tom, solemn as a backwoods preacher in his darkest suit, gestured for her to come in. "Thank you again for offering to do this."

"Oh, heavens. I'm happy to." Rose held up one of the two plastic bags she carried. "I brought burgers, milk shakes, and fries from Sid's for lunch."

The phone rang. Would it *never* stop?

"I'll get it," Agnes yelled from upstairs. "We've got to get a move on."

Rose headed for the kitchen. "Go do what you need to do. I'll be in here," she called over her shoulder.

"It's Russell, for you," Agnes announced loudly from the top of the stairs. "I tried to head him off, but he insists on talking to you. Better make it snappy."

Tom trailed Rose into the kitchen, which had already begun to smell like fried food.

Sid's was a fabled burger joint on Lynchburg Road. Years ago, for some reason to do with last-minute shopping, Tom had ended up there for a quick solo dinner on Christmas Eve. The place had been deserted except for two teenaged brothers. Tom had eavesdropped shamelessly as the older one carefully explained the intricacies of a cheap plastic watch he'd bought his brother for Christmas. The younger boy had seemed to listen with his whole *being*.

Tom picked up the kitchen phone. "Hello."

"Tom. It's Russell."

"I know. Agnes told me." The smells around Tom were distinctly counter-funereal.

"I just wanted to check in and be sure you and Agnes didn't need a ride or . . . or anything else."

Tom smiled. Russ had phoned with the same question yesterday. "No, thanks. It's very nice of you to offer, but Agnes and I feel we should be able to operate independently. She has a lot of Charlottesville friends, you know, that she might need to pay attention to."

"Oh, yes, of course. I just thought I'd ask." Russell cleared his throat. "Well then, you're sure everything else is okay?"

"Everything's fine," Tom said. "It's nice of you to be concerned about us, Russ." He had yet to tell Russell about Henry. It had simply been too much to talk about so soon after Marjory's death.

"Of course I'm concerned."

There was a pause. Tom imagined his friend gathering himself to say what he'd really called to say. Simple sincerity didn't come naturally to him.

"I'm really, really sorry about Marjory," Russell said eventually. "Not just that she's dead, but that she had such a struggle. I . . . I admire the way you stuck it out with her. I certainly wouldn't have done it. I . . . I'm much too . . ."

Tom lost the rest of what Russell said as Agnes marched in, dressed from head to foot in rebellious peacock blue. "Time to go," she announced, barely acknowledging Rose with a nod. Cantankerousness was 'Agnes's customary fallback emotion.

"I'm sorry, but I have to go now, Russ," Tom said, interrupting Russell, who was still going on about Marjory. "We'll see you at the cemetery. Thanks again for the offer of the ride."

Russell was still talking as Tom put down the phone. "Okay," he said, turning around, clapping his hands, "let's get these doggies rolling! 'Delays have dangerous ends!'"

Agnes scowled at him. *Henry the Sixth, Part One*," Tom said, thinking it was because he'd lapsed into Shakespeare.

The scowl deepened. "Aren't you forgetting something?"

Tom's mind felt unwieldy as a turning battleship. "What?"

"Henry?" Rose prompted.

Henry! Tom sprinted toward the door into the hallway and almost ran the boy down. Henry had been standing just outside the kitchen door, neatly dressed in Gap jeans, another plaid shirt, and his Nikes. Henry's hair, however, was *not* neat. Somehow, this gave Tom hope.

"Well, Henry," Tom said, way over-the-top heartily. "It's time for Agnes and me to get a move on. Rose is here to stay with you, and she's brought lunch. You remember Rose, don't you?"

Henry nodded but didn't move.

Then Rose was there beside him, holding out her second plastic bag. "I brought you something, Henry. It's something I wanted for Christmas when I was your age, but since I was a girl no one ever gave me one."

Henry looked first at the bag, then at Rose, then at Tom. *He's identified me as his boss,* Tom thought. *The one who has power over him.*

Tom nodded. Henry took a step forward, and Rose handed him the bag. He squatted down on the floor, folded down the plastic, and uncovered a red Tonka dump truck.

Rather than reaching for it, though, he looked up at Tom again, the whole history of human longing in his eyes. Tom smiled. "It's yours, Henry. Rose brought it for you to have."

Henry's hand hung in the air over the box. "Mine?" It was a question. But then he said "Mine" again, as a statement.

"Yes," Tom said "It's yours. So what do you say to Rose?"

"Thank you," Henry said, his eyes on the truck.

Rose squatted down in front of the boy, picked up the truck, and stuck it gently in Henry's lap. "Let's eat," she said, standing up again. "I'm starving."

Henry wrapped an arm around the truck and stood up. "Okay," he whispered, allowing Rose to take his other hand.

*　　*　　*

Iris looked out at the seventeen expectant faces and thought: *I don't care if Tom is at his wife's funeral, why the hell did I ever volunteer to take his RemWrite class?*

RemWrite stood for Remedial Writing. It was how the members of the English Department referred to the required course for first-years who'd demonstrated they'd yet to grasp the concept of the complete sentence. The class was gussied up in the college catalog by the appealingly vague name Creative Exploration, but no one—not even the students who were forced to take it—ever called it anything but RemWrite.

Tom, who alone among his senior colleagues regularly volunteered to teach a section of RemWrite, had e-mailed Iris late yesterday afternoon, explaining he was fine with canceling his Tuesday afternoon Shakespeare class, but he hated to cancel his Tuesday morning RemWrite. The students were so enthusiastic that it just didn't seem right to bail on them. Could Iris possibly take it for him? They were to turn in their first assignment, an essay on what they expected to get out of college. All she would have to do was have them read these in class and make suggestions for revising.

Reading Tom's e-mail, Iris, who'd bought two bottles of wine on the way home yesterday and was almost finished with the first, had been struck with a rare urge to help out. This, she knew, probably masked guilt, a feeling with which she was much more familiar.

How *had* she ended up in the Putnams' dreary guest room on Saturday morning?

Anyway, whatever she'd been feeling, she'd impulsively fired off a two-word e-mail back to Tom: No problem.

Except it *was* a problem. To begin with Iris felt fuzzy in the head, which would have been fine if the students staring at her had looked less full of expectations, less willing to prostrate themselves before the altar of the complete and grammatical sentence. Just the expressions on their faces made Iris want to shout, "Loosen up, will you! Complete sentences are *boring!*"

Iris cleared her throat rather savagely and stood tall in her red platforms. Why did innocence always irritate the bejesus out of her? Surely she'd once been innocent herself, expecting life to work out and other such nonsense.

The seventeen eager beavers continued to stare. Alcohol, Iris realized, had done it to her again. If she hadn't been almost through a bottle of wine when she'd read Tom's e-mail, she would never have chosen to accept this ridiculous mission.

Iris once again vowed to limit herself to two glasses of wine a night. Anything over that seemed to loosen her moorings. "Well," she said, "I'm sure you're all surprised to see me this morning. My name is Iris Benson. I usually teach women's issues in American Studies, but I'm filling in for Professor Putnam today, as he has family issues to attend to."

The seventeen heads nodded and smiled at her. First-years never, *ever* questioned anything or anyone.

Iris's head began to ache.

"Well," she said, doing her best not to sound as despairing as she felt, "I understand you have all written essays about what you expect of your college experiences. Who would like to go first reading hers aloud?"

Five eager beavers raised their hands. For just a moment, Iris looked into the face of one of them, a serious, bespectacled young woman with piles of red hair, and thought she was facing her own, resurrected self.

At one time, Iris remembered, she, too, had believed in almost everything.

*   *   *

Tom stood at the edge of Marjory's grave and wondered who all these people were who'd showed up at this small, quiet country cemetery to pay their respects to a woman who'd barely made a dent in the world's collective consciousness. Tom had never laid eyes on half of them, and they certainly were a motley crew—hippies, yuppies, artistic types, conservative business people, a flock of sour-looking, elegantly dressed older women.

Halfway through the service, it dawned on him that they were Agnes's old friends from Charlottesville. What a mark his mother-in-law must have left. These people couldn't have seen much of her over the last decade, and yet here they were, turned out en masse for her dysfunctional daughter's funeral.

Agnes stood on the other side of Marjory's grave, separate from him by choice, as though shunning anything resembling family support. She looked, Tom thought, utterly defeated and old.

The service was Episcopalian, which Agnes had been briefly during her marriage. The lovely, ritualized words of comfort and hope flowed on. Behind Agnes was the gravestone of one Joseph Hinton Tattle, born September 14, 1931, died January 1958; Agnes's flyboy, dead for all forty-seven years of his daughter's life, still mourned and missed by his wife.

Did Agnes now, Tom asked himself, deserve some time on her own again? Time to fight some more good fights with fellow comrades in rectitude, to flex her muscular character and charisma again, all those Agnes attributes that had rallied all these people to her side today?

His mother-in-law had never sold her house in Charlottesville. If he were truly a good person, would he encourage her to move back there, take up her lawyering and her life again? The thought panicked him.

"Amen!" the priest announced with finality. There was a collective sigh, and everyone but Tom and Agnes quickly turned away from Marjory's yawning grave. His mother-in-law was shortly surrounded by people he didn't know and most likely would never see again. His own crowd from the college hung back a bit, giving him the conventional last moment alone with Marjory. He stared at the mound of flowers waiting to be heaped on her grave, repressed a sigh, and, instead of thinking about his wife as he knew he was expected to, thought about Henry, at home and possibly—if miracles were still allowed in his world—*playing* with Rose Callahan.

Then, as though someone had fired a starter pistol, people from the college surged around him. For long minutes, Tom shook hands and murmured "thank you for coming" over and over and over, to kind face after kind face. Russell Jacobs gave him a hug, which was very un-Russell-like behavior. Tom hugged him back, surprised to find himself hanging on to his old friend for longer than was truly conventional. It felt to him as though their real selves connected during that hug, rather than their usual everyday selves.

Tom made a mental note to talk to him about Henry as soon as possible.

Just as Russell turned away, Tom felt movement at his side and looked down to find Agnes standing there. "Before we leave," she said, "I want you to come stand with me for a moment at Joe's grave. I sneak up here sometimes by myself to say hello, but today I need some company. Someone who's been right beside me during the Marjory struggles and knows I tried."

Tom took a risk and reached down for Agnes's hand. He took another risk and said, "Happy to. That's what family's for."

Agnes looked up at him. Stark gratitude was there and gone in her face as quickly as a passing thought. "Okay, then," she said, a trace of her old Agnes-ness returning. "And after we check in with Joe, Professor, can we please get the hell out of here and go home?"

part two

chapter 10

Tom, along with everyone else, had inspected *Harry Potter and the Sorcerer's Stone* when J. K. Rowling's first novel had appeared at the Book Store. He had not been impressed. Supposedly Ms. Rowling had begun it on the back of a paper napkin, and in Tom's opinion—formed on the basis of that hasty scan—napkin scrawl remained the level of her prose.

But this assessment had been made before Henry. This morning, the day after Marjory's funeral, Henry had pointed at a picture of Harry Potter in one of Marjory's magazines, and Tom had developed a sudden burning desire to read Ms. Rowling's books out loud to the boy. Prose, schmose. This was about Henry *wanting* something. So here he was at eleven in the morning, pushing through the Book Store's front door with Henry in tow, out together in public for the first time, on a mission to buy all the available Harry Potter books.

His whole life, Tom was beginning to realize, had been bifurcated by Henry's arrival. The years before Henry sat on one side; the thirty-some hours after Henry on the other. Despite reason, caution, Marjory's death, and all that alarming money, life again held promise; temporary promise, to be sure, as Henry was only temporarily in residence, but that did not make the promise any less real.

The Book Store, as usual these days, hummed with a cross-section of the college community enriched by a sprinkling of townies. "This is where Rose works, Henry," Tom said. "Would you like to go say hello to her?"

Henry nodded. "Yes, please." He spoke so softly that Tom had to read his lips.

They reached the archway into Rose's area, and there she was, rocketing around like a Pachinkoball, exuding composure and cheerfulness at warp speed among her chattering customers. Henry immediately broke free and flung himself at Rose's knees.

Rose swayed but did not fall—and, wonder of wonders, did not spill a drop of the three foamy coffees she carried. She put the coffees down on the nearest table, knelt, and hugged Henry back. People took their cues from her, smiling, nodding, clasping their hands together in demonstrable delight, then quickly turning back to one another to begin twittering about—Tom would have bet Henry's demi-million on this—the campus's newest odd couple: Rose Callahan and this small boy who was somehow attached to Tom Putnam.

The two were in front of him now, hand in hand, Henry chattering away as though he were someone who chattered as a matter of course. What *was* it with this woman? Was she the patron saint of misfits, here to rescue Henry and, who knew, himself?

"Rose," someone called from one of the tables, "when you get a moment, will you come settle this dispute we're having over Ann Beattie? You knew her in Charlottesville, didn't you?"

"Be right there!" Rose sang out, her eyes on Henry. "Obviously, I can't stay." She knelt down to give the boy another hug, looking up at Tom as she did so. Tom thought he saw longing sprint across her face. Once again he remembered the look she'd given him in class: *I'm in a bit of trouble here, but please pay no attention . . .*

"There," Rose said, rising. "Bye for now, Henry."

"Bye," Henry said—yes, *said*. "When will you babysit me again?"

Rose looked at Tom. "Soon, I hope?" she said, turning her words into a question.

"Soon," Tom said firmly. There it was again, that light around her. Watching Rose's face, he felt something in him reach out for her. He was almost certain something in her reached out for him in return, but before he could be sure, she turned her attention back to Henry. "See you," she said.

"See you," Henry said.

Still Rose hesitated, as though there were something else to say.

"Who's this?" a woman's voice demanded.

The mood shifted; intimacy shattered. "Hello, Iris," Rose said. And she was gone.

Tom felt Henry squeeze as close to his leg as the natural laws of the universe allowed. He put a protective hand on the boy's shoulder. A blast from Iris was often hard for him to withstand; he could just imagine what it would be like for a six-year-old. "This," he said, "is my son, Henry. Henry, this is my friend Iris Benson. She took one of my classes yesterday, so I owe her a big thank-you."

Iris threw up her arms, flaring the sleeves of her voluminous caftan, looking momentarily like a gigantic burnt-orange bat. "You have a *son?*" she bellowed. Once again heads turned.

Tom felt Henry stiffen and pull slightly away instead of shrinking closer, as any sensible child would do. "You talk too loud," he said, quite distinctly.

"Henry!" Tom was shocked in any number of ways.

Iris lowered her arms and regarded the boy appraisingly. Henry did not flinch. Then, to add to the sum total of the day's surprises, Iris grinned. "You're right," she said. "Sorry, Henry." Tom thought he saw admiration sneak into Iris's rather puffy eyes.

"I'm here to buy Harry Potter books," Henry said.

More surprises were to come. Iris reached down and patted the boy's shoulder. "Good for you. I've read every one of them twice."

That, Tom thought, *explains a lot.*

They left with all six Harry Potter books, three matching college T-shirts (one for Agnes), two Harry Potter posters, and a book called *Mapping the World of Harry Potter* that Iris had recommended. "It's quite a good atlas," she'd said, very seriously.

Classes were changing as they headed back across campus. Students streamed by, calling out "Hi, Professor Putnam" in various singsong tones. Tom answered back, calling most of the students by name. Henry, however, paid no attention to any of them. He held on firmly to his bag of books with one hand and to Tom with the other and did not say a word.

*   *   *

The college dining hall was annually ranked among the best in the country by *U.S. News*. The food was described as "southern healthy," whatever that meant. Everything was served cafeteria style, and as it was better than any restaurant food within a reasonable distance, the big, sunlit dining room was usually packed with faculty and staff as well as students.

Lunch was available from eleven thirty until one thirty. Russell waited until a few minutes after twelve to start through the cafeteria line. Rose's lunch hour, he knew, was noon to one, so hopefully, by the time he filled his tray and made it into the dining hall proper, she would be there.

Only she wasn't. Everyone he didn't want to eat lunch with was, but Rose was not. *Curses! Foiled again!* Snidely Whiplash shouted unexpectedly from Russell's early adolescence.

Well, now he was here, he'd have to sit somewhere and eat. Russell looked down at his tray. As his mind had been on Rose rather than food, he'd made a rather peculiar selection: kale, coleslaw, mashed potatoes with gravy, a small dish of over-mayonnaised tuna salad, two different kinds of pie, and nothing to drink.

Russell's usual lunch was a green salad, a piece of poached fish or a poached chicken breast, fresh fruit, and Earl Grey iced tea. It was prepared for him by his housekeeper (whom the college supplied—another perk!), who came in every morning to dust and tend to his larder.

"Russell, come sit with us!"

Russell looked around to see Nathan Eubanks, head of college public relations, waving at him from a nearby table. Nathan sat among a mixed collection of students and faculty—just the kind of cross-cultural confab he liked to bleat about in press releases. Usually Russell found the man mildly amusing, but not today. "Gotta do some reading for class!" he called out as he kept moving.

Thankfully he'd brought a book with him, so this did not look like the complete lie that it was. Russell moved on through the crowded room, fending off more invitations from both faculty and students, until he finally spotted a vacant table over by the big bank of windows that looked out toward the Quad. Perfect; sitting there he could easily spot Rose if she were running late, and then make a beeline back to the food line so as to "casually" bump into her.

Russell set his tray down on the table and went over to a nearby beverage stand to fetch a glass of water. While he was there, a group of third-years came over to ask him to please be their guest at some kind of dormitory high tea on Parents Weekend. They simply would not take no for an answer, so Russell was forced to accept in order to get back to his post. When he finally made it back to his table, Iris Benson was sitting there with a loaded lunch tray.

"What are you doing at my table?" Russell demanded.

"Eating lunch and annoying you," Iris said sweetly, pushing out his chair with her foot. "Have a seat."

"No, thank you."

"Suit yourself." Iris tucked into a huge plate of lasagna.

Russell folded his arms. "I wish you'd leave."

"I know you do." Iris spoke with her mouth full. It was done deliberately, Russell knew, to offend him further.

People at nearby tables were beginning to stare. Russell looked around to see if there was another vacant table. There wasn't.

Iris finished chewing and smiled up at him with wicked innocence. "So, Russell. Have you met Tom Putnam's new son?"

The world tilted. Russell sat down. "Tom Putnam has a *son*?" he roared. Heads turned several tables deep.

Iris was very pleased with herself. "Yes. His name is Henry, and he's soon to be seven. I met him this morning at the Book Store, naturally, which is where I meet most interesting people around here now that Rose has arrived to attract them. I rather liked the boy. He told me I talk too loud, which I thought showed surprising guts for a six-year-old."

Russell stared at her. "Tom Putnam has a son?" he repeated.

"Yep." Iris winked at him. "You should go introduce yourself. He might tell you a couple of useful things about your behavior as well."

"Tom Putnam has a son," Russell said for the third time.

Iris, however, had gotten distracted by the contents of Russell's tray. Her sweet tooth was legendary. "Yes, Russell. Tom Putnam has a son. And while you're absorbing this, would you mind if I ate one of those pieces of pie?"

*   *   *

When Rose got back to the Book Store after lunch, Susan Mason was sitting by herself at a four-spot in the corner of the coffee room. She had spread out books and papers to make it look as though she needed extra room to work and so sat alone from choice rather than from dorkiness.

Two other tables were occupied by glossy upperclasswomen, another by Dean Eagle and the president, who appeared to be yukking it up over something in *The New York Times,* and a fourth by three female science faculty members and a senior who had their heads stuck in *Vogue.* Everyone, even the president, looked up as Rose came in. Everyone smiled and waved in acknowledgment that Rose was . . . well . . . *Rose.* Then they went back to their conversations.

Susan looked up as well, but immediately looked down again. Rose recognized this as standard practice among shy persons. It was designed to guard against the anticipated public humiliation of being ignored. The sad thing was that by doing this, shy people guaranteed themselves the feared humiliation. How can you possibly greet someone who won't look at you? Part of Rose's self-imposed mission in life was to help the shy members of her current community stop such self-defeating behavior. She agreed with Bruce Springsteen, that everybody—even the most reclusive—has a hungry heart.

Social inclusion, of course, always begins with the *theater* of social inclusion. Which is where Rose knew she could *really* help. Because she was generally perceived as cool by already cool people (although who knew exactly why?), those with whom she associated would automatically become cool as well. So, in front of glossy students, the president, et al., Rose marched over to Susan's table, pulled out a chair, and sat down. "Hello, fellow Shakespeare scholar," she sang out heartily. "Thanks again for letting me copy your class notes. You really saved my bacon!"

Susan Mason's hand went to her chest: *You talking to me?*

Rose nodded. "And while I've got you, I have another favor to ask of you."

"Of me?" Susan's hand pressed harder against her chest.

"Of course, of you," Rose said, smiling. The glossy students, having duly noted that cool Rose Callahan was sitting with some frizzy-haired student they'd never noticed before, had gone back to their glossy conversations. But they would, Rose knew, never *not* notice Susan Mason again. Which was a good start. She didn't, of course, want Susan Mason to *become* one of the glossies; she just wanted her to become comfortable being Susan Mason.

"Okay," Susan said, looking worried.

Rose smiled again, encouragingly. "Here's the deal. I want to form a faculty-student advisory committee to come up with ways to bring people together in the Book Store who don't usually have much to do with each other. And I would like you to chair my committee. What do you say?"

"Me?" Susan Mason was stunned into abnormal forthrightness. "Why would you ask me? Nobody would pay any attention to anything I suggested."

"Yes, they would," Rose said. "Thanks to Mr. Pitts, I have a generous programming budget, so I can not only fund and publicize your committee's events, I can offer free cappuccino to anyone who participates. So getting people to come is not the problem. And the people I want to come are people like you."

"Like me?" Susan's incredulity was absolute. "Why on earth would you want to interest people like me? I'm not involved in anything around here."

"Exactly my point! That is such a waste."

"It is?"

"It is," Rose said firmly. Susan Mason had to know she was smart. She just didn't know how to make being smart useful outside the classroom. "Your brain, Susan Mason, is an underutilized community asset."

Doubt had begun duking it out with the first wisps of self-confidence in Susan's eyes. "Will you help me?" she asked. "Teach me how to chair a committee and all? You are so confident and easy with everyone."

"Of course," Rose said.

Susan's whole being began to glow. Or at least, it seemed to Rose that it did. Right here, right now, Susan Mason had begun embracing her own unrecognized potential.

It struck Rose, perhaps for the first time ever, that she might have something important to give the young women at this college that had little to do with her job description. She herself might be worth sharing.

Impulsively Rose reached across the table and squeezed Susan's hand. *Might I*, she wondered, *have finally fetched up somewhere I belong?*

Professionally, at least.

•   •   •

But then Ted Pitts, looking like thunder, asked the Book Store staff to stay for
an announcement after closing, and any feelings of belonging that Rose might
have had became irrelevant.

Once the eight women assembled themselves around the tables in Rose's
section, Mr. Pitts wasted no time. He needed, he said, to make an announcement that he wanted to make about as much as he wanted to set his hair on fire.
The college's VP of finance had informed him this afternoon that, as a cost-
cutting measure, she was seriously considering leasing the Book Store to some
big textbook company. Currently, she'd said, there was too much emphasis on
"building community" and too little on making money for the college.

Rose sat listening to purple-faced Mr. Pitts as her own future reverted
to type and thought, *So this is what someone looks like when their blood boils.* . . .

He had, Mr. Pitts was saying, made it clear to the Harpy of a veep that
if this happened, he would either resign or retire. The Harpy of a veep had
said they would be sorry to lose him, and that one more staff position would
probably need to be eliminated.

Every one of her colleagues, Rose knew, had gotten very busy *not* looking at her. Of course, she should be the one to go. She'd obviously been hired
as the future of the Book Store, and now its future was to be leased to a big
textbook corporation.

Rose walked home slowly through the slanted light of early evening. The days
were noticeably cooler now, the maples tipped with orange. *The seasons roll on,
no matter what,* she thought. *Life rolls on, no matter what.* Had she known that
at Rice? Probably not. She'd thought then that she would have something to
do with the grand course of it all, something to do with a larger picture than
the structure of her own day. That the way she'd briefly felt this afternoon, that
she belonged somewhere, was the way she'd end up feeling all the time.

It had been her last, perhaps her only, illusion. When had she let it go?
Rose had no idea. Someday, in some bookstore, when she'd realized that she
was now, always had been, and always would be a watcher; that other people
might be doers and participants, but she was not. She'd been briefly sad about
this, but then it had come to seem like the end of a long, gentle drift down-

ward toward the earth, at the completion of which she'd settled comfortably into her own adult life, with both feet firmly planted on the ground and no real regrets. Life swirled on around her, and there was only this occasional, bothersome sense that she was waiting for something.

For one thing, she'd never been in love, the kind of love that Mavis appeared to be in, where life expanded instead of fixated. She'd certainly liked all her lovers—and she liked having a lover—but Rose was uncomfortably aware that she'd never tipped over the edge into something that felt more necessary and richer than the comfortable, serene way she felt most of the time on her own. A lot of the other people she'd known seemed to cultivate crisis, to court agitation, to need something emotional going on all the time, while she just drifted along, peaceful, happy, interested, but always—well, except for rare moments—slightly detached from the furor.

Rose reached the edge of her scrap of lawn, in the middle of which sat her cottage. As always, she felt more squatter than occupant. Where would she go if—or rather when—Mr. Pitts accepted the inevitable and eliminated her job? Which was obviously the only chance he had to save everyone else's. Which was, in Rose's opinion, an absolute imperative. All her colleagues had children settled in school, mortgages to pay, PTAs that depended on them during fund-raisers. She could blow somewhere else as easily as tumbleweed.

Rose felt again the jolt of Henry tackling her around the knees. It had been such a surprise. She'd figured whatever else life had taught the boy, it had not been to hold on to other people. That was, however, what life had apparently not taught *her*. Mavis would never have meant that to happen; Mavis would have meant to teach her to throw open her arms and embrace the world in its great and wondrous entirety. But the best-laid schemes of mice and mothers do go awry, and she was, Rose realized only now, when it appeared to be too late, tentatively allowing someone to pry her arms apart.

Damn it, she was going to miss him!

Whether that him was Henry or Henry's father, she refused to speculate.

*   *   *

Agnes answered when Russell knocked on the Putnams' front door a little after nine that evening. "Oh," she said. "It's you. I suppose you've heard about Henry. I'll go tell Tom you're here. There's fresh coffee in the kitchen."

She turned to go, having, as usual, not-much-to-nothing to say to Russell.

Russell impetuously caught her arm. "How are you?" he asked, surprised to find he truly wanted to know.

Agnes considered this with her head on one side, reminding Russell of a thoughtful sparrow. "I'm okay, I guess. I've got a legal question to ponder, which is making me *think* for a change."

"Good luck with that," Russell said.

Agnes regarded him frostily. "Luck," she said, "has *nothing* to do with the law."

With that, she turned and stalked off down the hall.

Tom came into the kitchen improbably dressed in jeans and a T-shirt emblazoned with a chest-sized rendition of the college seal.

"What the hell is that you're wearing?" Russell glowered at Tom over his coffee mug. "You look like a billboard with legs."

Tom stopped where he was. There was no mistaking his friend was in a snit. "You've heard about Henry, haven't you?"

"Yes." Russell drew himself up with grand and petulant dignity. "Iris Benson had to tell me today, since you couldn't be bothered to tell me yesterday." Russell threw both hands into the air.

"I'm sorry," Tom said. "I simply didn't have the energy. Then, this morning, without thinking, Henry and I ran out to get Harry Potter books at the Book Store and there was Iris. Of course, I had to introduce Henry to her, which I suppose was like hiring the town crier to spread the news. I'm really sorry, Russell. You've been such a good friend. I should have thought things through better. I hope you'll forgive me."

Abruptly Russell's anger left him. Of course, what had really happened was that Tom had hurt his feelings, and when his feelings got hurt he usually got mad. It was just somehow easier to be mad than to be sad. The truth was that Tom hadn't *meant* to hurt him. The man did have a lot on his plate right now. Besides, what he really wanted, Russell realized, was for Tom to sit down and tell him *everything*.

"Okay," he said, "I forgive you."

"Really?"

"Yes, really. Now go pour yourself some coffee and let's hear all about this mysterious Henry. I don't suppose he's still up by any chance?"

Tom dutifully headed for the coffeepot. "Henry's asleep. He went out like a light about eight thirty."

"Damn!" Russell's eyes fastened on Tom's shirt. "You're not planning to wear that shirt out in public, are you?" he asked.

"Henry and I are planning to wear them whenever we go out in public. I'm thinking of asking him if he'd like to go to the college soccer game tomorrow." Tom pumped the air with a fist. "Go team!"

Russell, before Rose's arrival, had had zero interest in women's sports. Since her arrival, he'd been trying to learn a few scraps of information with which he might impress her—given her basketball background and obvious athleticism. "Do you know what the college mascot is?"

"The Belles, I believe," Tom said, selecting a cup from the open shelf above the pot.

"As in ring-a-ding or southern?"

"Southern. Belles with two *es*. Hoop skirts and all that. It's meant as an homage to the campus's days as a plantation."

"Oh." Russell tried to imagine himself perched on an uncomfortable bleacher, shouting *Go Belles!* Tom finished pouring his coffee. "May I top you up?" he asked, gesturing with the pot.

"No, thanks. One cup's my limit after dinner. Hope you don't mind that I popped 'round?"

"I'm very glad you did," Tom said, meaning it. On impulse, he reached into the drawer where they kept important household papers and fished out Retesia's letter. "Now you're here, I'd like to get your opinion on this," he said, returning to the table. "It came registered mail the day before Marjory died. You're the only person on campus I've ever told about my . . . my *thing* with Retesia Turnball. Would you mind reading it and letting me know what you think?"

Russell's eyebrows shot up. He reached for the piece of lavender paper. "Certainly. I'd be glad to read it.

Russell could feel Tom's eyes on him as he read and tried to imagine the pale, uptight Retesia Turnball with a makeover, sashaying forth into a world of romance novel readers. It seemed desperately improbable, yet here it was, all spelled out in black and white. Or, more accurately, brown and lavender. Which also seemed very un-Retesia-like, now that he thought about it. Russell remembered having a passionate discussion with her about engraved wedding invitations, of all things; about how they were the only *proper* invitations to send. How could anyone who clung to movable type over ink-jet printers possibly go in for lavender note paper and brown ink?

Russell handed the note back to Tom. "Well, it's pretty obvious from what Iris told me about Henry that he's not the biological offspring of you and Retesia Turnball."

"I know."

Silence again.

Russell found himself thinking about what Iris had said about Henry, about how handsome the boy was, with his great blue eyes and crop of Little Orphan Annie curls.

"There's more," Tom said.

"More?"

"Yes." Tom took the deep breath of someone about to detonate an information bomb. "Henry came with a half-million dollars in his backpack. Fifty thousand in cash and a cashier's check for the rest."

Kapow! "Oh. My," Russell said.

"I know. It's a lot of money."

"Do you think it's somehow . . . somehow criminal?"

Tom shrugged. "How would I know?"

"Have you asked Henry?

"Not yet."

Russell conjured up a picture of Retesia sitting primly across from him in departmental meetings. "I cannot see Retesia hanging out with gangsters. She was *so* uptight."

Even in the dim light, he saw Tom's cheeks flush violently.

So Retesia had not been all that uptight. At least in some areas. "Let's forget about possible criminal involvement," Russell went on hurriedly. "No need to invent complications."

Tom frowned down at his still-full mug of coffee. "Agnes and I *did* have enough sense to figure we shouldn't deposit the money in the bank. You know—federal regulations about cash deposits of more than ten grand and all. But it never occurred to either of us that Henry's money could come from criminal activity. We were just trying to keep the government out of Henry's business until we could figure out a bit more about what's going on."

AA Lewis spoke up in Russell's head, admonishing him again to *keep it simple!* "Good idea. Forget I said anything."

"Okay." Tom looked hard at the lavender paper. "Henry's from Picayune, Mississippi. At least that's where his ticket was from. But he was born in New Orleans."

New Orleans!

Russell's haunted and pathetic mother had been from the Crescent City. When he was growing up and things had gotten really bad at home in Atlanta, his grandparents had taken the train up and rescued him. The weeks he'd spent in their ramshackle robin's egg blue shotgun house had been his only childhood experience of reliable happiness.

He'd gone to treatment in New Orleans because of those memories. "How do you know Henry was born in New Orleans?"

"He brought his birth certificate with him. It's in the drawer over there. Would you like to see it?"

"Yes."

Tom got up, fished another folded piece of paper out of the same kitchen drawer, and handed it to him.

Russell took it, opened it, and read: Henry Thomas Putnam, born September 23, 1998, at Tulane Hospital in New Orleans; mother Serafine Despré; father Thomas Marvin Putnam.

Russell had been perfectly aware at the time that he and Serafine Despré had begun having sex mainly to flout the rules, being almost as addicted to subterfuge as they were to their substances of choice.

The sex had been good; the sneaking around to have sex had been terrific.

Russell hadn't used a rubber. He hadn't thought to bring any, and there certainly weren't any on offer at the treatment center. He'd never asked Serafine if she did anything toward birth control, because he hadn't wanted to know.

Serafine Despré.

What a bewitching creature she'd been, a Creole from right there in New Orleans, in treatment for an alarming array of cross-addictions, forced into rehab by parents who were willing to pay for endless stabs at sobriety. Serafine's problem had been that she'd had no interest in sobriety. All she'd been interested in was getting out again, and then getting her hands on enough of her parents' money to fund her various habits. Poor, poor Serafine had been so beautiful and so lost.

However . . .

During the three weeks their paths had intertwined at treatment, Russell had talked a lot with Serafine Despré about his best friend, Tom Putnam. At the time, he'd been going through a period of Tom adulation. Marjory's grip on the rails had become transparently precarious, but Tom's commitment to her remained unwavering. Tom Putnam, Russell remembered explaining to a rapt Serafine, had the fortitude to offer his crazy wife the kind of steady, warm, unconditional acceptance that every child dreams of getting from a parent. Or at least that he, Russell Jacobs, had dreamed of getting from a parent.

And it had evidently been Serafine's dream as well. She'd kept pumping him for information about Tom. It was, Russell realized, his fault that Tom's name was on Henry's birth certificate, and his fault that Serafine knew about Retesia Turnball, for he remembered holding up to her Tom's one, short slip in the fidelity department as a kind of oddball testament to his friend's superhuman steadfastness.

Seven-plus years later, Russell could still see Serafine's beautiful, intent face listening to him as he talked about Tom. What he remembered most vividly were her eyes, dark and full of unutterable longings.

It was now perfectly clear to Russell that while Serafine might have had sex with him, she'd dreamed of Tom Putnam.

Tom was rattling on. "Isn't that a wonderful name Retesia dreamed up? Serafine Despré? It's exotic and angelic at the same time."

Yes, Russell thought, *she was.* Where was Serafine now? She'd left treatment ten days before him and—the staff had whispered this to each other—disappeared a scant two days later from her group home. The orderlies and nurses, he remembered, had appeared stricken by this. But then, how could they not be? We all long to save beauty such as Serafine's from destruction, so as to have its light available to shine on our own less resplendent selves.

Russell realized Tom had stopped talking and was waiting for him to respond. "I suppose," he said.

This seemed to suffice. Tom barreled on. "Agnes did Google Serafine Despré just out of curiosity, but couldn't find anyone by that name who might be even remotely connected with Retesia."

Serafine shone at Russell from out of his murky past like a tiny pin-prick of light. She had been the real deal, completely genuine, in her own self-destructive way; everything he was not. Serafine Despré had shouted at the world that she was a junkie in need of help, while he, to this day, had not told a single person outside of AA—even Tom—that he was an alcoholic. Or, for that matter, begun to come clean about his chaotic, humiliating child-hood. "Did Agnes find anything out about anyone of that name when she Googled it?"

"She did. Some junkie by that name hanged herself in the St. John the Baptist Parish jail the same day as Marjory's funeral. Agnes said she was only thirty-two but had arrest records dating back over the last decade and a half. This Serafine Despré was the only daughter of two doctors who lost their lives in Katrina. Talk about a hard-luck family!"

So Serafine was dead. No more beauty. No more light. "Yes," Russell said. "Hard luck. Very sad." And an impossible loss for him to grieve in any open way. He couldn't even admit to *knowing* Serafine Despré without pub-licly exposing his secrets. And who would he be without his secrets?

Just at that moment a small, beautiful boy entered the room from the hall, clutching a bright red Tonka dump truck. Russell stared. So this was Henry! His heart reached for the boy in the same magically improbable way it had once reached for Serafine, for Henry was absolutely and completely a blue-eyed version of his mother. As far as any mark a father had made on him, the boy's conception could have been immaculate.

Henry was dressed in a smaller version of Tom's college T-shirt, all very father-and-son. Russell's first reaction was that this was just so wrong. He was the one who had slept with Henry's mother. Tom didn't even know she existed.

Rage rumbled inside Russell, even as he reached out in full-blown Rus-sellian persona to shake Henry's hand.

•   •   •

Usually Russell gloried in the status that had attached to him a little over four years ago when he'd moved into his current imposing residence. It had been built in 1913, a time when the college had been particularly flush, as an homage to Thomas Jefferson's Monticello, complete with a third-floor domed top hat of a reception room.

The Dean Dome (as Russell always referred to his residence, having been a fan of Tar Heel basketball since his graduate school days) sat a couple of imposing residences down from the president's house. It had been occupied for years by the late Dean Patrick, a straitlaced administrator with tremendous backbone whom Russell had deeply admired. When Dean Patrick had retired, his replacement, a shiny young history professor named Ralph Eagle, had expected to move into the house, but Russell had been tapped instead. Residency came with VIP hosting duties, and Russell had long been recognized as the college's most gracious host.

Russell had envisioned holding grand, inventive gatherings in the Dome Room stocked with fascinating people from business and industry, the arts, and the University of Virginia. Sadly, soon after he'd moved in, the Dome Room was declared off-limits by the college insurance company, so these days it functioned mainly as Russell's indoor track. He did not pace around it often, but he was pacing around it tonight—or rather this morning, for Wednesday night had turned into Thursday morning a good hour ago.

Russell had dutifully called AA Lewis as soon as he'd gotten back from Tom's. Lewis had promptly asked him if anything was bothering him. *Of course something's bothering me!* Russell had wanted to shout. *That's why I've called you!* But if he'd done that, Lewis would have asked him what that something was, and even if Russell had wanted to tell him, he couldn't. Because unloading what was bothering him could possibly do real damage to Henry, who could be—and once again Russell furiously did the math—his own son.

So instead of saying anything in response to AA Lewis's question, Russell had slammed the phone down, trembling with the certainty that God, whatever God was, really had it in for him.

Here he was, alone, pacing around the Dome Room like a hamster on a wheel, trying *not* to think about Serafine Despré or Henry, while a loop tape of disturbing episodes from his own childhood played over and over in his head. Usually these distasteful parts of his past stayed caged in the dark recesses of consciousness. Russell might dream about them, but he rarely thought about them. This evening, however, they had not only escaped but taken over.

Russell felt a great weight pressing down on him, forcing him to his knees. His mother had always been just sober enough on Sundays to drag him to church for their joint weekly wallowing in guilt. Her voice sounded now in his head, echoing across the decades. "We have left undone those things which we ought to have done; and we have done those things which we ought not to have done."

Oh God, Russell thought, *I need a drink . . .*

chapter 11

As reliably as death and taxes, Thursday afternoon at two o'clock rolled around.

Heeeeeeere's Shakespeare!

Rose sat bolt upright in her classroom chair and looked around. Here she was, face-to-face with *it* again, whatever *it* was. Could the difficulties she'd had with her first Shakespeare class have anything to do with the building itself? Not bloody likely, she decided. Elston Hall was a century old and had no reputation for weirdness. The second-floor seminar room, empty except for her, seemed as benign and sun-filled as a baby's smile. Its six enormous double-hung windows let in a flood of fresh air; its tall, transomed door was propped ajar. *It's just a room,* Rose told herself. *It's not a prison cell or a torture chamber. Any problems you have in here are all in your head.*

She'd sat down in the chair directly across from the table podium where Professor Putnam would stand. Surely if she sat here, right under the man's nose, then all would go well. He was about as nonthreatening as people got; very nice, not bad-looking, but not at all the type of driven man that she serially attached herself to. True, as far as attraction went, there had been that one moment at his house when he'd looked at her and said, "But you're Marjory's guest," in a way that had quieted everything and conjured up images of Mavis and her professor. And that other moment in the Book Store when she'd watched him attentively shepherding poor Marjory out the door. And, oh yes, that moment Monday at the Amtrak station when he'd smiled down at Henry. But surely here in the classroom Professor Putnam could be written off as innocuous.

Rose put her book and notebook and pen on the table in front of her. She had read and reread *Othello*, preparing herself to say something cogent about every aspect of the great tragedy, should she be called upon. Hopefully she would not be called upon. Hopefully she would sit here quietly, calmly, anonymously, taking notes and *not freaking out* while Professor Putnam delivered his lecture.

A breeze stirred and brought in the scent of fresh-cut grass. The grounds crew had been swarming the campus that morning like first graders let loose for recess. What, Rose wondered, if she was wrong in her assumption that simply being in a classroom gave her the jitters? What if her troubles last week in class had to do with something entirely outside this room? What if they were somehow tied into her rather abrupt decision to end things with Ray? She had been having some peculiar moments in the last few days, wrestling with *that look* of Marjory Putnam's, wondering what Marjory had seen in her that she herself had missed. Or—and this would be much, much worse—was hiding from.

Dust motes danced before Rose in the sunshine. Thoughts, reasons, explanations, understanding danced with them, tantalizingly ungraspable. No bells went off inside her head. Nothing announced: *That's it! I've figured it all out, and all is now well!!*

"Oh, get a grip," Rose muttered disgustedly. Her mother had always said the best way to solve a problem was not to think about it but to wait for revelation. Mavis was a strong believer in patience being rewarded by revelation.

Like mother, like daughter?

Rose folded her hands neatly in her lap, just as Mavis had taught her to do as a child when they were invited to an intimidating dinner at some academic's house. *I'm all right*, she told herself sternly. *I'm here because I want to learn more about Shakespeare, and this is the place to do it.*

The other students were wandering in now, chattering, giggling, dragging their feet. Rose looked out a window at the bright day and felt something uncomfortably close to unquiet desperation. Surely it would be easier to sit here after it got cold, easier when it rained, easier once she simply got used to it.

Susan Mason, resplendent in her role as chair of the Book Store Faculty/Student/Community Co-Curricular Program Committee, came in with an impossible load of books strapped to her back. The chair next to Rose was empty, and Susan plopped down in it. They *were* buddies, after all. "Did you *get* this play?" she whispered.

Rose looked at her blankly. What a question! Had anyone ever gotten *Othello*? She had seen four different productions of it. The best of them had thundered down upon her like a storm wave breaking off the point at Cape Hatteras. But was that the same as getting it? "I think so," she whispered back. "Pretty much, anyway."

Susan's hair was bundled up on the top of her head in a way that was quite carelessly attractive. The sunlight turned it into a frizzy red-gold halo. "Me, too. I didn't expect to, but I did. Maybe we should start a play-reading group in the Book Store, you think?"

"I think that's a terrific idea."

At that moment, Professor Putnam strode briskly into the room. Was she, Rose wondered, the only person at this college lacking in sass today? "Good afternoon, ladies," he said, reaching the podium and depositing his briefcase beside it. "Shall we begin?" The entire class snapped to attention. Everyone knew Professor Putnam's wife had been killed in a car wreck exactly one week ago today. Everyone also knew that he now had a son staying with him, a mysterious six-year-old.

"Did you notice," Professor Putnam began with great energy, bordering on charisma, "that we have quite a Shakespearean change of pace this week? What did you think of the play that is arguably Shakespeare's greatest offering, *Othello, the Moor of Venice*?"

This man, Rose thought, *is such a different animal in the classroom. He takes stage like a good actor.* Beside her, Susan Mason's hand shot up, and she strained forward like a leashed cocker spaniel who only wants to please. Later, when Rose tried to think about what happened next, it seemed as much of a disconnect as if a cabal of wizard troublemakers had pointed their wands directly at her and done their damnedest. Anxiety crashed down on her like a falling building, like Chicken Little's falling sky, like that devastating production of *Othello*. Rose's heart pounded and her breathing shrank to short, shallow gasps. The floor underneath her rocked and rolled like a room-sized

Tilt-A-Whirl. She grabbed the seat of her chair hard with both hands and held on, sure that if she released her grip one bit she would begin whipping around the room the way the doomed girl at the beginning of *Jaws* had been whipped around the ocean.

Professor Putnam began commenting animatedly on Susan Mason's surprisingly erudite response to his question. Rose forced herself to stare directly at his starched white shirt, which looked at least a decade old. As she watched with a pounding heart, Professor Putnam grasped the podium with both his large, square hands, leaned slightly forward, and spoke directly to her. *He knows what his wife knew,* she thought, drowning in panic. *He knows everything about me. Things I don't even know. Things I don't* want *to know.*

With that, Rose bolted. She got up from her chair and fled, leaving book, notebook, and purse behind. Once out of the room, she didn't stop running until she reached the bathroom at the end of the hall. She threw herself against the door and hurtled inside.

The bathroom was empty, thank goodness. Rose flung open the small window and leaned back against the wall beside it, spread-eagled, her arms and hands, the backs of her calves, the small of her back all pressed against the cool tiles. She took deep, shuddering breaths and waited. Waiting was something she was practiced in, something she did well. Once again, she had the fleeting sensation that she'd done nothing but wait her whole life. Gradually her heart slowed and her breathing became regular and easy again.

This is ridiculous, she thought, *but still, this is. What the hell am I going to do about it?*

Her mother had been a barrel racer in high school. Mavis had loved the thrill of competing, but she hadn't been very good at staying on a horse. Her best barrel-racing quality, she'd always said, was that she bounced, just the way Rose's grandmother had bounced when Rose's grandfather had run off with That Floozy the year Mavis was in fifth grade. Rose had grown up knowing she came from a line of resilient women. Mistakes and failures were okay. Accepting defeat was another matter.

There was no question of going back into that classroom. Even considering doing this made Rose feel like she might throw up or slide down the wall in a dead faint.

So what *could* she consider?

The goal here was to listen to what Professor Putnam had to say about *Othello*. Surely she could do that from *outside* the door? Rose tried visualizing this—she would creep back down the hall, sit on the floor outside the door with her back against the wall. No one inside would be able to see her, but she should be able to hear everything.

The visualization went just fine. The images brought on no palpitations, no dizziness, no symptoms of freak-out at all. Well, all right, then.

Was it Rose's imagination, or was Professor Putnam's Shakespearean fire burning particularly hot today? Last week's class had certainly been interesting, but nothing like today's. Today, Professor Putnam spoke passionately about *Othello*, skillfully energizing his flock of students to *think* about the complexities of both plot and language. Of course, he had a reputation for being a "fun" teacher, whatever that meant, and she wasn't taking notes and maybe that made a difference, but her fellow students inside the room did seem much less restless than last week. It wasn't just Susan Mason who asked questions, and there was less whispering, less fretful movement and scraping of chairs. Toward the end of class, some students got jittery, and when Professor Putnam finished there was the usual immediate stampede out the door, which forced Rose to scramble to her feet to avoid being trampled. She stood quietly to one side, and no one paid any attention to her until Susan Mason's giant backpack shifted suddenly and sent her through the doorway at such an extreme angle that Rose had to put her arms up in order to stop a collision.

"Oh, hi," Susan said, obviously surprised to see her. "I thought you'd gotten sick or something."

"No," Rose said. "Not really. I just needed to come out here for a while."

Susan was struggling to rebalance herself. "Your stuff's still in there," she said. "You want me to get it?"

"No, I'll get it. I guess I should speak to Professor Putnam. You know, apologize for bolting. I don't know what happened. All of a sudden I just couldn't be in there anymore."

Susan straightened up. "You couldn't? Wow! That's, like, so *strange*. You okay?"

Rose had started to really like Susan Mason. A lot of the other students were too contrived for real liking. "I'm okay," she said firmly.

"Well then, I better get going. I told a friend I'd meet her at the library right after class."

"Sure thing," Rose said. "See you."

"See you."

Susan trudged off down the hall, the tentative beginnings of what? Of an *attitude?* hovering around her like an aura. Rose smiled as students from other classes drifted by her, heading for exits. They walked in clumps, talking either to one another or on their phones. Most had also plugged in earbuds, as though silence were somehow dangerous.

As this was Thursday and the rest of the afternoon was reserved for labs, there would not be another class gathering in the seminar room. Rose had half hoped Professor Putnam would leave with the stampede so she wouldn't be able to speak to him privately, but no such luck. She peeked in the door and there he was at the far end of the seminar table, stuffing papers into a battered old briefcase that had too much in it already. His head was down and there was still time for her to slink away, wait him out in the bathroom, then come back and collect her stuff. She would talk to him tomorrow, maybe at the Book Store, which would be neutral ground and much less stressful . . . *Damn!* Now it was too late. Professor Putnam had looked up and seen her peering out around the door frame. She had lost her chance to enter the room with any dignity, along with her chance to run away.

"I'm sorry I bolted," Rose said, still hugging the door frame.

"Are you all right?" Professor Putnam immediately came toward her, lugging his loaded briefcase. He didn't look at all like a giant entity anymore. He looked like a nice man, deeply concerned about another person. What the hell had happened to her?

"Certainly I'm all right." Rose saw herself pressed against the tiles in the bathroom. Abruptly the floor shifted under her feet, threatening to begin its Tilt-A-Whirl activities again. "That is, no, I'm not, actually."

"Oh?"

Rose edged far enough into the room to grasp the back of a chair. The floor steadied itself. "I mean, I'm all right now, but I wasn't all right when I bolted."

"Can you tell me what happened?"

Professor Putnam had stopped about six feet away from Rose and put his briefcase down on the floor. He was looking at her expectantly, this tall, almost-handsome man, who needed a haircut and did seem so kind. "I don't know," she said.

"Really?"

"It had nothing to do with your lecture," Rose added hurriedly. "I've always been a bolter. From classes, that is. It's always been hard for me to sit in a room and listen to lectures. I bolted from college entirely at the end of my sophomore year. I have no idea why—I can sit still and read for hours—but classrooms have always felt a bit confining."

"I see." Professor Putnam looked no less concerned and confused.

Rose blundered on. "I did come back today and listen to your lecture from just outside in the hall." She gestured vaguely behind her toward the door. "I could hear everything perfectly." Rose felt herself blushing—yes, *blushing*! She hadn't been exactly accurate when she'd linked her panicky feelings today with what had happened to her during her first attempt at college. The anxiety she'd experienced today in Professor Putnam's class was nothing like the fierce case of the fidgets she'd sometimes gotten in lectures during her two years at Rice. It was, she knew, somehow connected to Professor Putnam himself. "I enjoyed your class today very much," she finished lamely.

"No kidding? You really liked my lecture?" His kind face lit up. "I'm glad to hear you say that. I enjoyed it myself today. I thought it was quite a good class."

"Yes, it was. I could tell that from behind the door." Rose smiled up at him and again felt that disturbing sensation of stillness. *But you're Marjory's guest . . .*

He smiled back. "I'm going to take that as a high compliment. Agnes says she thinks you are a truthful person."

"I hope I am. I was raised to be."

"Agnes said you were raised in apartments over bars."

"Over quite a few different bars. But that doesn't mean I wasn't taught to tell the truth." The stillness was gone, replaced by a riot of peculiar feelings. Love, hate, fear, longing, joy, sorrow, lightness, heaviness—all of them tumbled around inside her. Rose had to resist a strong impulse to bolt again.

"So the problem isn't crowded places, I guess," Professor Putnam said.

"I beg your pardon?"

"The problem you have sitting in a classroom isn't because the room is crowded?"

"Oh, no. I like crowds. I've always loved to watch people when they don't realize I'm there. When I was a kid, I watched people all the time while my mother was working, and I made up the wildest stories about them. I still do, to some extent."

"Me, too." Professor Putnam's whole face soared upward when he grinned. "When I was a kid, I'd give every stranger I saw an exciting life." Now he was laughing. *Really* laughing. "I hadn't thought about doing that in years. What an optimist I was back then! I thought when I grew up, I'd face all kinds of adventures. I had no idea how uneventful most days would be." He shrugged. "I suppose I've led a very boring life. The biggest adventure I've ever had is Henry."

Henry. That sweet, solemn little boy. Rose wasn't certain she was ready to ask Professor Putnam about Henry, about where he'd come from and why he'd shown up just now. Asking such things might trigger an exchange of truly personal information between them, not so much about their lives as about their hearts. "I'm almost never bored," she said. Which was also quite true. She could not remember ever being really, truly bored. At least, not for very long.

"Have you had a lot of adventures, then?"

"Almost none. I've done nothing but work in bookshops since I dropped out of college."

Professor Putnam nodded but didn't say anything. He seemed to be encouraging her to go on. Did he expect her to go on about bookshops? If so, there wasn't much to go on about. A bookshop was a bookshop was a bookshop. The building around them had grown very still. A door opened and closed somewhere down the hall. A telephone rang once. All of Rose's fellow students had escaped into the bright afternoon. Would it be all right if she escaped now, too? Surely escaping wasn't the same as bolting. Or was it? "Speaking of bookshops," she said, backing up a step, "I'd better be going."

"Of course." Professor Putnam immediately became professorial again. The strange, fragile, bothersome, intrusive intimacy between them dissipated, vaporized, retreated back into its inaccessible lair. "I'd better be getting along as well," he said, picking up his briefcase. "Although I do want to thank you again for looking after Henry on Tuesday during Marjory's funeral. Agnes and I didn't think he should go, but we also didn't feel right about parking him with a stranger so soon after he'd gotten here. And then you called, and we knew we didn't have to worry about Henry at all because he'd be with you."

"I was happy to do it," Rose said. "Henry's great. Really great."

Tom Putnam immediately put his briefcase down again and leaned toward her, radiating a kind of rusty *personal* intensity. "Did Henry say anything to you? You know, about his past?"

Well, this was odd. Surely Professor Putnam knew all about his son's past. "A little."

"What did he say?"

"Just stuff, like he didn't get to watch much TV and how he's never liked beets." Mavis shouted at Rose again from her childhood, something about speaking the truth and shaming politicians. "Henry reminds me of me," she added quietly. "Not that that's what makes him great."

"*How* does he remind you of you?" *Whap.* Back at her.

"I think Henry's had to work to keep a place inside him that feels safe," Rose said, and then immediately wondered what the hell she'd meant by *that*. Rose had never, as far as she could remember, felt unsafe. Or had she? Was unsafe what she was feeling right now, face-to-face with Professor Putnam?

"I think you're right," he said. "In fact, I *know* you're right."

"I am?"

"Oh, yes. Henry's got a lot of issues. An awful lot of issues for a six-year-old."

The question popped out before Rose knew she'd decided to ask it. "How much time have you spent with Henry?"

"You mean before this week?" he asked.

"Yes."

A group of students thundered by in the hall, laughing loudly at some communal joke, forcing Professor Putnam to speak louder. "Oh," he all but shouted, "I met Henry for the first time when he got off the train on Monday. So you see, Miss Callahan—Rose—anything you could tell me about him would be very helpful."

*   *   *

Iris Benson paused outside the double side doors of All Souls Episcopal Church. It was not too late to turn around and walk back to her car. Her Toyota was parked just one block up the street, wedged in between an old pickup and a jacked-up Firebird. Walking toward the church, Iris had seen no other cars she considered normal. They were all what she thought of as statement cars: big pickups stating *we have testosterone problems*; enormous SUVs stating *we have aggression problems*; or dilapidated, older American cars stating *we have money problems*. Even the ones Iris considered to be regular cars—relatively new Toyotas, Hondas, the smaller SUVs, the well-maintained, midsize American cars—had bumper stickers on them saying *I cruise without booze* or *I'm a friend of Bill's*, announcing to anyone who could read that their drivers had alcohol problems.

Her psychiatrist had been so adamant, though. Dr. Oakton had actually leaned forward while speaking to her, something he had never done before. The man hardly moved most of the time, and Iris kept waiting for his eyes to close, which would mean he'd finally nodded off. But this last time, he'd lunged at her just the way her colleagues did at meetings when they were trying to shout her down and make a point. And after he'd lunged, what Dr. Oakton had said was "The truth is we can't do any real work together, Iris, unless you stop drinking. And your best chance of doing that is to go into treatment and follow that up with regular attendance at AA meetings."

Well, treatment was completely out of the question. Treatment would mean going to the dean and telling him she was a helpless drunk at the same time she was up for tenure. She might just as well start sending out CVs now and applying for other jobs. The dean might be young, but he was an old boy if there ever was one. To him, a man who drank too much was a real man, but a woman who drank too much was—well, whatever she was, she wasn't tenure material.

That left AA. The sad thing was, Iris had almost stopped drinking for a couple of weeks on her own—keeping her daily alcohol consumption to a couple of glasses of wine, and that only after five o'clock—and life had begun to seem a little less stressful. She'd gone whole days without raising her voice. But then Marjory Putnam had been killed, and she'd accidentally gotten drunk out of her mind, and life had jumped right back into the toilet.

The last thing Iris remembered clearly about this past Friday was a colleague rushing into her office late in the afternoon to tell her the news about Marjory. What she had done after that was only there in bits and pieces that she didn't want to consider, ever, even in therapy. The ironic thing was that she'd been all set to tell Tom Putnam, who'd always been so kind, that she thought she might possibly have a tiny problem with alcohol. Iris had thought if she told someone, it might help her put the brakes on when she got the urge to really tie one on. Then Marjory had been killed, and she vaguely remembered shouting at Rose Callahan, of all people, in the entrance hall at the Putnams'. Her next memory was waking up in a strange room, which turned out to be the Putnams' guest room, with a head full of lead marbles banging about and a feeling that was uncomfortably close to despair. She'd lain there, staring at some god-awful ramshackle piece of furniture, and thought, *I have nowhere to go but down if I don't stop drinking, and I can't stop drinking.* But when she'd complained of this to her shrink, expecting him to help alleviate the bleakness of that moment, he had instead reinforced it, making her feel that if she didn't at least get herself to AA, she might as well hang herself and get it over with.

So here she was, poised to enter a church, something she hadn't done since she was twelve and old enough to rebel against *that* parental imperative. She would spend the next hour listening to a bunch of drunks, and somehow this was supposed to keep her from stopping at the ABC store on the way home? My God, it was hopeless. Just hopeless. She would have nothing in common with these people. Nothing. She could tell that from their cars. Her only real hope lay with her therapy, but now her shrink had lunged at her and given her the uncomfortable feeling that he didn't really want to see her again if she hadn't at least tried AA.

A middle-aged man in a faded flannel shirt appeared beside her. His stringy hair was cut very short on the sides and hung down to his shoulders in the back. When he smiled, Iris saw that he had very few teeth and none of those met. "I ain't seen you here before," he said cheerfully. "This your first meeting?"

"Yes." Iris was too startled to find herself speaking to this sort of person to evade the question.

The man stepped forward and pushed open one side of the heavy double doors. "Well, come on in," he said, still cheerful, as though this were no big deal. "All you have to do is not drink while you're here. There's no law that says you can't drink all you want just as soon as you leave." He stood there holding the door, smiling at her. Inside the room Iris could see a bunch of people sitting around a big seminar table. More people sat in folding chairs around the edges of the room. Heads had turned and were looking at her. "Thank you," Iris said, raising her chin, squaring her shoulders, tossing her hair, and brushing past him, making one of her grander entrances.

The first person to come into focus was Russell Jacobs, sitting against the wall on the far side of the room.

Iris stopped.

She stared.

She would never, *ever*, in a million trillion years, have guessed that Russell Jacobs, Professor Pompous, was an alcoholic.

It was awful. It had never occurred to Iris there might be someone she knew at an AA meeting. And having that someone be Russell made her feel as though Yahweh Herself were laughing at her.

At least she had the pleasure of seeing Russell look momentarily discomforted to see *her*. If she was blown, so was he, which meant that neither of them could out the other without outing themselves. But still, Russell would forever and ever know that she knew he was a drunk. Which, hopefully, would make him a tiny bit crazy. Or should she say, crazier?

But then, being the world's, biggest, fattest *fake*, Russell smiled and waved as though he'd completely forgotten they hated each other. Iris took the first seat she came to among the wall chairs, wedging herself in between an enormous man and an enormous woman who had obviously hoped they would be allowed a little extra space between them. Iris put her purse on the floor under her chair and then stared at her purple Birkenstocks while a piece of paper was passed around and different people read some mumbo-jumbo about Higher Power this and Higher Power that. *It's a cult*, she thought, *just like Aunt Suzy said*. Aunt Suzy was a Southern Baptist. She was married to Iris's mother's brother, who drank like a fish. Uncle Harry had gone to AA for a while and stopped drinking, but then he'd begun referring to his Higher Power, and Aunt Suzy had made him stop going to meetings, saying she'd rather be married to a drinker than to a man who put his faith in something other than Our Lord

Jesus Christ. Sure enough, in a couple of weeks, Uncle Harry was off on a full-blown toot, and Aunt Suzy had gotten what she'd asked for.

After they'd finished reading from the paper, the people who hadn't read introduced themselves. The introductions were obviously scripted. They started off as complete sentences—"Hi, I'm So-and-so (first name only), and I'm an alcoholic." A few people even stuck in "grateful, recovering" before the word "alcoholic." But by the time the first dozen people had finished, the introduction had shrunk to "So-and-so, alcoholic," the way academics introduce themselves to each other at conferences, stating their names and their colleges or universities, running the two together as though their place of employment were their true last names. Of course, academics could do whatever they pleased because they had nothing to be ashamed of, while these people had plenty to be ashamed of. Their cars, for starters.

The introductions whipped around the room like a runaway horse, reaching the enormous woman on Iris's right. "Myrtle, alcoholic," she said.

Silence fell. Everyone in the room looked at Iris. Even Russell Jacobs. Even the people at the near end of the table who had to turn around in their chairs. The almost-toothless man with the funny hair was nodding his head at her encouragingly from the other side of the room. Iris felt the pressure of her neighbor's shoulders on her own. What if she was stuck? Really stuck? Not just metaphorically stuck because of Dr. Oakton's ultimatum. Her shoulders certainly were mashed together, which made it impossible for her to sit up straight, which made it impossible for her to carry this moment off with any sort of aplomb.

Then dramatically—as though some inner-cranial intervention were taking place—the great black hole of last Friday night enveloped her, and a small voice spoke up very clearly inside her head: *Iris Benson, for once in your life, can't you just cut the crap?* She shrank back further against the wall. Oh, what the hell. As Martha and her Vandellas had sung so long ago, there was nowhere to run to, baby, nowhere to hide. "Iris, alcoholic," she mumbled, wanting very badly to add that she wasn't sure at all if that were true, and even if it were, she certainly didn't belong in this place with a bunch of losers and one pompous ass named Russell Jacobs.

The introductions galloped on around the rest of the room. Iris dimly heard, "Russell, alcoholic," intoned in Russ's rich, professorial baritone. She stayed pressed against her wall, almost hidden behind her neighbors. When they asked for newcomers to stand, she didn't move. Iris stayed mute and motionless as various people got up and addressed some hare-brained "topic" suggested by a pinched little man who spoke in a disproportionately booming voice. At the end of the meeting, when they asked if anyone would like to pick up a twenty-four-hour chip, signifying that they were going to give the AA way of life a try, she didn't move. When the meeting was finally over, she had to wait until her neighbors got up before she could. But then one of them grabbed her hand, and Iris found herself part of a giant circle embarked on the Lord's Prayer, of all things. Surely this was unconstitutional. Surely you weren't allowed to pray at a public gathering. Although maybe you were at this one, since they were meeting in a church. *Forgive us our trespasses as we forgive those who trespass against us. And lead us not into temptation, but deliver us from evil. For thine is the kingdom, the power, and the glory, forever and ever. Amen. Keep coming back. It works if you work it!*

Where did that last cheer come from? That wasn't part of the regular Lord's Prayer, was it? It was just too, too tacky for words. Iris grabbed her purse the moment her hand was released and raced for the door, but she wasn't quite quick enough. The flannel-shirt man nabbed her and thrust a pamphlet at her. "Nice to have you here," he said. "Keep coming back. This here's a meeting schedule."

Iris took the schedule and fled. Out of the corner of her eye, she'd seen Russell Jacobs chatting away with some mousy middle-aged woman who was looking up at him as though he were God's gift to AA. Iris didn't care if she spent the rest of her life drunk as a skunk. All she wanted was to get out of there.

chapter 12

Her daughter's struggles had been the organizing principle of Agnes Tattle's existence for more than forty years. Marjory's death had left her skilled at coping, not at living. Since Henry's arrival, she'd spent most of her time in her first-floor "office," a small, square room that had once been the house's china cupboard, trying to find some clue to the mystery that was Henry. But then, at some point late yesterday afternoon, it had occurred to her she might be more useful if she put in some time *with* Henry, so that Tom could get back to work.

So now, here she sat on the back porch steps, *not* smoking, watching Henry play politely with the new Tonka dump truck Rose Callahan had brought him. *Would that I,* Agnes thought, *shared Rose Callahan's ability to reach the hearts of small, damaged boys.* She'd been on her own with Henry for just under four hours and did not consider their time together a success. To begin with, she'd hovered, which was something she considered the hallmark of bad parenting. Children needed space more than overprotection. Parents who hovered were meeting their own needs, not their children's.

Agnes's one solace was that she'd been no worse than Tom in the hovering department. He had trailed Henry around like a besotted puppy, doing his best to "play" with him. Agnes had found the sight of her tall, semihandsome, thoroughly awkward son-in-law squatting, kneeling, crawling around after their small, strange cohabitant alternately unbearably endearing and unbearably pathetic. Midway through yesterday, overloaded with feelings, she'd fled to her converted china closet and mostly stayed there whenever she didn't have to entertain uninvited guests.

What Agnes wanted most was to stop feeling *anything* for a while. She thought she could probably have dealt with Marjory's death pretty well by itself. But that, coupled with Henry's baffling arrival and its attendant whiffs of renewed hope, had wrung her dry. It was as Tom had said, the boy had a *future*. This meant that, suddenly and alarmingly, so did she and Tom. Her own future might be very short—she was just turned seventy-two, after all—but there it was before her, as immovable as a mountain.

Oddly, of all the things that unsettled her, it was Tom's sudden *aliveness* that unhinged her the most. An energized Tom was much harder to deal with than an absent Marjory or an almost-silent Henry. Who was this strange man, chattering away about Barney and Transformers to a child who just *looked* at him? Last evening, after Henry had gone to bed, Tom enthusiastically confided to her that he'd had a couple of what he termed "mini-breakthroughs" with Henry while they'd been reading Harry Potter. This appeared to mean that Henry had spoken to him twice voluntarily.

Big whoop-de-doo! That oughta keep the child psychologists at bay another day, she'd thought at the time. But now Agnes asked herself, what right did she have to rain on Tom's breakthrough parade? She and Henry had yet to exchange a single word. A *single word!* At breakfast this morning, when she'd asked him whether he'd like cornflakes or Wheaties, he'd pointed to the cornflakes box rather than speak to her. Did Henry sense how bossy and controlling she'd become over the last forty years?

Agnes watched the boy cautiously push the Tonka dump truck up against the base of a derelict bird feeder. Weren't small boys supposed to *crash* their dump trucks into things while making loud motor noises? *Rummmmmm, rummmmmm?*

She sighed and wished with all her heart that she were expelling Camel smoke instead of air. At least, Agnes thought glumly, Henry *looks* a little less cautious.

The college bells began striking the hour. Agnes checked her watch. Good. Five o'clock. Tom's office hours were officially over. At this moment, he'd probably be racing home to resume "playing" with Henry. People would stop him, as they always did, but he would be in a hurry, so he would be uncharacteristically efficient in exchanging greetings. It was safe to assume Tom would be here in half or three-quarters of an hour, at which point she would go inside, mix up a meatloaf and watch *The News Hour* while it cooked. Talking back to nutcase politicians always revived her spirits. She was *good* at talking back to nutcases. In her bleaker moments, Agnes worried she no longer knew how to communicate with non-nutcases on anything other than the most superficial level. *How are you today? . . . My, isn't it hot? . . . Have you read* Blink *yet?* seemed to be about all she could muster by way of conversation with a regular person.

And Henry was much more important than a regular person. Henry was Henry.

*   *   *

Tom heard the college bells ring the hour through the open window. Five o'clock. There had been an early trickle of students showing up for his office hours, but then no one had come by after four o'clock.

Tom quickly packed his briefcase, closed his office door behind him, and walked down the hall with a spring in his step. Well, why shouldn't he? He was headed home after a surprisingly satisfying day, not to a bleak, predictable evening with Marjory, but to a completely unpredictable, possibly fun evening with Henry.

As he passed Iris Benson's closed office door, Tom briefly considered knocking, just to check up on her—an impulse that made him smile. Evidently his habit of feeling responsible for troubled people had not died with Marjory.

Marjory! How strange it was to think of her with something close to simple affection and regret instead of dread and guilt. The early fall sunlight slanted through the trees, pricking out light and shadow in ways that gave even Tom an artist's appreciative eye. Carried along on a miraculous tide of goodwill toward everyone, including himself, Tom realized that the reason he related to dead Marjory in a less complicated, more companionable way than he'd related to living Marjory might have nothing to do with him. It might, instead, have to do with some trick of memory. Perhaps in death, whatever she'd wished to be was allowed to stamp out the memory of what she'd been stuck with being? Which seemed, somehow, to release him from their shared, unhappy, pointless past. Perhaps it really was okay just to let go of all that worry and let a different, happier life begin?

Thinking this over—as much as he *could* think over something so illogical and fantastical—it occurred to Tom that embracing the possibility of a happy future might be the bravest thing he'd ever done. Change of any kind had always been a challenge for him, and this represented change on steroids, a shift in his entire habit of being.

Step by step, more and more, Tom began to feel that he *owed* it to Marjory to try; that allowing himself to be happy might, in some cockamamie way, be the most fitting tribute he could pay her. The hard truth was that, unlike him and unlike her mother, Marjory, for all her craziness, had always, *always* had the guts to hope that life would get better. Perhaps hope, thrust upon him in this queer *magical* way, was to be her lasting legacy?

A dog sniffed at his leg, then nipped him on the seat of his pants. Tom jumped and turned around.

"Sorry!" It was the president—teetering on stiletto heels, constrained by a short, tight skirt—out walking her greyhounds. Or rather being walked by them. The president's greyhounds had become a campus cross to bear. For two dogs who were never let loose, they caused a spectacular amount of ruckus. At the moment the president was ineffectually yanking the leash of the bigger one, who obviously wanted nothing more than to play with Tom. "I can't seem to control Romeo," she gasped. "Juliet is really much better behaved."

"That's all right." Tom resisted the impulse to finger his pants bottom and find out if the fabric was torn.

In the space of a couple of heartbeats, the offending Romeo lost interest in Tom and wrapped his leash completely around the president twice, binding her tightly about the legs, so that she looked like a bad fashion statement ready to be burned at the stake.

A squirrel ran by on the grass, tantalizingly just out of reach. Romeo lunged at it on his shortened leash. The president swayed dangerously. Tom dropped his briefcase and leapt to steady her, grasping her by the upper arms and bracing his legs. Romeo lunged and tugged. It was all Tom could do to keep the president upright.

"Why don't you just let Romeo run?" he suggested. The president smelled faintly of cigarettes. Was she a closet smoker? My, my.

"What if he runs away?" the president gasped. "I'd never forgive myself." Still, she unsnapped the leash, and Romeo shot after the squirrel. Or rather, he dashed about twenty feet and stopped, then veered to the right, dashed another twenty, and stopped. Then he sat down, thoroughly confused by his freedom. The president had rescued both him and Juliet from the racetrack. Romeo had spent most of his life in a cage. Now, actually given the chance to go anywhere he liked, the dog had no idea what to make of such options.

Tom stared at him. *We're two of a kind, Romeo,* he thought. A line from an old Dobie Gray song flashed through his head: *Looking back and longing for the freedom of my chains.* Then Henry and Rose Callahan wandered through his mind walking hand in hand, beckoning him to come with them . . .

The president, having extricated herself from Romeo's leash, was patting and pulling at herself and her clothes. Amazingly, Juliet sat calmly beside her like a working dog trained to *hup.* She looked up anxiously at Tom as though pleading with him. *Please, mister, don't let her release me, too. I couldn't stand it.*

Romeo came loping back to the president, sat down, and waited patiently for her to understand that he wanted to be put back on his leash. Once she got it and his wish was granted, Romeo immediately began charging off in all directions again. Everything interesting lay just beyond the length of his leash, which was just the way Romeo liked it. Juliet immediately joined him in the fun.

Tom leaned over to pick up his briefcase. When he unbent again, the president was still there, standing with her legs as far apart as her tight skirt would allow in order to brace herself in all directions at once. Her arms shot stiffly this way and that at the whim of her greyhounds. Why didn't the president just give up and go home? Hire some student with strong legs and sensible shoes to walk her ridiculous dogs. Then Tom realized the president was still looking at him, and, what's more, seemed to be *thinking* about him as well, for her eyes held genuine concern. "I just wanted to say again, Tom," she said, "how sorry I am that your life has had this dreadful disruption. I've had a few disruptions of my own, so I know how confusing it can be. So if there's anything you need, anything I can do, either personally or professionally, for you and your son, I do hope you'll let me know."

Tom was startled. The president hadn't made some greeting-card statement about Marjory's loss and Henry's sudden arrival. Instead, she had used the word "disruption." She'd figured out—who knew how—the thing he was only now fully coming to terms with himself: that his problem was not one of overpowering grief or a huge sense of loss, but was instead of deep confusion and disorientation at the possibility of something approaching happiness. This woman, who had only laid eyes on Marjory a couple of times at receptions, must have recognized her for what she was, not a wife so much as an extremely high-maintenance housemate, whose sudden removal would leave her husband not devastated so much as bewildered. Then, enter Henry, toting possibility in his backpack. Was it conceivable that under that ridiculous frosted hair and inside those ridiculous clothes and on top of those ridiculous shoes was a truly empathetic, observant human?

"Thank you," Tom said.

"You're welcome."

Both of them were pleased, but also slightly embarrassed, to find themselves capable of such surprising simplicity and sincerity.

"Well, good night, then," the president said. She turned to walk toward home. Tom was thankful to see both greyhounds run around her as she pivoted, but then each shot out straight in a different direction, so the president teetered away from him with her arms out as though she were in mid-swan-dive. She looked much less ridiculous to him than usual, however. She had, after all, rescued those dogs from life in a box and was doing her best to take care of them. If she looked foolish in the process, shouldn't this just add to her credit?

The college bells chimed the half hour. Doors all over the Quad opened and staff began to spill out. People immediately came up to Tom, patted his arm, welcomed him back, proffered dinner invitations, lunch invitations, even offers to clean his house. For the first time since Marjory had flown off Route 29, ending her life and redefining his, it occurred to him that all the inquiries, all the saccharine cards and stiff, formal flower arrangements, all the ritualized gestures of condolence might *mean* something. Of course, they were conventional offerings. His colleagues were conventional people, for the most part. They had to be. It was a question of survival, for if conventions weren't observed in this tiny, closed community, people would probably start killing one another pretty quickly. But might it not be possible that all those comings and goings during the last week, all that baking and flower arranging, all that bothersome curiosity and fuss about Henry, all meant that people, to some small degree, understood? Not everyone would have the chutzpah the president did; not everyone would come right out and say in so many words, *I know your wife was crazy as a bedbug and you couldn't really love her, and that this "son" of yours is a complete surprise, but still this is a terribly confusing time in your life, and I'd like to do what I can to help.* Maybe that was what all those casseroles and chocolate chip cookies and Jell-O had actually meant? He'd been so focused on maintaining Marjory for all those years, it had never occurred to him that he might have accidentally, and without intending to, made a lot of friends.

The wave of concerned people swept past him toward the parking lots behind the chapel. The president had disappeared. A few packs of chattering students had come out of the dorms and were heading for the dining hall.

Tom began walking toward home again, the thoughts in his head as disordered as the papers in his briefcase. It had been years and years and years since so much had happened to him, and he couldn't seem to sort any of it out. His brain had been dulled by two decades of trying *not* to think while, at the same time, finding the energy to do his duty and get through another day. And now there was Henry, who so obviously *needed* him. What did people *do*, exactly, that made them good parents?

"Hi, Professor Putnam!" Tom did not have to turn around to know he was being hailed by Susan Mason, the freckled second-year who'd had such interesting things to say in class about *Othello*.

"Hello," Tom said. "You on your way to the dining hall?"

Susan Mason shook her head. "Not yet. I'm trying to get to the Book Store before it closes to buy my little brother a college bill cap."

Tom was instantly attentive. "You have a little brother?"

Susan beamed. "I sure do. And he thinks it's very cool to have a big sister in college. He wants the hat so he can impress all his friends in second grade."

"Oh, he's in second grade."

"Yes!" Susan said happily. "Doesn't that make him the same age as your son?"

*   *   *

Hanging up the phone, Agnes wondered if the world might not be tilting as well as turning. How else could she explain her son-in-law's announcement that he was bringing Rose Callahan and a student home to dinner?

During their short conversation, Tom had raced through some loopy tale of going to the Book Store to buy Henry a hat with a student who had a little brother just ten months older than Henry. Rose Callahan had been working, and he'd impulsively—and who knew Tom Putnam *had* impulses—invited both her and the student to dinner. His thought was that Henry might enjoy the crowd, and that he and Agnes might pick up some tips from the student with the little brother on how to relate to small boys. So was this all right? And was there enough food or should he pick up some fried chicken?

When the phone rang, Agnes had had to force herself to come inside and answer it; force herself to leave Henry and his Tonka dump truck on their own for five minutes. Who knew hovering was addictive? Then, when she'd hung up and turned around to go outside again, there was Henry standing three feet away from her, truck tucked under one arm, regarding her soberly. Perhaps hovering was a family disease—if, indeed, they were a family.

Agnes folded her arms and regarded him soberly right back. "It seems we're having company for supper. You up for that?"

Henry blinked but otherwise didn't move.

"That's exactly how I feel," Agnes said. "But there you are. Shall you and I go get some potatoes from the pantry so we can start peeling them?"

Henry nodded solemnly. Well, surprise, surprise! Surely that counted as almost speaking. Agnes held out her hand, something she hadn't done to another person in probably twenty years.

Surprise, surprise again! Henry took it.

*   *   *

Supper was over, and something strange and wonderful had happened.

Henry, wearing his new hat, sat at the kitchen table playing Go Fish with Rose and Susan Mason. "Go *Fish!*" Henry screamed, hugging his cards and shaking with glee.

As far as Tom could tell from where he stood washing dishes at the kitchen sink, Rose Callahan really was a witch. A good witch, to be sure, but a witch all the same. Her powers had pried Henry open just as surely as they'd pried him open.

When Tom had given Henry his new hat, Henry had just stood there staring at it. Then Rose, the Good Witch, had stepped up and said, "Hi, Henry. I'm back. Wanna go play in your room?" and that was that. Henry had studied her briefly, slapped his hat on his head, taken Rose's hand, and headed for the stairs.

For the next half hour Tom had made distracted conversation with Susan Mason while listening to what could only be termed a ruckus coming from upstairs. Then, when Agnes had sent Susan upstairs to announce dinner, there had been a great clattering and the newly bespelled Henry had come sliding into the dining room in his sock feet, shouting, "I win! I win!"

Yes, Rose Callahan was a witch. She'd waved her roses at him and given Henry her hand and a couple of hugs, and *shazamm!* Both of them were *back!* Resilience, Tom had read somewhere, was first and foremost a matter of feeling safe, of feeling that just because things were different didn't mean things were dangerous. Was that Rose Callahan's gift? Bestowing a feeling that in her presence, whatever everything was, it was okay?

Henry obviously thought so. And Tom *felt* so. Sadly, he was too old to confuse feelings with reality. Still, while rinsing plates, he'd begun humming "Tecumseh Valley," an old Townes Van Zandt song he'd once plunked out on the guitar while dreaming of his ideal woman. *Her ways were free and it seemed to me that sunshine walked beside her.*

"Would it be rude to ask what song you're humming?" Susan Mason asked from the doorway.

The world jerked back into the here and now. Which was actually, Tom realized, quite a pleasant place to be. He rinsed the soap off his hands and turned to Susan. "Oh, just an obscure ditty by a singer-songwriter who drank and drugged himself to death years ago."

"How sad," she said.

Is it sad? Tom wondered. *Should you shed tears for someone who dies a bit young, but still manages to leave some truly grand songs behind him?* "I guess," he said, reaching for the hand towel Agnes kept on a hook planted within easy reach of the sink.

That was that. The dishes were done.

Susan was holding the Book Store bag that contained her little brother's ball cap. Tom made a mental note to search that boy out when Susan graduated and shake his hand. If it weren't for him this lovely evening would never have happened.

"I want to thank you for a lovely evening," Susan said.

"Are you leaving us?"

"Yes. I'm afraid I have to. I told a friend I'd meet her at the library to study for a French test tomorrow."

Tom put down the hand towel and gave her a little bow. *"Bonne nuit, mademoiselle,"* he said.

Surprisingly, Susan Mason, the gawky eager beaver, dropped a perfectly acceptable curtsy. Especially considering she was wearing jeans. *"Bonne nuit, monsieur."*

"Let me see you out," Tom said, offering her his arm.

He'd just shut the front door behind Susan when Henry—the new, verbal Henry—marched into the foyer from the living room and parked himself between Tom and escape. The child was still slight, still froth-haired, but he'd shaken off whatever voices from his past had been telling him to sit still and stay quiet. "Can Rose please spend the night with me?" he asked.

Tom's pedantic mind automatically noted with approval that Henry had said "please." Retesia appeared to have trained the boy well in the use of small courtesies. Only then did Tom move on to the question itself: *Could Rose Callahan spend the night?*

Some long-sleeping part of his heart woke up and banged hard against his chest, making it pleasantly difficult to breathe. Tom reminded himself sternly that this was Henry's idea, not his. He leaned over and picked the little boy up. Henry stiffened slightly but did not protest. Tom noted with pleasure that the boy's cheeks were flushed with outdoor rosiness, and that freckles were threatening to break out along the bridge of his small, straight nose. "Where would Rose sleep?"

"In my room. I got a big bed."

Tom felt deeply pleased that Henry had referred to the newly redecorated guest room as his room. And he was looking up at him as expectantly as *any* child would while asking permission of his father about something important. "Have you asked Rose if she'd *like* to spend the night?" Tom asked.

Henry shook his head vigorously. "Ask you first. Then ask Agnes. *Then* ask Rose."

Rose appeared in the foyer. "I think it's time for me to go. Thank you both for a lovely evening."

"*Can* she?" Henry hissed urgently into Tom's ear. "Rose is my friend."

Tom looked into Rose's eyes and everything he'd ever held sacred about convention flew away. "Henry would like to ask you to spend the night with him."

Henry wriggled violently to be let down. Once ambulatory, he scooted over to Rose. "Please, please, *please*, Rose. You could read Harry Potter to me."

Tom felt a stab of disappointment. Henry had asked someone else to read to him. Rose, however, did not miss a beat. "Henry, that is so nice of you. I haven't had a friend invite me to spend the night in years." Then, abruptly, she blushed and dropped her eyes. "I mean invite me for a sleepover," she corrected. "But tomorrow is a workday, so I better sleep at home tonight."

"I'll read Harry Potter to you," Tom said quickly.

Henry made what had to be his considering face. "Okay," he said. "But I'd rather have Rose."

Tom surprised himself by laughing. "Well, Henry, it looks as though you'll have to make do with me. Now say good night to Rose, run upstairs, put your pj's on and brush your teeth, and I'll be up in a minute to read to you."

Rose knelt down and held out her arms to Henry, who moved toward her. She pulled him into a hug, then released him. "Thank you for a lovely evening, Henry. I hope I'll see you again soon."

"Tomorrow?" Henry twisted around to look up at Tom. "Can Rose come over tomorrow?"

Rose smiled, first at Tom, then at Henry. "We'll see," she said. "Now run upstairs and get ready for bed like your father asked you to, okay?"

"Okay." That was that. Henry made for the stairs and ran up them. His clattering feet, Tom thought, was the best sound he'd heard in years. It was so boyish. For four days, Henry had made almost no noise.

He reached down for Rose's hand in order to help her up. Then, to the surprise of them both, he held it for a minute. "I don't know what magic you performed on Henry, but whatever it was has removed a very distressing spell from him."

Rose looked up at him and made no move to take back her hand. "I think the magic is you and Agnes and time."

"Really?" There was a sensation of something surrounding them as he held her hand that Tom had never experienced before. It felt as though he were living in two realities at the same time: the Regular World, which was rackety and confusing, and Rose's World, which was warm and calm. Tom felt the winds of enchantment blowing again. "Would you have dinner with me this weekend?"

"Dinner? With you? You mean just the two of us?"

"Yes," he said, *not* dropping her hand, quite amazed at how confident he felt.

Rose, however, looked troubled. "I . . . I don't know. I'm not sure. I mean, your wife just died."

"Ah!" Tom said. "Marjory. You're right, people might not understand. I guess the question is, how much should we care about that?"

That struck a spark. Rose was instantly defiant. "I don't care a fig about what other people think, but I do care about her. If I had dinner with you so soon after she died, I would feel disrespectful of her memory. I mean, she did her best, and don't both of us need to honor that?"

"Of course," Tom said firmly. "But I'd also like to start living. And I'd like to do that by having dinner with you whenever you're ready."

Rose's gaze drifted downward until she was looking at her hand, still surrounded by Tom's. "It could be that I'm so uncomfortable because I just broke up with my boyfriend."

Boyfriend! Tom dropped her hand immediately. It hadn't even occurred to him that Rose might have a boyfriend. But of course she would! She would have men lining up to bask in her sunshine. His confidence deflated like a punctured beach ball. "I'm sorry. I didn't know. About the boyfriend, I mean."

Rose had begun rummaging in her hair again. "I don't suppose you'd like to shoot hoops with me for an hour tomorrow morning around ten thirty?" she said, not quite looking at him.

Henry lay under his new Harry Potter bedspread beside his newly Harry Potter–curtained window. A giant poster of Dumbledore and the Hogwarts Castle gang hung on the wall opposite his bed, carefully positioned at Henry height.

Tom could *feel* those eyes as he read chapter two of *Harry Potter and the Sorcerer's Stone*, trying his best to bring those fabled characters to life. *This*, he thought, *is fun*.

It was ten o'clock by the time Tom closed the book; much too late for a six-year-old to be up, in his opinion, but as this was the first night Henry had actually *been* there in any way other than physical, Tom wanted it to last.

Henry was regarding him so seriously that Tom felt a riffle of panic. What if the boy only talked when Rose was around?

Oh well, Tom told himself, *there's only one way to find out*. "Did you enjoy the book?" he asked.

Henry nodded. "Can we read some more tomorrow? Please?"

A feeling he thought was probably joy flooded Tom. "We certainly can!"

"When?"

Guilt immediately replaced joy inside Tom. He would be deserting Henry for an hour tomorrow morning to go play basketball with Rose. And, if she'd said yes to dinner, he would have deserted Henry again tomorrow evening. What had possessed him to try to have a life and Henry at the same time? He thought of Romeo, the president's greyhound, completely freaked out by options.

Come on! Tom told himself sternly. *You organized anti-apartheid protests for several thousand students from five different colleges when you were only twenty years old. Surely you can organize your own life!*

"I have something to do tomorrow morning, Henry, so Agnes will take care of you while I'm busy. But I'll be back by lunch, and we can read some more then if you like. And then I thought we might take in the college's first soccer game tomorrow afternoon at four thirty. Do you like soccer?"

Henry brightened. "I've seen soccer on TV. With my pawpaw."

Tom was instantly alert. "Who's Pawpaw?"

"My grandpa. Down in Picayune."

"Oh." What, Tom wondered, was Henry doing here if there was a soccer-watching grandfather in the picture?

Henry's eyes had unexpectedly filled with tears.

"What is it? What's wrong?" Tom asked.

"My pawpaw's dead." Henry spoke in a barely audible whisper. "And my mawmaw."

Another peek at the chaos behind Henry's curtain. Tom was aghast. He reached for the nearest part of the boy, which was his shoulder, and held on. "I'm so sorry, Henry. So terribly sorry."

Henry said nothing. His eyes were far away.

"You okay?" Tom asked.

The boy came back from wherever he was. "Do I really get to stay here?" he asked.

Damn the torpedoes! "You do," Tom said, knowing full well that Agnes would have his head for promising this child something he wasn't sure he could deliver.

Henry's eyes roamed his face again, looking, Tom supposed, for any hint of adult codswallop. Something he saw must have reassured him. "Okay," he said.

"Okay," Tom said firmly.

Henry seemed to be considering something. "Is it fun?" he asked.

Tom had completely forgotten what they'd been talking about before Henry's curtain had fluttered. "Is what fun?"

"A college soccer game?"

"Of course. I think it's great fun," Tom said.

"Okay," Henry said. "We can go." He rolled over to face the wall, curling up around his pillow.

Tom reached down and smoothed the boy's fizzing hair off his forehead. "It's really nice to have you here, Henry," he said, his voice catching.

Tom continued sitting right where he was for another hour, his hand resting just at the edge of the gaudy Harry Potter pastiche under which Henry slept. He thought briefly about the backpack full of money under his bed, but then quickly decided to think about something else.

chapter 13

Agnes Tattle got up very early Friday morning and went downstairs. She felt miraculously reborn, as though this really was—may God forgive her the use of a hackneyed expression—the first day of the rest of her life. This was not a completely new feeling. She'd experienced it six times before: the day after her marriage, the day after her husband's death, the day after Marjory was born, the day after she'd decided to go to law school, the day after the doctors had finally convinced her that Marjory's illness was hopeless, the day after she'd decided to give up her practice and move into this house. Each of these mornings she'd opened her eyes to find the demands of life had changed dramatically, and a reinvented Agnes was required to deal with them.

This reinvention, she was pretty certain, had been caused not so much by Marjory dying as by Henry coming to life. It had meant he was on the road to being all right, and if Henry could be all right, so could she.

The kitchen was the same as it had been yesterday, and yet everything in it seemed strange to her. This did not surprise Agnes in the least. During a reinvention, every object and aspect of life has to be reevaluated. She stood by the kitchen door, examining the tidy counters, the worn tracks on the linoleum, Tom's decrepit galoshes and Henry's Tonka truck. So here she was at seventy-two, floating in this familiar, unfamiliar space again. She would most likely come down to earth in a day or two, reformulated, reinvigorated, ready to go—after what, who knew? Who cared, when you got down to it? Right now, there was nothing to do but float like the *petit prince* on his ancient, threadbare carpet and experience the unbearable lightness of creative dislocation.

Henry was still asleep, as was Tom. This, as he had no classes, was a good thing for him and also for her, as she would have some time by herself. In her experience (seven reinventions *were* rather a lot), input during the process polluted it. The point was to discover things within yourself, not to respond to other people.

Agnes turned on the coffee and sat down at the table to wait for it to drip. She had brought her cigarettes with her, but she decided not to go outside and smoke. Instead she placed the pack of Camels on the table and inspected them. What nasty things they were, seen in the fresh light of a new life—little white paper tubes stuffed with shreds of a noxious plant, designed to be set on fire so you could draw poisonous smoke deep into your fragile lungs. She'd been puffing away on them—taking the last few years off—ever since that tenth-grade afternoon in the attic of Martha Arnold's house. If she was going to reinvent herself, perhaps she should become a nonsmoker again? It would certainly be much, much better for Henry.

Maybe she'd become a vegan, while she was at it.

Or maybe not.

What she had to remember was that all options, except those firmly denied to her because of age—inconsequential things such as becoming an Olympic diver or a concert pianist or a Mandarin Chinese scholar—were open. She didn't *have* to do anything. This would probably be her last reinvention. At seventy-two, it was reasonable to expect she'd have no more life-altering experiences except death—which didn't count as far as reinvention went. And for once, there would be no kowtowing to necessity or duty or love or any other such foolishness. She would live completely as herself—as Agnes Tattle, plain and simple, whoever she was, and whatever she wanted to do. There were Henry and Tom to think about, of course. But only if that was what she *wanted* to think about. After last night, it was pretty clear to her that both would do just fine without her. Or at least without her *hovering*.

The Bunn spluttered and hissed. Agnes got up and poured herself a cup of coffee, automatically reaching for the mug that said "World's Greatest Mom!" This mug had stabbed her in the heart every morning for years. She hadn't been the World's Greatest Mom at all. She had been impatient, resentful, angry a lot of the time in her dealings with her daughter. But she had dutifully drunk her coffee out of that mug and smiled at Marjory and, at least three times a week, told her how much the mug meant to her. Now here she was, about to drink from it again on the first day of the last reinvention of her life.

Agnes poured her cup of coffee down the sink as though it had been contaminated. Then she stomped the trash-can lever to open the lid, dropped the "World's Greatest Mom" mug inside, took her foot off the lever, and watched it disappear with a bang. A familiar fierceness rose up inside her. She had a quick, bright vision of herself in boxing gloves, pounding something, before she moved briskly back to the counter and got down another mug, one that had no painful associations, white with the college logo. Agnes poured coffee into it and sat down automatically at the kitchen table with her back to the window. She stared at the wall opposite her, at its depressingly cheery yellow paint, at the perpetual calendar of saccharine kitten pictures that Marjory had thought so adorable. This was how she'd started her mornings for the last nine years, staring at those damn kittens and wanting to throw something at them while her poor, sick daughter sat beside her and talked about her magazines or a new hairdo or—haltingly, fearfully—about her latest imaginary catastrophe.

Agnes got up deliberately and moved to the chair facing the big window that looked out onto the neighbor's garden. The entire time she'd lived in this house, neither she, Tom, nor Marjory had ever sat there. In the self-sacrificial atmosphere of those long years, both she and Tom would have felt bad hogging the best seat, and contact with the outside had made Marjory nervous. Well, phooey on all that! This was the new seat of the new Agnes! Unless Tom or Henry wanted it, of course. Then, they would cut cards or draw straws, like the three *sane* people they were.

Time, glorious time, stretched before her like a lazy river . . .

The telephone rang, as insistent as a fussy infant.

Agnes got up and lifted the receiver. "Hello," she said.

"Agnes Tattle, please." There was a slight twang to the woman's *a*'s.

"Speaking. Who's this, please?"

"Rose Callahan. I didn't wake you, did I?"

"Of course not. What can I do for you?"

Rose got to the point immediately. "You can eat lunch with me, that's what. I don't go into work until two. That gives me time to entertain, and as

I didn't really get to talk with you the other times we've had together, I'd like a chance to talk with you today over a bowl of soup at my house."

Agnes was so surprised she almost dropped the phone. She hadn't been out to lunch with another woman in years. "You're kidding," she said, before she thought.

Rose laughed. "Why would I be kidding? I liked talking with you that Friday night out on your back steps, and I've already made the soup. Will you come?"

Agnes's recall of that Friday evening was fragmented, disjointed, scattered. She did remember going out to sit on the back steps in an effort to escape the stultifying atmosphere of the house, and finding Rose already there. She remembered Rose eating an extraordinary amount of mushy casserole while she had slugged back Scotch. Agnes didn't think she'd been drunk so much as uncharacteristically loose in the brain. She remembered feeling a lot better after their conversation, but what they'd talked about remained vague, submerged in the evening's river of banalities. But what the hell? Why not? "Sure," Agnes said. "What time?"

"High noon. Do you know where I live?"

"Yes. Tom mentioned the other day you had moved into that funny little shack at the end of Farmhouse Lane. How is it?"

"I like it. But you can see for yourself at noon today. I'll see you then."

The room around Agnes abruptly seemed cavernous and empty, everything in it unfamiliar and uncomforting. "I look forward—" Agnes began hurriedly, hoping to prolong the conversation for a minute while she got her bearings again, but there was a sharp click, and Rose Callahan had hung up.

"No," Agnes said. "Don't go yet." But it was too late, the connection was cut. And just like that, the conversation she'd had with Rose Callahan on the night Marjory had died came back to her. Agnes was stunned. Had she really talked with Rose Callahan about her *husband*?

The morning her flyboy had left her for good, they'd had that stupid spat. She'd given him only a grudging kiss and a lukewarm hug, and then he'd been gone forever. She never thought about that morning. *Never*. She'd loved him, he'd loved her, he'd been killed, she'd lived on. What was there to think about? But now—on this morning of the first day of the last new rest of her life—Agnes felt her heart sliding backward until suddenly she missed him as keenly as though he'd died only last week in the same crash that had killed his daughter.

Agnes stood frozen, as stuck as though turned to stone, staring at a yellow wall and clutching a dead phone. She'd lived with her flyboy for three years, four months, and twenty-seven days. He'd been gone almost half a century, and yet—right now—he seemed more real than any of the subsequent shadows that had wandered through her life claiming to be people. She unstuck herself enough to reach her hand out. Wasn't he right there with her now, only just unreachable from this box of space and time that passed for life?

Images flickered across from her on the yellow wall, just to one side of the smirking kittens. Agnes blinked and rubbed her eyes, looked again at that wall. Across it, as clear as a home movie, marched images of herself and her flyboy, astonishingly young again, walking hand in hand at the beach, in the mountains, out in the back pasture of his family's farm. When these faded, they were replaced by bright images of Marjory as a towheaded toddler lurching across green grass toward Agnes's outstretched arms. Marjory, her chubby pink arms and legs churning and flailing, laughing and babbling, toddling toward her mother from out of the golden time when untreatable illness was only a queer, flashing foreboding that came upon Agnes at odd times. It had been decades since she'd gone this far back in her own heart. My God, she had loved that child, that small, human connection with her vanished flyboy who somehow didn't seem so vanished right now, that tiny being who had been their daughter, had dispensed hugs and kisses with abandon, and whose first spoken word had been "A'nes."

"Reinvention, shmee-invention," Agnes said aloud. She hung up the phone, walked to the trash can, stomped on the lever, and retrieved the "World's Greatest Mom" mug. When she turned around, it was to find Tom standing in the doorway watching her. He irritated Agnes by smiling at her and not saying a word.

*   *   *

Iris Benson had to force herself to walk to the Book Store before going to her office and holing up for the day. Iris's office functioned as her womb. It was full of safe aggravations and familiar battles, and she liked to start the workday there, drinking coffee and firing off a volley of e-mails. Over the last week, though, she'd become fixated on the idea that she should apologize to Rose Callahan for shouting at her at the Putnams'. Iris's chief maxim had long been "Never apologize, never explain," but this stupid, aberrant apology idea had been pecking at her ever since she'd woken up Saturday morning in the Putnams' dreadful guest room, remembering nothing about the night before except that she had lambasted Rose—who was probably the one person on campus except Tom with whom she had never had an argument. And then at that damn AA meeting, she'd found herself staring at some ridiculous set of instructions tacked to the wall that said something about making amends, and it had been as though those words had writ themselves in fire across her brain. She'd hardly slept at all last night, despite two Valiums and two or three—she couldn't remember the exact number, it could have been more—tiny, *tiny* shots of bourbon. This morning she must have still been quite groggy from the Valium because, purely out of habit, she'd filled her antique silver pocket flask and tucked it into her purse. This had emptied the bottle of bourbon, meaning she had to have *spilled* quite a bit last night since the bottle had been full when she'd had her first drink, but this filling of the flask had turned out to be fortuitous, because she'd only gotten as far as the college's main entrance before she'd been forced to turn around and head back to McDonald's for another coffee and another shot just to have the courage to drive onto campus. If it weren't for that stupid apology, she wouldn't have even *thought* of drinking in the morning, Iris told herself as she sat in the parking lot of McDonald's (McDonald's!) gulping coffee and bourbon, but you had to do what you had to do to get on with things in this life. When the coffee was gone, Iris had badly wanted another slug from the flask, but she'd disciplined herself and refrained. She would certainly tell *that* to her psychiatrist! Imagine, the pompous jerk having the nerve to tell her she had no control over her drinking! What a crock!

Iris had dressed that morning in purple jeans, a violently colored silk and metal sweater created by a fiber-artist acquaintance of hers, and hiking boots. Iris called them her shit-kickers, and she made a point of wearing them to faculty meetings and referring to them by name whenever possible. She liked to wear clothes that made a statement. The meek conformity of this place drove her insane. Imagine wearing a skirt and sweater with matching pictures of puppies on them! Or the same tweed jacket every day for years! But shit-kickers or no, standing before the door to the Book Store, Iris felt as scared—yes, *scared*—as Alice must have after she'd shrunk herself down in that hole of a Wonderland and come face-to-face with a cat. Without really deciding to do it, Iris looked around to see if the coast was clear, then stepped behind the giant boxwood that shrouded one side of the Book Store front entrance, pulled the flask out of her purse, and drained it. If her natural courage was failing her again, surely it was all right to resort (one last time) to some of the liquid variety. Iris was lifting the flask to make sure it was empty when she heard a car stop, a heavy car door slam, and footsteps coming up the walk. Who on earth abandoned a car in front of the Book Store when people were arriving for work? She had just enough time to get the flask back in her purse, but not enough to get out from behind the boxwood, before whoever it was reached the door and stood opposite her.

"Good morning, Iris," Russell Jacobs said. "You have leaves in your hair." He gestured toward the Book Store. "Are you going inside?"

A couple of drivers blew their horns from the street. Russell turned and waved as though the honks were a greeting. Agnes saw a construction machine creeping by on the road in the other direction. Traffic was blocked and backing up behind Russell's car, but still he stood there, looking at her, waiting for her to answer him. Iris had no choice but to come out from behind her bush. She lifted her head and fixed Russell with a haughty glare. "Yes," she said. "I'm going in, thank you." Russell held the door open, and Iris was forced to walk very close to him. Too late, she realized the haughty glare was a mis-take. With her head up, even if she held her breath, he was certain to smell bourbon on her. But dammit, she was not going to slink past Russell Jacobs hiding behind her hair!

Russell surprised her by saying nothing. He simply walked behind her into the Book Store, nodded in passing, and then headed toward the coffee room. Unfortunately, that was also Rose's room. Iris wandered along in Rus-sell's path, trying to appear aimlessly interested in things, touching books on tables without reading the titles, studiously examining a hideous pottery plate, hand-painted with pink roses. When she reached the archway into the coffee room, she paused before a display of self-help books. The title of one caught her eye: *In the Jailhouse Now: My Prison of Addiction.*

Iris's conditioned response was to scoff at such books, but before her derision could gather much steam, she saw an image of herself, hiding behind a bush and slugging bourbon from a flask—this to work up the courage to face another human being and apologize for some equally ridiculous behavior of which she had only the haziest recollection, but which nevertheless made her burn with shame. The bourbon roiled in her stomach. A wave of nausea enveloped her. Oh my God, she was going to be sick, just like a first-year who can't hold her booze yet. Iris's stomach gurgled and pitched. She turned and raced for the bathroom, which was all the way on the other side of the Book Store.

*   *   *

Russell Jacobs was annoyed with himself for two reasons. The first was that he'd forgotten it was Friday and Rose would not be at work until after two this afternoon. The second was that he was here to see Rose in the first place. He'd had to deal with both of these annoyances when he'd gone into the back room, found she wasn't there, and realized he was astoundingly disappointed. And yes, a little desperate as well. Her not being there had forced him to own up to the fact that he really *needed* her to be there, needed a dose of her no-nonsense normalcy to counteract the disturbing ghost of Serafine Despré.

Russell looked around Rose's room gloomily while Sharon Some-thing—a skinny little woman with dyed too-black hair, who'd been at the Book Store for almost as long as he'd been at the college—poured him a cup of coffee to go and rattled on about the weather. Why, Russell wondered, did people talk about the weather so much? He could see for himself, just by look-ing out the window, that—as Sharon Something was tediously explaining—it might appear to be a bright, sunny day *right now,* but there *were* a few clouds up there and the breeze was really quite *brisk* and that might mean a *shower* later on. If Rose were here, Russell decided—chatting on about cold fronts and thunderstorms—they'd have spent a few pleasant moments talking about books. Rose Callahan was one of the few people who actually *listened* when he talked about books and so forced him to think about what he was saying instead of just rattling on. The fact that thinking felt peculiar made Russell realize what an old fart he'd allowed himself to become. Perhaps this should have made him sad, but it didn't. Eight years in AA had taught him to accept those things about other people that he could not change, and he, like everybody, generally rose to the level of the company he kept. Old Fartdom did just fine with most of the people around here, but it was nonetheless pleasant to discover that it did not pass muster with Rose Callahan. Russell had enjoyed feeling parts of his brain that had been snoozing for years rouse themselves and come up with new ideas while in her company. Or at least dredge up something interesting he'd forgotten about for a long time.

"I wish I'd brought my umbrella. I just know I'll get wet walking to my car this afternoon after work," Sharon Something said as she handed him his coffee.

"And then all your lovely wickedness would melt," Russell replied automatically. Witticisms from *The Wizard of Oz* had long been a staple of his when dealing with college underlings.

Sharon Something went off into gales of cracked laughter. "Oh, Russ! You are such a *card!*" As she was a heavy smoker, the laughter soon degenerated into loud coughing. Over this unpleasant roaring, Russell heard an even louder commotion in the front room. A couple of shrieks were followed by the sound of pounding feet.

"What on earth . . . ?" Sharon Something said, a veined hand flapping.

Together they rushed to the archway between the two rooms. "Oh my God, what has *that woman* done now?" Sharon Something said in a whisper, not even bothering to try to hide her disgust. And why should she? Jesus Christ Himself might have found the spectacle that greeted them difficult to accommodate gracefully. They got to the archway just in time to watch Iris Benson spew vomit on a shelf of glassware and then hurl herself through the bathroom door at the toilet, before which she then knelt and—as a student would have put it—puked her guts out.

"That woman is always doing *something*," Sharon Something hissed, watching Iris's shoulders and back spasm violently. "And I, for one, am not cleaning that mess up! I don't care *what* Mr. Pitts says!"

"My, my," Russell said, unable to keep himself from relishing the sweet victory of Iris Benson's complete humiliation. She had reeked of bourbon as she'd sailed past him. After this, she would never again dare make fun of him in faculty meetings. Forever and ever and *ever* she would look at him and know that he was there the day she got drunk at nine thirty in the morning and vomited all over the Book Store.

Iris finished throwing up and slumped over the toilet in full view of the few customers and staff. No one moved.

For eight years Russell had dutifully sat in AA meetings three times a week, listening to alcoholics talk about how humiliating it had been when they'd hit bottom. He himself had had rather a decorous bottom. Just before Christmas, eight years ago this December, good old Dean Patrick had called him in and announced it was obvious to him and to everyone else that he, Russell, had a problem with booze, and he was to get help immediately. That was it. No threats. No discussion. How Dean Patrick—not to mention everyone else—had known about his private late-night binges and the bottle in his desk, Russell had no idea. Before that conversation, Russell had always thought his drinking was under complete control, since it hadn't shown all that much—there had only been an occasional public overindulgence, and he had maybe missed a class or two—but looking into Dean Patrick's eyes, Russell had faced the dark truth: He had turned his life over to alcohol, and he would need help to get it back. Dean Patrick was that kind of authoritative presence. He was the last of the college's old-style, in-loco-parentis administrators so out of fashion these days. He had not been afraid to guide his students and faculty with a firm hand—which, in Russell's opinion, was something everyone, including himself, needed occasionally.

The next day had been the start of the college month-long winter holidays. Russell had checked himself (only slightly hungover) into that treatment center far, far away in New Orleans, delivering himself into the arms of abstinence and Serafine Despré.

Unlike Serafine, however, Russell hadn't had a drink since and had gone to AA religiously, at least three times a week. He'd always held himself slightly aloof at the meetings, as though they were more a lucky charm to ward off demon drink than a gathering where he might learn something. And Russell had always gone to closed meetings—ones with no visitors allowed—so that no one outside the program would know he was an alcoholic.

Now, however, staring at Iris and running through his derisive litany of all things connected with her, it occurred to Russell that he was *watching* another human hit bottom. With this realization came a rush of intense feeling like an epiphany, and he understood clearly for the first time that all alcoholics—yes, *all alcoholics*—suffered from the same disease; that he, but for fortune and Dean Patrick, could very well be hugging that toilet bowl instead of Iris; that his alcoholism was only in remission, which was not to be confused with being cured; and that if he didn't somehow align himself with Iris Benson *right now* and help her out of this humiliating mess then he, Russell Jacobs—especially now that he appeared to be standing on the brink of personal chaos—would drink again.

"Can't you see the woman is sick!" he said in a loud voice, startling everyone in the Book Store. People turned to stare at him with their mouths hanging open, looking dumb as sheep. Russell strode across the room toward the bathroom, all eyes following him. Ted Pitts had appeared at the door of his office and was staring at him as fatuously as the rest. "Ted," Russell called out, "can someone get us a nice big trash bag?"

As if by magic, one was produced and held out to him. Russell took the bag, swooped up a linen napkin with the college crest on it, picked up the soiled glassware from the display shelf, and dropped it and the napkin into the trash bag.

"Now," he said briskly, "may I have some kind of cleaner, please?"

This, too, was produced. Russell snatched up another crested napkin, squirted the soiled glass shelves, and wiped up the mess as best he could. He made rather a smeary job of it, not being much of a housekeeper, but at least most of the vomit was gone. He dropped the napkin into the trash bag along with the glasses, tied the neck of the bag, handed it to the astonished woman at the cash register, and said, "Put everything in here on my bill, please." Then he turned to Iris.

She was a horrible pale green color, and there was a sheen of sweat on her face. She looked up at Russell with the eyes of a beaten dog. "Help me," she said. And then, being Iris Benson and melodramatic to the core, she fainted.

*   *   *

The trouble was that in Tom's old life there had only been two legitimate ways to use up time—working and being with Marjory. Doing something for pleasure, except for his monthly poker game at Russell's, hadn't been an option for so long that Tom really had only a vague idea of what his pleasures were. He'd lost touch with the concept sometime early in graduate school, when he'd abdicated it willingly as one of the temporary sacrifices necessary to get a Ph.D.; then he'd married Marjory, and the next twenty years had been a blur of routine and anxiety. Not that Marjory—may God rest her sad, sad, soul—hadn't *tried*. He could see her looking up at him from her rocking chair—hands clasped so tightly around the arms that her thin fingers were bone white—and saying, "Go *on*, dear. Just because I'm not feeling quite up to snuff doesn't mean you can't go and enjoy yourself." She'd meant it, too, even though she'd known that if he threw caution to the wind and whooped it up at some colleague's party by himself, the price would be weeks and weeks of unreasoning fear and paranoia for her. What Marjory hadn't grasped, had probably never even thought of, was that as long as he lived with her, her price was his price, and an evening of fun simply wasn't worth it.

Breakfast was over. Agnes was upstairs with Henry, thumping around in his room, having announced that Tom was perfectly free to go out, but she would need him here from a quarter till twelve until about two fifteen as she was going to be out for lunch.

This, in itself, seemed as strange to Tom as a woolly mammoth appearing in the front yard. Agnes hadn't done anything social in a long, long time. He'd been too stunned even to ask her where she was going. He'd wondered briefly if he should feel guilty about not inviting Henry along this morning. But then it seemed to him that Henry was fine, and besides he might as well admit, since as Chaucer tells us, "Thou art a votary to fond desire," that he wanted Rose Callahan to himself for an hour, without Henry competing for her attention. Which seemed desperately immature of him, but there it was.

So anyway, here he was, sitting at the kitchen table at nine o'clock in the morning, full of Wheaties, feeling like a person who'd been sucked through a time warp, whooshed back to his college years. They had been delightful, those years, full of passion for learning, passion for his friends, passion for his occasional girlfriends (where, oh, where were they now, with their long hair and their black leotards he had ached to rip off?), passion against apartheid, and an especially pronounced passion for—there it was again—basketball! Tom heard again the satisfying *swunk* he'd dredged up last evening after Rose's surprise invitation to shoot hoops. He'd only played at the intramural level—but he'd been a pretty good shooter, averaging eleven points a game in the Amherst College winter league over the course of four years. Not too bad for someone who'd been a scrub all through high school.

The difference, of course, was that in college he'd finally grown into his six-foot-two-inch frame. Tom smiled warmly at the memory of those games. He'd blossomed, basketball-wise, at Amherst—at least that was what he liked to think.

Probably the truth was the other players had been just as bad as he, but why dilute a glorious memory with historical accuracy. The point was it remained his one experience with feeling good at something physical. Perhaps he was a fool to think he was up to a little one-on-one after so many years, but so what? It wouldn't be the first foolish thing he'd done, and appearing foolish was a small price to pay for an hour alone with Rose Callahan.

Tom got up from the table, moving as decisively as he had in years. It was time to find his old basketball, blow it up with the bicycle pump, put on a pair of gym shorts, if he could find them, go down to the gym, and see if his old baseline jumper still cooked.

*   *   *

Getting Iris to Russell's car was not easy. She was as limp as an overcooked noodle, unable to assist in the process at all. Russell drafted Ted Pitts to help him, and they ended up each grasping a side of Iris and more or less dragging her across the Book Store floor, out the door, and down the walk.

A crowd had begun to gather before they'd gone more than a couple of feet, as Iris kept raising her head and shouting, "Get your goddamn hands off me!"

This made Ted terribly nervous. "People are going to think we're kidnapping her," he whispered.

"No, they're not," Russell replied wearily. Really, Ted could be such a nudnik sometimes. No one with any sense would kidnap Iris Benson. She was too tiresome to be kidnapped. Someone might murder her, certainly, but kidnapping was out of the question.

Ted was terribly out of shape; he was sucking air like a three-hundred-pound lineman who's had to run ten yards. "She seems awfully sick. I hope she's not dying or anything. What on earth do you think is wrong with her?" he whispered.

"I think she's drunk."

"Oh my. I thought I smelled something, but it's awfully early in the day for that."

"Isn't it?" Russell said grimly.

His car was an old Mercedes. Usually it was his delight, but today Russell cursed the heavy passenger door that would not stay open. He would shift Iris's dead weight entirely to one arm and yank open the door, but before he could wedge a hip into it, the door would close again with the trademark Mercedes *thunk* he was usually so proud of demonstrating. "Damn!" he said in a loud voice.

Ted looked at him accusingly, as though this whole thing were his fault. "Can't you get it to stay open?" he asked peevishly. "My car doors stay open if you pull them back far enough."

Ted drove an old Toyota. Of course the doors stayed open. They weighed about two pounds. "No, I can't," Russell said in an equally peevish voice. All his AA-inspired tolerance was in use coping with Iris. There was none left over for Ted. "These doors are built for protection, not to stay open!"

Iris began to struggle. *"Where are you rapists taking me?"* she bellowed.

Russell suddenly had had enough. "Will you shut *up!*" he hissed. "You're drunk as a fart and sick as a dog, and we're trying to get you out of here before you lose your job!"

Terrible knowledge appeared in Iris's large green eyes. Tears welled and her nose began to run slightly. But she did stop struggling.

Ted opened the door again and this time held it. Russell grasped the limp but fully conscious woman under her shoulders, clasped his hands together behind her back, and bundled her into his car, falling in on top of her. For a brief moment he lay there, the two of them layered like some bad burlesque of lovers about to couple. She looked up at him. "Thank you," she whispered.

"You're welcome." Russell felt strangely moved in spite of himself. How much of what he hated about this woman was her disease? For that matter, how much of what she hated about him was his disease? Oh God, why couldn't the world be a simpler place?

He struggled to his feet again. The crowd of onlookers was dissipating. Ted, however, was still there, looking cross and relieved at the same time. "Thanks," Russell said, impulsively offering Ted his hand.

"What are you going to do with her?" Ted asked.

Russell had no idea. The idea of carrying Iris Benson into the Dean Dome repulsed him. "I don't know," he said. "What do you suggest?"

Ted shrugged, his mind already back at his desk, running numbers, trying to come up with a plan to ward off the Harpy's hovering hostile take-over. "Got me," he said.

*   *   *

Lord, what fools these mortals be . . .

Tom Putnam stood in front of the full-length, pebbled mirror in the cramped and deserted men's locker room and studied his legs. At least they weren't flabby—he did too much walking around campus for the muscles to have atrophied—but they were white as vanilla pudding. To make matters worse, the only gym shorts he'd been able to find were a pair he'd bought in the early eighties. They were the kind his hero Larry Bird would have favored in his heyday, but in today's world of jams, they looked ridiculously short and skimpy.

As a lark, Tom had also dug out his old basketball shoes from college. They were black, high-top Converse All Stars—a.k.a. Chuck Taylors. Putting them on—just sitting there on the bench in the locker room and lacing them up—had made him feel young again. *Looking* at them stuck on the end of his vanilla pudding legs was a different story. My, how he had aged! But even so, somewhere in that middle-aged, slumping body, he could still see the remnants of young Tom Putnam, good English student, decent basketball player, and all-around hopeful guy.

What the hell! Rose Callahan was no fashionista. She was likely to be as oddly dressed as he was.

Tom's basketball was on the floor, inflated and ready to go. He picked it up, gave it a tentative bounce or two, then tried a couple of moves that re-quired ball and feet to move in concert. It went better than he'd expected. He did not fall over a bench, or crash into a row of lockers or lose control of the ball. "'Put me in, Coach, I'm ready to play,'" he sang, dribbling the ball toward the locker-room door. John Fogerty, risen from the dead-songs file in the back of his brain.

The hall appeared to be deserted. Tom picked up his ball and walked briskly to the stairs. All was still clear. He took the stairs two at a time (feeling only a slight tug at his heart), double-timed it through the upstairs hallway, pushed open the door to the gym, and gave a short, victorious whoop. He'd made it onto the court unscathed. No one had seen him. No student would be describing him to her friends at lunch today.

It was then he saw Rose. She was in the process of driving toward the basket at the far end of the court. As he watched, she rose into the air and sank a lay-up. She caught the ball on the first bounce and dribbled out to the top of the key, turned, and sailed in a jumper. Tom was so entranced, he forgot to be embarrassed about his vanilla pudding legs. "That was wonderful!" he called out. "My goodness, where'd you learn to shoot like that?"

Rose started and dropped the ball, which rolled away. "You scared the living daylights out of me!" she said. There was even more Texas than usual in her speech. She made two syllables out of the "scared." *Scay-ard*.

"I'm sorry," Tom said, coming toward her. There again was that strange bubble of light around Rose so that she looked *displayed*. Space alien, beamed down in basketball shorts. Then, remembering her problems in class yesterday, he stopped and asked anxiously, "You're not going to hyperventilate or anything, are you, if I come over and talk to you?"

Rose considered this solemnly, reminding him of Henry, then shook her head. "I don't believe I am. At least, not right away. Let's try and pick up where we left off last night, shall we?" She looked up at him with a hint of a wicked gleam in her blue, blue eyes. "Disappointed?"

"No," he said. "Relieved." And, he could have added, strangely unconcerned about how ridiculous he looked. Sure enough, Rose looked pretty ridiculous herself, rigged out in a hideous orange and blue Virginia Cavaliers T-shirt and ancient, baggy gray shorts, her hair pulled up on the top of her head into a pom-pom.

Rose pointed at his basketball. She had, Tom thought, a challenging look in her blue eyes.

"I don't have a lot of time," she said. "I'm having company for lunch and I've got to be out of here by eleven thirty. So, would you like to play a little one-on-one?"

*   *   *

Russell took off Iris's repulsive shoes in the Mercedes so that she would not track anything into the Dean Dome. He then grasped her firmly under the arms, dragged her out of the car, eased her down his immaculately swept front walk, up the steps to his front stoop, around his beloved and carefully tended pots of red geraniums, in through the front door of his house, across the foyer floor, into his parlor, and dropped her none too gently into a wing chair. Iris was able to sit up on her own now, but only just. Russell couldn't tell if she was weak from throwing up or weak from shame. Probably it was a combination of the two. Iris had never been what one would call a stoic.

Russell sat across from her on an uncomfortable sofa and regarded her glumly. The last thing he wanted was a personal relationship with Iris Benson. He really had not thought this situation through at all well. It might have been better for both of them if he'd let somebody else bail her out of this mess, for now the two of them were inexorably bound by the chain of a rendered good deed. He'd rescued her, so now she'd feel crushingly obligated to him, and he'd have to take pains to act as though there were no such obligation, which she wouldn't be able to accept because, underneath, they still hated each other, and—as Kurt Vonnegut had so aptly put it—so it goes.

Iris was staring down at the bottom of her garish top, picking at the bits of bright metal attached to it. In Russell's opinion, the thing looked as though it had been dragged through the trash at a craft shop. It was, he supposed, what people in the Art Department would call "wearable art." In his opinion it was neither of those things.

Without looking up at him, Iris asked in a low voice, "How many people saw me?"

At least she remembered what had happened. That, in some cockeyed AA way, made the whole thing seem somewhat worthwhile. What was the use of disgracing yourself while you were drunk if you blacked out and forgot the whole thing? It was much harder to realize you'd hit bottom if you couldn't remember what it had felt like to be down there.

"Maybe a dozen," he said, not unkindly.

"Any students?"

"A couple."

"Did they realize I was drunk?"

If there was one thing students were savvy about, it was who was drunk. "Probably."

"Oh God." Iris let go of her sweater and covered her face with both hands. Russell actually felt compassion for her. It must be awful to be dependent upon the fickle admiration of students, to be an academic and yet have to compete with the likes of Kelly Clarkson and Reese Witherspoon for approval. It made what you did seem so *cosmetic*.

The college clock began to strike. Russell looked at his watch. Ten thirty. He had class today at eleven, which meant he needed to get going. He had no other choice but to leave Iris here, at his house, unattended for an hour. "I've got to go meet a class. Would you like to lie down while I'm gone?"

Iris fanned her fingers slightly so she could see out between them. "Yes, please."

"The guest rooms are upstairs. Do you think you can make it?"

"Yes." Iris lowered her hands and looked up at him, in dumb, unconscious mimicry of the kind of woman he was usually so taken with. "If you help me, that is. I'm a little weak."

Russell sighed. What would Lewis, his sponsor, have to say about this? A cardinal rule of AA was to place principles over personalities, and here he was helping another alcoholic and hating every minute of it.

chapter 14

Agnes stood in the middle of Rose Callahan's not very big living room and eyed a two-foot-long crack in a wall. "You say the maintenance people did a lot of work on this place? It still looks pretty primitive, if you ask me." Of course, Rose Callahan *hadn't* asked her, but neither did she look disturbed by the assessment.

"You should have seen it before," Rose said happily.

Agnes sighed and turned to look at the titles on Rose's bookshelves. Fiction, essays, science, history, travel, biography ran riot; there was absolutely no order. Her own bookshelves were methodically arranged. Might this literary free-for-all be a manifestation of the inner Rose Callahan, the woman standing over there with her calm, contained air that gave nothing away? Probably not. Probably the only accurate information you got about the inner Rose Callahan was what she chose to tell you. Agnes sighed again. Getting to know someone was a boxing match. You circled and circled, letting fly with a tentative jab every now and then to test your ring mate's reaction.

"I have to check something in the oven," Rose said. "You want to come with me?"

"Sure," Agnes said. They moved together into the kitchen. It was even more primitive than the living room. Agnes hadn't seen appliances like these since the eighties. The early eighties. "Do these things still work?"

"So far. It's pretty amazing, isn't it?"

There was so much color in the room it looked like a Matisse. Blue checked curtains, deep purple cupboards, harvest gold refrigerator, avocado stove, black and white linoleum squares on the floor. A rather adorable antique clock with a very loud tick was perched atop an old pine pie safe. A lime green covered pot of something simmered on the stove. Whatever it was smelled good enough to make Agnes realize she was hungry for the first time in over a week. "So, what are we having for lunch?" she asked.

"Chili. My mother's uncle's recipe. He taught me how to make it when I was a kid. We used to visit him every summer on his scrubby little ranch in the Texas panhandle. Of course, to follow the recipe faithfully, you're supposed to throw in some kind of rodent, but I had to leave that out."

"Pity." Agnes lifted the lid and looked in. She could see meat and tomatoes, but there had to be other things swimming around in there she could only smell. "What is it that smells so good?"

Rose shook her head. "I'm not telling. Uncle Luther would haunt me if I did." She looked at Agnes with great innocent eyes.

"Ah yes," Agnes said. "I understand. The ever-present departed, keeping us in line." Could she possibly *believe* such nonsense? It wasn't like her to even consider it.

Rose bent over and opened the oven door. The unmistakable smell of biscuits escaped. Rose poked at them with her finger, then straightened up again. "These'll be ready in about ten minutes. Would you care to sit here or in the living room while we wait? I've made some iced tea if you'd like something to drink."

"Brewed or instant?" The words were out before it occurred to Agnes that she might not know Rose Callahan well enough yet to be quite so direct. But the inscrutable, tousle-headed minx appeared undaunted. Why, Agnes wondered, had her daughter never been able to look like that when someone had given her a hard time? "What do you think I'd serve you?" Rose eyed her saucily.

Touché. A small hit, but a hit, nonetheless. "I'll sit right here and have some tea, thank you very much." Agnes sat down at the kitchen table.

"I'll get us some, then." The ancient refrigerator's motor kicked into action when Rose opened the door, making a muffled thumping sound. Agnes watched her get ice out of a blue bowl in the tiny freezer, get glasses down from a purple cupboard, pour tea from a yellow crockery pitcher. Color, color, everywhere. Even on Rose herself, today decked out in a purple T-shirt and voluminous ocher pants. From some angles she was almost beautiful; from others she was as plain as a stick. Her hair, Agnes noticed, was under no better control today than it had been at any other time.

Agnes leaned back cautiously, her wooden chair teetering on the uneven floor, or maybe it was the chair's legs that were uneven. None of the chairs grouped around the table matched. They looked like individual rescues from junk shops. So here she was at a ladies' luncheon—of sorts, anyway. What on earth were the two of them supposed to talk about? Please, God, don't let it be Marjory. Perhaps Henry? Although what would they say? Neither one of them actually knew that much about the boy. It was obvious they both—both what? Loved the boy? Was it possible to love anyone on a five-day acquaintance?

Rose set a glass of iced tea in front of Agnes and sat down across from her. "So," she said, her eyes bright with expectation—or maybe more mischief—"you're a lawyer. What do you think of Alberto Gonzales?"

Politics! Agnes was overjoyed. She did not think much at *all* of Alberto Gonzales.

She was off, in hog heaven, as one of her favorite pro bono clients would have said. Agnes hardly noticed when she began eating, she was so intent on pointing out the current administration's legal chicanery. Rose nodded and prodded and plied her with chili—which was extremely good, as were the biscuits (made with just a tablespoon or so of lard unless Agnes had completely lost her palate). There was real, honest-to-God, unhealthy butter for the biscuits and rich, gooey lemon bars for dessert. But the main sustenance was conversation, carried forward without effort or calculation. When the meal was over, Agnes felt almost completely happy. "So," she said, tipping back dangerously far in her rickety chair, "how come you're so interested in politics? Is your father a politician, back somewhere in Texas, doing righteous battle in the land of the Bushies?"

Rose had been reaching for another lemon bar but stopped with her hand hovering over the plate as though she meant to bless instead of eat them. It was an odd, awkward moment. Rose remained absolutely still, even to her disorganized hair. She reminded Agnes of the Kewpie dolls of her childhood, staring off into space with oversized, unseeing eyes. This was the trouble with good conversation. It had a life of its own that carried you along, willy-nilly, into the first, tricky stages of intimacy.

"Rose," Agnes said, "forgive me. I didn't mean to ask a personal question. I was simply curious about your interest in politics. I haven't met many women—or men, for that matter—who are interested enough to listen to me rant. Honestly, I wasn't trying to pry."

"I know that."

Rose's voice was expressionless. With half her face illuminated by the strong light from the window, she looked a bit like that Parmigianino painting, *Madonna with the Long Neck*. Why did Rose Callahan make her think of paintings?

A single bird began to sing outside the window. The ever-busy, peripheral, fact-gathering part of Agnes's brain registered that it was a cardinal. Long ago, a client had given her a record of bird songs, and she'd gotten quite good at recognizing them. It was part of what she thought of as her vast store of irrelevant knowledge. The birdsong broke the spell—or whatever it was that had frozen Rose's hand over the lemon bars. "It's nothing I'm at all ashamed of," she said, lowering her hand, turning to look out the open window, or perhaps to listen more closely to the bird's song. Her face still gave nothing away. "It's just—I think, anyway—it's just that I don't want people to misunderstand Mavis."

"Mavis?"

"Mavis Callahan. My mother."

"Oh?"

Rose squinted at the window as though trying to see something at a great distance. "I suppose it's a bit like what you told me about the morning your husband was killed. You know, out on the back porch."

Agnes nodded and waited for Rose to go on.

Rose was concentrating on her point in the distance very, very hard. "When you told me about that last morning you had with your husband, when you had that spat, I thought then about this thing that Mavis used to say after a long night of pouring drinks behind whatever bar she was tending. She'd come upstairs after hours and hours of listening to people cry on her shoulder, and she'd sit on the edge of my bed and shake her head and say that it was good for those lonely people to have someone to unburden themselves to, that we're all only as sick as our secrets. And I suppose that applies to me, too, although I've never thought of myself as someone who has secrets. But I do, I suppose. One, anyway. At least I have something I've never talked about to anyone, and I suppose that makes it a secret. You see, I don't know who my father is—and neither does Mavis. And I mean that quite literally. She really has no idea. She used to tell me that I was the child of a whole generation of love, which always sounded quite magical to me. And what I've realized just now—just as we've been talking—is that I couldn't bear to have my mother criticized for that, for the way I was conceived. She took very, very good care of me in her own post-hippie way. It was a lot of fun moving around the way we did. We were very self-sufficient and happy together, although I'm sure it accounts for a lot of my peculiarities as well."

This was the moment, Agnes decided later, when her great fondness for Rose Callahan began, while she sat there with no idea what to say to this strangely composed creature who'd just told her that she, perhaps like Henry, had no identifiable father because her mother had been, what? Promiscuous? A groupie? A flower child? Agnes found herself thinking about Russell Jacobs's silly insistence on knowing what people other people came from. And about that peculiar woman in the registrar's office who prided herself on the fact that her family had been right here in this provincial little county since the eighteenth century. And about her own in-laws, who'd gone on and on about their distant connection to Thomas Jefferson. And here was this self-contained Buddha of a woman, blown along with her mystical sidekick Henry into their neat, well-documented lives like tumbleweed. What difference did any of that historical pretentiousness make beside Rose Callahan's—and really Henry's—rare and fearless capacity to be themselves?

Rose got up and walked to the window. The cardinal sat on a branch of the lilac bush just outside, his red feathers bright against the blue sky behind him. "I know I'm put together a bit differently than most people. I . . . I never seem to expect much. People—and by that, I guess I mean men—say they never know what I want from them, and I guess the truth is I don't really want anything. This always seems to cause them problems, even though I don't mean it to." She put a hand up to her hair. It disappeared into her unbridled curls. "May I ask you a question, Agnes?"

"You can ask one. I don't promise to answer it. Especially if it's about Henry."

"It's not about Henry. It's . . . it's about your son-in-law."

"About Tom?" Agnes was instantly apprehensive, not of any harm Rose Callahan might do her son-in-law, but of the harm Tom, the Great Innocent, might do himself because of Rose Callahan. "All right. Though I need to warn you, I don't gossip. About anyone."

"I don't think this is gossip. Anyway, it's really more about me than about Professor Putnam. The thing is, he . . . he asked me to dinner tomorrow night, which was very nice, and I . . . I turned him down. The truth is, I . . . I *like* him, I really do, but I always feel so awkward around him. Do you have any idea why that is? Is it because of Marjory, do you think? I mean— she just died."

You feel awkward around Tom Putnam because he has a great honking, adolescent crush on you, Agnes almost blurted out, but even she, Lawyer Tattle the forthright, knew this wouldn't do. Looking up at Rose Callahan now, Agnes was mildly surprised to discover that she wouldn't mind *at all* if Tom eventually rode off into the sunset with this woman, wouldn't feel the slightest pang for Marjory's sake. But how likely was that? Tom was not a very probable candidate for romance. He was too indecisive. Agnes's own flyboy had met her, bedded her, and married her, all in three months. Tom Putnam couldn't decide which pair of shoes to buy in that length of time. Agnes could picture the two of them, inscrutable Rose, fuddle-headed Tom, perhaps mutually attracted, perhaps not, but certainly unable to process whatever it was they were feeling in any productive way. And then there was Henry stirring the pot. What he meant to each of them, and why he meant it, was a long, long way from being figured out. Anyway, Rose Callahan was probably already involved with someone. Agnes assumed this about every woman over twenty, except for herself and a few sad, buttoned-up creatures who reminded her of Marjory. And if Rose was involved, then surely Tom was toast in the romance department even before he had time to ruin things by being Tom.

Rose had turned back from the window and was looking at her as though she really would like an answer, really would like Agnes to explain why she felt so awkward around Tom. *What the hell,* Agnes thought. *People expect me to be peculiar and direct.* "I suppose you've got a lover, Rose?"

Rose's hand immediately moved to cover her heart. For the first time in their short acquaintance, Agnes thought she looked nonplussed. Agnes immediately filed this information away: *Nonplussed when asked about lover . . .*

"No," Rose said, "I don't. I mean, I did, but I broke up with him the day after I moved into this house."

"Oh?" Agnes was surprised by how pleased she was to hear this. "Interesting."

"Interesting," Rose echoed.

Agnes sat back and folded her arms. "I wouldn't worry too much about Tom. He's a bit bumpy around women, and it's easy to pick that up and feel it's somehow your fault. But it's actually my poor dead daughter's fault. I suspect Tom has forgotten how to be normal around any woman he finds attractive."

Rose blushed ever so slightly and nodded. "I see. Thanks. That clears up a lot." She smiled her Buddha smile. "About that lover, Agnes."

"Yes?"

"Do you know what a monad is?"

Agnes thought for a moment. "Some kind of biological unit sufficient within itself?"

"Close enough. What I think I want to say is, I'm not sure long-term connection with another person is ever going to be for me. It never has been before. I think the truth is that I'm a bit of a monad."

"I see." Agnes considered this. She was probably a bit of a crusty old monad herself, except for the three years, four months, and twenty-seven days she'd lived with her husband. With that thought, Agnes had to reach for the table to steady herself, as there he was, her tall, reckless, very much alive flyboy, come to visit her right here in Rose Callahan's colorful kitchen. This time it was his touch that came back to her, the feel of his hands, of his breath on her neck, of the wonderful fullness of climax. She'd had sex with quite a few other men since, but it had always been just sex.

Agnes smiled. *Monad, shmonad.* If what she'd had with her flyboy hadn't been true connection, then there was no such thing. Would it have lasted forever? Who knew? Besides, that was hardly the point. She looked across at Rose Callahan. Was the woman lonely? A bit, probably, but so what? There were much worse things for a person than being lonely. She really shouldn't meddle, Agnes told herself sharply. She should let Tom, Rose, and Henry muddle along as best they could. Of course, that didn't mean she couldn't *assist* them a little . . .

"Tom told me that the night before she died, Marjory came up to his office to say she liked you very much, and that she thought you needed friends."

"Really!" Rose's hand again rushed to cover her heart.

*   *   *

Iris Benson lay stretched out on top of what looked like a very expensive, hand-woven bedspread in one of Russell Jacobs's bewildering number of guest rooms. She still felt extremely weak, but she wasn't sleepy in the least. Iris saw herself as an undead corpse, laid out and waiting for the next bad thing to happen.

The room she was in was expensively and tastefully furnished. Russell, Iris thought, had to have had financial help from the college with furnishing all these guest rooms. He would be the type to finagle something like that, trading a night or two of overblown southern hospitality for thousands of dollars' worth of antiques. The furniture in the room Iris was in was all very old and beautifully preserved and not very comfortable. The bed was an imposing antique with a mattress hard as packed dirt. The pillows were down-filled. The feathers in them would start her sneezing violently at any moment, which meant she was going to have to get up shortly whether she had the strength to or not, because she certainly did *not* have the strength to sustain a violent sneezing attack.

Iris turned over on her side and looked at the room's far wall. Against it was a walnut bureau over which hung an antique mirror with wavy, not very clear glass. It was a lovely room. Peaceful, orderly, clean—something she couldn't claim for a single corner of her cabin. If she were truthful with herself, Iris unwillingly reflected, she would have to admit that it was sometimes depressing to wake up to the chaos in which she lived—particularly on the days she wasn't feeling quite up to snuff, which was most days, except for those few weeks she'd recently been able to lay off the booze.

Booze. Iris groaned aloud. Every detail of the morning came back to her, except, of course, for the few moments when she was passed out on the floor of the Book Store bathroom. *Passed out on the floor of the Book Store bathroom!* Oh God in heaven, what, oh what, was she going to do? She couldn't seem to drink anymore without making a fool out of herself, and she couldn't seem to stop drinking. And she had no one to turn to for help. No one. Even her shrink had deserted her.

A giant sneeze gathered at the back of Iris's head and burst forth, racking her entire body. She struggled to sit up. Another sneeze exploded, blowing her backward, but Iris managed to catch herself with her elbows and so keep semi-upright. She felt as limp as a just-dead goldfish, but she had to find the strength to get away from those pillows.

Iris pulled herself over to the edge of the bed. The mattress sat so high that her feet dangled like a child's. She carefully lowered herself to the floor, mussing the expensive bedspread in the process. This bothered Iris a lot; she didn't want Russell Jacobs to think she was a slob. Then the morning came rushing back to her again with all its bleak, unmistakable, and unavoidable truths: Russell Jacobs *knew* she was a slob. By now, the whole college knew she was a slob. Worst of all, *she* knew she was a slob, not the rebellious wild child she had always pictured herself as being.

Iris eased herself down to the floor and felt around for her shoes. Her shit-kickers were not there. She looked down at her feet to be sure she wasn't wearing them but saw only her socks, mismatched, with giant holes in them through which poked her grubby big toes. Iris never sorted socks when she did laundry, just bundled them into her sock drawer. She'd always thought of this as the successful flouting of another of womankind's meaningless tasks, but whether it successfully flouted anything or not, it left her wearing mismatched socks with holes in them. She shuffled down to the end of the bed, hung on to one of its stubby footboard posts, and carefully bent over so as to be able to see underneath the bed. That was a mistake. Bending over sent the first stabs of what was sure to be a monumental headache through her. And her shoes were nowhere to be seen.

Iris straightened up. Another stab, accompanied by a slight wave of dizziness and nausea. "Oh, stop it!" she said aloud, addressing her own miserable body. "Enough is enough!" Neither the headache nor the nausea responded. She felt another sneeze gathering. "I've got to get out of here," Iris said, again out loud, and she began to hand herself from piece of furniture to piece of furniture.

The door into the room was closed. Iris pulled it open and peeked out into what looked like the corridor of a small hotel. The stair landing, however, was mercifully close. Iris braced herself against the wall and crept to the top of the stairs. Once there, she eased herself down into a sitting position and bumped down the stairs on her bottom the way she used to at her grandfather's house when she was a child, except that each bump caused a fresh stab of pain in her head and a slight escalation of her nausea. At least there was nothing left inside to throw up.

Once at the bottom of the stairs, all she had to do was cross a rather grand foyer and then she would reach the front door and be able to escape. The need to get out of Russell Jacobs's house had become immediate and compelling, something very close to panic. Iris grasped the polished newel post and heaved herself to her feet. Without pausing to establish her balance, she let go of the newel post and tacked directly toward the front door, walking like a toddler who has leaned forward to get going and must now move her feet quickly to keep them under her. She reached the front door dizzily but successfully and flung it open, only to find Tom Putnam standing on the front stoop, his hand raised as though he were just about to knock. He was dressed in a pair of the skimpiest shorts Iris had ever seen on an adult male, and his shoes looked like a circus clown's.

"My God," he said. "Iris! What are you doing here?"

For just a second Iris let go of the door and stood on her own. "I'm visiting," she said, managing to sound quite dignified. Then the world abruptly telescoped, like the end of a Looney Tunes cartoon, and, for the second time that day, Iris Benson fainted. She fell forward, and as Tom Putnam was unable to react quickly enough to catch her, she smacked her head smartly on one of the large potted geraniums of which Russell Jacobs was so proud.

*   *   *

Agnes had gone to the bathroom, leaving Rose to, against her better judgment, stand at the window and think about what they'd just talked about. Or, more accurately, what she'd just said. All that atypically revelatory stuff about Mavis and Professor Putnam.

Rose had always defined her life through its movement: I came from here; I'll stay in this place for a while; I'll go there next. The rooms in which she lived were nests of carefully preserved keepsakes and carelessly researched future plans. It had never once occurred to her to stay put anywhere; never, at least, until her mother had announced her startling decision to marry her professor. Then the thought of staying put had begun to niggle at the edge of her consciousness, as unsettlingly persistent as the urge to jump was to a person with vertigo.

Mavis's professor, Dr. Stewart Rogers, had presented the one great complication in Rose's determinedly simple life. At first, the marriage had felt like a betrayal of her own value as a daughter (how *could* Mavis want someone else around permanently?), but then, once she'd gotten used to the idea, Rose was more bothered by a feeling that Mavis had betrayed herself, her own fundamental nature, or at least what Rose had always *thought* was her mother's fundamental nature. Mavis had always been a mossless stone, so surely that meant she should always *be* a mossless stone. It had only been in the last couple of months that Rose had begun to think she might have missed something important in her mother's character; that somewhere beneath all that hardy cheerfulness, Mavis had, in some mysterious way, been as lonely as her barfly customers. This thought had made Rose truly uncomfortable, for it had made her mother seem more vulnerable, less invincible, less fully insulated from the slings and arrows of everyone else's outrageous fortune.

If Mavis hadn't been able to insulate herself, then what did this say about her daughter? Just now, while standing at the kitchen window of this fairy-tale cottage with her back to Agnes Tattle, the most interesting person she had met in an age, Rose had been forced to realize what would have been obvious to her long ago if she'd had the courage to explore her own heart. The truth was that she herself was a tad lonely. Not in any devastating way, of course. Just in a way that made everything a bit more work. She kept all her relationships so carefully compartmentalized. There was no one person with whom she could completely let go. No one she could just *be* with without worrying about the awkwardness of mutual failure; without concern that she might ask too much, or be unable to give enough.

So this—her self-imposed separateness—was what Marjory Putnam must have seen in her when she'd turned back. This was, indeed, her deepest secret. And since Marjory had evidently told her husband about it and he had told Agnes, now Rose had to face the fact that three people had known her deepest secret before she did.

The simplest, most stripped-down life—a life such as hers without even so much as a house cat to look after—could not be kept complication-free. Rose, for just an instant, had a vision of all her nomadic drifting as nothing more than the long and winding road that had brought her, at last, to stand before Marjory Putnam to have this secret found out. It was simultaneously as obvious to Rose as a squashed bug on a windshield that Marjory's husband, Professor Thomas Putnam, for silly reasons of his own, had some kind of idiotic *thing* for her. And since the poor man was so vulnerable, so newly single, so unpracticed at the human mating dance, it was now her responsibility, in some screwy way, to protect him from coming to any harm because of her. It was the only kind thing she could do. Right on cue came her mother's voice inside her head, detailing the world according to Mavis: *Deliberate unkindness is the one great sin.*

None of this would ever have occurred to her if she hadn't had Agnes to lunch and Agnes hadn't started asking her about her sex life. One thing had led to another, and then *presto!* Everything she'd been muddled about in the loneliness department was clear. What was *not* clear to Rose was how she felt about her new understanding.

"Oh, stuff it!" Rose said aloud, addressing the cardinal who still sat outside the window in the lilac bush.

"I beg your pardon," Agnes said.

Rose whipped around to find Agnes back at the kitchen table. How long had she been there?

"Sorry," Rose said. "I was thinking out loud."

"Oh?" Agnes raised her eyebrows, letting Rose know she wasn't buying it.

Rose came reluctantly back to the table and sat down. *Well,* she thought. *What now?* Surely they didn't have to *talk* about this? She'd invited Agnes Tattle to lunch because she was certain that the two of them could have a rollicking good conversation without wandering off into anything personal. People so rarely talked about themselves accurately. They either made too much or too little out of everything. It seemed to Rose that you got to know people much more thoroughly by hearing what they *thought* and what they *did,* and then extrapolating the rest as a kind of interesting, intellectual puzzle. All you had to do was listen to the vehemence and passion with which a person talked about things other than himself or herself, and there the person was. Such impersonal conversations had the further advantage of keeping you away from messy moments such as this one; a messy moment that was, of course, entirely her fault, since first she'd spilled the beans about her father's unknown identity, and then, as though that had loosened some screw in her brain, she'd blatted out the awkward way she felt around Professor Putnam to his own mother-in-law. What *had* she been smoking? as Mavis used to say. In a few moments, if she didn't watch it, she would be telling Agnes everything.

"I'm sorry," Rose said.

"For what?" Every crease in Agnes's angular face lifted inquiringly.

"For bringing Professor Putnam up. For asking you why I feel funny around him. It's unspeakably rude of me to ask you such an awkward question about a member of your own family. Particularly at a time like this. Whatever problems I have around Professor Putnam, I'm sure they have nothing to do with him. He's always been perfectly polite and kind to me."

Agnes nodded. "Tom is kind. And polite as well. But he's a dolt around women and always has been, ever since I've known him. Even around me sometimes. So I hardly think it's your fault if he makes you feel awkward." She fixed Rose with what must have been her most penetrating, lawyerly gaze. The one she would have used to let clients know it was time to quit shilly-shallying and talk straight. "Exactly what do *you* think is going on between you two? It may not be my business, but I'd still like to know."

But Rose did not want to tell her. It wasn't that she had anything to hide; she was simply more at ease being a recipient of confidences than a giver of them. She hadn't had much practice confiding. Her heart had always puttered along so predictably on its comfortable, tight leash that there had never been much to confide about. Evidently this was no longer quite the case. Thoughts of her Shakespeare seminar room with its Tilt-A-Whirl floor intruded, and there were those bothersome, lingering moments of stillness between them that had brought her the same sharp relief a grape Popsicle brought to the heat of a Texas summer. "I'm not sure," she said.

"Oh?" Agnes leaned forward slightly. Again the eyebrows lifted. "Why?"

"Well, we were playing basketball, and—"

"Tom Putnam was playing *basketball*? You're kidding!"

"No, I'm not. I play a lot, and last night I asked if he'd like to play some one-on-one this morning—"

Again Agnes interrupted. "Was he any good?"

"Well, yes and no. He was terribly rusty and a bit out of shape, but he'd obviously been much better at some point. He made a really pretty mid-range jumper the one time I gave him a second to get himself squared up to the basket."

"Well, great jumping Jehoshaphat!" Agnes said, reverting to an allowed expletive from her childhood. "Who'da thunk it?"

"He said he used to play basketball in college."

"At Amherst? No kidding. I never knew that. Or maybe I did, and it just hasn't come up in the last decade or so. Okay, so you played some one-on-one this morning. Then what?"

"We played about thirty minutes, and then I had to go because you were coming."

"Did you tell him why you had to go?"

"No, I didn't. I thought if I did then I would have to ask him to come, too, and I didn't want to do that without checking with you, and besides there's Henry, and . . ."

Agnes finished for her, "And Tom makes you uncomfortable."

"Yes, Tom makes me uncomfortable. Well, it's more than that. He actually makes me rather nervous."

"Okay." Agnes nodded. "So then what?"

"He asked if we could play again sometime, and I said sure. And then . . ." Rose stopped. She could feel color rising in her face. "And then, I . . . I stood on my toes and kissed him. On the mouth."

Agnes gaped. "You did *what*?"

"I kissed him. And now I don't know how I'll ever face him again."

Agnes did not even try to suppress her glee. "What did Tom do?"

Rose covered her face with her hands. "Nothing!" she whispered through the cracks in her fingers. "He didn't kiss me back and then he just walked away."

Agnes sat back. "My, my. Silly old Tom."

Rose lowered her hands. "Why do you say that?"

Much to her surprise, Agnes Tattle leaned back in her rickety chair and laughed. "Why, Rose Callahan, you *are* female, after all. Or human, I guess I should say. You know perfectly well why I said, 'Silly old Tom.' Perhaps I should have said, 'Silly old Rose,' as well! Aren't you and Tom Putnam a *mess?*"

"Well, I don't know about that!" Rose said indignantly, wanting to protest that in the whole of her thirty-seven years she had never been a mess, that it was against her religion, her upbringing, her philosophy of life.

But Agnes continued to laugh, hugely delighted by whatever images danced in her head.

*   *   *

When Russell Jacobs got back to his house around three, he found broken stems in one of his precious pots of geraniums, what looked like a blot of blood on the front stoop, and an empty guest room. The bedspread was mussed, but otherwise there was no sign that Iris Benson had ever been there.

Russell immediately searched the house just to be sure Iris wasn't hiding in it somewhere, invading his privacy, discovering some revealing piece of his deplorable childhood he'd banished to the back of a closet. He finished his search in the kitchen, thoroughly going through the walk-in pantry and finding nothing objectionable but two commercial fruitcakes he'd been given last Christmas and had forgotten to throw away, a package of tissue paper party hats, and three unopened bottles of Wild Turkey some hired college bartender must have stowed there for a party and forgotten about. Russell made a mental note to throw the bottles out with the fruitcakes. He was not the sort of alcoholic, he knew, who would be safe for long with liquor stashed in the house. Even looking at the bottles conjured up images of his crazy mother, mascara slithering down her cheeks, clotted red lips smiling at him, drunk, as usual, by the time he was home from school.

His crazy mother . . .

Russell stood there, his hand on the pantry doorknob, feeling somehow that he had missed a golden opportunity to come clean with another human about his past. Could it really have been a good idea to talk with Iris Benson, of all people, about his childhood? Might it have been helpful to him as well as to her? Lewis, his sponsor in AA, was always droning on about how dangerous secrets were for an alcoholic, and, until this moment, Russell had more or less tuned Lewis out on that particular subject. He'd been in AA for years and had yet to own up to his real past, even to Lewis, even when doing his 12 Steps, even Step 4, which stated he was to make "a searching and fearless moral inventory" of himself. What *was* that anyway? Only AA could come up with such tacky and confusing language. Surely the fact that his mother had rivaled Blanche DuBois as Queen of the Crazies and his father had been a blue-collar nebbish was nobody's business but his own.

Standing there in his kitchen with his hand still on the pantry door, Russell began wagging his head up and down, agreeing with himself on this point, yet again. *Right?* The really annoying thing was that, no matter how many times Russell went through this perfectly sound line of reasoning, the nagging feeling that he should have talked with Lewis about his days as a desperately unhappy and pimpled nonentity still bubbled up. It was bubbling up right now—all because that shrew Iris Benson had been in his house.

Then, just like that, two pieces of chaos collided inside his head and together made a new kind of sense. He was, Russell realized, having another goddamn AA epiphany. *What if he'd completely misunderstood the fundamental AA nature of character defects?* He'd always thought of them as like the Ten Commandments, rigid taboos that make up a sort of one-size-fits-all AA moral code: *Thou shalt not put personalities before principles! Etc. . . .* But perhaps . . . ?

His mind struggled with whatever it was like a pushmi-pullyu; wanting, yet not wanting, to grasp that perhaps some character defects might be more in the nature of beauty, fluid concepts defined in the mind of the beholder, or, in this case, the transgressor. Perhaps whatever made you feel guilty or ashamed was what AA meant to be considered as a character defect. Perhaps AA expected you to be fully and completely before the world as you were to yourself.

Unexpectedly, like a beacon of hope, Rose Callahan was there beside him, smiling at him in that way she had of smiling that shot straight into the heart of the pimpled nonentity. Could he possibly talk to her about his secrets? Even about Henry? Might she be the One, come at last to save him from himself, after all these years?

The doorbell rang. Russell, certain it was Rose, rushed to answer it.

Tom Putnam stood on the front stoop, frowning down at the broken geraniums.

Russell's first thought was *He knows everything!* "What are you doing here?" he snapped.

Tom's frown deepened. "I . . . I wanted you to know I took Iris Benson to Student Health this morning." His eyes wandered past Russell into the orderly insides of the Dean Dome. "I dropped by and she was here and she fainted and . . ."

Russell's relief was immediate and almost overwhelming. He reached for his friend's arm and pulled him inside. "Come in here right now and tell me exactly what's happened."

Tom took a couple of steps into Russell's marble-floored foyer. "It's been quite a day. I can't seem to take everything in, so I thought I'd come talk to you. Agnes was out to lunch and she just got back or I'd have been here before now. I have to take Henry to the four-thirty soccer game, so I can't stay long. I hope it's all right that I stopped in? You're not busy, are you?"

"No. No." It occurred to Russell that he was rarely busy, that everything he did, he could do in his sleep. This seemed sad, somehow, now that he thought about it.

Why was he suddenly doing all this *thinking?*

Tom was still talking. "I came by this morning, but you weren't here and Iris was. I . . . I need to talk to you."

What Tom Putnam really needed, Russell thought, was a stiff drink. He did have those serendipitously discovered bottles of Wild Turkey in his pantry. But for some reason, Russell didn't want Tom to know about them. Nor did he want to figure out *why* he didn't want Tom to know about them. Anyway, coffee or a soda or water would do perfectly well, only now Russell realized he didn't want to go back into his kitchen for fear the whole childhood thing would start up in his head again. Then he remembered the paper cup dispenser in the powder room, something the college had insisted he have for official entertaining. "Do you want some water?" he asked.

"A glass of water would be nice," Tom said. "I am thirsty."

"I'll get you one, then. Go in there and sit down." Russell pointed through the set of French doors into the library, his favorite and most comfortable room. The one he would never, ever let Iris Benson enter. "I'll get your water and be right there."

Tom turned obediently and headed toward the French doors. Russell raced for the powder room and returned with a three-ounce cup of water to find that Tom had managed to make it into the library but was still standing up. Whatever resolve had driven him to make this visit appeared to be dissipating fast.

Tom looked up when he heard Russell's footsteps. "Iris hit her head on your geraniums," he said. "I think she may have broken some of the stems. There was some blood, too."

"That doesn't matter." Russell felt slightly relieved. At least one mystery was solved. He handed Tom the water. Tom looked at the tiny paper cup with wonder.

Russell took his friend's arm again and guided him to the room's most comfortable chair. "Sit down," he said gently, "and drink your water."

Tom sat and took a sip from the paper cup. "This tastes good," he said, looking up at Russell with kind, vacant eyes. Russell felt a sudden surge of fear. If Tom Putnam began acting weird, then the whole world would soon slide into insanity.

Russell sat down on the couch. "Why not start at the beginning and tell me what's happened?"

Something mulish came into Tom's eyes. "I don't want to."

"You don't want to what?"

"Start at the beginning. I'm not sure where the beginning is."

"Start wherever you want, then," Russell said in a somewhat louder voice. "Just tell me what the hell is going on!"

Tom seemed to focus. He took another sip of water. "This morning, I was over at the gym shooting baskets with—" he began.

"You were *what?*" Russell was astonished.

The mulishness returned to Tom's eyes. "Do you want me to tell you what happened or not?"

"Yes. Please. Go on."

Tom took a deep breath. "As I was saying, I was over at the gym shooting baskets, and something happened that I had to talk to someone about, and so—"

"*What* happened?"

"What happened when?"

"What happened that you needed to talk to someone about?"

Tom shut his mouth in a tight line. "I'm not sure I want to talk about it anymore. It's embarrassing."

"Okay." Russell spoke in what he hoped was a patient-sounding tone. "So this thing happened that you *did* want to talk about, but might not want to talk about anymore. Then what?"

"Then I came over here to talk to you about it. And I was raising my hand to knock when the door opened all by itself and Iris Benson fell out of it and hit her head on the geraniums and—" Tom's eyes clouded with misery again. "I'm so sorry about the geraniums. If I hadn't been so startled, I could have caught her and—"

"I don't give a damn about the geraniums!" Russell snapped. "Just get on with what happened."

Tom's eyes were those of a lost puppy. "Iris hit her head is what happened, and she bled and knocked herself unconscious. She was only out for a couple of minutes, but I was afraid she might have a concussion. So I got her into my car and took her to Student Health, and the nurse there called an ambulance. The nurse was very bossy about it. She said she'd heard that Iris had already been sick this morning—evidently there was some big to-do over in the Book Store that students in getting their flu shots had talked about. So off Iris went in an ambulance, and I . . . I didn't quite know what to do with myself." Tom looked up, and Russell was shocked to see tears in his eyes. "It's . . . it's been quite a week, and I . . . I guess I'm kind of overwhelmed by things, Marjory dying and Henry coming and all that money and now this. And so I came to find you." Something uncomfortably close to desperation appeared in Tom's eyes. "You . . . you are my friend, aren't you, Russ? I mean, it's all right to come talk to you like this, isn't it?"

"Of course it is. But you haven't really *said* anything yet."

Tom took a deep breath that seemed to settle him. When he looked up there was a firmness about him that Russell wasn't sure he'd ever seen before.

"I wanted to let you know about Iris, because she was in your house. But what I really came here to talk to you about is Rose Callahan."

*   *   *

There had been an eight-car pileup out on Route 29, and the Lynchburg emergency room was swamped. Iris Benson lay on some kind of high, hard surface in a tiny cubicle. Outside her cubicle, people were running up and down the hall, yelling commands at one another. Somewhere close by—perhaps even in the next cubicle—a huge commotion erupted, and a woman screamed. Iris would have liked to get up and get the hell out of there, even if it meant walking back to the college in her holey socks, but every time she lifted her head, waves of dizziness washed over her and she was forced to lie back down. An offensively cheerful woman had been in a couple of times, once to stab her in the arm and draw blood, the other to hook up an IV. This, she'd explained, held a saline solution. Iris needed it because she was dehydrated.

Other than that Iris had been left alone. She'd thought about asking the cheerful woman to call her psychiatrist and ask if she could see him today on an emergency basis, but then had decided not to. Where would she go, what would she do, if he said no?

Iris's ER cubicle had no walls. White cotton shower curtains hung on all sides of her. If she blurred her vision, Iris could imagine that she was floating in the clouds, somewhere—as poor, dead, drunken Judy Garland used to sing—*away above the chimney tops, where troubles melt like lemon drops.* Iris closed her eyes and was about to drift off into just such a place when a different young woman came in, as brisk and efficient as the first one had been cheerful. There was a smear of blood on the front of her smock. "I'm Dr. Laura Bennett, Ms. Benson," she said, in a voice that could have been generated electronically, it was so impersonal. "You evidently fainted because you were drunk and hadn't eaten for a while. You had a blood alcohol level of two-point-oh, and you were extremely dehydrated. We're going to fully hydrate you, and that's about all we can do here in the ER. When we've got you able to stand again, it will be up to you as to whether you want to go into treatment or go home. Do you understand?"

The doctor's steel gray eyes were serious. She had no time for Iris; she had lives to save. Only TV ER doctors had time to be nice to drunks. "Yes," Iris said. "I understand."

"You can leave as soon as you feel able to stand. If you decide to go home, it would probably be a good idea to get something to eat from the hospital cafeteria. If you decide you want to go into treatment, let the front desk know, and they'll get in touch with your psychiatrist. I assume you are seeing a psychiatrist?"

"Yes," Iris said. "I am."

"Good," the doctor said firmly. "I hope things go well for you, then. But that's up to you." With that she turned, glided through the white curtains, and was gone.

*   *   *

Russell felt the dark forces of complexity closing in around him. In his mind, he realized, Rose Callahan had become *his* Rose, and now Tom Putnam wanted to talk about her. "Yes?" he said cautiously.

Tom was almost himself again. "Last night," he said in a firm voice, "Agnes and Henry and I had Rose and a student to dinner. It was just a casual, impulsive invitation, but when Rose was leaving, I asked her to have dinner with me on Saturday. You know, like a date."

"A *date*!" Russell just stopped himself from gripping the arms of his chair.

Tom held up his hand. "Yes, I know. I only buried my wife on Tuesday, but the thing I need you to understand is that I think Marjory would be all for Rose Callahan and I sort of, you know, getting together."

"She would?"

"Yes, she would. You see, I think Marjory liked Rose. Really *liked* her. In a way I've never seen her like anybody else. I think she wanted Rose in our lives. In *my* life, even."

Russell was completely uninterested in what Marjory had wanted. He wanted to hear about Rose. "Go back to the dinner invitation," he said.

Tom looked bleak. "Well, she said no."

"She did?"

"Yes. No to dinner, anyway. But then she invited me to play some one-on-one basketball this morning. And I accepted, and we were playing, and then somehow something happened and she kissed me."

"She *kissed* you?" Again Russell resisted obvious physical reaction. The less he gave away of what was really going on in him, the better.

"Yes."

"Really?"

"Yes."

A childhood phrase invented when Russell was still struggling with the concept of truth came out of him. "For true life?"

Tom frowned. "I beg your pardon?"

Russell felt a bit light-headed. "Nothing. So what happened next?"

"Nothing."

"Nothing?"

"Nothing. I . . . I just walked away."

Russell wanted to make certain he had heard correctly. "You walked away?"

"Yes. I behaved like a complete dolt. Which I am. With women, at least. That's why I came to talk to you. You've had so much more experience with women than I have."

Not with this woman, Russell thought. *And she's the one woman who matters.*

Tom was still talking. "What I wanted to ask you was do you think she's interested in me—you know, as a man—or was she just being kind?"

Just as he used to as a child when preparing to lie, Russell crossed his fingers behind his back. "She was just being kind."

"Oh." If it were possible, Tom looked simultaneously disappointed and relieved. "You think?"

"I do."

"Well." Tom smiled ruefully at Russell. "I have no idea if that's the answer I was hoping for or not. But I guess it's the one I'll have to live with."

Russell kept his fingers crossed. "Sorry."

*　　*　　*

Rose gave the sheaf of flyers for the "Talking Writing" series another whack to bring them to order. They had, she thought, turned out nicely.

The series had been Susan Mason and her committee's idea. "Talking

Writing" involved the authors scheduled to give evening readings at the college throughout the academic year spending an afternoon hour sitting around the Book Store, drinking coffee and talking informally with whoever wanted to talk with them. The series had the Creative Writing Department jumping up and down, and Admissions reaching out to area high schools to suck in prospectives. How co-curricular could programming get?

Today, as soon as she got off work, Rose would make the rounds of the college bulletin boards and post the flyers. Then she would go home and start looking for her next job.

The morning in the gym came back to Rose, with all its awkward, disturbing moments compressed into a movie trailer. She felt her toes curling in her sandals, just as they once had in the presence of Jimmy Mason, a high school quarterback on whom she'd had a humongous crush. Why, oh why, had she *kissed* Professor Putnam? And why, in her heart of hearts, did she and her curling toes want nothing more than to kiss him again?

Rose still had a good dozen flyers left by the time she headed for her last and most far-flung stop, the bulletin board down by the soccer field. It was approaching six o'clock. Golden, slanted sunlight flooded the groomed gravel road that took her past Russell's house and the president's, then wound down toward the college lake. The field was off to the right and up a slight rise. Rose reached the bulletin board to find that a crowd was gathered. In her rush to get the flyers designed and printed, she'd completely forgotten that the college soccer season started today.

The scoreboard across the playing field showed the college up 2–1 with seven minutes left in regulation. Rose made her way down to the front of the bleachers. Her plan was to scan them for an empty seat, but instead she got stuck watching the team move the ball rapidly and expertly down the field. Imagine, speeding along, controlling a ball so completely without using your hands! Perhaps, if she hadn't been scarfed up by basketball, she might have played soccer more seriously. But then, why shouldn't she give it a serious try now? Soccer was everywhere these days. There had to be a low-level adult league close by that would let her practice with them. She was already in pretty good shape and—

Something tugged at her shirt.

"Rose," a voice piped up from south of her hip bone. "Rose. We're watching soccer. *Please* come sit with us."

It was Henry, of course. Who else did she know besides his father who could make her heart go quite this funny?

*   *   *

Illogically, considering the ruckus it caused inside him, the sight of Rose Callahan filled Tom with joy. He'd been stunned to see her, too stunned to come up with an acceptable reason for Henry *not* to ask her to sit with them. He could hardly explain to the boy that he'd made a fool of himself this morning in the gym and simply needed more time to recover before he faced Rose again.

Tom watched her kneel down to talk with the boy, putting a hand on his shoulder and tousling his hair while Henry gestured animatedly at the field behind her. The two were so easy together, so comfortably themselves in each other's company. It would be perfect if his own relationship with Rose could be the same, only—well—different. Why, why, *why* had he not kissed her back this morning? Why had he stood there like a complete blockhead and let her walk away? If he'd kissed her back and she'd pulled away, at least he would now be one hundred percent certain that Russell had been right in his assessment of their relationship, instead of just, say, ninety-seven percent certain. There would have been no options open to him besides forging ahead with their "friendship," whatever that constituted when one party teetered on the brink of perhaps—however inappropriately—falling in love with the other.

Now Rose was before him, papers in one hand, Henry firmly attached to the other.

"Hello, Professor."

Tom managed what felt like his usual smile and patted the seat beside him. "Won't you sit down?"

Rose hesitated. "I was just posting some flyers. I hadn't planned on staying. I don't want to intrude."

"But Rose!" Henry all but bellowed. "We *want* you to stay. You sit there and I'll sit on the other side of you, so I can explain the *rules* to you!"

Still Rose hesitated. All Tom could think about was how much he wanted her to stay. Why shouldn't his muddling give way before that one simple truth? *Why?* "Henry's right," he said. "We want you to stay."

Color flooded into Rose's face. "Well then, I guess that settles it. I'm staying."

Just as the two of them sat down, a great roar arose. The college had scored a hard-won goal. All around them, the crowd rose in unified exaltation and began the Wave.

"What are they *doing?*" Henry wanted to know.

"The Wave," Tom shouted, impulsively hugging the small, mysterious child.

And just like that, he, Rose, and Henry were laughing, standing, flinging their arms high into the bright, warm air.

The three of them walked back up the hill toward the Quad holding hands. Henry was in the middle, and every fourth or fifth step, cued by some jointly felt impulse, Tom and Rose swung him high in the air between them the way all children crave to be swung. Those around them smiled to hear Henry's high-pitched glee, then turned and whispered to one another.

The day was just falling into dusk. Hospitable lights were on in the president's house. Beside it, Russell's grand house remained a dark and formal directive to stay away.

Henry was in full chatter mode, going on and on about soccer and how he was going to play it professionally one day now that he knew the rules. When they reached the intersection at which the road to Tom's house went one way and the road to Rose's house went another, unextended invitations hung shyly in the air.

"Well," Rose said, after a pause. "I'll say good night, then."

Henry was not a cautious issuer of invitations; at least, not to Rose. "Can Rose come home for supper, please? I can split my food with her, so it's not any trouble and Agnes doesn't have to fix anything extra."

Tom's heart flopped yet again. Wherever Henry had come from, he certainly had been taught to think of others. Before he could answer, Rose had put her stack of papers down on the ground and taken Henry's hands in hers. "Thank you, Henry, but I have some things at home tonight that I better see to."

"Tomorrow? Can you come tomorrow?"

Rose looked up at Tom. There was much they should talk about, he supposed, but that didn't mean they couldn't just let this moment be. He shrugged his permission.

Rose turned back to Henry. "How about this?" she said. "How about I come over about ten tomorrow with my soccer ball, and we go out on the Quad and I can see your moves?"

"*Really?*" Henry gave a little jump.

"Really." Rose smiled first at Henry and then at Tom.

"Is that okay, Dad?" Henry's eyes were fastened on Rose.

Tom had to exercise great discipline to avoid whooping it up as it dawned on him that Henry had just called him "Dad" for the first time. Inside, his heart seemed to grow larger and stronger until it filled his entire being. "Of course. Maybe I'll come with you."

"Okay!" Henry sounded as though it really *would* be okay, as though he didn't need to keep Rose all to himself.

Rose was still smiling. "Okay, then. Tomorrow it is!" And with that she turned and walked away. Ten paces down her road, she turned and waved. Henry and Tom, who were standing hand in hand and watching her go, waved back.

Only after she disappeared did Tom realize that Rose had left her flyers on the ground. He scooped them up and tucked them under his arm.

*   *   *

Russell hung there, feeling rather like his own ghost, behind the heavy silk drapes of the largest of the guest bedrooms that marched across the front of the Dean Dome.

When he saw Rose walking hand in hand with Henry and Tom, he felt something inside him break and something else inside him quicken. Just like that, he was on fire with a confusing and consuming jealousy. Rose and Henry, it seemed to Russell, should be walking with *him*.

Rose's smiling face floated before Russell, beckoning to him like his own private Star of Bethlehem. Or, perhaps, his Star of Perdition.

Russell suddenly fixed on those bottles of Wild Turkey, still stashed at the back of a pantry shelf.

He took a deep breath and resolutely put them out of his mind, knowing full well that they would regularly pop back in until he either settled himself or poured their contents down the sink.

Or, some long-quiescent imp pointed out, poured them down his throat.

*   *   *

Supper conversation had been mostly about soccer.

Agnes had made a real effort to follow Henry's rather confused explanation of the game's workings. "But why can't they just catch the ball and throw it?" she'd asked at one point.

"Because," Henry said, exhibiting the kind of elaborate patience required of small children in their dealings with grown-ups, "it's against the *rules!*"

Immediately after ice cream, however, Agnes had chased Tom and Henry out of the kitchen. Tom had protested, saying that since she had cooked, he should clean up, but Agnes had flapped her arms at him until he'd left. She needed a few orderly moments to herself, and really, when you thought about it, washing dishes was a very orderly process. Besides, it was time for her after-dinner cigarette.

She was down to two Camels a day—one after lunch and one after dinner. Agnes had resolved to be shunt of them entirely by the time it was too cold to sit out on the back steps, but it wasn't that cold yet. She slid on the sweater she kept hanging by the back door, grabbed the tuna-fish can she used as an ashtray, and took herself outside.

It was almost full dark. Summer was losing its grip. Agnes sat on the top step, lit her Camel, and inhaled deeply, enjoying the feel of smoke scratching around inside her lungs. Then she blew the smoke out and watched darkness gobble it up.

Small pleasures, deeply enjoyed. How old was she before she recognized this as the true joy of living?

Perhaps she should write a book.

Or perhaps not.

Too many people wrote books already.

But surely she should do *something*.

The world around Agnes was peaceful, but far from quiet. Night-shouting insects screeched away fortissimo, aware their screeching days were numbered.

It was easier for Agnes to think out here in this dark, solitary spot. Life lost its insistence; people who weren't there kept her comforting company, Joe, Marjory, her parents, friends whom she hadn't seen for years before her daughter's funeral. Rose Callahan appeared to be the newest attendant, for there she was, hovering companionably alongside Marjory.

Agnes chuckled. So, Rose Callahan had kissed her son-in-law! What a hoot! Deep down, under the layers of acquired cynicism, Agnes knew she was still the same hopeless romantic who in the course of a single afternoon had fallen for her flyboy like a felled tree. Why, this part of her wanted to know, should Tom and Rose and Henry *not* live happily ever after? What was wrong with their three separate lives intertwining, turning this poky old house into a place where occupants experienced the kind of safety and warmth and *interconnectedness* of which everyone, in their heart of hearts, dreams?

Of course, Henry's past was murky and his future unsettled, and there was that mysterious money to be dealt with, but she, as a lawyer, could help sort that out. It was obvious from the child's behavior that, after only a few days, he felt quite at home with them. There was also the fact that Tom's name was on his birth certificate, which counted for a lot. If no other man came forward to challenge Tom for paternity, then Henry was legally his. And it seemed likely that poet-cum-romance-novelist Retesia had pretty much lost interest in being a full-time mother.

Agnes took one last deep drag and stubbed out her Camel in the tuna-fish can. The problem with allowing herself only one cigarette after dinner was that one cigarette was too quickly smoked. As soon as it was out, she wanted nothing more than to light another.

Well, phooey on that! A resolution was a decision. She would get up and find something to keep her mind off cigarettes.

Back inside, Agnes looked around the orderly kitchen. There were a few Henry leavings—his Tonka truck, some crayons, a brand-new soccer ball still in the box—but she liked having those around. The truth was she, Agnes Tattle, crusty old broad, liked having *Henry* around, liked it a lot. Maybe even, as startlingly uncharacteristic of her as this would be, she was beginning to love the boy a bit—love being construed in her lawyer's mind as a heartfelt commitment to someone's current and future well-being.

Just as she was about to turn out the kitchen lights and head upstairs for the evening's *Masterpiece Mystery* fix courtesy of Netflix, Agnes spied a stack of papers that Tom had brought home with him, put down, and forgotten. Or perhaps meant to throw away. Impulsively, Agnes walked over and picked them up.

They appeared to be some kind of flyer for a series of events at the Book Store.

*   *   *

Tom was still surprised by how much he enjoyed reading Harry Potter to Henry. He'd expected to enjoy Henry's enjoyment of the book, but not to enjoy it himself. Something, however, appeared to have put a sock in his persistent pedantry, allowing him to dive uncritically into the story as though he, too, were a child. His favorite character was Ron Weasley, the perennial sidekick. It had probably been his own role in life. If, that is, he'd *had* a role and not just a muddle. He'd definitely not been leading man—or leading boy—material.

At the completion of tonight's ritual two chapters, Tom closed the gaudily jacketed book. "Okay, that's it for tonight, Henry. Time for you to go to sleep."

Henry's blue, blue eyes were not at all sleepy. "Just one more chapter? Please?"

Tom looked at his watch. He loved these small parental routines. *Loved* them. The devil might be in the details, but so were the angels. It was nine fifteen. Henry's official bedtime (a concept with which he appeared familiar) was nine o'clock. Tom shook his head. "Not tonight."

"Tomorrow?" Henry's voice was high and piping. He still needed reassurance that tomorrow things would not revert to whatever they'd been before the train delivered him into Tom's keeping.

"Tomorrow," Tom said firmly, reaching a hand out to stroke the boy's springy hair.

"Okay, then."

He trusts me, Tom thought, leaning forward to kiss the boy on his forehead. "Good night, Henry. Sweet dreams."

"Good night." Henry turned on his side.

Tom waited hopefully for him to add "Dad" to the end of "good night," but it didn't happen. Oh well, he hadn't called Henry "son" either. Such things would fall into place naturally in their own time. As the Supremes had put it, you can't hurry love.

Henry fell asleep almost immediately. Tom tiptoed out of the room, not quite closing the door. The newly installed night-light burned steadily in the hall, and in its dim glow Tom was startled to see Agnes standing there, holding a stack of papers.

*   *   *

Agnes sat in her usual spot at the kitchen table and watched Tom dialing Retesia on the phone. One of Rose's flyers was before her and there it was, second from the top: November 23, Retesia Turnball, winner of the 2000 Dorothy Prize and 1995 Writer-in-Residence, 2:30 P.M. "at home" in the Book Store, 7:30 P.M. Library Reference Room. Reading new, unpublished poems as well as selections from her prize-winning book, *Fading Flowers.*

Tom had taken one look at it and immediately called John Thomas, head of the college Creative Writing Department and reading series sponsor. Of course, John had contact information for Retesia Turnball, who—surprise, surprise!—was not off on tour as a romance novelist but was instead remarried and living in Ann Arbor.

Agnes could not remember a time when she had been involved in a real crisis but had not been the one in charge. It felt weird to sit here and watch Tom dial Retesia. With uncharacteristic diffidence, she'd suggested he wait until morning, but Tom—also uncharacteristically—had waved her suggestion away, making it clear that he was going to find out what part Retesia played in Henry's life, and he was going to find out *now.*

"Hello," Tom said into the phone. "This is Tom Putnam, a professor at a college where Retesia Turnball will be giving a reading in November. May I please speak to her?"

There was a pause while Tom either listened or waited. He did not look at Agnes but stared rather fixedly at Marjory's kitten calendar, which neither of them had yet had the heart to take down.

"I'm sorry if she's gone to bed," he said finally, "but I still need to talk with her. This is an emergency!"

Was it an emergency? Agnes wondered. Well, yes, it probably was. If Henry did not belong to Retesia, then they'd have to get cracking and find out where he had come from. And where all that money had come from as well.

There was another pause in the action, during which the only sound was the ticking of the kitchen clock. Agnes found herself thinking about the funny old clock in Rose Callahan's kitchen.

"Hello, Retesia," Tom said firmly into the phone. "This is Tom Putnam. Do you remember—"

There was a short pause.

"Yes, it has been a long time," he said. Agnes wondered if Retesia could hear the impatience in his voice as clearly as she could.

Another pause.

"That's very nice. I'm delighted you won the Dorothy Prize, and that you've remarried."

Pause.

"Marjory is dead, I'm afraid. She was killed in a car wreck just a short while ago. But listen, I didn't call just to chat, I called because I need to ask you something important. Did you send me a letter two weeks ago about a boy named Henry?"

Agnes could hear Retesia's answering squawk from where she sat.

"So you did not send me any letter?" Tom, rightly in Agnes's opinion, wanted to be very clear on this point.

Another squawk.

Tom soldiered on. "Okay then, I have just one more question. Are you by any chance the mother of a six-year-old boy, and if you are, did you send him up here for a visit?"

This time there was a more prolonged squawking, during which Tom held the receiver away from his ear, looked at Agnes, and shrugged. Finally there was a pause. "I do understand, Retesia," Tom said. "I do know it's late. But I trust *you* understand I wouldn't be calling you with these questions if it wasn't terribly important."

Pause.

"Certainly, I'd be happy to explain when you get here. I look forward to seeing you again." Without waiting for more, he put the phone down and leaned against the kitchen wall.

"Liar, liar, pants on fire," Agnes said.

"What?"

"You will *not* be glad to see her again, will you?"

Tom actually thought this over. "Not really, I suppose. It just seemed like the polite thing to say."

"I take it Retesia is not Henry's mother?"

"She is not."

"So if you are not Henry's father and Retesia is not his mother, then who is Henry, what's he doing here, and where did that money come from?"

Tom shrugged again. Was he pleased, Agnes wondered, that Henry was—as it were— up for grabs? "It's a complete mystery," he said.

"Isn't it just?" Agnes said. "Where's Inspector Morse when we need him?"

Tom came back to the table, pulled out his chair, and sat down. "The most important point is that Henry's here."

Agnes's legal mind immediately hummed into action, ticking off other points that had to be considered important as well. But then she caught sight of her dead daughter's disgusting kitten calendar and all those points just flew away. "I agree. Everyone needs a home, including Henry, and, furthermore, I think it is entirely possible that you and I need Henry."

Tom nodded.

Silence. Agnes watched Tom worry some thought like an old bone. Finally he spat it out. "What do I owe Marjory in all this? It feels funny to be so swept up by something that has nothing to do with her. It's not disrespectful of her memory, is it?"

"You mean, do I think you and I should do nothing about Henry's situation, or feel nothing for him, either, until we've observed an official period of mourning?"

Tom smiled. "Well, when you put it that way, it sounds absurd, doesn't it?"

Agnes nodded. "It does. Conventional, but absurd. I don't know about you, Tom Putnam, but I've been in mourning for my daughter for decades."

A look of pain crossed Tom's face. "Me, too, I guess."

"Enough is enough, in my opinion. And one more thing, while we're getting down to brass tacks here."

"Yes?"

"I had lunch with Rose Callahan today."

Tom gazed at her like a dumbfounded donkey. "You did?"

"I did. And we had a very nice talk about you."

Dumbfounded gave way to worried. "About me?"

"Yes. I hear you are quite the basketball player."

"I am?"

"Yes. And that you asked her out to dinner and she turned you down."

Tom turned the color of cherry licorice and said nothing.

Now what?

Agnes plowed on. If she didn't, who would? "I think you should ask Rose out a second time."

"You do?"

Agnes read confusion, a plea for help, and, yes, hope in his eyes. Hope was good. Hope gave her something to work with. "Yes. I do."

"Where?" Tom asked.

Did she have to do *everything*? "You figure that out."

"Oh. Okay."

Agnes could see Tom's mind ticking through restaurant options. "Take her to some interesting place in Charlottesville," she said.

The relief in his face was immediate and immense. "Good idea."

"So, can we get back to Henry for a moment?"

"Certainly," Tom said.

"I'm thinking it's time we sat him down and asked him about himself. What do you think?"

Tom considered this. "He's had some real troubles, you know? I mean *real* troubles."

"Yes, well. It's hard for us to help him with those troubles if we don't know what they are, right? And there is that money. We know *nothing* about that now because Retesia's out of the picture."

Tom surprised her by nodding quickly and decisively. He really was,

Agnes thought, coming along when it came to making decisions in all things except those that had to do with Rose Callahan. "You're absolutely right," he said. "We'll sit him down tomorrow right after breakfast."

*   *   *

Henry knew something was up as soon as Agnes whisked away his empty Cheerios bowl. Tom watched him get up, fetch his Tonka truck from over by the back door, and sit back down at the kitchen table. He clutched the truck fiercely and stared, wooden-faced, at nothing.

Agnes fussed pointlessly at the sink. Could the fearless bearder of soon-to-be-ex husbands possibly be *stalling*?

Eventually she came over and sat down.

The three of them were almost equidistant from one another around the table. Tom slid his chair closer to Henry, so as to be within easier reach.

"Henry." Agnes spoke in the gentlest tone Tom had ever heard come out of her mouth. "Can you tell us where you come from?"

Henry's eyes were round as gumballs. "My pawpaw and mawmaw's house," he said. And stopped. And looked off again at nothing.

Tom hung an arm across the boy's rigid shoulders.

"Okay," Agnes said. "Where's that?"

Henry addressed the tabletop. "214 Grover Street, Picayune, Mississippi." His small shoulders hunched even tighter.

"It's okay," Tom said. "Just take your time."

"They had a old house that was really big, and I could play in any room I wanted, even the study. And when they had to work, Laura Ann stayed with me. She was real nice. Sometimes my mama would visit when she had her act together."

"Were Pawpaw and Mawmaw your grandparents, Henry?" Agnes asked. Tom noticed she'd caught Henry's use of the past tense in referring to them.

Henry's head sank lower. "Yes. They went to help in the hurricane."

"Hurricane Katrina? The really bad one that just happened?"

"Yes."

"How were your grandparents helping, Henry?" Agnes asked.

"They were doctors. They went down before the hurricane came, so they would be ready."

Henry stopped. A tear splashed down on his Tonka truck. Tom smoothed the boy's hair and tried to hug him closer, but it is difficult to hug a statue.

"And?" Agnes prompted.

"They got drowned."

Tom immediately looked at Agnes, who was looking at him. What a collision course with calamity this child's short life had been. "Oh, Henry," he said, leaning down to nuzzle the child's ebullient hair. "I'm so, so sorry."

"Me, too," Agnes said. "They must have been very good people."

Henry said nothing. Another tear hit the truck.

Still, it was important to press on. They had to know. "Then what happened to you?" Agnes asked.

Henry sighed deeply. "Then my mama came and stayed. This time she said she'd got her act together for good, and she brought some report that said that, too, but Mr. Brownlow looked worried and said he'd see."

A new character in the Henry play. "Who's Mr. Brownlow?" Agnes asked.

"He's the man at the bank. He said he was legally in charge of me after Mawmaw and Pawpaw got killed as long as my mama was away. Laura Ann was staying with me, but then Mama came and Mr. Brownlow said, as she had the report, they had no choice but to give Mama my money and let me stay with her."

"Your money?"

"Yes. The money in the backpack."

"And do you know where that money came from?" Agnes asked.

Henry nodded but didn't say anything.

Tom held his breath.

"Where did it come from?" Agnes asked.

"From Mawmaw and Pawpaw. Mama didn't spend any of it. She said it was my emergency money. There's more when I get older."

Tom exhaled. He and Agnes exchanged a look.

"What is your mama's name, Henry?" Agnes asked.

Henry's eyes flew upward to look at Agnes. "Serafine Despré. Don't you *know* her?" He suddenly looked quite desperate.

Agnes shook her head. "No, Henry, we don't. That is, I don't. Do you know her, Tom?"

Tom remembered Agnes's Googled hit on the junkie who'd hung herself in a parish jail. She'd been the only child of doctors, the article said. Bingo. Henry's mother. But why had she sent Henry to him? "No, I'm afraid I don't know her, Henry. But I'm sure if I had, I would have liked her very much."

Henry glared down at his truck. "She really tried," he said in a surprisingly fierce voice. "She just couldn't. And she knew Mr. Brownlow wouldn't let me stay in Pawpaw's house with Laura Ann, and Mama didn't want him to put me somewhere that wasn't nice, so she sent me here. She had to buy tickets because I'm so young. She got on the train with me to fool them, but then she got off again."

"But, Henry, how did she *know* to send you here?" Agnes's voice was gentle as a falling snowflake.

Henry was not one to be sucked in by anyone's tone; he knew an alarming situation when he landed in one. He pulled away from under Tom's arm so as to be able to look up at him. "She said I *belonged* here, because your name is on that certificate. The one I showed you. Isn't that right?"

Tom was careful to look Henry straight in the eye and speak directly from his heart. "You do belong here, Henry. Agnes and I are very, very pleased that you are staying with us."

Henry picked up immediately on Tom's careful choice of words. "Does that mean I have to go *live* somewhere else? That I don't get to live *here*?" His voice was shrill.

In all his helpless years with Marjory, Tom had never felt quite *this* helpless. He opened his mouth to say something both truthful and comforting, but there *was* no truth that was comforting. And he wouldn't lie. He wouldn't. Children knew when people lied; Tom was certain of that. Who knew how they knew, but they did.

Agnes cleared her throat. "Look, Henry. Here's the deal."

Henry immediately sensed there would be no humbug coming at him from Agnes. "What?"

"Tom and I hope very much that you can stay with us, but we need to find out how you happened to get here. You've already said you know that Tom is not your real father—"

Tom could not stop himself from interrupting. "Not that that changes anything about our great joy that you're here," he said, giving the boy's shoulder another squeeze.

Agnes plowed on. "So do you have any idea why Tom is listed as your father on your birth certificate?"

Henry shook his head. "I didn't see the certificate until my mama put it in my backpack. She told me to hang on to it even harder than I hang on to the money. She said the certificate was my real future."

"What exactly did she say about the certificate when she gave it to you, Henry?" Agnes asked, as casually as though they were discussing a routine part of a routine day.

"She showed me the place where it said Tom Putnam was my father. She said he would meet my train when it was time to get off. And she said he was the nicest man in the world and would take good care of me. And then she started to cry and say 'I'm sorry' a lot."

Tom was thunderstruck. Who was this sad and mysterious Serafine Despré, and how had she come to think of him as her son's savior? And what was she sorry for?

Agnes once more rushed headlong where her son-in-law feared to tread. "Do you know what your mother was sorry about, Henry?"

Tom could *feel* sadness leaking out of the boy. "She said she knew she was 'going out' again, and when she did, it wouldn't be safe for me to stay with her. I think she was sorry that she couldn't keep me safe."

Tom heard Agnes catch her breath. This small being sent to them by a desperate junkie mother had somehow beamed himself into Agnes Tattle's crusty heart. "I'm so sorry, Henry. About your mother. I hope—" She stopped midsentence.

Henry was immediately transformed into a small human question mark. "Is what she did okay?" His concern, Tom realized, was for Agnes.

"It's great." Agnes stood up abruptly and stalked over to the Kleenex box on the kitchen counter.

The Tonka truck tumbled to the floor as Henry scurried over to where Agnes stood with her back to the room, blowing her nose loudly into a tissue. He pulled at the hem of her ancient hoodie. "Agnes, please don't be sad. I don't want to make you sad, too."

Agnes turned to the boy, squatted down, and scooped him into a fierce hug. When she spoke, it was over the top of Henry's head and to no one in particular. "I'm sad for your mother, Henry. I know what it's like to lose your child, and I'm sorry she had to lose you."

Henry pulled back to study Agnes's face. Whatever he saw made him reach out and stroke her cheek. "Agnes," he said, "you can say you're *borrowing* me, if that makes you not be sad. Okay?"

chapter 15

Rose slept soundly and woke Saturday morning with the certain knowledge that her karma had long ago been writ. Like Popeye, she was what she was: She had always been, and would always be, a wanderer. Her heart could do whatever it wanted to make things more difficult and painful, but it was only a matter of time until she, Rose Callahan, was outta here.

The realization was almost a relief.

Almost.

"Oh, suck it up, Rosie," she said aloud to the new day.

The Rolling Stones obligingly began shouting in her head about not always getting what you want but, provided you try, sometimes getting what you need. Mavis, as Rose remembered it, had worn out two separate recordings of *Let It Bleed*. Rose would come home from school to find her mother getting ready to go to work, moving free-form with the Stones.

Mavis had been fired just once, when Rose was about seven. She'd been working at a bar in Austin, Texas, and the two of them were living in a two-room apartment on the building's third floor. One night, Rose had been sitting at the bar coloring when a ruckus broke out. Mavis was refusing to tell a homeless man to move on so a couple of frat boys could have his table. When the owner intervened on behalf of the frat boys, Mavis called him an uncharitable pig in a very loud voice and was fired on the spot.

Upstairs in their apartment, Mavis had put on the Stones so she and Rose could dance and pack at the same time. The stereo system had been the last thing into the station wagon. They had left town that same night; moving on, Mavis had said, to their next adventure.

Her mother would have been, what, when she was seven? Twenty-six? Eleven years younger than she was now. Twenty-six years old with a seven-year-old kid and no savings to speak of. No wonder she'd danced, since cowering or wailing or worrying was not an acceptable option in the World According to Mavis.

Just like that, Rose's perspective on the past shifted slightly, uncovering a heretofore unimagined possibility. She'd always thought her mother danced to the Stones before work because she loved to dance. But might the real reason have been to fend off fear and worry? Might Mavis actually have had to *work* to be Mavis?

Could all her wandering have been less about freedom and more about necessity?

It was just ten o'clock as Rose reached for the knocker and pounded three times on the Putnams' front door. Henry and Professor Putnam opened it together, Henry resplendent in college gym shorts and T-shirt, Tom dressed as she was, in a pair of sagging gray sweats.

Astonishingly, Professor Putnam stepped forward and hugged her hard. It was not a romantic hug but a relief hug, one human claiming another human as his willing partner in circumstance. "Oh, Rose," he said, stepping back and looking down at her with that *thing* in his eyes that reached straight into her heart and shook it. "We're both so glad you're here. It's been quite a morning."

. . . *his willing partner in circumstance* . . .

"I made Agnes cry," Henry announced.

"You did?"

"Yes. She didn't want me to know she was sad, but I saw."

Professor Putnam ruffled the boy's hair. He didn't, Rose noticed, try to steer the conversation toward some safer haven. He just wanted Henry to remember he was there. "What was Agnes sad about, Henry?" she asked.

Henry's eyes drifted away toward the safety of some anonymous spot on the foyer wall. "She said she was sad because her daughter died and my mama lost me." His eyes flew back to her; his chin jutted. For the first time ever, Henry looked mad. "Mama didn't *lose* me. She was 'going out,' so she *sent* me here."

"Going out?"

"It means she can't take care of me because something happens to her and she gets sick," Henry said, obviously parroting words he didn't understand.

Oh, *that* kind of "going out." The kind Mavis had witnessed—and enabled—from behind her many bars. "Did you think Agnes meant your mama couldn't find you? That she lost you as in mislaid you?" Rose asked.

"She *didn't!*" Henry actually stamped his foot. "She didn't lose me. She put me on a train and sent me here for Tom to take *care* of me."

Professor Putnam put his hand on the boy's shoulder. "Why don't we all go sit down in the kitchen so you can tell Rose what you just told us?" he said gently. "I'm sure Rose would want to know."

Would she, Rose wondered, ever plumb the depth of Tom Putnam's capacity for kindness and, yes, for love? Henry and he, it seemed, had no biological connection. Which meant that Tom had taken in the boy simply because the boy was there. And this morning he was struggling to convince Henry that, in their case, a biological connection was not necessary to make them father and son.

Rose could not stop herself. Out it came. Everything she'd never told anyone before she'd told Agnes.

Rose kept her eyes on Henry as she explained how her own situation in regard to fathers had been a bit—and she did have to struggle to find the right word to use with a six-year-old—*unusual*. "So you see, Henry, I haven't the slightest idea who my father is," she finished, as though this would somehow make it easier for this child, who wore trouble as comfortably as old clothes, to deal with everything he had to deal with.

They were seated—where else?—at the kitchen table, Henry and Rose quite close together, Tom somewhat removed, as though he wanted to be supportive and present but not intrusive. But then, since he wasn't deaf, Tom Putnam would now also know about her unconventional inception. Could that really be why she'd told Henry?

The boy regarded her solemnly. "What did you tell other kids?"

Ah yes! Other kids. Those pint-sized iterations of judgment and convention. Rose grinned at him. "The truth. But only when they really backed me into it. I got to be quite an expert at not answering that particular question."

Henry was still thinking. "Was it hard on you to be a kid who didn't have normal parents?"

With anyone else, Rose might have launched into a discussion of what was meant by "normal parents." But since it was Henry, she answered the question. "Sometimes it was very hard. But still, I wouldn't swap childhoods with anyone."

"You wouldn't?"

"Nope."

"Why?"

Now it was Rose's turn to think. "Because then I would have been living someone else's life and not my own?" She heard what she'd meant as a statement come out as a question. Had she meant to ask a six-year-old's opinion about this? Was this the one babe whose mouth really did spout wisdom?

Henry's face scrunched with thought. "It's sort of like we each get our own adventure, isn't it?"

Exactly! "That's it!" Rose said, finally daring—yes, she *had* been chicken before now—to look at Tom. When she did and found him smiling at her as though they were together in this business of Henry, it felt as natural as breathing to smile back.

A phrase from some long-ago history class floated between them, a phrase she'd always loved for its vivid representation of the unknown.

Here be dragons . . .

*   *   *

That evening, after supper, after Harry Potter, after Henry was asleep, Tom grabbed his briefcase from his usual drop-off spot just inside the front door, climbed the stairs to his office, and settled in to grade the latest batch of Rem-Write assignments. He had just finished unloading the stack of papers—seventeen attempts at a five-hundred-word autobiography—when he heard the hall door open and Agnes's step on the stairs. "Is Henry all right?" he called out, as any parent would.

Agnes's head appeared. "Henry's fine. He's sleeping." She glared around her. "I need to sit for a moment. Where am I supposed to do that in this rubble pile?"

Tom got up and removed a stack of books from the room's chair and gave it a quick dust with his sleeve. "How about here." He resisted the urge to give Agnes a quick peck on the cheek as she stalked past him and sat down.

Agnes, having read his mind, rolled her eyes at him. "You. Sit. This might take a while."

He sat and watched her pull some papers from her reticule.

"I've been in touch with an old contact in New Orleans. A colleague of a friend from law school."

Tom sat up. "Yes?"

Agnes eyed him in the dim glow of his desk lamp. "This colleague of the friend is a private investigator who evidently knows some pretty spiffy hackers. Anyway, there's no such thing as privacy anymore—if you're willing to throw enough money around."

"How much money?" Tom felt he should pay whatever had to be paid to disinter Henry's past.

"None of your business. Do you want to know what he found out or what?"

"About Henry?"

"And his mother. There was quite a lot to find out about the late Serafine Despré."

"Are you sure the Serafine Despré you had those people research is Henry's mother?"

"I'm sure." Agnes held out the papers. "You wanna read this stuff for yourself or you want me to give you the CliffsNotes?"

"Let's start with the CliffsNotes." Tom realized he was gripping the arms of his desk chair, quite literally bracing himself for whatever was to come.

"Okay." Agnes fished reading glasses from her reticule and perched them on her nose. "Serafine Despré, the only child of Drs. Honoré and Prudence Despré, was born on May 14, 1973. Both parents were forty. He was Creole; she was white. Serafine was their only child.

"Honoré and Prudence met and married during their respective residencies at Tulane Medical School, where both trained as internists. Mrs.

Dr. Despré came from lots of old money—rice plantations with a little fishing thrown in. The couple eschewed the high life, however, and settled in Pica-yune, Mississippi, where they proceeded to use a chunk of Prudence Despré's family money to set up a series of clinics serving surrounding rural areas that had no other reliable access to medical care. Evidently they both worked their asses off in these clinics. No one has a bad word to say about them; they were always together, always working, never out for personal gain. In other words, Henry's grandparents were saints."

"Hmmm," Tom said, feeling he should say something.

"Hmmm, indeed." Agnes kept her eyes fixed on her papers. "Not so Henry's mother. Serafine appears to have been a bit like Marjory, in that she was semi-okay until puberty, then, after puberty, anything but okay. Se-rafine has a sealed juvenile record, but the public record of her numerous arrests begins six weeks after her seventeenth birthday. It's all for drugs and drug-related offenses—mainly possession, possession with intent, and, when her parents cut off all direct financial support after Henry was born, for prostitution. She was *not*, I'm happy to say for Henry's sake, HIV-positive when she died."

"Good Lord."

"Or not so good." Agnes scowled at her papers. "Poor woman."

"What do you think happened to her?" Tom couldn't stop himself from trying to fathom how the child of such decent people could zoom so far off the rails.

"Life happened to her." Agnes looked up at Tom, the bleakness of a Siberian winter in her eyes. "It's not for everyone, you know."

"I do know," Tom said gently. "I'm sorry."

"Nonsense." Agnes fished a tissue out of her reticule, blew her nose loudly, balled the tissue up, and threw it at the distant trash can. It didn't make it, but so what? Tom knew it had done her good to throw something.

"Well then," she said. "You ready for me to go on?"

"I am."

Agnes adjusted her glasses. "Honoré and Prudence sent their daughter away for her first rehab stint to a posh and very expensive place called the Manor, when she was fourteen. Alcohol appears to have been her drug of choice at that time, obtained while her parents were off being saints. Accord-ing to the Manor's records—"

Tom was astonished. "You mean your person got a look at a private hospital's records?"

Agnes eyed him over her glasses. "I suggest we save bemoaning the sorry state of privacy these days until we finish sorting this out."

"Sure. It's just that I'm shocked."

Agnes was unable *not* to enjoy jerking her son-in-law's infinitely jerkable chain. "Well, if a little well-intentioned peeping shocks you, get ready to be *fried* by what's coming. Serafine appears to have been a raging alcoholic by the age of fourteen. There are also mentions of coke, weed, and a snort or two of heroin in her doctor's notes from the Manor"—Agnes held up a hand to forestall another interruption from Tom—"but alcohol was her most pressing problem. Serafine stayed in treatment for three months. Honoré and Prudence were very involved, visiting an average of four times a week and attending twice-weekly family therapy sessions. The doctor gives them high marks as parents but also notes his general worry about Serafine's inability to resist relapsing once she returns home. Which is just what happened. Serafine was back at the Manor a couple of weeks after discharge, this time for nine months. During her second stint, at the doctor's suggestion, there was much less parental involvement." Agnes stopped reading to look up at Tom. "Not sure what *that's* about. Maybe they *hovered*," she said, the pot acknowledging the kettle when it came to that particular parental failing.

"Maybe they did. I'm beginning to grasp how easily paved a parent's road to hell is."

Agnes snorted. "Amen to that. But we digress again. This time, Serafine was discharged into a boarding school called Mount Olive, which appears to have been run on a combination of tough love and Outward Bound. She did well there, staying put long enough to get her high school diploma at the age of seventeen. Her parents, overcome by optimism, allowed Serafine to attend Tulane, and stupidly—there's really no other way to say it—gave her a generous monthly allowance and a new Mazda Miata." Agnes eyed him angrily across the gloom of his office and waved her hand dismissively. The Després' parental flounderings struck too close to home for her to tolerate without judgment. "What were they thinking, Tom? They were *doctors*, for God's sake, dealing with addicts every day. How could they *not* know they were inviting their daughter to party her way into oblivion?"

"They probably just wanted to believe she was all right," Tom said mildly. "I guess parents don't always think straight when it comes to wounded children."

Agnes bit her lip.

Tom thought it best to move on. "So I take it nothing good happens to Serafine after that?"

"Wrong!" Agnes triumphantly smacked her papers. "Henry happened."

Of course! Henry! Serafine's chance of redemption, and, perhaps, his own. Children at least made you *try* to be your best self.

Agnes was off again. "It appears Serafine got pregnant during yet another stay at a New Orleans rehab center, although it may have been just after, because Henry was born a bit prematurely. By this time, her parents had cut off all direct financial support of their daughter, as any money they gave her went for drugs, but they were still paying for her rehab stints and any health care she needed. It looks as though Serafine got serious about sobriety as soon as she discovered she was pregnant and went home to Mom and Dad. Society articles in the local paper, the *Picayune Item*, document that the Drs. Despré were showing up at community events around this time with their long-lost daughter in tow. And from the one picture of the three of them, it's obvious that Serafine is pregnant."

"You've got a picture of them?" A picture offered a chance to catch firmer hold of Henry's past.

"It's faxed newsprint, so it's not very good."

"May I look? Please?" Tom held his hand out. Agnes fished one of her papers out of the pile and handed it to him. He turned and held the paper directly under the desk lamp.

It was a photograph of three people at some kind of garden party. Two of them were kindly-looking people in their early sixties, made lusterless by newsprint and fax. Not so the ethereal sprite who stood between them, looking off at some distant spot over the photographer's shoulder. Here, indeed, was Cleopatra in the flesh; a woman whose infinite variety could neither be withered by age nor staled by custom.

Serafine Despré was dark and cloud-haired, with enormous, haunted eyes. Slender as a reed except for her basketball of a tummy, she seemed too insubstantial to survive the knock-around life endured by mere mortals. She was not so much beautiful as magical. But Tom had absolutely no doubt that she was Henry's mother. She was a dark-eyed Henry, made female.

"My goodness," he said.

"Or not," Agnes said.

"Or not," Tom echoed.

They sat in silence for a moment, Tom staring at the photograph, trying to grasp that this lovely, delicate creature had hanged herself in a parish jail. Marjory visited again, young and beautiful and differently doomed. Tom knew that no matter how long he thought, such waste and cruelty would never make anything approaching sense. The thing to do was to grieve for the lost and then get on with doing what you could for those within reach. Like Henry. And Agnes. And, even, himself.

"When the going gets tough, the tough suck it up," Agnes said. "The rest get run over."

He looked up to find her watching him. "You think?"

"I know. There's all kinds of ways to die, and most of them don't involve actual death, just the handing over of the soul to fear and anger and greed. Or despair. Very few people have the guts to deal with life on life's terms."

Tom immediately thought of Rose Callahan. Agnes, of course, read his mind. "Yes, we're lucky to have met Rose. She's just what we both need in our lives at the moment. And, perhaps, for a great many more moments in the future."

"You think?" Tom heard the hope in his voice. My God, could he truly be in love with the woman? Or was he just in love with the possibilities of his new life?

"Shall we go on?" Agnes asked.

"Yes." Tom handed the picture back to her without looking at it again. One stare at a grainy picture, and Serafine Despré was forever lodged in his heart.

"Okay, where were we?" Agnes made a show of rattling pages, finding her place. "Henry was, as I said, born a bit prematurely. Serafine was admitted to Tulane Medical Center as soon as she went into labor, as the Drs. Despré were concerned that both baby and mother might need more sophisticated medical care than their local hospital could provide because of Serafine's history of drug abuse. Henry's birth, however, appears to have been uncomplicated. Serafine was sent home the next day, Henry in two weeks. Both baby and mother were discharged to the Despré family home in Picayune. Serafine's next arrest was in Slidell, Louisiana, six months later. This was her first arrest for prostitution."

"Oh dear."

Agnes looked at Tom over her glasses. "Shall I go on, or do you need a moment to wrap your mind around the way Serafine was now supporting her various habits?"

"It's . . . it's just hard to hear."

Agnes had never been one to encourage sentiment. "And even harder to live," she snapped.

"Sure. Of course. Go on."

Agnes cleared her throat. "Anyway, this appears to have become Serafine's pattern after Henry's birth. She would get herself arrested, clean up, go home to her parents and her child, stay for a couple of months, go out, get herself arrested again. As her parents had stopped posting bail, her jail sentences ranged from five to ninety days. A couple of times she went from jail into treatment again, but there were no long residencies. Thirty days appears to have been her longest treatment sojourn. She was at home and clean when Katrina struck and the Drs. Despré were killed. But, as we know, not long after, she put Henry on the train for Charlottesville, and then she was dead. Henry evidently has quite a sizable fortune held in trust until his twenty-second birthday, and a whacking great allowance until then. Not to mention the five hundred grand currently under his bed." Agnes took off her glasses. "That's it."

"That's it? Doesn't it say how Henry ended up here?"

"Nope."

"But surely there's something in all those papers that connects us to the Drs. Despré or to Serafine or to *someone* connected with Henry?"

"Nope."

"Not one thing?"

"Nada. Zip."

Once again, Tom found himself trying to grasp reality by its greased tail. "Okay. I'm stumped. What do we do now?"

Agnes was ready for this. "Well," she said, "the good banker, Mr. Brown-low, must have been out of town, because it took him until yesterday to notice that Henry and his mother were not in residence at the Despré family home. But boy howdy, was he quick to call the police in after that. So what I'd sug-gest is that we phone the Mississippi state cops just as soon as we figure out what we want to say. And I suggest we figure that out right now."

So here it was: the future. Those two roads in the yellow wood were diverging right here, right now! "Holy smoke," Tom said.

"That's helpful."

Tom laughed. "So what do you suggest?"

Agnes made her considering face, a kind of crooked moue, her many wrinkles pulled to one side. "You up for a question?"

"Sure. Fire away."

"Is there any chance you want Henry to stay here permanently?"

Tom was stunned. Certainly he'd fantasized about this, but he'd never *thought* about it. At least not in any logical, orderly way that went forward through adolescent rebelliousness into paying college tuition. He was forty-four years old. Did he really want to plunge into full-time fatherhood?

Visions of future battles over loud music, curfews, and car keys danced in his head. Then abruptly they dissolved, vanquished by the reality that was Henry. This decision was not tied to some abstract child; it was tied to the very real child asleep upstairs. The question Agnes had asked him was not whether he wanted to father *someone* but whether he wanted to father Henry.

"I do," he said.

Agnes was watching him. "You sound like you're marrying Henry."

"I am."

chapter 16

Ray's housewarming present, the old shoe box clock, banged away in the kitchen. Every day Rose told herself she would let it run down, and every day she wound it again. Time does pass; why should she avoid being reminded of that? The clock on her bedside table announced it was 6:22 in the morning.

Rose sat up in bed and looked around at the little, low-ceilinged room that had been her bedroom for the last few days. Its walls were bedecked, as all the walls of all her various bedrooms had been, with framed photographs. The morning sunlight moved across these captured moments of her life; pictures of people and places that had meant a lot at the time, but not so much they couldn't be left behind.

Fairly soon she'd be leaving here as well. All she had to do was wait a couple of months and this confused ruckus inside her head would simply become irrelevant. She didn't *have* to be involved with these people; involved, that is, in the sense of feeling that her life was intertwined with theirs.

Tick! Tick! Tick! reminded Ray's clock. Time, if not flying, was at least marching briskly along.

Without really thinking about it, Rose picked up the phone and dialed her mother's number. Mavis answered on the second ring, wide awake, on top of things as always. "What are you doing awake at this hour on a Sunday morning?" she asked before Rose even said hello. Stu must have gotten them caller ID.

"I'm just up," Rose said.

There was no beating around the bush with Mavis. "You didn't sleep well, did you? That's not like you, Rose. What's bothering you?"

Out it came. All of it. Tom, Henry, Agnes, Marjory's death, her job—everything that had happened over the course of the last two uncharacteristically tumultuous weeks. Rose had already told Mavis most of it in bits and pieces, but this morning she felt a great need to tell the whole story again to her mother. Or maybe she just felt a great need to tell herself, and telling Mavis was easier.

The Sage of San Marcos was silent when she finished. This, Rose knew, could mean only one thing. Her mother was thinking.

"I'm sorry you're quitting your job, child," Mavis said at last. "You seemed to really like it there. That have anything to do with *why* you're quitting?"

"Of course not," Rose said, a bit too quickly.

The sun shone now on a picture of a friend from Nashville. When Rose had left, he'd been in love with the husband of his wife's best friend, who, he'd thought, was also in love with him. Rose had felt so sorry for him—he'd allowed his life to become so higgledy-piggledy. But it had, she'd heard, all ended rather well. The two men were still together. The two wives had rolled with the punches and gone on. One was in medical school; the other had remarried and given birth to twins. "I'm sure I'll be fine," she said into the phone. "I just thought you'd like to know what's happening down here."

"I would like to know. I always like to know."

Rose heard Mavis draw in a deep breath as though she were about to launch into something, but all that traveled south from Williamstown, Massachusetts, was more silence. Rose had an impulse to leap into it and tell Mavis truly *everything*—whatever everything was—but just as she opened her mouth to do that, the impulse died away. "So," she said, "how's your stock portfolio these days?"

"My *what?*"

"I said, how are your investments doing?"

"Not well. And yours?"

Rose laughed. She had no investments. What little money she had was in a money market account drawing a whopping three-quarter percent.

There was another silence. Usually the two of them chattered away like squirrels.

"Rose," Mavis said. "Why did you really call me?"

"What?"

"I said, 'Why did you really call me?'"

"Just to chat?"

"Nonsense! It's still dark. I don't remember you ever calling me when it's still dark on a Sunday morning."

"Oh."

"So why did you call me?"

Despair rose up inside Rose like a sullen beast. If she couldn't talk to Mavis right now, she might never, *ever* be able to talk to anyone. And yet she had no idea what to say. Mavis's own voice rang in her head, a loud blast from the past. *Tell the truth, Rose.*

"I don't know," she said.

"Uh-huh." There was a pause. "You really mean that, don't you, Rosie?"

Mavis only called her Rosie in her rare moments of deep maternal worry. "Yes, I think I do."

"You're bothered about leaving that place, aren't you?"

"A little, I guess."

Mavis laughed. "And probably more bothered by the fact that you're bothered, right? You've finally landed with people you can't take pictures of and then leave behind."

"*Yes!*" How had Mavis known this when she hadn't known it herself?

There was a long sigh. "Look, Rosie," Mavis said. "People change. Or maybe I should say, *I* changed. In my thirties, I began to want different things than I did in my twenties, but it took me a while to realize it. I don't think I realized it fully until I met Stu." Mavis paused. Was she, perhaps, remembering the moment she'd first laid eyes on her professor, the moment he'd put his hand on her arm, and she'd felt the rackety old world slow, then stop, then change forever . . . Rose could hear the smile in her mother's voice. "I can remember thinking, *Why am I, Mavis Callahan, attracted to this nice, smart, quiet, normal guy? I'm not usually attracted to nice, smart, quiet, normal guys. I'm usually attracted to interesting, difficult, creative, self-centered guys who make my life hell.* Sometimes they were smart, but not always. One or two were dumb as dull thumbtacks. You remember that guy in Ann Arbor? That artist who painted those big, ugly pictures and was always bad-mouthing people because no one bought them? Now, there was a dim bulb! It amazes me now to think I put up with him for five minutes. But I did. And had a pretty good time doing it—hanging out with weird people, smoking a little dope, drinking bad wine, talking irrelevant nonsense." Mavis laughed. "You remember him, Rosie?"

Rose did. He'd drawn her pictures of dogs and cats on bar napkins. She'd tolerated him because she'd known he wouldn't be around long. She and Mavis were the team. The others in their lives who came and went were just groupies. "Sure, I remember him," she said.

Mavis sighed. "You know, Rosie, I don't think it was until Stu asked me to marry him, and I immediately said yes, that I realized how much I'd changed. And that what I wanted now was some kind of permanent home and a permanent partner who made life easier instead of more difficult. Oh, eventually I would have found some nice place and settled down even without Stu showing up and giving me a shake by proposing, but I must say, I find my permanent home is much nicer with him in it, even though he can annoy the dickens out of me. As long as I had you, Rosie, I guess I didn't need anyone else permanently. But when you struck out on your own wandering ways, what I really missed, I think, was shared history. You know the way we'd always laugh and talk and remember things? Well, without you, it was as though I had no history."

My photographs, Rose thought, staring at herself surrounded by her high school basketball teammates. *My photographs are my shared history.* "Were you ever lonely, Mama?"

"You mean without you? God, yes. I missed you terribly."

Rose smiled. "We were quite the team, weren't we?"

"That we were, child. That we were. Good for many a mile and many a laugh."

"I loved my childhood, you know?" Rose said impulsively. Surely Mavis knew that, but it felt important to say it anyway.

"I do know. But you're not a child anymore, Rosie, my dear. And you're also almost not young anymore."

"I know. I suppose I should dread turning forty in a couple of years, but I just don't somehow."

Another laugh. "Speaking for myself, I found not being young anymore a great relief. It allowed me to get rid of a lot of ridiculous expectations I'd set for myself. I was always pushing myself to *do* something—what exactly that something was, I had no idea. I found I was a lot more comfortable once I got rid of all that ridiculous excess baggage."

"Really?"

"Really."

Rose felt calm again, all the way through. It was the way she was used to feeling. But she felt quite different in other ways. How, she wasn't sure yet, but that didn't worry her. Pippi Longstocking piped up, *Don't you worry about me. I'll always come out on top!* "Thanks," she said.

"For what?"

"For talking."

"You're welcome. Do you feel any better?"

"Yes. I think I do."

"Good. Well, I gotta go. I just heard Stu stirring around. We're on a tight schedule today. Gotta go pick apples with friends."

My goodness, her mother and her professor knew how to enjoy themselves. "Okay. Give him my best," Rose said. Someday she might even say "love." "May I ask you one more thing before you hang up?"

"Shoot."

"Why haven't we talked like this before?"

Would Mavis, Rose wondered, tell Stu about this conversation in great detail? Probably. And it came to Rose with a sense of wonder that she wouldn't mind in the least.

She heard Mavis chuckle. "We have, Rosie. I haven't said anything today to you that I haven't said before. I've always pretty much told you everything I felt."

"You're kidding."

"Nope."

Rose had absolutely no memory of her mother ever talking to her about being lonely, or describing her old boyfriends as dull thumbtacks. "But why don't I remember it?"

She could picture Mavis standing in her own bright kitchen, shaking her head, smiling. "Because, as I just said, people change, Rosie. Maybe it just wasn't anything that interested you until today."

*   *   *

Sunday morning at breakfast, Tom and Agnes had another talk with Henry. Agnes took the lead, explaining that Mr. Brownlow at the bank had learned he was missing and, out of concern that he was all right, had alerted the

Mississippi State Police. In order to keep things as simple as possible, Agnes said, she was going to call the police in Mississippi as soon as they'd finished their pancakes, just to let them know that Henry was here with his legal father, that his mother had sent him, and that he wanted to stay put. "We don't expect any real trouble from anyone about your living with us," she added. "Although it may be a bit confusing to Mr. Brownlow and the police at first, and could take some time to sort it out."

Henry shoveled in pancakes nonstop while Agnes talked.

"So," she finished, "does that sound like a plan, Henry? You ready to tell the police that you want to live here?"

Henry stopped eating, put his fork down carefully, and appeared to be thinking. Tom and Agnes watched him and waited. Children, Tom suspected, made big decisions in increments, dealing only with the question of the moment. For Henry to tell *them* he wanted to stay here was one thing; for him to tell the police was quite another.

The kitchen faucet dripped; a car rumbled down the back alley. Finally Henry nodded. "After I tell the police I want to stay here, can we call Rose and see if she'd like to play soccer?"

"Sure," Tom said, flooded with relief, wonderfully aware of the doomed Serafine Despré's delicate stamp on her son's hair and mouth and skin and *being*. Surely her parents had tried as hard as Agnes had to keep their daughter safe. And neither one had managed to hold damage at bay.

So what had made Serafine think she could best keep Henry safe by sending him here? How had she even known that *here* existed?

*   *   *

A woman answered when Agnes called the Mississippi State Police. Agnes identified herself and went right to the point. "Six-year-old Henry Putnam is playing upstairs in my home."

There was an intake of breath in Mississippi. "Hold, please."

Agnes was not on hold for very long. Sergeant First Class Hoskins's voice was deep and male. "I'm told you have information about Henry Putnam, a six-year-old boy reported as missing yesterday by Mason Brownlow of Picayune."

"Well, not exactly," Agnes said, enjoying herself. "I have Henry Putnam. He's upstairs at the moment, getting dressed to go play soccer." There was a slight click on the phone line. "I can give you my address if that would make it easier for you to come check us out," Agnes said sweetly.

"Yes, ma'am," Sergeant First Class Hoskins said. "Please."

Agnes gave it to him. "It's the fourth house on the left, just at the end of Faculty Row."

"Yes, ma'am." Agnes pictured a red alert speeding throughout law enforcement. The address she'd given verified that Henry had crossed state lines, so FBI involvement was now officially permitted. Sergeant Hoskins cleared his throat. "And what, may I ask, is your connection to Henry Putnam, who is, I'm sure I don't need to remind you, a minor?"

"Certainly you may ask. I am his father's mother-in-law, housekeeper, and lawyer," Agnes said, with a slight emphasis on "lawyer."

"You are with Henry's *father?*"

To Agnes's finely tuned ear, Sergeant Hoskins sounded nicely disconcerted. "Yes. My son-in-law, Tom Putnam, is Henry's father."

"According to who?" Sergeant Hoskins demanded.

Agnes had to enunciate carefully around the big lump of butter in her mouth. "According to his birth certificate."

Papers rustled briskly in Mississippi. Voices murmured as well. A female voice declared, "Got it!"

"I'm going to put you on hold for a moment," Sergeant Hoskins announced briskly. "I'm sure we can straighten all this out, but please, do not attempt to change locations or move Henry Putnam. The police are on their way." The phone line went briefly mute before an annoyingly sweet-sounding female voice came on offering safety tips for highway driving.

The Putnams' doorbell rang. Agnes waved to Tom to answer it. With her free ear she heard him cross the foyer and open the front door. "Good morning, Clarence," Tom said. "Come in. Come in." Agnes could picture him offering his hand to affable Clarence Mayhew, a retired elementary school teacher and the college's chief of police. "I'll bet you've been told to come here and investigate me for kidnapping."

Clarence Mayhew made a soft choking sound that was probably meant to be laughter.

Sergeant Hoskins was back on the line. "Is your name Tom Putnam?"

"No," Agnes said sweetly. "My name is Agnes Tattle."

Out in the foyer, Tom and Clarence laughed in chorus, probably at some gentle joke of Tom's about his status as a wanted felon. Henry thudded down the stairs. "I'm ready to go play soccer when you and Agnes are done with the police," he shouted. Agnes heard Tom introduce the boy to Clarence.

Down in Mississippi, Sergeant Hoskins drew in a sharp breath. "I'm sorry, ma'am. I meant to ask if you're *related* to Tom Putnam. Henry Putnam's birth certificate does name a Tom Putnam as his father, but we were told by Mason Brownlow that it was a made-up name. That Tom Putnam wasn't a real person."

"Well, he most certainly *is* real," Agnes said, theatrically indignant. "He's right here! And, as I told you before, I'm Tom Putnam's mother-in-law, housekeeper, and lawyer." Again the slight emphasis on "lawyer."

"I see," said Sergeant Hoskins. "Is Mr. Putnam available to speak to?"

Distant sirens sounded.

Henry appeared in the doorway. He looked excited. "The police are coming!" he said happily.

"Excuse me a moment," Agnes said into the phone. She pressed HOLD and beckoned the boy to come over. "Henry, I've got a policeman from Mississippi on the phone. Would you like to talk with him? I'm sure he's got some questions you could answer better than anyone."

The sirens were coming closer. "Sure," Henry said.

Agnes took the phone off hold and handed it to him. Henry drew himself up to his full almost-seven-year-old height. "Hello."

There was a short pause.

"This is Henry Putnam. Agnes says you're a policeman in Mississippi, and you're looking for me."

Another pause. Slightly longer. The sirens reached screeching level, then stopped abruptly.

"My mama put me on the train. She put my birth certificate in my backpack. She says it shows I belong here with Tom and Agnes. Would you like to see it?"

A man's face appeared at the kitchen window. Another man's face appeared at the back door. Both faces were topped with Virginia State Police hats. Agnes smiled and waved them in. The faces disappeared, the back door opened, and a half-dozen troopers filed in, each one carefully wiping his feet on the doormat. Guns and various other weapons hung from their persons like Christmas tree ornaments.

Agnes made a shushing sign and pointed to Henry. "He's on the phone with the Mississippi State Police," she mouthed.

Tom and Clarence Mayhew appeared in the hall doorway. Clarence looked abashed to find himself in the presence of the state police. Tom, however, went over to each officer and shook his hand, introducing himself sotto voce as "Henry's legal father, Tom Putnam."

"Yes, I want to stay here," Henry said emphatically. "I belong here. My name is Henry *Putnam*."

Agnes went over to inspect the coffeepot. There was only a cup or two left from breakfast. She picked the pot up and used it to gesture, first to Clarence and Tom, who both nodded yes, and then to the state police, who pretended not to notice. Agnes shrugged and went about making a fresh pot.

"Forever!" Henry announced in a loud, strong voice.

He listened again and then held the phone out to Agnes, who was in the middle of emptying old grounds into the wastebasket.

Tom stepped forward. "I'll speak to them."

Henry shook his head. "He wants to speak to Agnes."

"Okay. Agnes it is. I'll finish making the coffee."

Agnes and Tom did a do-si-do. Agnes took the phone from Henry. "Yes?"

There was a loud clunk. Tom had hit his head while opening the kitchen cabinet where the coffee was kept. "Daggone it!" he muttered.

"Do you know Tom Putnam's present whereabouts at this time?" Sergeant Hoskins asked from down in Mississippi.

Agnes could not remember a time when she'd enjoyed herself more. "Why, Tom Putnam's right here, banging his head on cabinet doors. Would you like to speak to him?"

"Yes, please." It was pleasantly obvious to Agnes that Sergeant Hoskins was losing his cool.

Agnes held out the phone to Tom. "He wants to speak to you."

They did their do-si-do again, and Agnes went back to putting the coffee together.

"Hello. This is Tom Putnam."

At that exact moment, Clarence Mayhew farted. Loudly. Henry, who had inched over to stand beside Clarence so as to be able to examine his holstered gun, giggled. One of the Virginia state troopers also snickered involuntarily, then turned red. There was a general shifting of feet among the police.

"Sorry," Clarence said, turning scarlet as a tanager. Henry continued to giggle.

Agnes smiled. How many major turning points in human history, she wondered, had been enlivened by farts? Probably most, and yet not a single one had been recorded.

"Certainly I can prove I am Henry's legal father," Tom was saying. "My name is on his birth certificate, and his mother sent him here. I have the—"

He stopped midsentence as Sergeant Hoskins obviously interrupted him. Tom's face darkened as he listened, and he shot Henry a quick, protective glance, but Henry, who had finally stopped giggling, had also stopped listening. He was busy inching the tip of his finger toward Clarence Mayhew's weapon. "Yes, I am aware of what happened in the St. John the Baptist lockup," Tom said. "But there hasn't been an opportunity yet to talk with Henry about that. And I'd appreciate the time to do it."

Henry's finger reached its goal. He was standing there, his pointer on a real gun's shiny leather holster, lost in a six-year-old's nirvana.

"Certainly, I understand," Tom said.

The front doorbell rang. "I'll get it!" Clarence offered, happy to get out of the room.

Agnes, busy pouring water into the coffeemaker, nodded her thanks. Clarence trotted off. Henry, his shoulders drooping, turned and watched him leave.

"I understand that Mr. Brownlow was named as his legal guardian," Tom was telling Sergeant Hoskins. "And he's welcome to call me or come and visit us anytime. But Mr. Brownlow also needs to understand that I'm Henry's legal father, his mother sent him to me, and Henry wants to stay right here. And, according to my lawyer"—here he shot a look at Agnes, who gave him a thumbs-up with her free hand—"as I am named as his legal father on his birth certificate, I have every legal right to have him live with me."

Tom, Agnes noted with approval, had not told a single lie. He'd claimed legal, not biological, parenthood. If Sergeant Hoskins or Mr. Brownlow chose to muddle the two, it was too bad; or, actually, in this case, too good.

Clarence returned with Rose Callahan in tow.

"Rose!" Henry sang out, skipping across to her. "Have you come to play soccer with me and Tom?"

Rose immediately knelt down and hugged Henry. Their two heads looked like a platter of froth.

"Certainly, I'd be happy to talk with Mr. Brownlow anytime," Tom said. "I completely understand his concern. As I said before, he's more than welcome to call or come visit."

Henry pulled back from Rose's hug. "Have you come to play soccer?" he asked her again.

Clarence Mayhew tapped the boy on the shoulder and made a shushing gesture with his finger. "Oops!" Henry whispered loudly. He clapped his hands over his mouth and did a little dance.

"There are actually six Virginia State Troopers here, Sergeant," Tom said. "Would you like to speak to one of them?"

Rose's hand had drifted protectively to Henry's shoulder, but her eyes, Agnes noticed, were on Tom.

Tom held the phone out toward the line of Virginia State Troopers, who had begun to remind Agnes of the Village People. The trooper in the middle stepped forward and took the phone. "Trooper Davison."

This was it, Agnes knew; the moment they found out if they were in any immediate trouble. And if they were, how much.

Everyone stared anxiously at Trooper Davison. Even Henry.

"Yes, sir!" Trooper Davison said. "Certainly, sir!" He hung up the phone.

No one breathed.

Trooper Davison turned to his men. "I think we're done here," he said. "Mississippi will notify the FBI that the child is safe and with his legal father."

There was a collective sigh of relief, followed by a general buzz of congratulatory chatter. Even the state troopers seemed pleased with the outcome.

Prying eyes be damned. Tom and Rose threw their arms around each other. Agnes smiled. It was at moments like this that people did what they had to do.

She herself was going outside for a smoke. To hell with resolutions!

*   *   *

When Tom opened the front door for the state troopers, he found a good-sized crowd gathered on his front lawn. Knots of grown-ups murmured together while children raced about among the troopers' cars.

Tom shook hands with each trooper in turn as they filed past him; then, feeling rather like the pope on his balcony, he stepped out on the front porch and waved briefly to his assembled neighbors. "All's well," he called, knowing that everyone, constrained by their good manners, would now have to go home. Concern was permitted; nosey-parker-ness was not.

Back inside, having closed the front door, Tom stood for a moment in the cluttered foyer and tried to figure out how he felt. This had been irrelevant for so many years, he wasn't quite sure how to do it anymore. At first he tried to *think* about how he felt, to figure it out intellectually. But then it came to him that the thing to do was to do nothing; he simply needed to stand there and feel.

Just as he reached the point of realizing that what he felt was *alive*, Rose Callahan slipped in from the kitchen, came straight toward him, put her arms around him, and kissed him as he had not been kissed since . . . since *never*. This was what he'd dreamed about as a teenager upstairs in his room staring at Farrah Fawcett in her bikini, combined with the calmest, steadiest realization that he needed to hang on to this woman, forever and ever, amen. Was this how true love happened? Could it possibly be this uncomplicated?

Who knew? At this moment, who cared? Tom wrapped his arms around Rose and kissed her back unreservedly, heart, head, passions all funneled from his lips to hers. Then he stepped back, keeping his hands firmly on her shoulders, needing to look at her, look into her. "Are we beginning to fall in love, Rose?" he asked.

"I . . . I don't know," she said, looking right back at him. "I think maybe, yes, we might be. I know I want to keep kissing you."

Tom smiled. "And I, you."

He no longer felt any need to monitor how he was doing or even what he was doing. He drew Rose to him and kissed her again, longer, deeper. The kind of kiss that subsumed everything else into it.

Henry giggled. "You two are *kissing*!"

Tom and Rose broke apart, but Tom captured Rose's hand and held on to it firmly. "Yes, we were, buddy. And you better get used to it."

Henry continued to giggle.

chapter 17

The four of them were on their way home from Sunday dinner at Golden Corral. Henry (strapped into the new safety seat Agnes had thought to buy) and Rose were in the backseat of Tom's ancient Subaru Forester, Tom and Agnes in the front.

Agnes, who'd eaten two brownies and a big bowl of ice cream, was in full planning mode. What they had to do, she declared, was develop a comprehensive plan to settle Henry quickly into his new life. This included setting up doctor and dentist appointments, enrolling him in peewee soccer, encouraging him to make friends and invite them over; all the things good parents did for their children. They needed to be able to show Mr. Brownlow that Henry was in a good place, not just a legally justified place. Their first priority should be to enroll him in school.

Tom and Rose nodded in agreement. Henry failed to respond. He was absorbed in looking at *Celtic Football Club, 1887–1967 (Archive Photographs: Images of Scotland Series)*, a book Tom had discovered among the piles shoved into the corners of his attic office.

They were stopped at a red light. "How do you feel about starting school, Henry?" Tom asked, turning around to face the boy.

"Fine," Henry said without looking up.

"What about enrolling Henry in Ed House?" Rose suggested. "I'll bet Henry'd like being able to walk to school. And the teachers there seem really nice."

Ed House, as it was unofficially called, was a K–3 school run by the college's Education Department. As Education regularly claimed more majors than any other department, the staff-to-student ratio was unreal.

"What a good idea," Agnes said. She approved of Ed House because it welcomed children from the entire area, not just the campus.

It was a long red light. Tom was still regarding Henry. "You have *been* to school, haven't you?"

Henry looked up long enough to give Tom the what-a-dumb-question eye. "I finished first grade at Westside Elementary School in Picayune with all check marks," he said. "Of *course* I've been to school." Then he went back to his book.

Tom telephoned Betty Price, the Ed House administrator, as soon as they walked in the house and got the all-clear for Henry to attend. Agnes was adamant that, if possible, he should start tomorrow.

"So," Tom said, as the four of them sat down to play Parcheesi, "Henry? How would you feel about going to school tomorrow?"

Henry placed his four blue Parcheesi pieces in their nest and thought this over. "Fine. If you and Agnes and Rose will walk me over."

"I can," Tom said. "I was planning to, as a matter of fact. And I'm sure Agnes will. But Rose has to work tomorrow."

"Actually, I don't," Rose said, looking up at him and smiling. "I have tomorrow off."

Tom's heart did a double backflip. The promise of the ages was in that smile.

"I'm sorry, Henry," Agnes said immediately, "but I have to be somewhere tomorrow."

"Where?" Tom asked in surprise.

"Somewhere," Agnes said firmly. "And I have to be there early."

Monday morning, Henry, dressed in his college T-shirt and blue jeans, wearing his Nikes and carrying his brand-new soccer ball, woke Tom up at six forty-five, announcing he was ready to go to school.

Tom, jerked out of a sweet, charged dream involving Rose Callahan, tried hard to refocus himself on the here and now. "It's a bit early, isn't it? School doesn't start until eight thirty."

"Oh." Henry thought for a few seconds, then brightened again. "You wanna go play soccer until then?"

Tom sat up. So *this* was parenting. "Maybe I should take a shower and then we could have some breakfast?"

"I already ate. Cheerios and orange juice. My mawmaw always says if you don't eat a good breakfast before you go to school, you won't learn as much." Henry delivered this wisdom in a singsong voice, obviously repeating something that had been said to him on a regular basis. Then, very softly, with no warning, "I miss my mawmaw. I don't understand why they had to go help other people instead of staying home with me."

"Oh, Henry," Tom said, holding out his arms. He had no answer for that one. People did what they did.

Henry hesitated, then stepped forward. Tom hugged him, soccer ball and all. "I don't know why," he said into Henry's cloud of hair. "All I know is that I'm very, very glad to have you here."

Henry stood there for a full moment, not moving, not responding at all. Then he stepped back. "Can I have some more Cheerios?" he asked, almost happy again.

Rose left her cottage at ten till eight to walk to the Putnams'. She was dressed in a new white T-shirt, her best skirt, a swoop-hemmed, rusty red cotton number bought on extreme sale from Sundance, and her cowboy boots, bought years ago in Austin. She had ironed the skirt and polished the boots, as this was a special day. She and Tom were to walk Henry to school, then walk back to the Putnam house and—Rose felt pretty sure this would happen—have sex for the first time.

As Rose headed down Farmhouse Lane, it came to her that she felt more as though she were *going* home rather than *leaving* home. Evidently, when she wasn't paying attention, "home" had stopped being the cottage and started being the Putnams'. She reached the end of Farmhouse Lane, crossed the road, entered the campus proper, waved and nodded and chatted her way along.

This is like living in a village, Rose thought. Or at least like living in a village the way she'd always imagined it; a place where people had no choice but to know one another, where you couldn't go anywhere without having chats about the weather or people's children or how insufferable skateboarders were. Would such serial sociability feel suffocating after a while? Perhaps. But she, conditioned to be anchored to a place by employment, would have drifted away long before that happened. Karma was karma.

Still, when Rose rang the doorbell and Tom opened the door and took her into his arms and Henry danced around and shouted, "Rose is here," and Agnes called out, "Morning, Rose," from the kitchen, Rose felt something dangerously close to heartbreak at the thought of the three Putnam house resident stilled, captured, and framed on some faraway bedroom wall.

"Rose," Henry said, "you got dressed up!"

"I did," she said, leaning over Tom's arms, which still encircled her. "It's a big occasion, so I put on my big-occasion outfit."

Tom smiled down at her, and suddenly—whether from insight or fear—Rose's vision of the two of them zoomed out to her usual, comfortable no-nonsense perspective. She'd known happy times before she'd come here, and she would know happy times again after she left. The thing to remember was that, when dealing with her own heart or someone else's, her reach really must be kept in line with her grasp.

A new firmness enveloped her; Rose felt almost, but not quite, calm. She was what she was; honest, forthright, caring, just not, in the end, someone who allowed herself to become *involved*.

Rose stepped back from Tom's arms, turned to Henry, and offered her hand. "You think Agnes has any coffee left?"

Tom gave her a look, as though he'd heard her thoughts. But surely, if he had, it was all to the good? It would be a terrible mistake for this lovely, kind man to imagine that she, Rose Callahan, could be part of his future.

*   *   *

The three of them crossed campus hand in hand, Henry in the middle, Rose carrying his lunch in her free hand, Tom carrying the soccer ball in his. "*Every* kid plays soccer at school," Henry had announced with authority.

It was one of those energizing days that come with the change of seasons. Knots of students chorused, "Hi, Professor Putnam! Hi, Rose! Hi, Henry!" as though the three of them had been a fixture on campus forever. In fact, no one seemed startled anymore by the sight of him walking hand in hand with Rose and Henry. Marjory was dead; long live Professor Putnam, and whoever.

Do they even remember her? Tom wondered, giving yet another nod and smile to an assistant professor of chemistry heading past on his way to the Quad. Just as the three of them were crossing the miniature formal boxwood garden attached to the president's house, some internal imp reminded Tom that he and Rose had yet to say things to each other that perhaps, given the circumstances, they needed to say. Or at least, he needed to say his things and see how she responded. The truth was that Rose mostly still showed him only what she showed the rest of the world. Still, there had been enough glimpses behind the curtain to give him hope. And he would gladly settle for hope after so many years of combating despair.

Impulsively he squeezed Henry's hand. "Swing me!" Henry shouted happily. And they did.

Ed House was tucked in behind the president's house at the top of the road that led down to the college lake. As they passed the Dean Dome, Russell stepped outside onto his portico and turned to lock his door. Which was unusual. No one on campus ever locked anything.

"Hi, Professor Jacobs!" Henry called. "I'm going to school."

Russell either didn't hear Henry or didn't want to hear him. He fussed on with his door, still with his back turned, flanked by the urns of geraniums. Those geraniums marked an aberration in Russell's behavior. He'd always been as regular as Old Faithful in replacing them with mums the second week of school. Russell's hair had gotten shaggy as well, Tom noticed. He'd always worn it long, but romantically so, not raggedly.

"Hello, Russ," Tom called out. "Come with us to take Henry to Ed House for his first day."

"I'm going to be in second grade," Henry added. "If you come, you can meet my teacher."

Finally Russell turned to face the three of them. Years ago, when Tom had been playing croquet in Charlottesville, there had been a slight earthquake. He would never forget his reaction. His first thought had been: *This is just wrong.* That was how Russell looked now; as though seeing the three of them together on a Monday morning was just wrong.

Henry broke free, ran up to Russell, took one of his hands, and pulled it gently. "You feel all right?"

Russell snatched his hand back. Then, looking at Rose, he reached into Henry's hair and gave a yank.

"Ouch!" Henry backed up. "You pulled my hair!"

"I did not," Russell said. "My hand got tangled."

Henry wasn't having it. "You did *so* pull! Look, you've got my hair in your hand."

"Sorry." Russell put his hand in his jacket pocket. "I have to go now—I'm late for a meeting."

What is all this about? Tom wondered, as he watched Russell's eyes drift downward until they rested on Henry. "Henry, I—" Russell began, but then broke off abruptly and hurried down the portico steps. "I have to go," he muttered as he strode past Tom and Rose.

Tom watched him go. Was Russell losing it? He felt Rose's hand on his arm. He turned to find her looking up at him.

This, Tom thought, *is it. If I'm going to have a relationship with Rose Callahan, I have to trust not only her, but life. I can either give up right now or go forward, accepting that whatever is going on with this woman might end gloriously or it might end badly.*

A line from an old Doobie Brothers song floated into his head. *You'll always have a chance to give up, so why do it now?*

Why indeed, Tom thought, catching up Rose's hand.

He and Rose walked back together, not hand in hand, but something closer, their world a separate one from everyone else's.

They didn't talk much. Tom wholly gave himself up to the swishing sound of Rose's skirt, the smell of her lavender shampoo, the sight of her boots appearing and disappearing beneath the hem of her skirt.

"You do know, Tom," Rose said, "I won't be here much longer. My job at the Book Store isn't very secure."

Tom was too happy to let the future bother him. He could *think* about it, but he wasn't going to *feel* about it. Not right now, anyway. "Something will work out," he said.

Rose touched his arm, stopped him, made him look at her. "Just so you understand that I'm not a permanent fixture around here."

"Okay." The future could jolly well take care of itself. It always had, after all.

"You need to hear me, Tom. I don't want to make you unhappy."

He laughed. He couldn't help it. "Oh, Rose," he said, putting his hands on her shoulders, "I'm *good* at being unhappy. Please, please just let me enjoy you right here, right now." He watched her eyes as he spoke, trying harder than he'd ever tried before to peer into someone's soul. He thought he saw promise, hope, warmth, caring—all the things he hungered to give and receive.

Rose reached her hand up and touched his cheek. "You are a remarkable person, Tom Putnam."

He liked that she'd said "person" instead of "man." It meant she found him remarkable in ways that really *mattered*. "As are you," he said.

They turned and walked on, in sync, not saying anything until they reached the turn onto Faculty Row. Tom felt all the underutilized parts of himself waking, stretching, springing into action.

Then, "I think we should go to bed," Rose said quietly.

"What?" Tom stopped dead, not quite able to look at her.

"I think we should go to bed," she said again.

Tom took a deep breath. He had no idea whether *that* part of him was ready or even able to spring into action. "Rose," he said, finally daring to look at her, "I haven't had sex with a woman in years."

"So?" she said, looking up at him, her whole face twinkling.

The front doorbell rang while he and Rose were still in bed. Tom—awash in happiness and, yes, triumph—ignored it. Then he remembered it was Henry's first day at school, visions of the boy tumbling off the jungle gym elbowed their way into his head, and he jumped, naked, out of bed.

"I'll just see who that is. I won't be gone a moment."

Rose's skirt poofed before him on the rug like a huge rusty red mushroom. "I think your trousers are in the doorway," she said.

Tom turned to find her raised up on one elbow, smiling at him, her hair spilling across her shoulder in a rush of unmanageable curls. He stopped, mid-hurry, transfixed. "You are so beautiful."

Rose blushed. "No, I'm not. That's just lust talking."

"No, it's not. It's—"

The doorbell rang again. "You better go see who that is," she said. "Better make sure Henry's all right."

"Don't go anywhere."

Rose smiled. "I won't." She caught her breath. "Not for a couple of months, anyway," she added in a voice just loud enough for him to hear.

Tom opened the front door to find a short, round man about Agnes's age, dressed in a suit and tie and holding a briefcase. "I'm Mason Brownlow," he said, beaming a cautious smile up at Tom and sticking out a soft, pudgy hand, "from Picayune, Mississippi. May I come in?"

Tom's first move was to check his fly.

Mr. Brownlow noticed this. "Am I disturbing you?" he asked mildly, his hand still hanging in the air. "The state police said you'd invited me to visit anytime."

"Of course!" Tom grabbed Mr. Brownlow's hand and shook it vigorously. "I'm sorry. I was just . . . just changing."

"Ah, I understand." Mr. Brownlow retrieved his hand. His eyes twinkled. "I am delighted just to lay eyes on you, you know. I always thought Tom Putnam didn't exist. That you were just a name Serafine made up to have something to write on Henry's birth certificate. And now, here you are in the flesh."

"Yes!" Tom gave an awkward little flourish. "Here I am!"

Mr. Brownlow gestured vaguely behind him. "I could certainly come back later, if that would be more convenient. I wanted to have a little talk with you about Henry. As his grandparents' executor and friend, and, I hope, also a friend of Henry's and his late mother's, I felt I needed to come up here and see for myself how Henry's getting on."

"Of course." Tom's mind stampeded through his immediate options. Putting Mr. Brownlow off would only make him think he, Tom, had something to hide. Which he *had*, as Rose was upstairs, but surely that was not something Mr. Brownlow need find out.

"No, no." Tom gestured for Mr. Brownlow to enter. "Come in. Come in. Henry's at school, I'm afraid. Today's his first day. And my mother-in-law, Agnes Tattle, who lives with us, has gone . . . gone shopping. But *I'm* delighted you're here. Delighted to meet you. Delighted you made the trip. And I'm sure Henry will be delighted to see you as well. And I know Agnes will be delighted to meet . . ."

Stop babbling! a voice yelled inside his head. *Start over!*

Tom took a deep breath. "Come in. I'm very glad to meet you."

Mr. Brownlow stepped inside and shut the front door firmly behind him. He stood there beaming, both hands clasping the handle of his briefcase, calmly inspecting Tom and what he could see of Tom's house. Tom turned around and inspected it with him, taking in the piles of junk mail, Henry's Tonka dump truck, the coat tree holding Agnes's thirty-year-old Harris tweed, the dust balls in the corners—their housekeeping efforts never quite made it this far. Yet when he turned back to Mr. Brownlow expecting the worst, the little banker gave a decisive nod. "Let me assure you, Mr. Putnam," he said, in the same cheerful, hopeful tone, "that I am not here hoping to make trouble for you. I'm here only to make sure Henry's all right. He's such a dear boy and there's all this money involved and his grandparents were my dear friends and—" At this point, Mr. Brownlow abruptly broke off to gape at something behind and above Tom's head.

Tom turned around to see Rose, wearing a bedsheet like a ball gown, standing at the top of the stairs.

"Hello," Mr. Brownlow said, not unkindly. "I see I *am* interrupting something."

"I'm—I'm so sorry," Rose said, speaking in a rush. "I heard the door close. I'm Rose Callahan. I—I do community-building work for the college bookstore and run the coffee bar."

Tom whirled back to Mr. Brownlow and was shocked to see he was still smiling. His good manners evidently ran deep. "I'm Mason Brownlow from Picayune, Mississippi. You said you do community building for the college bookstore?"

Tom turned back to Rose. It was worse than watching a tennis match. "At least for now," she said. "The Book Store serves everyone around here."

"Interesting," Mr. Brownlow said. "A good bookstore is so vital to a community's life of the mind, don't you think, Mr. Putnam?"

"I do," Tom said. With conviction.

Mr. Brownlow went back to Rose. "And are you a friend of Henry's as well as Mr. Putnam's?"

"Oh yes!" Rose almost let her ball gown slip in her enthusiasm. "Henry's great. We play soccer together."

"Indeed," said Mr. Brownlow. "Well then, perhaps you'd like to join us.

I've come to check up on things here for my own satisfaction. But let me assure you right from the start that any real friend of Henry's is a friend of mine."

"Oh, lovely," Rose said. "I feel exactly the same way."

"Would you like to see the rest of the house?" Tom asked. "I'm afraid we're not very neat."

"Neither am I," said Mr. Brownlow. "At least not since my wife died ten years ago. My housekeeper says the hardest part of her job is picking up after me."

"Oh," Tom said. The two of them still stood in the foyer. Rose had disappeared from view, presumably to put on something other than her bed-sheet.

There was a slight pause. "Might I trouble you for a glass of water?" Mr. Brownlow asked.

"Of course," Tom said. "Where would you like to sit?"

Mr. Brownlow thought about this. "Do you have a kitchen table?"

"Yes."

"Well then, let's sit there. The kitchen is the heart of a house, don't you agree?"

Tom flashed back to his parents' kitchen table thirty years ago, to Eddie and Louise and their friends plotting the liberalization of all New England over the remains of supper. "I do!" he said, relaxing slightly, relieved that Mr. Brownlow was not a parlor kind of guy. He was also relieved he'd thought to clear the cereal bowls away this morning and put them in the dishwasher. "This way," he said, leading Mr. Brownlow down the hall toward the back of the house.

The pudgy little banker trotted behind him, his leather-soled shoes tap-tapping along the hardwood floor. *This whole place needs painting,* Tom thought, looking around him. At least there were no dust balls lurking in the corners once they left the foyer. He had vacuumed just yesterday, and Agnes had trailed behind him with a dust mop.

"What a nice kitchen," Mr. Brownlow said as they entered the sunny room. He made a beeline for the refrigerator and peered at a drawing Henry had done showing himself, Rose, Agnes, and Tom dancing around a giant soccer ball. "Did Henry do this?"

"Yes," Tom said. "He really likes to draw."

"And has fallen in love with soccer, I see." Mr. Brownlow turned and smiled at Tom.

"Yes," Tom said. "He insisted on taking his soccer ball to school with him this morning."

"And where is he in school?"

"We've just enrolled him in second grade in the campus school, which has an excellent reputation."

"I see." Mr. Brownlow blinked his bright little eyes. "And who's we?"

Tom stared. Who *was* we? "Why, myself and Agnes—my late wife's mother—and, and Rose," he added, just as she entered the room reclad in her red skirt, T-shirt, and cowboy boots.

"Rose what?" she asked.

Mr. Brownlow spoke up. "Tom was just telling me that you were part of the team that enrolled Henry in school this morning."

"Yes." Rose walked over to Tom and took his hand. "I was."

"You two, I take it, are a couple?" Mr. Brownlow inquired affably.

"Yes," said Tom firmly.

Rose said nothing.

"And how long has your wife been dead, Mr. Putnam? If I may ask?"

Tom felt the walls closing in on him. "She was killed in a car wreck three days before Henry got here."

Mr. Brownlow considered this information, his face unreadable. "I see. Interesting. Perhaps I might trouble you for that glass of water now."

Just at that moment the back door banged open and Agnes backed into the kitchen carrying several recyclable bags of groceries. "Yoo-hoo! I brought smoked turkey for lunch. Is it all clear in here?"

"No," Tom said. "It's not, actually."

Agnes spun around to find Tom, Rose, and Mr. Brownlow all staring at her. "Ooops," she said, grinning puckishly. "What have I walked in on *this* time?"

For some reason Mr. Brownlow appeared charmed by this. He put down his briefcase and bustled forward. "Let me help you with those, please." He reached for Agnes's bags.

Agnes backed away from him. "Who are you?"

The little banker beamed. "Mason Brownlow, from Picayune, Missis-sippi. Come to check up on Henry."

Agnes dropped her groceries. "Holy Mother of God," she said, staring at the little man. "Why the hell am I trying to quit smoking?"

*   *   *

Russell found Luellen Mars, chair of the Biology Department, in her base-ment lab, busily directing a half-dozen students in the pursuit of some truth that could be demonstrated in a petri dish. *I should have been a lab technician,* Russell thought, as he stood in the doorway and watched the students recon-structing an experiment that was guaranteed to turn out the same way every time. *Or perhaps a line worker, putting the same part in the same place of the same thing, all day every day. Anything with a predictable outcome.*

Russell had been arguing with himself about the merits of knowing unpredictable outcomes ever since he'd pulled the hair out of Henry's head that morning. A line from an old hippie-dippie Youngbloods song kept run-ning through his head, something about holding the key to love and fear in your trembling hand.

He'd always hated that song for its sappy, one-size-fits-all inclusivity, its call to "try to love one another right now."

Today, however, that business about holding the key to love and fear in your trembling hand could not have been more appropriate, for in his own trembling hand were two envelopes containing Henry's hair and some of his own. This was it. He had to decide right now: Did he or did he not want to know whether he was Henry's biological father?

As long as the question had remained a hypothetical one, Russell had pretty much been all for knowing. Paternity had seemed somehow a picture-perfect completion of all that he'd wanted himself to be. It would be so . . . so *Jeffersonian* to have fathered a beautiful little person of color with blue eyes. But then this morning, with one impulsive yank, he'd replaced a theoretical argu-ment with a concrete one. Russell, along with the rest of the world, watched *CSI* and so knew that hair follicles contain DNA and DNA proves paternity. Ambivalence had immediately gripped him like a pair of giant pliers. He'd stood looking down at Henry—at that beautiful little boy, properly outraged at having his hair pulled out by the roots—and felt for the first time in living memory that someone else's well-being might be more important than his own.

It had been an awkward—no, an *awful*—moment; Russell hadn't had the slightest idea what to do next. He'd scraped for acceptance, indeed for love, for so many decades, that this onslaught of selflessness incapacitated him. His first impulse had been to go back inside the Dean Dome, find those bottles of Wild Turkey, and down half of one in a single mindless gulp. The only thing that had stopped him was the thought that Henry deserved better of him, whether or not he was his father. Henry deserved better of everyone.

"Russell? May I help you?"

Luellen Mars had spotted him and begun walking toward him. This was it: Did he or did he not want to know?

Time slowed. Russell watched Luellen swim toward him leisurely and thought—God help him—of his own nonentity of a father. Oh, how much he'd wanted *not* to be that man, patiently dealing with his alcoholic wife, doing what he could to make life easier for his loser of a child, cheerfully going every day to his dead-end job. "Son," his father had said to him over and over and *over*, "you've got to do the best you can with the hand you're dealt." Standing there in the doorway of the biology lab, Russell saw in a flash that his whole adult life had been one massive effort to disprove that statement; he had spent the last fifty years refusing to play the hand he'd been dealt and, instead, pretending he'd been dealt a different one.

"Russell, are you all right?" Luellen asked.

She stood in front of him, a little pinched-faced woman with a bad permanent. Whoever could have guessed that Luellen Mars would be the gatekeeper of his fate? Russell looked down at her and the stakes ratcheted skyward; he didn't want to be just Henry's *biological* father, he wanted to be Henry's *actual* father. He wanted Henry to occupy his life in much the same way he dreamed of Rose occupying it. He wanted—he needed—*somebody* to stage a takeover of his being; someone to force him to fess up, face up, start over, get it *real* this time. In a flash, Russell made his decision: He would have the test, and when it came back proving he was Henry's father, he would demand physical custody of the child. "I'm fine," he said briskly.

"But you were talking to yourself just now," Luellen said, real concern in her voice.

"No, I wasn't. You're imagining things."

Luellen opened her mouth to argue, but something in Russell's face turned argument into concern, and instead she asked again if she could help him.

"Yes, actually you can." Russell handed her the envelope. "There's hair in here from two different people. Could you run whatever tests are needed to determine whether they come from people who are biologically related?"

Luellen opened the envelope, fished around, and came up with several long, straight silver hairs and several other long, curly brown hairs. "Russell," she said, obviously worried, "what are you up to?"

"The pursuit of truth. How long before you can do the test?"

"*I* can't do the test. I'll have to send it to a lab. It'll cost a bundle."

"I'll pay. How long?"

Luellen shrugged. "A few days. Unless you want to pay to messenger the hair to the lab and have it expedited?"

"I'll pay." Russell thought again of those bottles of Wild Turkey. He'd been sober for years. Surely he could now have a couple of drinks, to help the time pass? Inside his head, AA Lewis began shouting something, but the sound was muffled and without its customary cautionary power.

Luellen put a hand on his arm. "I have no idea what you're doing, Russell, but are you absolutely one hundred percent sure you want to do it?"

Russell stared at her. What did this woman mean by "one hundred percent sure"? As far as Russell could remember, the last thing he'd been one hundred percent sure of was that he really liked good bourbon.

He turned and left without another word.

*   *   *

Henry came out carrying the soccer ball and walking beside Sam Driskell, the son of a French professor. Tom waved and walked over to the two boys. "Sam and I are best friends," Henry announced. "Can he come over and play soccer?"

And so the invasion of small boys begins, thought Tom. *We're not going to have just Henry thundering around, but Henry's friends as well.*

Today, however, was not a good day. "Not today, I'm afraid," Tom said. "You already have company."

"Who?" Henry was immediately suspicious. "I don't *know* anybody else."

Tom turned and gestured for Mason Brownlow to come forward. "Hello, Henry," Mr. Brownlow said, with a cheerful little bow. "I'm delighted to see you again."

Instantly, a Henry mask replaced Henry's face. *This,* Tom thought, *is what he will look like when he's old if his life hasn't gone well.* "Have you found my mother?" Henry asked, his voice as lifeless as his expression. "Do I have to go back?"

Mr. Brownlow stopped smiling immediately and glanced up at Tom. Tom shook his head: *No, he doesn't know his mother is dead.* "Only if you want to, Henry," Mr. Brownlow said.

"You sure?" Henry's own brand of street smarts was out there, ready to mix it up with Mr. Brownlow or anyone else who might want to move him around again like a piece of furniture.

"I'm sure," Mr. Brownlow said. "I just came up to see how you are doing. And as long as I'm satisfied that you're doing well, I don't see any reason why you can't stay. For a while, anyway."

Tom felt the implied threat. Or was that too strong a word? If you thought about it, the little banker wouldn't be doing his job if he didn't view Henry's current situation with energetic skepticism.

Henry had no desire to pussyfoot politely around. "You didn't come about me," he said mulishly. "You came about the money."

Now it was Mason Brownlow's eyes that were unreadable. Abruptly there was something of steel about the round little man. "I was your grandparents' closest friend, Henry. Surely you understand what that means as far as the money goes."

Surely not? Tom thought. *At slightly under seven years old?*

Sam Driskell shuffled his feet. "Uh, Henry, I better get going," he said in his high-piping seven-year-old voice. "My mom worries if I don't get home or call before much after two thirty."

"I'm sorry about today, Sam," Tom said. "Perhaps you could come home with Henry tomorrow? If it's okay with Mr. Brownlow."

"Of course it's okay," Mr. Brownlow said quickly, back to his old cheerful self.

Sam looked at Henry. "Is it okay with you?"

Tom watched a whole short lifetime of disrupted longings parade through Henry's eyes. "Sure," he said, in his guarded, old-man voice, "if I'm still here."

Agnes cut right through the awkwardness and tension of the walk home from Ed House by stopping abruptly, kneeling down, looking Henry right in the eye, and saying, "See here, Henry. There's two separate legal issues here, and I think you're feeling bad because you're wopsing them up into one. Okay?"

Other parents and children drifted past, the children gawking, the parents determinedly not looking. "Okay," Henry said doubtfully.

"All right, then." Agnes plunged on. "Now, as I'm not only your sort-of grandmother, but your lawyer as well, you need to pay close attention to what I say. The first legal issue is where you are to live; the other is what to do about all that money you have stowed under your bed."

"And the income from the sizable trust your grandparents left you," Mr. Brownlow stuck in, uninvited, back to being the round little man of steel.

To Tom's surprise, Agnes didn't object to the interruption. "That, too," she said.

Henry's thoughts were as easy to read as a Dick and Jane adventure. *Grown-ups do all this talking, and then—poof!—there you are, living somewhere else.*

"Henry," Agnes asked, "you following me here?"

"Yes, ma'am."

"Okay, then. Here's the deal. Tom Putnam is legally your father. His name is on your birth certificate. If you want to live with him, no one can take you away. Not Mr. Brownlow; not anyone."

"Well, I'm not sure it's quite that simple," Mr. Brownlow said mildly. "But if you like living here and you want to stay, that certainly gives us a place to start."

Henry eyed him no less suspiciously. "You used to say things like that about living with my mother. And then you'd take me away again."

Mr. Brownlow looked truly stricken. "Your mother was struggling with an illness, Henry. I couldn't let you go on living with her if she couldn't take care of you, could I?"

Henry was becoming mulish again. "I can take care of myself. Ask Tom and Agnes how I got my own Cheerios this morning."

"He did," Tom felt compelled to add. "And he dressed himself as well."

Agnes shot him a look. "Could we stick to the point at hand, please? Which is legal custody of Henry."

"Of course," Tom said.

"So, Henry," Agnes said, "you understand that while you are here, no one can legally take you away, and that, furthermore, no one *wants* to take you away. Right?" She looked up at the three other grown-ups for confirmation.

"Right," said Tom and Rose in chorus. Mr. Brownlow said nothing. Both Tom and Rose instinctively maneuvered themselves closer to the boy.

Henry looked up from beneath lowering small-boy brows. "So what about the money?"

"As far as the money goes," Agnes said, "just as you are Tom's legal responsibility now, the money is Mr. Brownlow's legal responsibility until you are much older. Which is just fine with Tom and me. However, just because he can make decisions about the money does *not* mean he can make decisions about where you live."

Henry looked over at Mr. Brownlow. "Is that for real?"

"Well," Mr. Brownlow said. "It *is* true, Henry, that where you live is a completely different issue from the money. Ms. Tattle and I may come to have different views about where you should live, but she's right that when it comes to your grandparents' money, it's my legal and moral responsibility to see that it does the most good for you that it possibly can. Within the terms they specified, that is."

"And," Agnes cut in, "it's my job as your personal legal representative, Henry, to keep an eye on every move Mr. Brownlow makes to be sure he doesn't cheat you out of one single penny that's rightfully yours once you grow up."

There was a collective intake of breath. Were battle lines being drawn?

But Mr. Brownlow appeared to be regarding Agnes with something very close to admiration. The battle, if joined, was going to be conducted civilly. On his part, at least. "Well, now," he said, extending his hand. "It seems we all know where we stand. So shall we put our heads together and see what we can work out that is in Henry's best interests?"

Agnes hesitated, then held out her hand. Agnes Tattle, lawyer and fierce champion of the bullied and the oppressed, was on the case.

As for Henry, he'd marched over to Rose, collected her hand; turned to Tom, collected his. And there they were again, the three of them, a sort of family setting off for home before all the world and Mason Brownlow.

chapter 18

That afternoon, Tom had just gotten back to his office after teaching his three-fifteen section of RemWrite when someone knocked on his door. It wasn't Russ, Tom was sure of that. Russ, even in his current state, would have opened the door and walked in. Besides, there really was no need to knock, as the door was partially open.

The knock came again. "Come in," Tom called.

The door opened slowly and Iris Benson's red head appeared. "I'm sorry to bother you," she said with uncharacteristic politeness, "but do you have a moment?"

"Iris!" Tom shot out of his chair, took her hand, and drew her into his office. "How the hell are you? I've been worried about you."

Iris wore tailored black slacks, black flats, and a green sweater—clothes that almost any woman on campus might have been seen in. "I guess I owe you an apology," she said.

"You do?" Tom smiled. If Iris Benson owed him one apology, she owed him a thousand.

"Yes. For causing you trouble last Friday at Russell's. When . . . when I fainted."

"Oh, don't worry about that." Tom had never realized before what a tiny person Iris was. She couldn't be any more than five foot two or three at the most. It must have been all the bombast that had made her seem taller. For the bombast, he realized, was no longer there. "Iris," he said, gently, "what's going on?"

"May I sit down?"

"Of course." He indicated a chair.

Iris sat, her spine straight as a steel rod, her ankles crossed, her hands folded in her lap. The Iris Tom had known and been wary of for years was simply gone.

He sat down in his desk chair and swiveled around to face her.

"Could we close the door again?" Iris whispered. "Please?"

"Certainly." Tom hopped up, closed the door, and sat down again. "What's up?"

On the rare times Tom's mother had been extremely upset, she'd had a way of clasping her hands together so tightly that the tips of her fingers turned pink, then white. Iris's fingertips, Tom noticed, had already progressed to white. "I've been in a kind of a . . . a resting place over the weekend," she said, not looking at him.

Oh my. "Are you all right?"

"I'm okay, thank you," she said quite primly. Then, as though an invisible hand had plucked out the steel support, Iris slumped in her chair. "It was a treatment place," she whispered.

"Pardon?"

"A treatment place." Iris looked up at him with a welcome trace of her old bravura. "For alcoholism, Tom. I'm a drunk. Making a fool of myself in front of you was the last straw. I realized, lying there in the emergency room, that you were the only person at the college I could possibly call a real friend. That morning, I'd already puked all over the Book Store, but falling down in front of you was even harder to think about than that. So for the last two days, I've been getting some help in trying to imagine life without alcohol." She stopped and sat there looking at him with the great lost eyes of motherless Bambi.

Tom's brain had gotten stuck at "puke." "You vomited all over the Book Store?"

"Yes." Iris was looking at him rather as Henry had looked at Mr. Brownlow when he'd been expecting the worst. "I was drunk at nine o'clock in the morning. Russell was there, and he took me to his house. That's why I was at the Dean Dome when you showed up."

Last Friday seemed far, far in the past. Trying to remember it felt like trying to remember his eighth birthday party. "I see."

Iris's next words came out in a rush. "I'm not sure I can stay sober. It's hard being back at this place. Everybody looks at me so strangely. The dean said I can hang out in a day treatment thingee in town between classes, but that closes at six. There are AA meetings, which are dreadful, but at least they keep me from drinking while I'm in one. But the thing is, I'm scared to go home. There are bottles everywhere and lots of Valium. And I can't have either one."

Tom knew nothing about alcoholism or day treatment thingees, but he did know about mental hospitals. Marjory had always been at her most paranoid just after coming home from one. It had taken a catapult to get her out of the house. She'd been so sure everyone had nothing better to do than say mean things about her. And here was Iris, in what must be a similarly terrible muddle.

Tom's mother had been a master of irrational kindness. When Louise Putnam had been concerned about someone, she'd always offered companionable food. "Why don't you come home to dinner, Iris? We've got company already, so you won't have to talk much. And Rose will be there. And Henry. It would give you a safe place to be around people for a while. Sort of get used to it again, you know, without—without anything," he finished lamely.

Iris reached out and grabbed Tom's hand in both of hers. For a horrible moment, he thought she was going to kiss it, but she settled for squeezing it unpleasantly hard. Her great Bambi eyes filled with tears.

"Thank you," she whispered. "Thank you, so *much*."

*   *   *

During her Charlottesville period, most people had taken Agnes Tattle for an extrovert, because she'd led such a busy social life. Agnes, however, had known better. Years ago, she'd read somewhere that the difference between an introvert and an extrovert was not what one does with one's energy, but how one recharges. Extroverts get energy from being around people; introverts, from being alone. Agnes knew she was definitely a social being (look at all the nonprofit boards she'd been on—nonstop yakking there), but she most definitely recharged alone. This made her, as she liked to put it, a human oxymoron: a social introvert.

Her son-in-law, alone of all the people who'd passed through her life, had gotten this immediately, even before he'd married Marjory. And so today, as soon as he'd come back from the office, Tom (whom Agnes classified as another oddball, a shy extrovert) had obligingly herded Iris (what was *she* doing here?) et al into the living room so as to give his mother-in-law her space.

The price of an hour of solitude was cooking dinner—pork chops, sweet potatoes, green beans, bakery rolls, a final flush of tomatoes from a neighbor's garden. Dessert would be apple dumplings from the same bakery and vanilla ice cream. Agnes had planned on serving wine with dinner, but Tom had quietly put the kibosh on that, so she would offer iced tea instead.

It took some doing to squeeze six places around the kitchen table. Agnes had briefly considered moving the meal into the dining room, but dinners there tended to be weird, and there was enough weirdness floating around already. Iris Benson, for example, looked and moved like a wooden marionette mistakenly costumed in some other marionette's clothes. (What *were* those meek little flats about?)

Shortly after 7:00 P.M., Agnes removed her apron and went into the living room to announce that dinner was served. Everyone greeted this news enthusiastically except for Iris and Henry. Iris said nothing; Henry immediately bolted out of the room and thundered up the stairs. No matter—the boy was *not* one to miss a meal. And sure enough, just as Agnes finished seating everyone, Henry reappeared carrying the blue lunch box with the dinosaurs that, as far as Agnes knew, still contained the demi-million. "Here," he said, handing the lunch box to Mr. Brownlow. "This is all that money my mother gave to me, and I don't want it. I really, really, really want to stay *here*."

Mr. Brownlow hesitated before taking the lunch box, looking first at Tom, then at her.

Agnes had nothing to say about the matter. In her experience, money had always come with strings attached, and Henry—at least in her opinion—dragged enough strings around already.

"Thank you." Mr. Brownlow took the lunch box, leaned down, and tucked it under his chair. *Oh well,* thought Agnes, remembering her very rich in-laws, *sic transit pecunia*. The entire Tattle family (except for Joe, of course) had been shanghaied by their pots of money into leading very dull lives. They never did anything that wasn't expensive.

"You're welcome," Henry said. "My mawmaw and pawpaw would rather help lots of people with that money than just me. They liked helping other people better than anything."

*   *   *

"Tell me about the college Book Store," Mr. Brownlow said to Tom, apropos of nothing.

He might as well have fired a starter pistol. Tom was off and running, happy to be talking about something that couldn't possibly lead Mr. Brownlow to think him an unsuitable parent. "The Book Store is the soul of the college and the community, in a lot of ways," he said, waving his fork for emphasis, slinging mashed potatoes dangerously close to Henry's arm. "It's where everyone comes together comfortably. And Rose was hired just this year, as a kind of community organizer. Higher education is increasingly viewed as a business—its worth to students more and more tied to the dollars they can earn postgraduation—which may be important, but it's not *all* that's important . . ."

*   *   *

As she listened to Tom go on and on about the Book Store, it occurred to Agnes that the college's people—students, faculty, and staff—did indeed have a group soul that was threatened with extinction by the college's bottom line. Agnes dismissed the idea that Mr. Brownlow's questions were motivated by idle curiosity. If Mason Brownlow indulged in idle *anything*, Agnes thought, then she was a monkey's aunt. But for the life of her, she couldn't figure out why he was so curious about something that had nothing to do with why he was here.

Patience, patience, Agnes told herself. *She who waits longest learns most.*

Iris Benson sprang to life when dessert was served, inhaling her apple turnover as though it were so much clear mountain air. Seeing this, Rose, who Agnes suspected might be almost as compulsively kindhearted as her son-in-law, stealthily switched her own full dessert plate for Iris's empty one.

As Iris kept right on eating without so much as a nod of thanks, Agnes was pretty certain she wasn't aware the switch had taken place.

*   *   *

Iris Benson, looking as insubstantial as a shadow, sat perched atop the ever-present stack of junk mail on the foyer bench. Rose, who had been on her way to the living room, stopped, moved a stack of *The New York Review of Books* onto the floor and sat down beside her. After a moment, without saying a word, she took Iris's hand.

They sat there, once again, face-to-face with the grandfather clock while the minute hand moved three clicks through time. Finally Iris said, "I am so scared," and took back her hand.

Rose kept her eyes on the clock. "Of what?"

"Of everything."

"Everything?"

Iris shrugged without spirit. "Of being alone, of being with other people, of working, of not working, of going home, of having nowhere else to go other than home where I'm *wanted*."

Rose was her mother's daughter, cognizant since childhood that sometimes people needed temporary shelter. "You can stay with me at the cottage," she said. "My couch is quite comfortable. And you'd be most welcome."

"Really?"

"Really." Rose stealthily crossed her fingers to ward off the bad karma of a well-meant fib.

Iris was no fool. "You don't mean that. You're just saying that."

The needier they are, the more they resist, Mavis had always maintained. "Iris, I'm happy to have you if you'd like to come." Which was more or less true, although probably mostly less.

Iris began fussing with an unopened envelope, plucked from the pile beneath her. "I guess I don't have any place else to go," she said almost crossly.

This woman has no idea how to take help, Rose thought. *Fishing around for help is the best she can manage.* "Would you like to tell me what's going on?"

"No." Iris gave a truculent toss of her red hair. Then she sagged again. "Yes."

She fell silent. Rose watched her chew on a nub of a fingernail and waited.

"I'm a drunk," Iris muttered. "I've been in a drunk place all weekend."

For years, Rose had watched and listened as stricken, terrified people had poured out their alcoholic confessions to Mavis. Her mother's reaction had been uniformly practical. *The last thing a drunk trying to stay sober needs is sympathy,* she'd always said. *What they need is practical help.*

Rose reached for Iris's hand. "Am I right in assuming that you have liquor bottles stashed all over your house?"

"God, yes, as well as about a ton of Valium and oxycodone. Which I'm not allowed to take anymore either."

"What were you taking all that medication for?"

Iris shrugged again. "Life."

Ah yes! Life. There was that to be gotten through. "So how long have you been clean and sober?"

"I don't know. What day is it?"

"Monday."

Iris counted it out on her fingers. "Two and a half days," she said.

"Are you having withdrawal symptoms?"

Iris snorted. "You mean other than feeling cracked as the Liberty Bell? No. I'm not seeing purple elephants or anything. The doctors said I'm not in any medical danger. You know, of seizures or anything."

"That's good," Rose said. "So how's this for a plan? You come home with me tonight. Tomorrow morning, we'll get up early, run out to your house, round up all the bottles of alcohol and pills, and take them to the dump." Rose took a deep breath. "And while we're out there, you can pack enough stuff to stay at my house until you feel up to going home. How does that sound?"

Iris stared at her. "You'd do that, for *me?*"

"Of course."

A light snapped on in Iris's eyes. "You'd do that for *anybody,* wouldn't you, Rose?"

Would she? Surely not. "No, not for just anybody. At least, I don't think so."

Another thought struck Iris. "I have animals."

"You do?"

"Yes, six dogs."

Rose had visions of dehydrated animals lying prone beside empty water bowls. "Oh, goodness! Perhaps we better go out to your house tonight."

"They're all right. I called my down-the-hill neighbor's boy on Saturday, and he's been taking care of them." Iris looked particularly bleak. "They like him a lot better than they like me."

"Oh, I don't believe that," Rose said automatically. She, who'd never had so much as a housecat.

"Oh, yes, you do," Iris said darkly. "Animals are not stupid."

*   *   *

Tom and Henry were upstairs getting Henry ready for bed. It seemed to Agnes this was the natural time for Mr. Brownlow to leave as well. But no, he asked for an apron and insisted on helping her wash up. So here they were, hip to hip; she washing, he rinsing.

She was, Agnes decided, *not* going to make small talk with Mason Brownlow. There was, after all, nothing small between them to talk about; there was only Henry. As they progressed through the pile of dishes, she was both pleased and not pleased to note that Mr. Brownlow wasn't saying anything either. But then all the dishes had been washed and here they still were with nothing to say. What on earth was the man *thinking*?

"What I'd like is to table all discussion of Henry's living situation for the moment and talk about Henry's money," Mr. Brownlow said, as though answering her unasked question.

Game on! "Okay," Agnes said cautiously. She had shepherded too many women through too many ugly, big-money divorces to have much faith in the financial generosity of human beings. Conversations about money, in her experience, had always been, and so would always be, rancorous.

Mason Brownlow was making quite a lot of work out of drying his hands. "The Després' will is a bit ambiguous."

Of course it was. Every will was ambiguous if you wanted it to be.

"There's a *lot* of money involved," Mr. Brownlow said.

Agnes crossed her arms. "How much?"

Mr. Brownlow carefully folded his damp hand towel and put it down in a puddle on the counter. "Henry's chunk is around twenty-five million, all but that five hundred thousand in cash held in trust."

"Held in trust, how?"

Mr. Brownlow chose his words carefully. "Well, there are strings, you see."

Agnes hadn't engaged in a good legal joust in years. *What the hell?* "Would you like a Scotch?" she asked.

Mr. Brownlow twinkled. "I'd rather have bourbon, if you've got it."

*   *   *

It was well past midnight. A low murmur from below announced to Tom that Agnes and Mr. Brownlow were still talking in the kitchen while he lay in his bed, wide awake and full of yearning.

For Rose, of course. And not for sex with Rose as much as for Rose herself, the solid feel of her both in his arms and in his life. It felt unnatural to lie in his bed without her, even though he'd only lain *with* her for a little over an hour.

So here it was, the witching hour, when the human heart is at its most defenseless. And there it was, the truth: No matter how illogical and inconvenient his timing might be, he was full-blown in love with Rose Callahan. And he would never sleep again until he knew whether or not she was in love with him.

Tom threw back the covers and got up.

Marjory's frilly dresses still hung in the closet; her shoes crowded his on the floor. "Listen," he said softly, "I know you did the best you could. And so did I. And I'm sorry that I couldn't figure out how to make our life together better, but . . ."

His final "but" hung in the air. But what? But everything that had happened since Marjory had sailed off Route 29. Rose and then Henry and all they'd brought with them, everything that had colluded over the last two weeks to flood his own being with . . . with *life!*

Tom touched one of Marjory's dresses, the fussy sprigged number she'd worn that afternoon in the Book Store when she'd so pleasantly shocked him by inviting Rose Callahan to dinner. Now that he thought about it, Marjory was the one who'd set everything in motion. If Rose hadn't shown up that Friday night for supper he never would have invited her to join them at McDonald's; she and Henry might have never become friends; he and she would probably never have had a relationship outside the Book Store; most likely, his long-cramped soul would never have found the courage to fly free again.

"Thank you," he said to Marjory. Not, surely, for dying—Tom could not bring himself to believe he was grateful to her for that—but rather for that one moment in the Book Store when she had dared to live more completely than either of them had in a long time.

Suddenly Tom Putnam was a man in a great hurry.

*   *   *

Iris was finally asleep, curled up on the couch around a pillow like a baby around a binky.

Rose got up from the chair where she'd been keeping vigil and went into the kitchen to check the time. Ray's clock sat in its place on the pie safe, shrouded under a quilt. Iris had complained about its ticking. "That sound is making me crazy!" she'd said.

Crazier, Rose had added to herself.

Bang! Bang! Bang! went the clock as soon as Rose liberated it. *Tempus fugit-ed*, as it always did, twelve forty-eight heading lickety-split for twelve forty-nine. Rose had set her bedside alarm for six thirty. This meant there were less than six hours to go before it was time to wake Iris up, yet Rose still didn't feel sleepy. Instead she felt a strange, precarious, tilting sensation that she might or might not want to know the cause of.

Perhaps, if she just waited awhile, it would go away.

Moonlight flooded the kitchen linoleum, calling to her to—to what? Rose went over to the window, opened it, and stuck her head out. The last of the summer insects sawed away; an owl hooted, a whippoorwill answered. The moon, a huge, round, mottled silver plate, floated above her in its vast sky, showering earthbound humans with mad and wondrous possibilities, theirs for the risking.

Risk. That was it! In a flash Rose understood: Risk for her involved staying put, not moving on. She wasn't the fearless maverick she'd always thought she was; instead, she was just another scaredy-cat. Perhaps, deep down, she didn't feel anyone would *want* her around long-term. Except, of course,

Mavis. But then Mavis was her mother, not some regular person she'd happened to bump into like Henry or Mr. Pitts or Agnes, or—or Tom Putnam.

"I love you, Tom Putnam," she said into the night, trying out the words.

"What?" a man's voice said.

Rose immediately pulled her head back in the window and slammed it shut. Feeling a desperate need to clutch, she snatched a cookbook from the shelves below the window and clutched that. She felt dizzy with fear, the way she'd felt in her second Shakespeare class, only more so; not because she didn't know who was out there, but because she did.

Tom Putnam peered at her from the other side of the window, dressed in jeans and a pajama top. His almost handsome, overwhelmingly dear face hung there, separated from her by a pane of glass.

"Open the window," he mouthed, flapping his hands upward to sign what he meant.

Rose clutched the cookbook harder. The question came to her like a gift: WWMD? *What would Mavis do?*

Mavis would open the window, of course, reasoning that opening a window meant nothing more than opening a window. Mavis did not carry actions far into the future, did not turn simple decisions into complicated ones she might never have to face. Mavis would remind her daughter that just because she might love Tom Putnam, it did not automatically mean that she had to stay with him forever. It didn't even mean that Tom Putnam loved her back.

Oh dear. There it was. Her Big Fear, revealed at last: *I'm afraid that, I, Rose Callahan, am not truly lovable.*

Tom flapped his hands again.

Rose put down her cookbook, leaned forward, opened the window, picked up her cookbook again, and clutched it to her chest like a shield.

Tom Putnam, Romeo in a pajama top, wasted no time. "Did you just say you loved me?"

*   *   *

Agnes and Mr. Brownlow were seated directly across from each other at the kitchen table. Mr. Brownlow's briefcase sat beside his chair; Agnes's reticule hung from the back of hers. "I have an idea," Mr. Brownlow said.

"Lay it on me," Agnes said.

Surprisingly, Mr. Brownlow responded by holding up his Old Fashioned glass of bourbon and branch with no ice (a good southern gentleman, at least when it came to his drinking habits). "To Henry's happiness and well-being," he said.

Well, there was certainly no harm in drinking to *that*. "To Henry's health and well-being," Agnes echoed, raising her own glass of iceless Scotch.

They each downed a healthy swig and put down their glasses.

Mr. Brownlow looked around him appraisingly, as though whatever he saw in the Putnam kitchen could have real weight in his decision to say whatever it was he wanted to say. Agnes followed his eyes with her own, passing over Marjory's calendar, Henry's Harry Potter lunch box (waiting on the kitchen counter to be filled), a half-finished *Times* crossword abandoned by the toaster (which obviously had not been crumbed in several days), Tom's ancient and slightly muddy galoshes by the kitchen door, the well-worn deck of cards on the little table under the phone. As far as Agnes could tell, there was nothing to see except the unconscious litter of daily life. Nothing in the room was up-to-date (except Henry's lunch box); the floors and counters were respectably, but not spit-and-polish, clean. All in all, it was the kitchen of people who liked to eat together, perhaps enjoyed talking or playing cards around a table, but were massively unconcerned with décor.

Did it look like a good place for a smart six-year-old to grow up feeling safe and secure? It *was* a good place—Agnes was as sure of that as she was of anything in this weird old world—but that didn't mean it *looked* that way to a banker from Picayune, Mississippi.

Mr. Brownlow cleared his throat. "You do know that I really want to do the best I can by Henry, don't you?"

Did she? Agnes thought back to the parade of devastated and angry women whom she had shepherded through their divorces. She had certainly wanted to do her best by them. But that didn't mean that was what she'd done. How could this round little man really know how much—as suddenly and unexpectedly as they'd come together—Henry and Tom and Rose meant to one another? Separately, they would each be fine in the faltering, limited way lots of people are fine. But together, they had a chance to fly. "Mr. Brownlow," she said, "all I can say is that you have the power to do great harm by trying to do what's right. I'm old enough, experienced enough, and have been through enough grief to know that it's rare for life to serve anyone as well as it's served Henry Putnam by washing him up here. I'm asking you to trust me on that."

Mr. Brownlow held his bourbon up to the light and squinted at it. "I just can't," he said. "Not quite. Not yet. I'm sorry, but that's the way it is."

Agnes felt uncharacteristically—what? Helpless? Surely this round little man had lived long enough to know that the greatest things in life just happened? And that more often than not, people broke rather than fixed. "The last thing Henry needs is more yanking," she said. "He's safe here; he's loved. What else could you possibly want for him?"

Mr. Brownlow chose not to answer. Instead, eyes still on his bourbon, he asked, "You done any nonprofit work in the state of Virginia?"

Agnes gave a huff of annoyance. "Of course." What did that have to do with anything?

Mr. Brownlow put down his bourbon, leaned over, picked up his briefcase, placed it on the table, lifted its hinged lid, and almost completely disappeared behind it.

It occurred to Agnes she was beginning to like this little man, which was odd since he was still possibly—*probably*—the enemy, as far as Henry was concerned.

Mr. Brownlow came out from behind his briefcase and handed a folder across to her.

"What's this?"

"It's a folder containing the Després' will and the terms of the trust they set up for Henry. What I'd like is for you, as Henry's lawyer, to read it while I sit here and drink this excellent bourbon and do a little thinking."

Well! Agnes thought. And got no further. Well, *what?*

She opened the folder and began to read.

*   *   *

Russell had another slug of Wild Turkey, then hunkered down at his kitchen table to contemplate the bottle's lovely label with its wild bird just taking off. It felt so good to be on a break from total sobriety, to let off some steam, to release some of the pressure that had been building, building, building—now, it seemed to Russell with a goodly dram of bourbon swimming around his veins—since he'd had his last drink years ago. Goddamn Tom Putnam with his sly attempts to co-opt Rose and Henry! Goddamn AA Lewis with his pious patience! Goddamn his students! Goddamn his job! Goddamn the college! Goddamn his parents! Goddamn everyone in the whole world except Henry and Rose Callahan!

Rose! What a wondrous creature she was. Imagine being the child of a bartender and just *telling* that to people. Where did she get the courage? He could never in a thousand years of sobriety and AA meetings develop enough honesty to puncture other people's assumptions about his past. Except, maybe, for Rose. He might, someday, be able to tell her who he really was, where he actually came from. She alone (except for Tom, who no longer counted) appeared to like him best when he talked about ideas or literature or his work. He'd even begun having ideas again, just to have something new to bring up in their conversation. But now rumor had it that Rose was leaving—resigning her job because the administration had a cash register for a brain.

Russell glanced at his watch—a Roven Dino he'd bought himself for Christmas two years ago. It announced the time to be one fifteen on Tuesday morning. There might only be hours left to get through before he'd be able to prove that he, not Tom Putnam, was Henry's father. Which would mean that, if he wasn't a real southern gentleman, he was, at least, a real *something*. He would demand custody of the boy, take him shopping at Eljo's in Charlottesville, send him to boarding school at Woodberry Forest and then to the university, where he would play soccer and join Kappa Sigma.

Russell took another slug from the Wild Turkey bottle and stood up. All the energy generated by years of pent-up outrage surged through him. All he wanted was what was rightfully his! Then he thought of Rose and immediately sat down again. Rose looked right through all his . . . his *guff* and still seemed to like him all right. When Rose was around, he almost relaxed. And wasn't that what he really, really wanted—to be able to relax in the company of another human being?

*   *   *

They'd had no choice but to go immediately to bed. After all, they were officially (tentatively?) in love; star-crossed, as it were—or perhaps, more accurately, moon-struck; brought together against all reason by dumb luck. This morning, sex had been sweet, perhaps a trifle tentative and polite; tonight, lying together under the enchantment of a full moon, they gave in to full-blown need and loved like Olympians. After all, Tom had climbed in a window and Rose had let him. Now they lay in Rose's bed, his front to her back, as close as two sardines.

"Are we in love?" Tom asked. He felt for the first time at one with the universe, as though he were as much a part of the natural order of things as a rock or a tree.

"Are you asking me if I love you?" Rose said.

"God, yes! Do you? Please say you do!"

It seemed to Tom she stiffened slightly. Had he asked too much, too fast? "Does that mean you love me?" she asked softly

"Heavens to Betsy, yes!" Tom held her even tighter. "Yes, yes, *yes!*"

"Yes, you *think* you love me, or yes, you *know* you love me?"

"Yes, I *know* I love you."

Rose rolled over on her back and looked at him. There was something in her eyes he'd never seen before, something vulnerable. "What does being in love with me feel like?"

What did being in love with Rose *feel* like?

Instantly Shakespeare supplied a couple of possible answers. *I would not wish any companion in the world but you.*

A heart to love, and in that heart, courage to make love known.

That's the trouble, Tom thought, *I've never had words of my own.*

Of course, he'd also never had anything quite so magical to talk about before. Surely he could find the right words now if he just opened his mouth and let them out. "It feels like being really truly alive, and really, truly safe, no matter what. It feels like something wondrous that will stay with me, sustain me, give me peace, and make me happy for the rest of my life."

Rose bit her lip. The vulnerable look intensified. "Really? You *really* feel all that for me?"

Tom smoothed back the hair that framed her face with its usual rebellious frenzy. "Oh, Rose. I really feel all that for you. And a lot more that I don't know how to talk about yet. But please give me time to figure the words out. Please, say you love me."

Tears and wonder shone in Rose's eyes. She reached up and touched his shoulder with just one finger, as though needing to prove he was really there. "Oh, Tom," she said, whispered so softly he could only just hear. "God help me, but I think I must love you. I really think I must."

*   *   *

Mr. Brownlow took himself off to the College Inn shortly after two in the morning. Standing at the open front door and watching the little man trundle down the front walk, Agnes impulsively called out an invitation to come back for breakfast.

Mr. Brownlow turned back. "Thank you. I'd be very pleased to breakfast with you." Then, with a brief wave, he was on his way again.

Back inside, Agnes poured herself one more Scotch, her third, and took it upstairs. On impulse, she poked her head into her son-in-law's room and was surprised and pleased to see his empty bed. Tom's absence could only mean one thing: He'd gone to Rose Callahan. Tom Putnam, man of muddle, had mutated into Tom Putnam, man of action!

Agnes raised her glass in a silent toast.

Henry's door was also open, and she checked on him as a matter of course. The boy slept on his side under the watchful gaze of Albus Dumbledore and the rest of the Hogwarts crowd. His soccer ball sat beside his shoes on the floor, ready to roll with Henry through his second day at school.

Agnes smiled down at the sleeping boy. He would be done a great wrong by the probably well-meaning Mr. Brownlow if he decided to whisk Henry back to Mississippi. Which, despite her legal bluster, Agnes knew might well be possible. For a time, anyway. The estate could simply sue Tom into bankruptcy and give him no choice but to cave.

Would she, Agnes wondered, be willing to bankrupt herself for Henry's sake? Now, there was an interesting question. And, wonder of wonders, the answer wasn't a definite no.

The boy was, in her opinion, adapting to his new surroundings and his new people with remarkably good sense. For the most part, Henry seemed to trust Tom, which was a smart move on his part. After all, she, who trusted almost nobody, trusted Tom Putnam. Once that man took people on, he took them on for life. At supper, Henry had talked on and on about play period and how he'd read aloud to the other children (only the *good* readers got to do that), and about what the other children had brought in their lunch boxes.

Agnes was still amused that Henry had traded his slice of apple pie *and* his banana for two Double Stuf Oreos. Eventually he'd gotten around to asking her (shyly) if she might buy him some Double Stufs at the grocery store. If, that is, he'd added hastily, it wasn't too much trouble, and if Mr. Brownlow didn't mind paying for them—and *only* for them—out of the money that Henry had given back to him.

He'd also several times referred to Sam Driskell at dinner as his "best friend," which Agnes thought was probably a bit premature, but still, it was nice that Henry had enough social gumption to claim a best friend.

Agnes impulsively reached down and touched the sleeping boy. Just a touch, no more. Just to try on how it felt to think this child might be within reach for the rest of her life. Henry stirred, then rolled over on his back, dragging his covers with him. Agnes bent over him and carefully undid the tangle, just as she'd once done for Marjory, who'd been a restless sleeper until medication had begun conking her out.

Henry had come to them trailing so many unanswered questions. How old would he be before he realized what remarkable people his grandparents had been? When should they tell him his mother was dead? And above all else, why had he been sent to them? Why had Serafine Despré picked Thomas Marvin Putnam to be her son's guardian and hope? The two had never met, as far as Agnes could tell, and Tom wasn't exactly someone people in Mississippi would have heard about. Mr. Brownlow might be able to figure out why Serafine had picked Tom to raise her child, but asking him to try would mean admitting publicly that Tom was not Henry's biological father. Which, Agnes suspected, Mr. Brownlow had probably already guessed, but for some reason had chosen not to talk about. For the last three hours, she and Mr. Brownlow had tap-danced around admitting what was what with Henry while, at the same time, supposedly working out what to do with his money.

The idea they'd come up with was quite wonderful, Agnes thought. It was a way to counteract what Mr. Brownlow had termed the sad digitalization of community while incidentally saving Rose Callahan's (and so Tom's) bacon. This life thing was so strange. Today at breakfast, no one in the

Putnam-Callahan-Tattle household had laid eyes on Mason Brownlow. To-night they were going to bed with a big chunk of their collective fate in his hands.

"I need to sleep on it, Ms. Tattle," Mr. Brownlow had said, standing at the front door to say good night, "and do a bit more research before I'm certain it can work, but right now it seems clear to me that what I've tentatively proposed fully meets the Després' requirements. The language of the trust is very clear. There's that chunk of money set aside to provide for Henry's raising, but the bulk of the twenty-five-million estate is to be held intact for Henry until his twenty-second birthday. Until that time it is to be 'invested in ways that will do real people some actual good.' I did encourage them to be more specific about 'real people' and 'actual good,' but they refused. They said they trusted my ability to know 'real people' when I saw them, and 'actual good' when it presented itself."

Mr. Brownlow had looked steadily at Agnes while he'd said this, then held out his hand.

She'd shaken it, and much to her amazement (Agnes found herself smiling as she remembered this) Mr. Brownlow had held on for a moment longer than necessary before wishing her good night.

Agnes reached down now and gave Henry's covers a final straightening tug. Then she turned and crossed the hall to her room, leaving both her own and Henry's room doors open since her love-struck son-in-law was not available and the boy might need something in the night.

chapter 19

A bird woke Iris, shrieking away in that annoying, bright-eyed, early morning way birds have. And then what sounded like a tractor rolled by.

Her brain immediately registered whispers of alarm. Her cabin was too far out in the woods for any tractors to be rolling by; ergo, she wasn't in her cabin.

Iris lay there for a moment with her eyes squeezed shut, trying to figure out her location from the feel of whatever she slept on. Had she been on a really bad bender and had another blackout? Was she still drunk? She didn't *feel* drunk or hungover, just weird.

Then, with the force of Superman's punch—*Zowee! Blam! Kaboom!*—reality was back: She was completely sober. What's more, she'd been completely sober for almost four days and had been told by several doctors, her counselor, and Dean Eagle to think hard and long before she ever drank again.

The goddamn bird shrieked again, and Iris's entire being cried out for alcohol. Or Valium. Or better yet, for both. She opened her eyes to see if any mood-altering substances might be handy, only to discover that it was still mostly dark.

Where the hell *was* she?

Wherever she was, she was lying on her back. Iris reached out tentatively with one hand and felt nothing but emptiness. She reached out with the other and felt a vertical wall of puffy upholstery.

Was she on a couch?

Whose couch?

Could she have blacked out from habit?

Iris swung her legs around and sat up, unconsciously bracing herself for a wave of nausea followed by engulfing pain in her temples. Neither occurred. Well, *that* was certainly different.

The first strands of real daylight had begun wandering about. The room Iris was in was smallish, rather jumbled, its walls entirely covered either by bookshelves or framed photographs. There were three open windows that she could see; one directly across from her looked out on a small front porch. The goddamn bird had started shouting again, now joined by a disgustingly energetic choir of other birds. No two of them sang the same notes; it was, in effect, a blab school of tweets. Why had so many poets gone on about this racket for so many centuries? Iris vowed right then that she would never again teach any poet who'd written as much as a phrase in praise of birds!

The day was strengthening rapidly, light flouncing into the corners of this funny little space. Iris had a sudden, vague memory of a woman sitting in that chair over there, looking up from her book to smile at her. The woman had a lot of dark hair and was badly dressed. Nothing she'd worn matched, and she'd kept hiking her cowboy-booted feet up on the coffee table so her face appeared to sit on top of a couple of pointy-toed boot soles. . . .

Rose! Rose Callahan had been the woman sitting in that chair.

That was it; she was sleeping on the couch in Rose Callahan's living room.

All of last night came scampering back to Iris. She was here because she'd been worried that if she went home, she'd drink. She'd gone to Tom's office to ask for help (possibly for the first time since she'd learned to tie her own shoes), Tom had taken her home for dinner, and then Rose had brought her here. It appeared that alcohol and drugs had reduced her, macho Iris Benson, to uncomfortable dependence on the kindness of others.

Well, didn't that go along with what the treatment people had yammered at her all weekend? *You can't go back to alcohol, Iris, without destroying yourself and your life, and you can't go forward without help from other people.* Might this morning signify the start of, if not a *brave* new world, at least a *new* new world?

Iris was engulfed by a great yawn that began in her mouth and spread to the tips of her fingers and toes. She looked at her watch. Six fifteen. Much too early for any civilized person to get up, but the chance of her sleeping again in her present, unmedicated state was about the same as the chance of pigs flying.

Immediately a covey of tiny winged pigs flew across the room's ceiling.

Heavens, could this be the D.T.'s? Should she wake Rose up and ask if she had any Valium? Hadn't she read somewhere that people in danger of going into the D.T.'s should be put on a Valium drip? Perhaps it would be better if she just poked around Rose's bathroom to see if she had any suitable downers. There was always the chance that if she woke Rose up and asked for pills, Rose might misunderstand the medicinal nature of her request and go all moral on her and flush any stray downers she *did* have down the toilet.

Just at that moment Russell Jacobs walked briskly by the window that looked out on the diminutive front porch. A few seconds later, there was a tentative tapping on the front door beside the window. "Rose! Rose, open up and let me in! I must talk with you!"

Even sober, Iris was able to enjoy the prospect of discombobulating Russell Jacobs. She padded over to the door, assumed what was left of her hauteur, and opened up.

Russell Jacobs's horrified stare was everything she'd hoped for. "My God!" he said. "What are *you* doing here?"

"Having a sleepover with Rose," Iris said grandly. "What do you want?"

Russell hesitated, giving Iris a moment to realize he was—there really was no other word for it—a mess. Russell Jacobs, Professor Natty, stood before her, greasy-haired, unshaven, with bloodshot eyes and a wrinkled white shirt that hung half in, half out of wrinkled khaki pants.

Iris frowned. She needed *her* world to change if she were to stay sober, not the *whole* world. Russell Jacobs looking insufferably spiffy was one of the maypoles around which reality danced.

She held open the screen door. "Why don't you come in, Russell? You look terrible."

Russell's bleary eyes focused on her chest. "Well, you don't look so hot yourself," he said, with a flash of his old self. "What are you doing in that T-shirt? I never took you for a groupie."

Iris looked down to find she was wearing a large Dave Matthews Band
T-shirt that must belong to Rose. She did not remember putting it on, but,
as she rather liked DMB, it wasn't the tackiest thing she could be wearing.
The band had, after all, played at this very college not so many years ago.
Still, as Russell had obviously meant his remark as a dig, she needed to come
up with a suitable rejoinder.

Didn't she?

Or should she just give it a rest?

Oh, what the hell! Iris opened the screen door a little wider. "Come on
in, Russell. Rose and I have to get up soon anyway. I'm trying to get sober, and
we're going to my house to clean out the whiskey bottles."

Russell trailed bourbon fumes as he pushed past her. Wow! Professor
Natty had fallen off the wagon with a big *clunk*. "Where's Rose?" he said,
rounding on her from the middle of the room. "I need to speak with her."

"Russell," Iris said, feeling ineffective and silly, "you can't just barge
into Rose's bedroom. She's still asleep."

But Russell was already through the archway on the other side of the
room. "Have to speak to her," he flung back over his shoulder. "Up all night
thinking. Need to relax."

Iris trailed after him. "But Russell . . . ," she said, and stopped. But Russell, what? But Russell, Rose's job today is to keep *me* safe, not you.

Russell flung open the door to Rose's bedroom and stopped so suddenly
that Iris bumped into him.

"Hello, Russell," a man said groggily from inside the room. "You're up
early."

It took Iris a moment to realize that it was Tom Putnam who'd spoken,
and that he, too, was having a sleepover with Rose.

*   *   *

One moment Rose was asleep; the next she was up to her chin in complexity,
which, for her, was the deepest sort of trouble.

First of all, there was the fact that she was naked, and Tom Putnam
(also naked) was in bed beside her. That, all by itself, was quite a lot to sort
out. But to make things even more complicated, a wild-eyed Russell Jacobs

was staring down at her from Tom's side of the bed while Iris Benson hovered behind him saying, "I'm sorry, I couldn't stop him," over and over like some talking doll whose computer chip has malfunctioned.

There was movement beside her as Tom propped himself up on his elbows. "Are you all right?" he asked Russell, which was unnecessary as Russell was obviously *not* all right.

Rose decided to stare at the ceiling for a while, at that long crack that suggested the Florida peninsula. It struck her as odd that Tom sounded so *normal* talking to Russell, like someone who, against all available evidence, remained confident that God was still peacefully tucked up in heaven and all was right with the world.

Footsteps sounded. Here came Iris, rounding the bottom of the bed, fluttering her arms like a distressed chicken. ". . . and I'm so sorry, Rose. I woke up and there he was. I let him in, and he barged right past me and came in here."

Rose decided to smile at Iris. "It's all right. No harm, no foul."

This reassured Iris enough for her to snap to and realize Rose was not alone in bed. She clapped her hands in delight. "I didn't know you two were lovers. Why, that's . . . that's *luscious*!"

"Isn't it?" Rose said.

Iris did a little dance of joy. "Who'd have thought old Tom Putnam had enough gumption to snag a woman like *you*!"

Rose felt Tom grasp her hand under the covers. "Thank you, Iris," he said happily. "It *is* pretty amazing, isn't it?"

Tom reached out his other hand to high-five Iris, who then offered a high hand to Rose. *Why not?* Rose thought, smacking Iris palm to palm.

All eyes turned to Russell.

My goodness, Rose thought, *something really bad has happened to him.*

Russell Jacobs's wild eyes were shifting rapidly from her to Tom and back again. Rose had seen similar looks in the eyes of roped calves on Uncle Luther's ranch.

Was that bourbon she smelled? Had Russell been drinking? She'd never seen the man so much as sip a glass of sherry. Of course, the only time she'd really been around him socially was that night at the Putnams'. For all she really knew, having booze on his breath at first light was business as usual for Russell Jacobs.

Iris evidently didn't think so. In a fit of what Rose took to be unaccustomed selflessness, Iris trundled back around the end of the bed and put a hand on Russell's arm. "You look even weirder than I feel. Do you need some help?"

Russell opened his mouth again to speak, but nothing came out. His eyes stopped their roaming and fastened on Rose. He raised both hands in mute appeal.

And then he was gone, so rapidly he was out the front door before anyone else could move.

*   *   *

Tom Putnam walked happily through the golden light of a bright new morning, heading home. At the top of Faculty Row, he stopped for a moment to prepare himself for whatever was coming. Tom felt fairly certain that both Henry and Agnes would be pleased by his decisive action in the romance department—Henry, openly and immensely; Agnes, less openly, but no less immensely. The only real cloud in the sky was Mr. Brownlow. If he found out, would he think him irresponsible for taking off in the middle of the night to go sleep with Rose? But then, how on earth would he find out? Henry and Agnes certainly wouldn't tell him.

"Good morning, Professor Putnam," a cheery male voice sang out from the other side of the street.

It was Mr. Brownlow, naturally, proving again that life was essentially a comedy. His own, Tom thought, tended toward farce, full of improbable situations and ridiculous complications that still somehow managed to lead logically one into the next. "Good morning, Mr. Brownlow," he said, acutely aware he was wearing jeans and a pajama top.

Mr. Brownlow came toward him, indicating they should walk together. "I've been invited to your house for breakfast. You're certainly out early."

"Yes," said Tom. "I am." Would Mr. Brownlow expect him to say *why* he was out at seven thirty in the morning, wearing jeans and a pajama top?

The little banker's round face would have made a perfect Buddha mask; cheerful inscrutability made human. He was unexpectedly decked out in madras pants *(madras pants!)*, a bright blue polo shirt, penny loafers, and a London Fog windbreaker. When did he think it was, 1962? "Is that a pajama top you're wearing?" Mr. Brownlow asked mildly. "Or some new style of shirt I'm not familiar with?"

Tom briefly considered lying, but what was the point? Mr. Brownlow was no dummy; he wouldn't believe any lame whopper Tom came up with. "It's a pajama top."

"Ah!"

Mr. Brownlow began walking again. Tom wordlessly fell into step beside him, Mr. Brownlow's "Ah!" dragging on his happiness like Marley's chains. Halfway down Faculty Row, he could stand it no longer. "Look here, Mr. Brownlow, you might as well know. I spent the night with Rose Callahan."

The little banker regarded him evenly. "I see," he said, without breaking stride.

Tom trundled miserably alongside him, his eyes firmly fixed on his own feet. This impenetrable *impenetrability* must be what Mr. Brownlow laid on customers he suspected of trying to hustle him.

Just then Mr. Brownlow touched Tom's arm very lightly. "Good for you," he said in his cheery way, giving Tom's pajama-clad arm a little pat. "Good for you."

Of course it's good for me, Tom thought miserably. *But do you also think it's good for Henry?*

*   *   *

Rose was not a fastidious housekeeper, but she *did* keep house.

Iris evidently did not. Her cabin was one enormous room with closets and a bathroom. Stuff was everywhere; books, notebooks, junk mail, dirty dishes, dirty socks, dog toys, empty wine bottles. Rose got a trash bag from the box she'd brought with her and went to work. Iris took one look around and immediately shot out the back door.

A great and joyful yelping commenced immediately.

One filled trash bag later, Iris marched back inside, muddied but, Rose thought (with a nod to Gertrude Stein) with much more *there* there. A few moments with her dogs had restored some of her Iris-ness. There was, Rose suspected, real toughness and single-mindedness in Iris Benson that would serve her well as she worked out who she was without booze.

Who *was* Iris Benson without booze?

Now that she thought about it, who was Rose Callahan without flight?

Iris had pointlessly wiped her feet before stepping onto the cabin's grubby floor. "I'm letting the puppies run in the woods for a while. They're good about coming right back when I whistle."

"Good idea," Rose said. Was Iris, she wondered, scared of the future? Did she realize that sobriety would change everything about *everything*?

"Why are you looking at me like that?"

"Like what?"

"Like you're trying to figure me out or something."

"Oh. Sorry."

Iris shrugged. "What are you sorry for? You're not doing anything I'm not doing. I'd like to figure me out, too. Although the people this weekend kept saying that *thinking* about things was the stupidest thing I could do at the moment."

"They did?"

"Yeah. Can you imagine that? Telling an academic not to think is like telling a fish not to swim."

Rose stared at the other woman. Iris was supposed not to *think*? What else was there to do in a crisis? She did, of course, often end up thinking about why she was thinking about what she was thinking about. "What are you supposed to do if you're not supposed to think?"

Iris snorted. "This is the beginning and the end of what those bozos had to say about *that*: One fucking day at a time, don't drink, go to meetings, and wait until you get over the shock of not drinking and going to meetings. Period. End of story. God bless us every one."

The question was out before Rose could stop it. "Are you scared?"

"Of not drinking?"

"Well, more of the huge change that not drinking represents in how you go about . . . about everything? I guess what I'm asking is, are you afraid of such a huge change?"

Iris didn't hesitate. "Hell, yes. But the people this weekend took pains to point out that *anything's* an improvement over publicly upchucking in the Book Store at ten o'clock in the morning."

Anything's an improvement over . . .

Rose thought of her bedroom walls, of all those photographic remnants of lovely people she'd allowed to slide out of her life. What had ever made her feel that *photographs* could sustain a heart?

Iris was checking her watch. "It's ten minutes after nine. Didn't you say we needed to get out of here by nine thirty?"

"Yes," Rose said. "I did."

"Well then, as pleasant as it is just to talk, I better start packing. Believe it or not, I gotta teach two classes this afternoon. And I'm not teaching my first class sober without wearing something absolutely smashing!"

Iris waited a beat. When Rose didn't respond, she poked her in the ribs. "Get it, Rosie? *Smashing?* Since my problem is getting *smashed?*"

It took Rose a moment. "Of course. *Smashing.* Sorry. I wasn't *thinking.*"

It took Iris a moment to get that. Once she did, she broke into a huge grin. "My, my, aren't we a couple of smarty-pants?"

Rose gave up thinking about thinking and grinned. *Why not?* "I certainly hope so," she said.

*   *   *

Russell's first drink remained the brightest of his teenage memories, standing out from the parade of small and large embarrassments that had constituted his adolescence. It had been a Thursday evening in his junior year. He'd just gotten his driver's license, and he'd been trying for hours to get up enough courage to call Sally Stutford, an attractive but unspectacular girl in his Latin class, and ask her to go to the movies with him on Saturday. Finally, in desperation, he'd gone to the low kitchen cupboard, where his mother kept her "hidden" vodka stash behind cans of Silvo and Bab-O and a welter of cleaning brushes, fetched out a half-full bottle and taken a goodly swig. A lovely, lightening warmth had instantly spread through his limbs, but what Russell remembered most vividly was how *hopeful* he'd felt; hopeful enough to march over to the kitchen wall phone, pick it up, and dial Sally's number. She'd answered, he'd asked, she'd turned him down flat. He'd put down the phone, gone back to the kitchen sink, fished out the bottle, had another slug, and not cared.

Not cared . . .

That was really what alcohol did for him, allowed him not to care. And now that he'd allowed himself to care, he needed alcohol again. Only this time, he didn't want alcohol to help him *not* to care; he wanted it to give him the courage to do what needed to be done *because* he cared. He'd started out to Rose's this morning thinking he would talk to her about his own confusion. And now here he was, back home, without a shred of doubt that the time for talk had passed and the time for action had come. Radical action, to be sure; action that no other person on this cautious little campus could even conceptualize, let alone consider, but then he wasn't any other person, was he?

Russell thumped the kitchen table with his fist and went upstairs to shower and shave and dress himself appropriately for what lay ahead.

chapter 20

Against all odds, Rose made it to work on time. She spent the rest of the morning and the first hour of the afternoon trying not to worry. Worrying, Mavis had always maintained, meant you were trying to control something you had no business trying to control.

William Shatner in his girdle and *Star Trek* outfit smiled knowingly at her, reminding Rose that, yes, she had boldly gone where she had never gone before.

> *Scotty*: [*the USS* Enterprise *is being sucked into a black hole*]
>   I'm giving her all she's got, Captain!
> *James T. Kirk*: All she's got isn't good enough!!

There it was, niggling doubt that would not leave her alone. *What if what she had wasn't good enough?*

Around one o'clock, Rose was watching the espresso machine wand whipping two-percent milk into froth for a student's vanilla latte with extra syrup and whipped cream when Russell Jacobs came in. He marched right up to her, looking better than he had for a week, dressed in a rough gray tweed sport coat, one of his signature monogrammed shirts, lightweight gray wool gabardine pants, and spit-polished black shoes. Russell's hair was still long, but it was washed and brushed, and he was freshly shaved. He still smelled slightly of booze, but mostly of citrus cologne.

"Hello, Russell. What's up?"

Russell wasted no time in the usual Russellian banter. "Are you on Henry Putnam's approved pickup list from school?"

"Yes," Rose said, her hand flying to her heart. "Is Henry all right?"

Russell gave her shoulder a reassuring pat. "I'm sure he's fine. It's just that Tom phoned to ask if you and I could pick Henry up from school and keep him at my house. It has something to do with the goings-on about his future."

Rose's customers had reported that Mr. Brownlow had been snooping around the college asking questions about the importance of her job to the college community. And Mr. Pitts had told her Mr. Brownlow was planning to come by and talk with her—in her lair, as the lawyer had phrased it—later today. So something was afoot on that front. Still, Rose didn't hesitate. "Of course! Just let me deliver this and ask Susan to cover, and I'll be right with you."

"Good," Russell said. "There's no time to waste."

A few leaves had begun to fall. Henry scuffed along beside Rose, kicking at them, but then Henry kicked at *everything*. "I drew a dinosaur today," he said. "We're studying brontosaurus. Did you know they only ate grass and leaves?"

"Will I ever get to see your picture?" Rose asked.

Henry turned coy. "If you come to my school's art show, you can. We each get to choose a picture to put up, and I'm going to choose that one."

"When is the art show?"

"Just before Christmas."

Rose smiled. "Don't you think you might paint a picture you like better before then?"

"No *way*."

That was the end of that.

Henry carried his soccer ball. "How come we're not going home? Then we could go out in the backyard and practice head shots."

"Because—" Rose began.

Russell interrupted her. "Because we're going to my house. I have a great big round room at the top of my house with lots of round windows that I thought you'd like to see. It's big enough so that you can practice head shots inside."

"Cool!" Henry was obviously impressed. Rose involuntarily tightened her grip on his hand. Something didn't feel right about this, but what did she know? Nothing had felt right for several days now.

"I've got cookies and milk already laid out up in the Dome Room," Russell said for Henry's benefit.

Henry, the cookie connoisseur, was immediately interested. "What *kind* of cookies?"

"Double Stuf Oreos."

"Wow!" Henry, like everyone, had his price. "How much further, Professor Jacobs?"

"We're here." They stood in front of the Dean Dome. Russell pointed to the top of his house, which stuck up over everything else around it. "That's where we're going."

Henry's mind was still on Double Stuf Oreos. "How many can I have?" he asked.

"As many as you want." Russell smiled at the boy, offering his hand. Henry took it, and together they trotted up the Dean Dome's front walk.

Russell opened the front door with a flourish. "Come in, come in! Welcome to my home."

The space Rose entered was dominated by a curving staircase, the kind you floated up rather than climbed. Facing sets of French doors opened into what looked like a parlor on her right, a library on her left. From what she could see of it, Russell's house was exactly as people had described it—not so much a home as a stage set for the Russell Show.

"Excuse me, Professor Jacobs," Henry said, "but I need to use the bathroom."

"Right this way." Russell gestured up the stairs. "There's a nice bathroom up in the Dome Room that you can use."

"Okay! You show me where!" Henry turned and raced up the stairs.

Russell gave Rose a little shrug, as though to say *what's a host to do?*

*   *   *

It was pleasant to be among the gaggle of parents waiting at Ed House for school to let out. Tom supposed that at some point he'd have to let Henry walk home by himself in order to foster independence. Unless, of course,

Henry had *enough* independence already, and needed other things—such as a sense of belonging—fostered more.

Good Lord, parenting and being in love were fraught with decisions. Life with Marjory had been simple. He'd only had to be kind and keep her safe. Everything else had been so screwed up by fate, he didn't have to worry about making anything worse.

"Henry's already gone," a thigh-high voice announced.

Tom looked down to find Sam Driskell standing before him. "Hello, Sam. What did you just say about Henry?"

"He's already gone. Someone came and got him during reading."

Tiny wisps of panic rose in Tom. "Who got him?"

Sam gave the elaborate shrug of a seven-year-old pleased to be involved in a *situation*. "I didn't see who it was. Teacher just said Henry needed to go."

Tom was still having trouble grasping what Sam was trying to tell him.

"Didn't he go home?" Sam asked.

"No, he didn't." Tom had come from home.

"You can check with Teacher," Sam said. "She might know."

Tom was off. "Thank you, Sam," he called back over his shoulder. "I'll do that."

*   *   *

The second set of stairs Rose climbed was a much tighter spiral and emptied directly into the Dome Room. There was no landing; you just climbed until there were no more stairs, took one last step, and stood at the edge of a round space perhaps twenty-five feet in diameter. Russell's Dome Room had eight chest-high circular windows evenly spaced around its circumference, and one narrow door leading into the promised bathroom, contained by the little bump in the room's roundness you saw from outside.

Russell had furnished the space with only one couch and a scattering of comfortable chairs. There were lamps but no pictures. He evidently considered the space its own best decoration.

A rather incongruous apartment-sized refrigerator was off to Rose's right, and a single table was on her left. This had been laid with a cloth, a champagne bucket full of ice holding an old-fashioned bottle full of milk, and two unopened packages of Double Stuf Oreos.

The room's beauty was such that it trumped even the lure of Oreos or the need to use the bathroom. Henry's face shone with delight. "It's like a room in Hogwarts!"

"Isn't it?" Rose put her hand on the boy's shoulder.

Then there was a sound like a hospital trolley rumbling down a corridor. Rose turned to find that Russell was no longer there, and the hole in the floor opening to the spiral staircase had completely disappeared.

Something clicked into place, something turned, and it was as though that hole had never been.

*   *   *

Tom found Henry's teacher, Mrs. Parker, hanging gaudy tempera-on-newsprint pictures on a clothesline strung across the back wall of her classroom. "Professor Putnam," she said, without the slightest trace of anything even approaching alarm, "how nice to see you. Come and look at Henry's lovely picture."

Mrs. Parker moved to stand beside a picture of a big green blob with a long tail on one end and an improbably toothy smile on the other. "It's a brontosaurus. Henry's quite proud of the fact that it has very small teeth because brontosauruses were vegetarian. I'm sure he'll tell you all about it at supper."

Tom forced a smile. "Er, where is Henry, Mrs. Parker?"

There can be no more alarming question to ask a teacher. "Why, he's with Rose. Rose Callahan. She came to fetch him about an hour ago, saying you'd called and asked her to pick him up. Was that not true?"

It was not. But surely, if Rose was involved, Henry was fine, whatever was going on. Perhaps she and Henry were in cahoots with Agnes and were planning some sort of surprise for him? "No worries, Mrs. Parker. I'm sure we've just gotten our wires crossed."

Mrs. Parker, a thirty-year veteran of elementary school teaching, was not so easily fooled. "Surely you'd know if you had called Rose? Was she making that up? I thought it was fine since she's on Henry's list, and you and she are . . . are . . ." Mrs. Parker ground to a halt.

"I'm sure everything's fine," Tom said, to reassure himself as much as her. "Tell you what, I'll leave now and get this figured out."

"Will you call me when you do?" Mrs. Parker said. "Please? I won't sleep a wink tonight unless I know everything's all right. Henry's such a dear little boy, and he's been through so much."

Tom was already on his way out. "Yes, he has," he called back over his shoulder. "And yes, I'll call you as soon as I find out what's going on."

He went directly to Rose's cottage. She was not there, but her car was. Which meant she was probably at work.

At the Book Store, he was told that Rose had left abruptly around one o'clock with Russell Jacobs. Her reason for leaving had been something vague about an emergency. Ted Pitts told Tom he'd expected her back shortly, but so far there had been no sign of her. He promised to call Tom as soon as she showed up.

Tom went next to Russell's and knocked on the front door. Russell opened it immediately. "Well, hello, Tom," he said, sounding much like his old self. "Sorry I can't ask you in. I'm kind of in the middle of something."

Tom was by now too worried for polite preliminaries. "Have you seen Henry, Russ? Or Rose? They left school together and I can't find them. The Book Store said Rose left work with you."

"She did. We went to a late lunch."

The panic returned, less wispy and more robust. "You went to lunch? Ted said Rose told him there was some kind of emergency."

Russ shook his head. He smelled heavily of cologne and something else that could have been whiskey. But he seemed sober enough, and Tom had more important things to worry about than Russell Jacobs's drinking. "I don't know anything about any emergency," Russell said. "Rose and I parted company outside the dining hall. She said she was headed back to work. Did you check at the Book Store?"

"Yes, I checked at the Book Store," Tom snapped. "I just *told* you I talked to Ted."

Russ looked offended. "Well, don't bark at *me*, Tom. You could, after all, have talked to Ted on the phone, you know."

"I know," Tom said. "I'm sorry. I'm just worried about Henry."

"As well you should be," said Russell evenly. "Would you like me to call the police?"

Tom's first instinct was to say yes, but then he remembered Mr. Brownlow and immediately changed his mind. Things had been going so well, but that didn't mean they couldn't turn sour once Mr. Brownlow found out that Tom couldn't even keep track of Henry. "No," he said. "I need to think first."

"Are you going to start a search?" Russell asked.

Tom shook his head. "Not yet. I have to think things through."

"You do that," Russell said. "Now, if you'll excuse me, as I said, I'm kind of in the middle of something."

"Certainly," Tom said. "I'll call you if I find out anything."

"You do that," said Russell, smiling at Tom as he firmly closed the door.

*　　*　　*

The bathroom door closed behind Henry.

Rose was instantly on the move, hurrying over to the rectangle of floor where the entrance had been. There was no visible way to open it, no handle or even a bit of mismatched edge to grab on to. Rose jumped up and down on it, testing its sturdiness. Solid as the Rock of Ages.

"Russell," she called softly, "are you out there?"

No answer.

"Russell! Are you there?" Louder this time.

Still no answer. Had he gone downstairs and left them locked up in this top hat of a room without even telling them *why*?

It was then Rose noticed a sheet of stationery taped to the wall. She snatched it down and found that it was a letter to her, written in a hard-etched, emphatic scrawl on Russell's elegant letterhead.

Dear Rose,

What you are doing with Tom Putnam is not real, and it is also wrong—wrong for you, wrong for me and wrong for Henry. I'm sure you will realize that I'm right about this as soon as you have had time to think.

I'm sorry to have to do what I have done, but everything was happening too fast, and this was the only way I could figure out to slow things down, and keep them from going past the point of no return! Which would have been a great tragedy!!!

Tom Putnam may be a very nice person, but he is wrong for you and wrong for Henry. You both need someone with more substance, and I feel strongly that I am that someone!

I have instigated a DNA test which will prove once and for all that I am Henry's real father and that Tom is just a pretender. So that situation is relatively simple and straightforward.

With you, however, the situation is more complicated. The relationship you have begun with Tom Putnam is not so much an error of taste, as an error of judgment. I feel certain that given time to reflect calmly, you will realize that I am the one for you!!

Over the last few days it has become crystal clear to me that I would not be able to feel as comfortable with you as I do, if you did not feel equally comfortable with me. I'm not saying you need to marry me, just that people who are as comfortable together as you and I are cannot marry anyone else!!!

My plan is to keep you and Henry safely away from distraction for a few days so as to give you time to think things through. Given this time to reflect, I'm sure you will reach the same conclusion I have: Tom Putnam is not the man for you and I am.

There is plenty of food and drink in the fridge, and there are fresh towels in the bathroom.

With the greatest respect and affection,
Russell Jacobs
(your loving Protector, Russ)

The toilet flushed. Pipes gurgled. Henry was washing his hands.

Rose took a deep breath. She could not have been more wrong about Russell being back to normal. This thing in her hand announced he'd flipped his lid, big-time. He evidently planned to hold her and Henry captive up here in this tower like a modern-day Rapunzel and child.

Rose immediately thought of her great-aunt Miranda, who'd flipped her lid in a similarly bizarre fashion when Rose was about Henry's age. Family history had it that Miranda, an early widow, had been living quietly by herself for decades in a minute house in the tiny Texas town of Wellspring. Rose had an indistinct memory of "Miss Prissy," as the family had called her, sitting buttoned up to the chin and down to the wrist among the raucous Callahan clan, a frail, faded woman, who never said a word.

Then one morning in early June, wordless Aunt Miranda had taken off all her clothes and marched out her front door into family legend. She'd walked across town and sat herself down in a rocking chair on Tom Dyson's front porch. Tom Dyson was a fiftyish, thrice-married local druggist who everyone said looked just like James Dean would have looked if he'd lived to be Tom Dyson's age. Great-Aunt Miranda had sat and rocked calmly on Tom Dyson's front porch for a couple of hours while a large crowd gathered and gawked.

The problem was that no one knew what to do. Great-Aunt Miranda had always been so shy, so unassertive, so religious, it seemed wrong for a bunch of men to just go up and tackle her while she was naked. Wife Number Three had screamed at her through a front window to go away a couple of times, and the sheriff had gone up on the porch at some point and asked her politely if she'd like a ride home. But Miranda had ignored them both and continued to sit serenely in her rocking chair, wearing her long history of modest timidity like a protective force field.

Eventually someone had thought to call in the Methodist minister, and that had done the trick. Miranda left the porch on the preacher's arm and allowed herself to be returned home. After the Dysons threatened to sue if she wasn't put away, the family reluctantly packed Miranda off to a secure unit at the Baptist home, where she'd had the good sense to die within a year.

Granny Callahan had been the only one of Miranda's siblings to speak out in support of her rampage. "At least Prissy had the good sense to bust loose *once* before she died!" Mavis's mother would say whenever the subject of Great-Aunt Miranda came up. "It's just too bad it landed her locked up with a bunch of Baptists."

Over the years, Rose had found herself thinking frequently about Aunt Miranda and wondering if she'd enjoyed herself sitting naked on Tom Dyson's front porch. Rose also wondered if she'd inherited any of her great-aunt's propensities to "bust loose," and if so, what she might need to bust loose from.

Just in the last decade, Rose had concluded that her great-aunt had done what she'd done because she'd finally gotten the courage to be all that she could be, not just the parts of herself she'd gotten used to. And just in the past few days, as Rose had felt herself getting more and more emotionally entangled with the Putnams, she'd wondered if emotional entanglement might be her own version of Great-Aunt Miranda's "busting loose." It was hard to imagine anything more unlike her.

Of course, right now, it was more important to consider whether Russell Jacobs might be doing a Great-Aunt Miranda, breaking free of a part of himself he'd always denied was there.

It certainly made sense, Rose decided, but it didn't get her and Henry out of here. In a rush of anger at Russell, she balled up his note and bounced it off the nearest wall.

"What are you doing?"

Rose turned to find Henry looking at her. "Nothing." Which, after all, was true. She retrieved the letter, unballed it, folded it, and stuffed it in the pocket of her pants.

Henry watched her. "Where's Professor Jacobs?"

"He had to go do something."

"Oh." Henry looked longingly at the table.

The thing I must *not do,* Rose thought, *is panic Henry.* "Are you hungry?"

"Yes!" Light shone in Henry's eyes.

"I don't think Professor Jacobs would mind at all if you started without him. He might be quite a while—you know, doing what he's doing."

"Okay," Henry said, "if you're sure he wouldn't mind."

"I don't think he would at all." How long, Rose wondered, would it be before the two of them were missed? And then, after they'd been missed, how long would it take for someone to figure out where they were? And after people knew where they were, how long would it be before Russell let them go?

Perhaps she could open a porthole and yell at a passerby and speed things up? "I'm just going to look out a window, Henry, and then I'll be right over."

Henry didn't miss much. "Why are you going to do that?" he asked, with the slightest trace of worry in his voice.

"Just to see the view," Rose said, airily channeling Annie Hall. La-di-dah! La-di-dah!

She walked quickly to the nearest porthole. So much for shouting at passersby. The thick circle of glass was unopenable and would have withstood a direct hit from a man-of-war.

*   *   *

Tom got home to find Agnes settled at the kitchen table, drinking coffee and looking through a stack of papers.

"Is Henry here?" he asked.

Agnes looked up and took off her glasses. "No. I assumed he was with you."

"Well, he's not. Rose picked him up an hour early saying something about an emergency, and no one seems quite sure where either one of them is now."

Agnes frowned. "Who's 'no one'?"

"What?"

"Who's 'no one'? The people who don't know where Henry and Rose are. Whom have you talked to?"

"Oh. Ted, Mrs. Parker, and Russell."

"*Russell?*" Agnes, Tom knew, distrusted anything involving Russell Jacobs.

"Yes. He was with Rose when she left the Book Store."

Agnes leaned back in her chair and folded her arms. "Well, what did Russell have to say for himself?"

"That he and Rose had lunch, and then he left her."

Agnes thought for a moment. "That doesn't make any sense."

"What doesn't make sense?"

"That Rose would leave work with Russell because of some kind of emergency and then go off to lunch with him."

Tom considered this. "Well, that's what he said just now when I talked to him."

"Where did you talk to him?" Agnes asked.

"At his house."

"Did you go in?"

Tom shook his head. "No, he said was in the middle of something, so I just talked to him at the front door."

"Hmmm." Agnes pushed her chair back and stood up.

"Hmmm, what?" Tom asked, trying hard not to snap at Agnes, who, after all, was just being who she was.

"Hmmm, nothing in particular. That just seems a bit weird, even for Russell."

Tom clamped both hands on the back of one of the kitchen chairs and squeezed hard. "You're right, that was a bit weird, even for Russell. But now can we discuss how to go about finding Henry?"

"Certainly." Agnes began moving toward the phone.

"Who are you calling?" Tom asked, thinking again of Mr. Brownlow.

"Mr. Brownlow. Henry's his concern as well as ours. And then I'm calling Clarence Mayhew."

"But—" Tom began.

"But nothing," Agnes said, and picked up the phone.

*　　*　　*

Russell's parlor window was shut and locked. He stood before it, glass in hand, and watched people rush up and down the sidewalk in front of his house. Russell could read lips well enough to realize that when they raised hands to mouths and called out, what they called out was "Henry!"

Russell felt bad that so many people had been sucked into searching for Henry when Henry was upstairs safe and sound. He wished he could let everyone know that there was absolutely no reason to worry about anything, that this was a private matter between him and Rose and Henry.

Russell reached down and touched the pair of nineteenth-century dueling pistols he kept displayed on the small table beneath the window. They weren't loaded, but that didn't mean they wouldn't come in handy if things came to a head. Meanwhile, it was important to carry on as though nothing at all were out of the ordinary.

The phone rang. *Business as usual*, Russell reminded himself, taking a generous sip of bourbon while he moved toward the phone and picked it up. *Business as usual.* "Hello," he said. "Russell Jacobs here."

"Russell, this is Luellen Mars."

"Hello, Luellen." Russell felt his heart quicken. Surely this couldn't be DNA test results already?

"I just got back the results of the DNA test you wanted."

Russell sat down in the prim little chair beside the telephone desk. "Yes?"

"The two people whose samples you gave me are not biologically related."

There it was. No Jeffersonian fatherhood for him. Whatever else he was, he wasn't Henry's father. A great calm enveloped Russell; for some unquantifiable amount of time he felt nothing, knew nothing, was nothing. Then, gradually, he became part of the world again. Somewhere a clock ticked. More people rushed by outside his window, their mouths open in wordless appeal, *Henry! Henry!*

"Russell, are you still there?"

The enveloping calm retreated, leaving him feeling quietly invincible. He, Russell Jacobs, was the one who could make things right for all concerned. "Yes, I'm here," he said to Luellen.

And then he put down the phone.

*   *   *

Susan Mason was walking by the Dean Dome thinking about where she should search for Henry next when Henry appeared on the porch carrying his soccer ball. The door shut immediately behind him.

"Susan!" Henry called out.

"Henry!" Susan began running toward him. "You're alive!"

Henry, who'd begun trotting down the Dean Dome's front walk, stopped and frowned. "Of course I am. I was up in Professor Jacobs's tower."

"Really?" She'd reached the little boy and didn't quite know what to do next.

"Yes. Really."

What Susan really wanted to do was hug Henry, but that might not be a good idea. Her little brother didn't always like to be hugged in public anymore. So instead, she knelt down in front of him, took both his hands in hers, and said, "We've all been so worried about you. The whole campus is looking for you."

Henry looked troubled. "We were locked in. But then Professor Jacobs came up and said I wasn't his son and I could go, but Rose had to stay."

"What did he mean, you weren't his son?"

Henry shook his head. "I don't know. But I'm glad I'm not. I'd rather be Tom's son."

"Of course you would." Susan's brain was processing information and exploring possibilities at a pace she would never have thought possible. "Did you say Rose was still up there? In Professor Jacobs's tower? Is she locked in, do you know?"

"Yes." Henry looked anguished. "He told her she had to stay up there until she came to her senses."

Susan stood up. Rose Callahan was her hero. "Well, let's go get her out," she said, reaching for Henry's hand.

Henry shied back. "We can't," he said in a tiny, crumpled voice.

"Why not?"

Twin tears rolled down Henry's cheeks. "Professor Jacobs has a gun."

"A gun!" Susan pushed Henry behind her and began backing up, her eyes scanning Professor Jacobs's battlement.

"Could we go and get my dad, please?" Henry asked. "He'll know what to do."

"Of course," Susan said, still backing up, still keeping Henry behind her. It was only when they'd gotten across the street and behind cover that she turned around, took Henry's hand, and began lickety-splitting it across campus, ignoring the delighted cries of other searchers.

*   *   *

It was now full dark in the Dome Room except for stray gleams from the streetlights. Rose stood at one of the round windows, watching the crowd gathered below. The campus police had set up velvet ropes borrowed from the college museum to keep people from trampling the ancient and valuable boxwoods that ringed Russell's house. Onlookers were massed in a neat semicircle about ten feet back from the front entrance.

Many people carried lit flashlights. The scene below reminded Rose of a Grateful Dead concert.

Mavis had liked the Dead almost as much as she'd liked the Stones. "Truckin'" and all that.

Rose sang softly to herself. *Lately it occurs to me, what a long strange trip it's been . . .*

One of the Dome Room's lamps flared. As there were no light switches in the room, Rose knew Russell had to have switched it on from below. A few people spotted her silhouetted against the window. Word spread quickly; soon everyone was looking up and pointing, like a crowd of movie extras standing around Metropolis pointing up at Superman. Rose waved a hand; those below waved flashlights, littering the world with dancing points of light.

There was a rumbling sound, and Rose turned to see that Russell had opened the floor just wide enough for him to stand at the top of the staircase. In his hand was an old gun that was not pointed at her but still made its point: She was a prisoner.

"Fools," Russell muttered. "They're all fools. I could spend the next thousand years explaining what's going on between you and me, and not one of them would understand."

"Could you explain it to me, do you think?" Rose asked from her window.

Russell stared at her. "Surely you must know. I mean, you are the one who *started* it."

"Started what, Russell?" Rose began moving slowly toward him. If she could get close enough she could kick the gun out of his hand. "I promise you I don't have a clue what you're talking about. Please tell me what's going on."

Russell tossed his head. His hair flew about. "This," he said, "is about destiny!"

Abruptly, Rose lost patience. Gun or no gun, this had gone on long enough. "Russell Jacobs, you let me out of here!" she said, making a rush at him. "You have no right to keep me locked up like this."

Now Russell pointed the gun at her as though he meant it, stopping Rose a good ten feet from freedom. "I have *every* right! It turned out I did *not* have the right to keep Henry, and so, as you saw, I let him go. But I *do* have the right to keep you!" He loosed a stentorian belch. "Oops. Can't have that. Must go now. Have one more tiny drink, while you stay put!" He waved the gun purposely at her again. "Read my letter again. Think about things. Have some more Oreos."

And he was gone, closing and locking the floor behind him.

*   *   *

Tom kept his arms around Henry and his eyes fastened on Rose standing in the window of the Dome Room. As long as he could see her, he knew she was all right. Tom thought the chances that Russell would hurt Rose were slim, but still, it was obvious that Russell had temporarily lost any connection to reality, and so who knew what he might do? There was that gun to consider.

Henry had said it was an old gun, and Tom suspected it was one of the pair of matched black-powder Mortimer dueling pistols that Russell was so proud of. He liked to give the impression they'd been in his family for the better part of two centuries, but Tom had been with him when he'd spotted them in a Christie's catalog. Had he been wrong not to call Russ on his guff? Isn't that what real friends did, call each other on their guff?

Rose moved in the window, lifting a hand, pushing back her hair, a gesture that went straight to Tom's heart. "Can you see me?" he whispered. "Do you know I'm here?"

Henry pulled at the sleeve of his sport coat. Tom bent down and put his arms around the little boy. Henry's face was scrunched with worry; no one could tell him this situation was not his fault. "Can't you *make* him let her out?" he asked yet again. "Can't we just go in and get her?"

Tom answered just as he had the other times Henry had asked these questions. "I think it would be better if we give it a little more time."

"That's what you said before."

"I know." Tom stroked the boy's hair.

"But he's got that gun."

"It's an old gun. I don't think Professor Jacobs has any bullets for it."

"But you don't know for *certain*." Henry spoke in an almost-whisper.

"No, you're right. I don't know for certain. But if he did have bullets, don't you think it would be better not to make him feel attacked?"

Tears glittered in Henry's eyes. "But Rose must be scared up there by herself. I should have stayed with her, even though she told me to go."

Tom brushed a tear off Henry's cheek. "No, no, you did the right thing. You let us know where Rose is so we can figure out the best thing to do. If you hadn't done that, we'd still be looking for her."

Henry, who had yet to crumple, crumpled now. "I'm sorry," he wailed.

Tom picked the boy up and held him close. "Everything will be all right," he said, over and over. But he stopped short of promising this. Everything being all right was hope, not certitude. Tom wasn't going to pretend to Henry he had powers he didn't.

He caught Mr. Brownlow's eye over the top of Henry's head. Agnes had, indeed, phoned the little banker. He'd come over immediately and, much to Tom's relief, had flung no blame at anyone for Henry's disappearance. Instead, Mr. Brownlow had searched like everybody else. Then when Henry had turned up, he'd beetled over to Russell's house with Tom and Agnes like the adjunct family member he appeared to have become. Temporarily, at least. Until he blew the family apart. How could he leave Henry in the care of someone whose friends kidnapped him?

Russell usually pulled his Mercedes into the Dean Dome's double garage, but today he'd conveniently left it in the drive. Clarence Mayhew had set up an impromptu command post on the car's wide trunk. Tom, Henry, Agnes, Mr. Brownlow, and Iris Benson (who also seemed to have joined the family) were all clustered around it, along with the president and Clarence Mayhew. As chief of the college police, Clarence was titularly in charge, but it was obvious he deferred to the president.

Mr. Brownlow, however, deferred to no one. Just as the college bells began to strike eight, the little banker ducked under the museum ropes, marched up to the Dean Dome's front door, and pressed the doorbell.

The crowd hushed and held their collective breath.

Nothing happened.

Mr. Brownlow rang the bell again. "Professor Jacobs," he called out, "I'm Mason Brownlow of Picayune, Mississippi. Might we speak for a moment?"

"Go away!" Russell shouted from behind the closed front door.

His voice sounded amplified to Tom. Could Russell still have that megaphone left over from his long-ago days at the University of Virginia?

Tom had a sudden vision of Russ, sitting in the student section of Scott Stadium, correctly dressed in Cavalier colors, yelling his head off in support of a bunch of football players who wouldn't care if he lived or died.

Why hadn't he seen it before? Russell was the way he was simply because he wanted to *belong*. He wanted someone, anyone, to put his arms around him and say: *Russell Jacobs, I know you're full of it most of the time, but I still like you a lot.*

Was this why Russell had locked Rose up in the Dean Dome? Could it possibly be as simple as that she'd made him feel she *liked* him?

This morning, had Russell been on his way to explain this to her, talk to her about it, when he'd barged into her bedroom and found the two of them together? Had Russell looked at Rose in bed with him and seen his own rare real connection with another person slipping away? Was that why Russell had flipped out and kidnapped her?

Of course, Russell had kidnapped Henry as well. But then he'd let the boy go again, telling him it was because he wasn't his real son. Which meant that, for a time, Russell had thought Henry was his real son.

This would, of course, have to be sorted out later.

Later. That was the operative word for the Henry part of this mess. For right now, Tom was dimly certain the most helpful thing he could do was face his *own* part. The truth was that he, Tom Putnam, had been an iffy friend to Russell Jacobs. He'd spent the first twenty years of their relationship immersed in his own troubles, the last two weeks immersed in Henry and Rose. The bottom line was he'd been completely wrapped up in his own doings while Russell had floundered along beside him, a runaway train heading for to-night's crash.

Of course, Russell's breakdown was not *all* Tom's fault; Russell had de-liberately made himself difficult to know. But wasn't that the point? Wasn't Russell's stagy behavior how his corrosive loneliness had manifested itself?

And wasn't Tom's chief transgression that he'd never thought to question it?

Surely, Tom thought, if he'd been paying even a modicum of attention sometime over the last twenty years, he would have seen Russell's behavior for what it was—a plea for acceptance. Aren't the messed-up ways people behave always cries for help?

Oh, whatever. Right here, right now, it was time for him to ac-knowledge that Russell Jacobs had been *bellowing* for help for years, and that he, Tom Putnam, had essentially stuck his fingers in his ears and ig-nored him.

Mr. Brownlow was leaning on the doorbell again. "Professor Jacobs, we cannot let this continue. Please, won't you talk to us and tell us what's going on? Tell us why you're holding Rose Callahan captive? If you don't, we'll really have no choice but to call the state police."

"Rose Callahan is not my captive, she's my guest," Russell boomed. "My *acolyte,* as it were, in the church of the human heart. She is here to learn."

"But what if she wants to leave?" Mr. Brownlow shouted.

"Too bad."

The whole assemblage loosed a sigh. Mr. Brownlow shrugged, turned around, walked back to the museum ropes, ducked under them, and rejoined the group around Russell's Mercedes. "He's really *out* there, isn't he?" he said to Agnes.

"Yes, he is," she said. "Poor, poor Rose. I just hope Russell doesn't do anything stupid."

"He's *already* done something stupid," the president pointed out to no one in particular.

*   *   *

Iris Benson was uncomfortable on a lot of levels, but the most pressing was that she alone seemed to know that Russell was an alcoholic off on a toot. The problem was she knew this only because she'd seen him at that AA meeting, and so saying anything about it would be a big AA no-no. On the other hand, saying something might also help Russell in the long run, for surely being a drunk on a toot aroused more compassion in people than being a gun-waving, lunatic kidnapper.

Iris badly wanted to do the right thing. Russell had helped her out big-time during the Book Store debacle. However, whenever she tried to think, all she thought about was vodka.

Indecision hung thick in the air around her.

Oh, what the hell! She meant to help, and that would have to do. "Russell Jacobs is an alcoholic," she announced in a loud, clear carrying voice, "and he's back on the booze. I think that's probably at least part of what's going on with him."

All eyes within earshot turned toward her. "How do you know he's an alcoholic?" the president asked.

So here came her own walls a'tumbling down. "I know Russell's a drunk because I'm one," Iris said.

Tom gasped. "I had no idea. I thought he'd stopped drinking because of the calories or something."

The president, however, nodded her manicured head decisively. "Well, that's certainly good to know. I understand a lot about alcoholics, as it happens."

Iris stared at the president. "You do?"

"You bet. Both my father and my uncle died of drink, and I had to learn about the disease in order to come to terms with that. So how long have you been sober, Peony? Not long, if what I hear is right."

"Iris," Iris corrected her. "It's Iris. I've been sober four days."

"Good for you," the president said. "It explains a lot, doesn't it?"

"About me?" Iris asked.

"Yup. And about Russell Jacobs." The president turned to the rest of the group. "Well, now that we know a bit more about what we're dealing with, does anyone have any suggestions? It seems to me that if Russell's an alcoholic who just started drinking again, we should call the police in before he gets any drunker. I hate to do it because of what it will mean for the college and for Russell, but that's pretty small potatoes next to Rose Callahan's safety."

"No," Tom said.

All eyes turned to him, but it was Agnes who spoke. "Thomas Putnam, have you lost your mind? It's Rose in there. Locked up with a drunk who's got a gun."

"I know, but I'm pretty sure from what Henry said that it's just an old dueling pistol that isn't loaded. I'd like to try talking to Russell before we call the police."

"But Mason just did that." Agnes had unconsciously put herself on a first-name basis with Mr. Brownlow, who noticed and smiled.

"True, but I'm still going to try." Tom reached into his pants pocket and pulled out a key ring. He and Russell had traded house keys years ago. "Besides, I can get in."

"Oh, you don't want to do that," Clarence said quickly.

Tom smiled. "Oh, but I do. Russell's been my friend for twenty years, and I owe him that much at least."

"Russell Jacobs isn't *anyone's* friend," Agnes snapped.

Tom lifted the museum rope. "I know. And if that is not my fault, it certainly is my responsibility."

•   •   •

Tom heard the doorbell shrill inside the house. As had been the case with Mr. Brownlow, however, nothing happened.

Tom rang again.

Nothing.

He fumbled the big, old-fashioned key into the lock, turned it, twisted the door's big, polished knob, and pushed.

The door swung open. Lights blazed around him; the megaphone sat abandoned on the beautiful Turkish carpet. Russell was nowhere to be seen.

"Where are you, Russ?" Tom called.

"Go away," Russell shouted, evidently sticking to a script. His voice came from above.

"No," Tom shouted back. "I'm not going away. I'm coming up."

He climbed the steps two at a time. Once on the second-floor landing, he headed directly through the archway that led to the Dome Room stairs. The stairwell's lights were off, so Tom switched them on.

Russell sat halfway up the Dome Room stairs, a two-thirds empty bottle of whiskey on one side, one of his Mortimers on the other. He had what looked like a wilted paper party hat stuck on one side of his head. Tom could not help but feel pity for his friend. How fast the mightily arrogant had fallen. There he was, just another sad and struggling drunk.

"Hello, Russell," Tom said.

Russell said nothing. He sat looking down at Tom as though not quite sure who he was.

"It's Tom. Your old friend, Tom Putnam."

Russell touched the pistol. "I've got a gun."

"I can see that. It's one of your Mortimers, isn't it?"

Russell smiled but said nothing.

"Is it loaded?" Tom kept his tone casual.

Russell looked sly. "Yes," he said. "It is."

"When did you get the ammunition, Russell? I remember you saying you didn't have any ammunition."

"I lied," Russell said, still sly.

"Ahh," Tom said. "Well then."

Russell picked the gun up and waved it vaguely in Tom's direction.

"She's mine," he said. "You can't have her."

Tom knew enough to grasp that arguing was not going to move things along. "Is that a party hat you have on your head?" he asked.

Russell had forgotten what was on his head. He reached up, touched it, and broke into a truly happy smile. "Yes. I'm having a party. For Rose."

"Well, isn't that something?" Tom hoped he sounded impressed.

Russell immediately pointed the gun directly at Tom. "You're mocking me."

Tom, in spite of his best efforts not to, felt momentarily afraid. Agnes was right. This wasn't his friend he was dealing with; this was a drunk with a gun. "I would never mock you, Russell."

Russell wagged his head. "Would, too. Everyone else does." He began to cry silently. Even from the bottom of the stairs, Tom could see the great drops rolling down his cheeks. One bounced off the Mortimer.

"No one mocks you," Tom said, aware he might not be telling the truth.

"Do, too. 'Cept Rose. Rose is real."

Tom spoke from his heart. "You do know I love her, don't you, Russell?"

"Too bad. You've got lots of other people to love. I've only got Rose, now that I haven't got Henry."

Tom was careful to keep his voice cheerful and relaxed, an effort to project a calm decisiveness he didn't feel. "Look, Russ, it's hard work standing here, shouting at you, so I'm going to come up about halfway and sit down on a step. That will make it pleasanter for us to talk."

Russ had retreated into dullness again. "Don't want to talk to you. Only want to talk to Rose."

"Well, I'm coming up. Just halfway, remember. I'm not going to try to tackle you or anything."

Russell waved the pistol. "Better not!" He sounded more like a child pouting than a grown man threatening someone with a gun.

Tom kept his eyes on Russell as he climbed. For a moment, he thought Russ might be falling asleep, but no.

"That's far enough!" Russell barked.

Tom was six steps below him. He held up both his hands in the classic gesture of surrender. "Sure. I'm just going to sit down now."

He sat.

Neither said anything for perhaps a minute, during which Tom thought of Rose behind the locked door of her aerie. She was so quiet. Was she listening? Could she hear anything? Probably not. The Dome Room, as he remembered it, was one solidly constructed manifestation of architectural ego.

"So whaddaya want?" Russell demanded truculently.

The best thing to do, Tom decided, was to speak the truth. "I think what I want first is to say I'm sorry."

Russell gazed down at him, scratching his head with the barrel of his Mortimer before he spoke. "What are *you* sorry for?"

The devil peered out from just behind Russell's left shoulder, daring Tom to tell the truth and shame him, big-time.

Or shame her, big-time.

Or it.

A bossy offstage voice piped up. *Will you for once get on with it, Tom Putnam?*

"I'm sorry I was so preoccupied with my own business that I didn't notice how unhappy you are, Russ."

Russell glowered at him. "*I'm* not unhappy. I have Rose. Up there." He gestured upward with the Mortimer. "*You're* who's unhappy!" He smiled his sly smile again.

The same offstage voice spoke again. *Just tell the truth, and it shall set Rose free. Eventually, anyway . . .*

"Look, Russell," Tom said, "why are you doing this if you're not unhappy?"

Russell stared at him. After a moment he reached up to touch his head. When he felt the wilted paper hat, his face crumpled as Henry's had done not that long ago. "Rose doesn't mind things about me as much as everyone else."

"What things?" Tom asked gently. "What things do other people mind?"

Russ looked around him vaguely. "Oh, you know. Things."

"No, I don't know. What things, Russ?"

Russ said something in such a soft voice that Tom couldn't catch what it was. "What was that, Russ?"

Russell put the Mortimer down beside him and sat there looking off into his past. This time, he spoke loud enough for Tom to hear. "My mother."

"Oh? What about your mother?"

"You wouldn't understand." Some of Russell's belligerence had come back. He leveled what Tom took to be a sneer down at him. "Your mother was so wonderful all the time, baking cookies and wearing the right clothes when she went out."

"Wearing the right clothes?"

"Yes. *Wearing the right clothes!*" Russell yelled. "What's the matter with you? Are you deaf?"

"No. I'm not deaf, I'm just trying to understand."

"I know. I talk too much. I'm sorry."

"There's no need to be sorry, Russ," Tom said mildly.

"Talked about *you* too much," Russell said, following some illogical train of thought.

"What's that?"

"To Serafine. Talked about you too much to her."

Tom was immediate alert. "How do you mean, Russell? You mean you talked about me too much to Serafine Despré, Henry's mother?"

"Yes. Thass what I mean." Russell's final *t*'s were disappearing. "Serafine Despré, Henry's mother. *Bragging* about you."

Tom was astonished. "Bragging about me? Why?"

"About how nice you were. How *normal,* and steady, and kind. Not like anyone else in this place, let me tell you! How you were married to Marjory all that time, only had one affair, years ago, with that poet Retesia somebody. Slam, bam, then back to Marjory!"

"What place?"

"Treatment center in New Orleans. What place you *think* I mean?"

"You were in *treatment* for alcoholism with Henry's mother?"

"Yes." Russell had gone sly again. "Had sex with her, too, which was . . . like . . . *way* against the rules!" He was briefly proud, then collapsed into wretchedness again. "That's why I thought I was Henry's father. Not true, though, so I had to let him go. Luellen told me."

"Luellen Mars?"

Russell wagged his head. "She's the one who did the test."

"A paternity test? Is that what you're talking about?"

Russell frowned. "Henry isn't mine, isn't yours. Serafine just *wanted* him to be yours, because I told her you were nice. She didn't *know* anyone nice herself, so she had to go with *my* nice person."

There was one big fat mystery explained. "I see," Tom said. "Well, thank you for saying that about me."

Russell had begun shaking his head like an old, sad dog. "Henry isn't mine, isn't yours, isn't *anybody's*."

Even under these circumstances, Tom could not let this pass unchallenged. "As far as I'm concerned, Henry Putnam is my son. And that's the end of that."

"Okay, okay. Don't get all steamed up about it."

"I didn't get steamed up," Tom said, even though he knew had. A bit, anyway. "I just wanted to be clear about Henry. You know, have things straight between friends."

Russell peered down at Tom. "Are you really my friend?"

"Yes," Tom said, in the same clear, firm voice he'd used to claim Henry. "I am your friend, Russell. I've been your friend for a long time, just as you've been mine."

"I have?"

"Yes. You have. You've been a very good friend to me."

Russell looked even more muddled. "Really?"

"Yes."

The crumpling happened again. Only this time, Russell's whole being collapsed. "I don't know what's going on anymore. It's all broken. Please, somebody, help me!"

Tom crawled up the six stairs that separated them and put his arms around Russell much as he'd put his arm around Henry not very long ago.

*   *   *

When Tom brought Rose out there was a loud cheer from the crowd. Clarence and his force (three other school system retirees and one Marine Corps reject) attempted with middling success to hold back Rose's well-wishers sufficiently to allow her and Tom to make their way over to the command post.

Tom kept his arm tight around Rose as they pushed through the crowd.

"I'm fine. I'm fine," she kept saying, over and over. Which wasn't true—Tom could feel her shaking. Rose would *be* fine, of that he was sure. But right now, what she needed was a good dose of Agnes's no-nonsense care, a warm bath, and a stiff drink.

Tom had to work hard to keep the two of them moving. Rose kept stopping to defend Russell's actions to people. "He was just a little over-*involved*," she kept saying. And although this made no sense, people seemed to catch her meaning, which Tom construed as *don't be too hard on the man.*

Then there was a sudden parting of the crowd, and Henry came scrambling toward them. The boy sparkled with joy, jumping up and down, hugging whatever parts of Rose he could reach. "Rose! Rose!" he shouted again and again. "My dad rescued you!"

Tom, in spite of four decades of entrenched modesty, could not stop himself from swelling with pride. Technically, at least, the boy was right—he had rescued Rose.

Tom allowed himself a second or two of macho satisfaction before he scooped Henry up and boosted the cheering boy onto his shoulders.

*   *   *

Iris slipped unnoticed through the crowd, made her way up the Dean Dome's front walk, and strolled in through the gaping front door. Russell sat on the bottom step of the grand curving staircase with what looked like a rumpled paper napkin clinging to one side of his head. Beside him were a megaphone and a bottle of Wild Turkey that looked to be about a third full.

Iris marched up to him and scooped up the whiskey bottle by its neck.

Russell roused himself. "What are you doing?"

"Pouring this down the sink."

"Why?"

"Because I might drink it." Iris gestured with the bottle. "You got any more of these?"

Russell glowered at her. "No."

"Promise?"

"Yes."

"Are your pants on fire?"

chapter 21

"I suppose Russell will be in some sort of trouble," Mr. Brownlow said.

He, Tom, and Rose sat at the kitchen table. Henry was bouncing around the room like a Ping-Pong ball; Agnes stood at the stove smashing grilled cheese sandwiches in an iron skillet.

"Some, probably," Tom said. "I hope just enough to force him into, you know, getting appropriate help. It'll be up to the president, I guess. And she's able to understand his situation better than most. I'm hoping her main interest will be in making it clear to Russell that he has to face up to what's bothering him if he wants to keep his job."

They were speaking in a kind of code, as Henry was around. It was not a time to resurrect his mother's struggles by talking about such things as "alcoholism" and "treatment."

"Iris certainly seems to have taken Russell in hand," Mr. Brownlow said.

"Yes," Tom said. "Perhaps they'll be good for each other."

Agnes marched over from the stove, carrying the skillet. "Here you go," she said, shoveling a grilled cheese sandwich onto Rose's plate.

"Eat, Rose!" Henry commanded from her elbow. "Grilled cheese is good for you!"

Rose looked up to find Tom smiling at her from across the table. She looked down at her plate. The sandwich was impossibly huge.

Wonderland's Alice spoke up inside her head: *I can't explain myself, I'm afraid, Sir, because I'm not myself, you see.*

For a book Rose had never much liked, it did seem to haunt her. Perhaps, in this instance, it was because she didn't feel much like herself either. Could she possibly have taken up residence in someone else's life?

Agnes was making the rounds with her skillet. "Come here, Henry," she said, depositing a sandwich on his plate. "Sit down and eat your supper."

But Henry was not finished with Rose. He threw his arms around her in what was more tackle than hug. "I'm so glad my dad rescued you," he crowed. "Now we can all live happily ever after."

Henry's words seemed to come at Rose from a great distance. From another galaxy, perhaps, one that was far, far away.

Anyway, she was way too removed to notice that Mr. Brownlow, rude as it was, suddenly blew his nose into his napkin.

Agnes, however, missed nothing. "Okay," she said. "Let's have it."

"I can't do it," Mr. Brownlow said, wiping his eyes.

Everyone at the table, even Rose, even Henry, knew what Mr. Brownlow meant. What he couldn't do was take Henry back to Mississippi.

"I shall monitor the situation closely, of course," said Mr. Brownlow with a snuffle, "because things are a bit, shall we say, *unconventional*. But, you know"—and here he turned to look directly at Agnes—"I quite like it here myself. Everyone seems to care about everyone else so very much."

Tom turned toward Agnes, expecting some tart reply, but she was too busy doing something Tom would have bet the Putnam family fortune she'd never done before in her life.

Agnes Tattle was blushing.

Finally Tom had succeeded in stowing the overexcited Henry in bed under the watchful eye of Albus Dumbledore. Rose, who was very tired and wanted nothing but to sleep for days, had been about to leave when she and Tom were summoned to the kitchen table by Mr. Brownlow and Agnes. Now she sat there while an avalanche of what others seemed to take as very good news tumbled around her. The two of them, Agnes and Mr. Brownlow had gleefully explained, were to be cochairs of a new nonprofit corporation funded by Henry's millions. Their mission would be to save endangered bookstores that were deemed culturally essential to their communities. And the first bookstore to be saved would be hers.

The idea for the corporation had first popped into Mr. Brownlow's head when he'd met Rose on the stairs in her sheet and heard about the community relations part of her job. He'd spent every spare minute of his time at the college talking about the Book Store with college faculty, staff, students, and administrators who did not report directly to the VP of finance. And he had not talked to a soul, Mr. Brownlow said, even the president (with whom he'd wangled a half hour), who didn't see the Book Store as an integral part of what made this college *this college*. It was the only place on campus where the pecking order disappeared; the only place where, as the president put it, she could be who she *was* instead of what she *did*.

Tom sat there, clutching Rose's hand, saying over and over, "I can't believe it. I can't believe it."

Neither could she. The conversation floated around her like so many bubbles. Rose knew intellectually there was a reason to celebrate, but all she felt was dull and creeping outrage. This was *her* life they were messing with, these two tiny, elderly fairy godparents. Of course, Henry's corporation would do a lot of good for other people as well, but the good it did for her was not a good she'd ever asked for or contemplated. It felt more like a *complication* than a blessing.

Mavis had always maintained that "Thou Shalt Not Meddle" should be the Lord's Eleventh Commandment. According to Mavis Callahan, "I was only trying to help" described one of humanity's most destructive impulses. What these people were doing, Rose realized, was cutting her off from the familiar course of her own life. They'd *bought* her baloney that she was only moving on for professional reasons.

But then, Rose realized, until this moment, she'd mostly bought it, too.

The Animals sang tinnily at her from out of the past about getting out of this place if it was the last thing they ever did. Their rebellious Vietnam-era anthem had been another of her mother's favorite packing ditties.

*　　*　　*

Rose hesitated, standing there on her mother's front stoop beside a pot of bronze chrysanthemums. Once Mavis Callahan was involved, there would be no more pussyfooting around. Her mother would support her no matter what she did, but she would have to do *something*. Mavis would not approve of running away when it worried other people.

Come to think of it, Rose didn't approve of that kind of running away either. It was one thing to move on; another thing entirely to worry a six-year-old boy who'd just lost his mother—and didn't even know it yet.

Rose lifted her hand and knocked.

Mavis opened her front door holding a ball of yarn, which she dropped when she saw her daughter. The yarn scuttled over the doorsill and rolled down the front porch steps. Rose bent to retrieve it.

"Never mind about that, Rose," Mavis said. "Tell me what's wrong."

Rose picked the yarn up anyway. She felt compelled to pretend, at least to herself, that *nothing* was wrong, that everything was *fine*, just as it been fine for the first thirty-some years of her life. *You're okay, so I'm okay*, had become her new mantra. Which she'd repeated to herself as she'd watch other, bona-fide-ly fine people pumping gas along I-81 and I-78 on her way to Williamstown, Massachusetts. In fact, she was so okay, she'd made the trip in just under eleven hours, which was something of a personal record.

Mavis snatched the yarn out of her hand and chucked it through an open doorway off to her right. "You look terrible, Rosie," she said, drawing her daughter into her house. "You need to come and sit in the sunroom and tell me what's going on."

"Is—" Rose began, looking around.

"Don't worry. Nobody's home but me." Mavis took her daughter by the hand and led her through the old, comfortably cluttered New England saltbox to the sunroom. This was the old back shed, tapped for renovation because of its southern exposure. Three walls of windows let the sun in throughout the day. Fall, Rose noticed, was much further along in Massachusetts than it was in Virginia. Brilliant maples ringed the bright green back lawn.

"Sit!" Mavis pointed to a saggy, overstuffed armchair, shrouded with afghans.

Rose sat. Mavis pulled a footstool over so that she could perch in front of her daughter and take her hand. "Now, Rosie, let's hear it."

Rose stared out the window at the maples. What would it have been like to grow up here, watching those same trees turn every fall? How would it have been, going to school with the same friends, getting to know them through and through, becoming known through and through? She'd always felt it would have been beyond boring to stay put, but now she was no longer sure.

The truth was that she, intrepid Rose Callahan, was scared. Which was why she'd jumped in her car and driven north lickety-split in the predawn hours. But what, exactly, did she expect her mother to do—make all her fears go away? This wasn't some imaginary bogeyman nibbling at her heels, this was real life.

Rose picked at an afghan with her free hand.

"Take your time," Mavis said. "Stu's away at a conference till tomorrow around lunch. So there's nobody here but us chickens."

The phone rang. "Let the machine get it," Mavis said, her eyes on her daughter.

Five rings later, Mavis's voice invited the caller to leave a message. "This is Tom Putnam," a male voice said. "I'm a friend of your daughter's, Miss Callahan. And I was just wondering if, by any chance, you'd heard from her?"

"Should I pick up?" Mavis asked.

Rose, dumb with misery, shook her head. "No. Not yet."

"He sounds worried," Mavis said. "Is he that professor who was giving you fits because you liked him?"

"I might love him," Rose whispered, leaning her head forward so that her words came out from behind the curtain of her hair. "It's all so fast."

To her surprise, Mavis threw back her head and laughed. "Oh, honey, it always *is*. I had to talk myself off the *ceiling* when I figured out I was in love with Stu."

Rose peeked at her mother through her hair. "You did?"

"Yes. I was scared to death. To *death*, I tell you!" Mavis reached her free hand out and lifted Rose's chin. "We Callahan gals do like to pretend a lot."

"We do?" Rose stared into her mother's eyes. Was that what she'd been doing all these years? "Pretend what?"

Mavis stroked her daughter's cheek lightly with the back of her hand. "Oh, you know, that we're invulnerable. That no one's going to slow *us* down, even though we don't have a clue where we're going."

"Really? You were scared of Stu?"

"To death," Mavis said again. "I mean, how could I have gotten myself into a situation where it really *mattered* whether some man was around or not?"

Rose sat up. "That's it. That's what I've done."

"Well, there you go!" Mavis patted her daughter's knee.

"I guess."

"So, are you on the lam from that man who just called?"

"Yes. I guess I am. And from his kid and his mother-in-law and from my job, and from everything and everyone at that college." Rose started to cry.

Mavis drew her close. "Oh, child, are you worried if you let yourself settle down with this fella and his entourage that you'll wake up one day to find your little magic kingdom's jumped in the toilet?"

"Yes," Rose wailed. "I am."

Mavis put her hands on her daughter's shoulders and gently pushed her away so as to be able to look her in the eye. "See here."

Rose sniffed. "Yes?"

"The thing is, that could happen. But the other thing is, that's not the point. The point is, do you love this man?"

Rose caught her breath. "Yes! Oh, yes! At least I think I do!"

Mavis waved this away. "Thinking, schminking. What does your gut say?"

Rose bit her lip. "It says I do."

"There you go! The only advice I can give you, Rose Callahan, is the advice I gave myself nineteen years ago when I married Stu. After years of chasing a vague dream of freedom, I woke up one morning thinking about how much I'd loved being with Stu yesterday and the day before, and how likely it was that I was going to love being with him today and even tomorrow if I stuck around. And that was that. One day at a time, I've been sticking around ever since. Some days with Stu have been better than others, but they've mostly all been better than they would have been without him."

"But you married Stu. That's not just hanging around one day at a time. That's commitment. That's . . . that's *trust*."

Mavis fingered her wedding ring. "Well, Stu's traditional and kept asking me. And at some point, I said to myself, 'Mavis Callahan, get *over* yourself. Admit you love this guy with your whole heart, he loves you back, and your wandering days are over.'"

Rose involuntarily held out a hand to push Mavis's words away. So much of who she thought she was had always been tied to movement.

Mavis chuckled. "The thing I had to learn to trust, Rosie, is that every good day I get really *is* a good day. I don't have to enjoy it any less just because yesterday wasn't so hot and I don't know what tomorrow will bring. We do get to just enjoy ourselves, you know."

Rose thought of Henry; of how when the boy was kicking a soccer ball around, he was so *there*, unburdened by all the things that *weren't* there. It seemed to her that being like that took either great courage or great faith. "So what should I do, Mama?"

Mavis took both her daughter's hands in hers. "Do what you *want* to do, Rosie. Just don't shoot yourself in the foot because what you want scares the pants off you."

Rose smiled. "Can I hide out here for a couple of days?"

"Of course. But don't you think you better let that nice man know you're all right?" Mavis grinned. "Well, maybe not all right in the head, but at least you're still in one piece."

*   *   *

Tom and Henry were somewhere around New Paltz on Interstate 87 when Henry spoke up from the backseat. "My mother's dead, isn't she?"

Every ounce of Tom felt immediately and fiercely protective of the small person behind him, strapped into his safety seat. He put on his emergency blinkers, pulled over, got out, and got in beside Henry. So here they were, face-to-face with the truth that would set Henry free from both the hope and the worry that Serafine Despré would someday show up to claim him again. "Yes," he said. "Your mother is dead."

Henry was staring out his side window. "What did she die of?" he asked in a toneless, old man's voice.

The world might be willing to show Henry mercy, but Henry was evidently not going to show himself any. Was this *really* the kind of truth that sets you free? "Drugs and alcohol," Tom said. Which, he told himself, was the actual truth even if it wasn't the exact truth.

Henry nodded. "She wasn't ever happy," he said, his face still turned away from Tom. "She said she was, but she wasn't. I could tell. Mawmaw and Pawpaw always said she couldn't help it. That she was sick, just like she had cancer or something."

"That's right," Tom said, not knowing what else to say.

"Just the way your wife was sick," Henry said.

"Yes."

An enormous semi rumbled by them on the left, followed immediately by another. *People die; life goes on,* Tom thought. *Or at least commerce does.*

"Is Rose dead?" Henry asked.

"Heavens, no," Tom said.

"Are you going to die?" Henry's voice was small and tight.

How much truth could one almost-seven-year-old handle? Tom reached over, unbuckled Henry's seat belt, and pulled the little boy out of his safety seat onto his lap. Henry was stiff as a board, as stiff as he'd been the first time Tom tried to hug him.

Tom stroked his hair. "Listen, Henry," he said. "Everybody's born at the beginning of life and everybody dies at the end of it. So death isn't bad or unnatural; it's just . . . just unknown. And it's hard on the living because when people die they are gone and we miss them."

A strange sound came out of Henry; part sob, part howl. And then he crumpled as completely as though his bones had turned to Jell-O. "I don't want you to die," he wailed.

Once again Tom could think of nothing to do for his small son but hold him close. And so he did.

*   *   *

An older version of Rose opened the door when Tom and Henry knocked. "Well, well," she said. "Good for you!"

Tom agreed, at least partially. He hadn't really had any doubts about *doing* this since talking to Rose last night. His only doubts concerned how she might respond. Still, he was somewhat taken aback by such forthright approval from someone he'd never met. Nevertheless, he politely stuck out his hand. "I'm Tom Putnam."

"Of course you are," the woman said. "And this must be Henry."

Henry, in full on-a-mission mode, got straight to the point. "We've come to see Rose and ask her to come home."

"Of course you have," the woman said, taking Tom's hand. Instead of shaking it, though, she held it in both of hers. "I'm Mavis, in case you couldn't tell. And Rose is right back through there talking with Stu. If you don't mind, I'll come back with you, so Stu doesn't mistake this for a *social* call."

"Of course," Tom said.

Mavis reached out for Henry's hand. He gave it to her without the slightest hesitation. "Tom and me are skipping school, but my teacher said it was okay."

"Of course she did. Your teacher's no fool." Mavis led the way deeper into the warm old New England house. Tom felt right at home. Books were everywhere. Just as they were bearing down on what appeared to be a back den, Mavis called out, "Stu, Rose has got company, and she needs her privacy. So you need to keep me company out here, okay?"

"Okay!" a pleasant male voice responded. Almost immediately, a tall man in a gray sweater appeared in the doorway. Thinking back later about this first glimpse of Stu, all Tom could remember was how *cheerful* he'd seemed, and how he, Tom, had irrationally willed that his own future resemble this man's past. The man extended his hand. "I'm Stu. You must be Tom," he said. The two men shook hands. "And you must be Henry," he added, smiling down at Henry.

Henry offered his hand to Stu without prompting.

Mavis took her husband firmly by the arm. "That's enough of that for now. Stu and I will be out in the kitchen for as long as we can stand it. Both of us are naturally nosey." She winked at Tom. Stu smiled happily down at the top of his wife's head, and the two were gone.

Henry, back in mission mode, didn't hesitate. "Rose," he shouted, running into the room, "Dad's come to rescue you again!"

Tom, older and perhaps less wise, hesitated before he could make himself enter. He'd worried on the way up about whether or not this might overwhelm Rose, be too much love thrown at her too quickly.

But really he'd had no choice but to come. He was who he was, and who he was was in love with Rose Callahan.

And there she was. Seeing her sitting there with her arms around Henry, her nose buried in his curls, it was much as it had been that first day in the Book Store. Except that this time Tom felt his heart flex, bursting free from all the stupid constraints routinely imposed upon it by his head.

When Rose looked up at him over Henry's frothy head, he saw something suspiciously close to joy in her eyes.

"You know what I've decided?" she said.

Tom held his breath. This was it. "What?"

Rose gently pushed Henry away from her so that it was clear she was addressing them both. "I've decided," she said, her eyes dancing, "that it's okay for me to be happy."

"With me?" Tom could hardly breathe.

Rose nodded. "With you. And Henry, of course."

Henry looked perplexed. "But you don't need to *decide* that, Rose," he said. "We *are* happy. All of us."

"Exactly," Rose said, taking a deep breath, crossing her fingers for luck, hoping against hope that life really might be that simple.